# Love AT THE 20-YARD LINE

by
SHANNA HATFIELD

***Love at the 20-Yard Line***



ISBN-13: 978-1495217777
ISBN-10: 1495217779



Shanna Hatfield
shanna@shannahatfield.com
shannahatfield.com

*To those who surrender to love...*

Special thanks to Travis Vance and the Tri-Cities Fever Football team for answering my many questions!

For more information about Indoor Football, check out the Indoor Football League website at: http://www.goifl.com/

*Books by Shanna Hatfield*

## FICTION

***HISTORICAL***

**Hardman Holidays**

*The Christmas Bargain*

*The Christmas Token*

**Pendleton Petticoats Series**

*Aundy*

*Caterina*

***CONTEMPORARY***

*Love at the 20-Yard Line*

*The Coffee Girl*

*Learnin' the Ropes*

*QR Code Killer*

**Rodeo Romance Series**

*The Christmas Cowboy*

**Grass Valley Cowboys Series**

*The Cowboy's Christmas Plan*

*The Cowboy's Spring Romance*

*The Cowboy's Summer Love*

*The Cowboy's Autumn Fall*

*The Cowboy's New Heart*

**The Women of Tenacity Series**

*The Women of Tenacity - A Prelude*

*Heart of Clay*

*Country Boy vs. City Girl*

*Not His Type*

## NON-FICTION

*Fifty Dates with Captain Cavedweller*

**Savvy Entertaining Series**

*Savvy Holiday Entertaining*

*Savvy Spring Entertaining*

*Savvy Summer Entertaining*

*Savvy Autumn Entertaining*

## *Chapter One*

"I need you to take care of this."

Haven Haggarty lifted her gaze from the report in front of her, wondering what could possibly be so important her boss delivered his request to her office in person.

"What is it, Mr. Young?" Haven asked, hoping he wasn't sending her out on another assignment. One of the top consultants at the brand analysis company he owned and operated, she often worked long, hard hours. With close to sixty hours of work already completed that week, she planned to spend the weekend relaxing.

As her boss stood in front of her desk holding an envelope in his hand late on a Friday afternoon, it didn't bode well for a peaceful start to her weekend.

"Tickets. We're an event sponsor and someone needs to represent us tonight. I forgot about it until a few minutes ago and since you're still here..." Frank Young said, dropping the envelope on Haven's desk and giving her an encouraging glance. He turned and left her office before she could verbalize an objection.

"But, sir, I..." Haven snapped her mouth shut as she watched him stride back to his office.

Rolling her blue eyes, she prayed this event wouldn't turn out like the time he made her go to what they both thought was a networking event and ended up being an exclusive preview for a new adult-only store. He'd given her an entire month of free evenings and weekends after that humiliating debacle.

Fortifying herself with a deep breath, she opened the envelope and removed four packets of season tickets. Her neck muscles tightened and her stomach clenched with nerves as she read the details.

Football tickets.

Mr. Young expected her to attend an arena football game that would begin in less than two hours. And not just her, he wanted four bodies warming the seats that he'd purchased.

Fighting the urge to scream in frustration, Haven quickly scanned the letter accompanying the tickets. It appeared Mr. Young was a sponsor for the entire season. She certainly hoped he didn't expect her to attend every home game.

Haven glanced at her watch and grabbed her phone, calling her oldest brother. Maybe Wes and his wife, Tammy, would be interested in going with her. Waiting for someone to answer, she stuffed the report she'd been reading into her bag with a few other projects she planned to review before Monday.

As the phone rang for the fifth time, she gave up and dialed her middle brother.

"Please pick up, please pick up," Haven chanted as she willed Hale to take the call.

"Hey, sis, what's up?" Hale asked, sounding out of breath. Haven could hear his pounding footsteps and knew he was probably on his evening run.

"Hale, I need the hugest, biggest favor tonight," Haven said, sounding desperate as she gathered her things and turned off her computer.

"I've got a date with Abby. What could possibly be more important than that?"

"Mr. Young gave me four tickets to something tonight and expects me and my guests to be there. He just now gave them to me and I really, really need you to go with me. You can bring Abby." Haven locked her desk and looked around her office to make sure she wasn't forgetting anything.

"Where are you going?" Hale asked, maintaining a neutral tone. From experience, he knew to ask questions before he consented to accompany Haven to one of her work-required functions. The last time he blindly agreed, he ended up as the only male at an all-women luncheon and fashion show.

"A football game," Haven said, trying to shove her arm in her coat sleeve, hold the phone to her ear, and not drop the stack of files in her other hand.

"You're kidding, right? It's February. In case you and your boss aren't aware of the fact, football season is long gone."

"Arena football, dork. Tonight's the first game."

"Name calling won't help your cause, baby girl."

"I'm sorry. It's just I had plans to… never mind," Haven said, swallowing down another sigh. "Can you go or not?"

"Sure. Sounds like fun. How about if Abby and I meet you there?"

"Great, I owe you one," Haven said, giving her brother directions and the game start time. "I'll meet you about twenty minutes before the kickoff."

"And you'll buy us dinner," Hale said, knowing Haven would go along with anything he suggested as long as she didn't have to attend the game alone.

"Fine," Haven said, disconnecting the call. Leaving a stack of files on the receptionist's desk to file on Monday, she rushed outside, wrapping her scarf around her neck against the cold.

In a hurry, she didn't take time to let the car warm up before pulling into evening traffic.

Haven swung by the grocery store to pick up a few things on her way home. She planned to spend the entire day Saturday tucked away in her cozy apartment enjoying quiet solitude and a good book.

Racing down the aisles of the store, she filled her cart, trying to decide if she should resort to begging her brother Tom to go with her to the game. A year her senior, he seemed to think his mission in life was to torment his younger sister.

Impatiently waiting in the checkout line, she called her brother before she could change her mind and even thanked him when he agreed to go.

"But you have to come pick me up, feed me whatever I want to eat, and make sure I get home safely," Tom said, knowing it would annoy her to drive out of her way to run by his apartment.

Biting her tongue to keep from telling him she didn't need him to go after all, she forced herself to remain calm and assured him she'd be there as soon as she changed.

Loading her purchases in her car, she rushed back into the busy after-work traffic. Since it seemed to be moving at a snail's pace, it took twice as long to drive home than she'd planned. Finally reaching her apartment, she filled her arms with groceries and work projects, managing to get inside and the door closed behind her by nudging it shut with the toe of her shoe.

Quickly putting away any groceries that might spoil before she got home, she left the rest of her purchases on the counter and glanced at the clock on the wall in panic. If she ran out the door and sped to Tom's apartment, she might get to the game before it started.

Kicking off her heels and jamming her feet into a pair of flats she kept by the door, she ran back to her car and made it in record time to Tom's place. Pulling into the parking lot, she took out her phone to let him know he needed to hurry, but he was already jogging toward her car.

"Hey," he said, climbing in and buckling his seatbelt. "Thanks for inviting me. You know I love football and totally forgot about the arena games."

"You're welcome," Haven said, driving toward the arena. "You can thank Mr. Young. He demanded I go at the eleventh hour."

"Cool. It's not like you have a life or anything," Tom teased, giving his sister a mischievous look.

Haven speculated, as she had so many times, about the possibility of a secret adoption, or maybe her parents got the wrong baby at the hospital when they brought her home.

Her mother and all three of her brothers had brown hair with hazel eyes and olive-toned skin. They loved to joke and tease, and she often wondered if they had a serious bone in their bodies.

She, however, was blonde with blue eyes and fair skin that burned if she even thought about going outside. Her dad had blue eyes, but his hair was dark and his skin bore a permanent tan from working outside on their potato farm. Like her brothers, he was big and tall, as well as a terrible tease.

Wes, Hale, and Tom all looked so much alike, there was no denying the fact they were brothers. If it weren't for the difference in their ages, they'd probably be mistaken for triplets.

That's all the world needed, a triple dose of her three ornery brothers. It was going to be bad enough sitting between two of them during the football game.

Taking a shortcut into the parking lot at the event venue, Haven found an empty space far from the door and parked the car.

"What's the deal? You can't even drop me at the door?" Tom asked, trying to sound like he'd been mistreated as he got out of the car and waited for Haven to walk around to his side. "I think I should get curb service."

"No way, lazy bones. You can hoof it. Besides, you wouldn't want me to walk across this parking lot all by myself, would you?" Haven asked, grabbing her brother's arm when her foot slid on a spot of ice.

"Steady there, kiddo," Tom said, taking her hand in his and keeping her upright. Glancing down, he shook his head with disapproval at her dress coat, skirt, and ballet flats. "What are you wearing?"

"Work clothes. Didn't have time to change," Haven said, glad they were almost to the door. She looked up to see Hale wave at them. "You know Hale's current girl of the month, don't you?"

"Can't say that I do. How long has he been dating her?" Tom asked, studying the tiny redhead standing next to his brother. The three Haggarty boys all topped six-feet and the petite girl standing next to his brother might make five if she stretched.

"I don't know. A couple weeks, maybe," Haven dug in her bag for the tickets and clasped them in her hand as she stepped next to Hale.

"Thanks for coming, Hale. You are a lifesaver," Haven whispered as her favorite brother engulfed her in a hug.

"Anytime, baby girl," Hale said, turning to introduce Abby to Tom.

The four of them proceeded inside with Tom and Hale making a beeline for the concession stand selling pizza.

Haven stood with Abby, making small talk, until the guys were ready to order. Tom gave Haven a look that let her know he fully expected her to make good on the promise to buy his dinner. She paid for the food then led the way to their seats. Sitting close to the twenty-yard line, they had a great view of the playing field.

"Why is the field so small?" she asked, turning to Hale as he settled into a seat between her and Abby.

"It's arena football. The field is about half the size of a regular football field and they only use eight players instead of eleven," Hale explained, pointing to the end zone nearest their seats.

"I see," Haven said, not really caring about the field size, the number of players, or anything else related to football. Her biggest concern was if they would have to stay for the whole game.

She could feel a headache coming on and wanted to go home where she could indulge in some hot chocolate, a good book, and a peaceful weekend alone.

"Do they play four quarters, like regular football?" Haven asked, looking up at the digital scoreboard, catching a glimpse of her company's logo as it flashed across the screen.

"You bet they do. I heard they have a great halftime show, too. Dancing girls, drummers, and giveaways," Tom said, winking at Haven.

"Fantastic," Haven said with mock enthusiasm, smiling a little too brightly.

Removing her coat, Haven tugged down the hem of her skirt and straightened her sweater before glancing around. She noticed a banner with their company name stretched over the stands on the far end of the arena. Pleased to see Mr. Young's business well represented, she made a mental note to tell him about it Monday.

Accepting the breadstick Tom held out to her along with a bottle of water, she mumbled a word of thanks. Stifling a startled gasp as the arena lights went off, she winced when loud music began pounding over the speakers.

Digging in her bag for a pain reliever, she rubbed her throbbing temple and decided it was going to be a long, long evening.

## *Chapter Two*

Wide receiver Brody Jackson caught a pass and grinned, spinning the ball around in his big hands as he and his teammates warmed up before the first game of the season.

"Check out cougar town, dude," he said, inclining his head toward the stands as a group of middle-aged women dressed in too much makeup and not enough clothes sashayed toward their seats.

"Ripe for the picking, man. Just your type," Marcus Smith teased, smiling at Brody. Not only were the two of them teammates, they were also best friends.

"Hardly," Brody said, glancing around the bleacher seats, trying to decide what girl currently filled the role of his type. He'd dated blondes, brunettes, and redheads. He'd charmed tall girls, skinny girls, short girls, and voluptuously curved girls. Smart, pretty, sassy, and brainless - he was sure he'd dated just about every type of girl out there, but it was all in fun. Not one girl had ever reached beyond the surface and touched his heart.

Brody planned to keep it that way. Women were a distraction he could ill afford in his quest to play football with the pros. Someday his dream of playing at the Super Bowl would come true.

His current gig, playing with a well-respected arena football team, took him a step closer to making his dream a reality.

"How about that one?" Marcus asked pointing to a tiny redhead taking a seat in the sponsor section.

"Hmm. She's got potential," Brody said, not really interested in the girl. She looked so petite and fragile, he'd be afraid he might break something shaking her hand.

"Sure she does." Marcus chuckled, then stopped and pointed to a girl taking off her coat near the redhead. "Now, talk about high maintenance, there it is."

Brody glanced at the woman who looked as out of place at the game as he'd be at the symphony. The woman appeared classy, polished, and refined in her professional attire.

She wore a sleek black skirt and one of those sweater set things that looked all soft and expensive, even from across the field. Curly golden ringlets escaped from a bun at the back of her head and the glasses framing her eyes gave her a reserved air.

He couldn't see her hands, but Brody would bet money she had long, fake nails and a gaudy ring on her left hand.

Assuming she was probably someone's trophy wife, he looked away.

"You're such an idiot," Brody shook his head. "I don't want any part of that."

Before they could further speculate on the dating material available at that night's game, the coach motioned them off the field.

Excited as the first game of the season rolled into high gear, Brody played hard, having a great time. Waiting for the quarterback to throw him a pass, he flexed his long fingers and took a deep breath.

With one eye on the guy planning to block the pass and the other on the quarterback, Brody grinned when the football spun through the air his direction. Leaping up, the ball went into his hand like he'd tugged it by a string. He hit the ground running.

Knowing a tackle was coming, he pushed himself to keep going then absorbed the impact as he hit the turf at the twenty-yard line. Pleased with himself at the yards he covered, he lifted his gaze and looked straight into the prettiest blue eyes he'd ever seen.

Forgetting everything around him for a moment, Brody gazed behind the glasses and saw warmth in the girl's eyes. She was the girl he and Marcus had joked about being high maintenance before the game started.

This close, a sweet innocence about her drew his attention. Something stirred deep within his heart, leaving him breathless.

When a hand clamped on his shoulder, he rolled over, coming up on his feet and tossing the ball to a referee. He grinned as his teammates slapped him on the back and Marcus lightly tapped twice on his helmet. It was their way of saying job well done.

The cheering crowd was like a shot of pure energy surging through Brody, driving him on as his team trounced their opponents.

Trying to keep thoughts of the blonde-haired girl with the soulful eyes from knocking him off his game, he continually found his gaze wandering her direction through the second quarter.

Glad for halftime and the opportunity to regroup, Brody blocked out the people around him and attempted to center his thoughts back on winning the game.

"Dude, s'up with you?" Marcus asked as he bumped shoulders with Brody.

"Nothing, man. I'm cool," Brody said, taking a drink from a bottle the water boy handed him. Tipping back his head and closing his eyes, the cool liquid slid down his throat. A pair of blue eyes immediately filled his vision so he opened his eyes and sat up straighter.

"You don't look cool, bro. Something going on you need to tell ol' Marcus about?" Marcus knew all of

Brody's moods and he could tell his buddy tossed some idea around in his head. They were far ahead of the visiting team and unless something disastrous occurred between now and the end of the fourth quarter, he was confident they'd win the game.

By rights, Brody should be on top of the world and shouting it from the rooftops, not sitting with a look of concern etched across his face.

"I'm fine, man, but thanks for asking. You better pay attention to Coach and look snappy about it because he's giving us the evil eye." Brody grinned at the coach and nodded his head, attempting to listen to the direction they received for the last half of the game.

Further conversation ended as they headed back out to the field. Stretching while he waited to go out to play, Brody happened to glance into the stands, trying to steal a glimpse of the mystery girl. He knew she was sitting in the sponsor seats section, so if he wanted, he could ask the sales manager about her.

That smacked too much of an interest Brody was determined he wouldn't admit to, though.

Glancing over his shoulder, he could see her sandwiched between two hulking guys who looked like twins. One of them was trying to shove a mini doughnut dripping with chocolate topping in her face while the other waved a tray of nachos in front of her.

Pushing at both of their hands, she shook her head. The one with the doughnut touched it to her mouth, forcing her to take a bite. Brody stood mesmerized as her tongue came out to lick away a drop of chocolate lingering on the corner of her pink lips.

She glared at the guy with the nachos then laughed at the one with the doughnut. Her face transformed as dimples filled her cheeks and the serious lines softened. She took the doughnut and ate it, then licked the sticky frosting from her fingers. Brody had the most insane desire to do the same thing.

"Dude, you gonna play or not?" Marcus asked, slapping Brody's shoulder as the coach motioned him onto the field. Grabbing his helmet, he gave himself a mental lecture about blocking out the girl and focusing on the game.

Far ahead of the other team as the fourth quarter wound down, Brody stood waiting for the next play, doing his best to ignore the blonde sitting three rows up, two seats over, between the twin terrors. He wanted to beat the stuffing out of the guy who kept bumping her shoulder and trying to get her to share his drink.

When the man placed a hand on her arm and leaned closer to her ear, Brody clenched his fists to keep from climbing up the bleachers and knocking him unconscious.

Now the other one was saying something to her, but she seemed to like him, smiling at him with a look on her face that bordered on adoration. That particular twin turned to the redhead next to him and kissed her cheek.

Brody forcibly returned his attention to the game before he got involved in something that was none of his business. None at all.

Catching a pass seconds before the buzzer signaled the end of the game, Brody ran to the end zone, making a final touchdown as the crowd went wild.

Enjoying a round of high-fives and congratulations with the team, Brody returned to the bench and grabbed a pen, signing his name on the football. Taking off his helmet, he glanced up to see the girl who captivated his interest trying to put on her coat while one of the twins held the back of it against her seat. She had her arms in the sleeves, trapped by the big dolt.

Jumping over the dasher boards surrounding the field, Brody ran up the steps and stood looking down at the girl and her friends.

"Hey, thought you might like the ball from the last touchdown," he said, holding it out to the blonde staring at him as if he was speaking in tongues.

Up close, her skin resembled smooth porcelain and her eyes glowed behind the frames of her glasses. Springy curls escaped the messy bun on the back of her head and Brody battled a nearly irresistible urge to reach out and see if the golden strands felt like silk.

She got to her feet and he experienced a moment of pleasant surprise to see she was considerably taller than the tiny redhead who stood next to one of the look-alike brothers. Leaning forward, he caught a whiff of a soft, tantalizing fragrance that raised his temperature several notches.

Brody still held the ball out toward her, so she worked her hand out of her coat sleeve and took it in a tentative grasp, offering him a polite smile. Relief washed through him to see no wedding ring adorned her left hand and her nails were, in fact, short and unpainted.

"Thank you, Mr. Jackson," she said. Brody felt inordinately pleased she at least knew his last name.

"Call me Brody," he said, accepting the hand the more obnoxious of the brothers held out to him. Studying the two men, he could see they weren't the same age, although they definitely bore a strong resemblance to each other.

"Congrats, man, that was a killer game. I'm Tom and this is my brother Hale."

'Thanks, man." Brody said, shaking hands with the second brother and smiling at the redhead.

"There's a party starting in a while. You'd be welcome to come as my guests," Brody offered, hoping for the chance to spend time with the girl away from the field. If he had his way, he'd be taking her home instead of the Neanderthal duo.

"Please, Haven?" Tom asked, nudging her in the side with his elbow. "I promise we won't stay too late."

Although he hoped she would agree, the urge to punch her boyfriend returned with a vengeance. The guy treated her as if she was an annoying kid sister, not a beautiful woman who, for all appearances, seemed refined and very feminine.

Rolling her name around in his head, he thought it suited her well, although he'd never heard it before. Prepared to plead with her, he looked into her face and could see fatigue around her eyes.

He wouldn't pressure her to come to the party, but he wouldn't let her leave without knowing her full name. He wanted to know how he could get in touch with her, if he was so inclined.

"What's your name?" Brody asked, giving her his most charming smile. He'd been told when he used it women practically fell at his feet, ready to do his bidding.

"Haven Haggarty," Haven said quietly, wondering why this particular player decided to bring her an autographed ball and invite them to a party. Maybe it was something each player did for a corporate sponsor.

Despite the dull roaring of her headache, she couldn't help but be aware of the very cute Brody Jackson out on the field. She'd watched him play with interest and noticed him gazing into the stands their direction, but had no idea he was remotely aware of her or her brothers. Abby was a dazzling little beauty. Maybe she'd caught his eye.

In his uniform, Brody appeared to be ten feet tall and sinfully handsome. His jet-black hair was tousled and sweaty, but thick. His chiseled jaw ended with a firm, ridiculously square chin. Sensuously full lips and dark brown eyes added to his appeal, as did his deep, gravelly voice.

The symmetry of his face was perfect for modeling and she wondered if he'd ever considered posing for an ad campaign. She was always in need of good models for their clients.

When he flashed that megawatt smile her direction, Haven found it difficult to swallow, let alone speak. Managing to push her name out her lips, she frantically tried to engage her brain after he'd scrambled it with both his presence and that husky voice.

She felt her hand engulfed in his large one and an immediate stream of sparks licked up her arm, exploding in her head.

"It's nice to meet you, Haven Haggarty," Brody said, trying to gauge her reaction to him. Other than her eyes growing a little wider, she looked calm, cool, and collected. And ready to go home. "Maybe you'll come to the party another time."

"Please?" Tom begged, picking up her bag and handing it to her, trying to be helpful.

Shifting the football beneath her arm, she took the bag in the hand Brody hadn't captured, and stood staring at him, unaware of the look passing between her two brothers.

"Maybe next time," Haven finally said, pulling her hand from Brody's. She'd never seen such long, capable fingers. Handing Tom the football, she dug in her bag and pulled out a small case. Removing a card, she handed it to Brody.

"If you ever want to consider doing some modeling, I'm always looking for a handsome face like yours," Haven said, flushing as the words left her lips. Now she sounded like one of the ditzy flirts who enjoyed the attentions of men like Brody Jackson.

"So, you think I'm handsome," Brody teased, waggling expressive eyebrows her direction, noting Haven's flushed cheeks.

Rather than respond, she finished putting on her coat, shoved the football into her big bag, and pushed against

Tom's side, trying to get him to step into the aisle and go up the steps so they could leave.

"Thank you for the ball, Mr. Jackson, and congratulations on your victory," Haven said, giving him a smile that had lost most of its warmth before turning to follow Tom out of the stands.

"Great game, man, and very nice to meet you," the other brother said, turning with his date toward the exit.

Looking at the crisp white card in his hand, Brody smiled. He might not be seeing Miss Haven Haggarty later tonight, but he'd definitely see her again.

## *Chapter Three*

First thing Monday morning, Haven sent Mr. Young a brief email about how well represented the company was at the game Friday night. She was surprised to glance up from her desk that afternoon and see her boss smiling at her from the doorway of her office.

"Have fun at the game?" Mr. Young asked, stepping into the room and sitting down in a chair across from Haven.

"Well, um... I... my brothers had a great time, sir. Thank you for the tickets," Haven said, taking an envelope from her desk drawer and sliding it across the tidy surface to her boss. "These are the tickets for the rest of the season. I'm sure you want to give others the chance to attend."

"Actually, Haven, I'd prefer you go to all the games. You can take whomever you want with you, but just work them into your schedule, please," Mr. Young said, giving her a look she couldn't quite decipher.

"Are you certain, sir? Seth and Adam both love football." Haven knew her two coworkers would enjoy the games much more than she would. "They might..."

Mr. Young cut her off, holding up a hand to indicate her silence. "Nope. I want you to go. You really need to stop putting in so many hours here, Haven. I know you worked more than sixty last week. Judging by the volume of emails from you first thing this morning, I'd guess you also took work home with you this weekend. Is that correct?"

"Yes, it is. I wanted to get the Clemson account settled and I need to…"

"Not work so hard," Mr. Young said, smiling at her again. "I appreciate your loyalty and dedication to your job, but you're going to burn out and I don't want to lose such a valuable employee. That's why I'm hiring an assistant for you and Seth to share. I'll let you know when I have some candidates to interview. I want both of you to be in on my decision."

"Mr. Young, I…" Haven struggled to sort out her thoughts and feelings at this announcement. She finally found her voice. "Thank you, sir. I appreciate your thoughtfulness."

"It's not thoughtful. It's entirely selfish. You and Seth carry the bulk of the work around here and I want to keep you both happy. We're a good team, but you both need to get out more and stop spending every moment working. Get a life, date someone for goodness sakes," Mr. Young said, getting to his feet and walking to the door, amused by Haven's shocked expression. "While I'm at it, get out of here and enjoy an extra hour or two of free time."

"But sir, I have to…"

"Put on your coat and go. I insist," Mr. Young said, crossing his arms over his chest and waiting for Haven to do his bidding.

Reluctantly, she turned off her computer, straightened her already neat desk and started to grab a file to take home with her. Mr. Young strode across the room and grabbed it from her hand.

"Nope. No homework tonight. Go. Go out to dinner. Go to the spa. Go shopping," Mr. Young suggested, holding her coat as she slipped her arms in the sleeves then picked up her purse and handed it to her. "Go do something completely fun and frivolous. Then be back here, raring to go tomorrow. I have a new client coming in I want you and Seth to meet."

"Yes, sir. Thank you," Haven said, walking down the hall and shrugging at the receptionist as Mr. Young entered Seth's office. She assumed he'd soon be shoved out the door, too.

Deciding to take the unexpected time as a welcome gift, Haven couldn't decide what to do. Driving to the mall, she spent an hour browsing through stores.

When she shopped, it was normally because she needed a specific item. She would race into the store, get what she needed, and hurry back out. Nevertheless, today she could browse to her heart's content. She found two blouses and a pair of jeans she liked and purchased them along with a new pair of shoes.

Pleased with her unexpected shopping trip, Haven wandered to the bookstore and browsed, selecting a title from the romantic suspense section. She bought it and a big hot chocolate on her way out the door.

Hurrying home, she changed into jeans and a sweatshirt then curled up on the couch with the book and drink, immersing herself in a world much different from her own.

Lost in the story, she failed to notice the afternoon light grew dim. At an exciting point in the tale, she had no awareness of anything beyond the book in her hand.

A knock on her door made her scream as she dropped the book on the floor and glanced around, wide-eyed.

The pounding resumed and she rushed to the door, smiling at Hale as he stood on her step, holding bags of Chinese food.

"I come bearing gifts," he said, grinning as he stepped inside. "I wasn't sure you'd be home yet since it isn't obscenely late and you're usually still hunched over your desk at work, but I took a chance."

"I'm glad you did," Haven said, leading the way to her kitchen and taking two plates out of the cupboard, setting them on her small table. "What brings you to my humble abode?"

"Can't I drop by for dinner with my favorite sister without having a reason?" Hale asked, removing his coat and sitting down at the table. Helping Haven take the food out of the bags, he passed her the fried rice with an innocent shrug.

"You're joking, right? I'm your only sister so don't try buttering me up with that favorite business. The only time you guys come over is when you want me to do something."

"True," Hale said, smiling as he helped himself to some orange chicken and broccoli beef. "But I really did come over without any ulterior motives tonight. It's been a while since just the two of us have hung out and I wanted to see how things are going for you."

"Oh," Haven said, setting down her fork and staring at her brother. While Tom and Wes could be obnoxious and thickheaded most of the time, Hale was the one who offered his support when she needed it and often gave her good advice. Picking up her fork, she continued eating but still wondered what brought Hale to her door. He rarely dropped by just to visit, but maybe this was one of those far and few between instances.

"So, did you enjoy the game Friday?" Hale asked, knowing Haven wouldn't have gone unless she had to. "It was fun to meet that player. What was his name?"

"Brody. Brody Jackson," Haven supplied, too quickly. She'd never admit it to anyone, least of all one of her brothers, but the football player had been in her thoughts since the game Friday evening. She kept picturing that head of dark hair, square chin, and rich brown eyes. If she closed her eyes, she could hear his gravelly voice and it made gooseflesh ripple up her arms. "At least I think that was his name."

Hale looked at her with a narrow, knowing glare. "Yep. That was his name. What did you do with the ball he gave you?"

"Tommy tried to keep it, and I would have let him, but he irritated me before I got him home, so it's in my closet," Haven said, realizing that even if her brother hadn't annoyed her, she still would have kept the ball. It had Brody's name and the date scrawled across it and for some reason, Haven couldn't part with it.

Hale laughed and shook his head. "You know, someday the two of you are going to have to learn to play nice together."

"Someday, maybe." Haven gave Hale an impish grin. "But that day has not yet arrived."

"Are you going to the game this weekend?"

"Yes." Haven speared a piece of broccoli with force. Although she did enjoy the game and was secretly thrilled at meeting Brody, she didn't want to go back.

If she did, it would be extremely hard for her to keep pretending she wasn't interested in the gorgeous football player. She knew even if she managed, by some miracle, to catch his eye, she'd just be a conquest for him then he'd move on to the next girl. She didn't intend to become involved with him. Ever.

Men like Brody Jackson were bad news. Especially to softhearted, sensitive girls like Haven.

"Don't sound so excited about it," Hale teased, sitting back in his chair and studying his sister. He and Tom both noticed her interest in the ballplayer and planned to find out if she was going to do anything about it.

He could count on one hand the number of dates his sister had been on in her lifetime and the girl was almost twenty-six. Smart, pretty, and funny, he didn't know what was wrong with the men she encountered. She should have them beating down her door.

Instead, because she tended to be reserved around strangers, most of them didn't give her a third glance. Those big blue eyes and curly blonde hair always got her a second look, but that was as far as it tended to go.

"I'm not, but Mr. Young decided I was going to be the official office representative at all the games. I tried to talk him into letting Seth or Adam go, but he wouldn't even discuss it. He is, however, finally hiring an assistant for Seth and me to share and told me to stop working so many hours."

"That's great news, baby girl. You work far too hard. It's about time you quit hiding behind your desk and get a life."

"I've got a life, Mr. Know-It-All. I've got… stuff going on," Haven said, trying to think of what she did have besides work and the occasional trip out to the farm to visit her parents or a random evening spent with her cousin Allie and her crazy friends.

"Yeah, I know all about your stuff, missy. Admit it, you are a workaholic and need an intervention. I'm just grateful Mr. Young doesn't take advantage of that. He must really value your work," Hale said, finishing his dinner and reaching for a fortune cookie. Breaking it open, he chuckled as he read his fortune, handing the message to Haven.

She rolled her eyes after reading, "*Your wisdom exceeds your years*," on the little slip of paper.

"Don't let that go to your already swollen head," she said, opening her cookie. The message it contained made her choke on a bite of rice, causing it to go down wrong. Hale thumped her on the back and snatched the fortune from her fingers.

Holding it out to her, he grinned broadly. "Guess you better start enjoying those football games, Haven. Brody Jackson is your best prospect."

Haven's cheeks flushed at the words written on the fortune in her cookie. "*True love comes to those who tackle it.*"

"Who writes these stupid things, anyway?" Haven asked, wadding up the little piece of white paper, suddenly losing her appetite. "That's ridiculous. What's it supposed to mean? I hope you know I'm not tackling anybody."

Hale laughed again, patting Haven's arm. "That's what you've got big brothers for, isn't it? To do the tackling on your behalf? You just tell us who to take out and we're there."

Haven giggled as Hale made a funny face then started cleaning up the leftovers from dinner.

He helped her with the dishes and they sat visiting in her living room for a while before he got up to leave.

"I'm glad things at work are going to get better for you. You really do work too much."

"I know, Hale. Thanks for your support. And for going with me to the game Friday. You want to go this week? The game's Saturday night."

"Can't. I promised to take Abby to see that new chick flick that's out," Hale said, vigorously rubbing a hand over Haven's head, mussing her hair. Watching as she tried to brush it out of her face, he pulled on his coat and stood at the door. "I'm sure Tom would be willing to go."

"Yeah, but I can't afford to feed him every time there's a home game. I'll see who else I can round up," Haven said, feeling only marginally guilty for not inviting Tom. She knew she could call him if she couldn't find anyone else to go with her.

"You're a good sport. Have a great week at work," Hale said, as he opened the door and cold rushed inside.

Haven shivered but waved at him. "I will. Thanks for dinner tonight, big brother. I'm glad you came over."

"Me, too. But you can buy or cook next time," Hale called as he opened his pickup door.

"It's a date," Haven said, waving one last time before closing her door and returning to the couch and the book she'd spent the afternoon enjoying.

Picking it up, her thoughts continued to wander to one extremely fit and handsome football player instead of the story.

Disgusted with herself, Haven tossed down the book and turned on her television, seeking anything to divert her thoughts away from Brody Jackson.

## *Chapter Four*

"Think she'll be here tonight?" Marcus asked as he tossed a ball to Brody before the game started.

"Who?" Brody feigned ignorance. He'd spent the entire week thinking about Haven Haggarty. He didn't know what it was about the girl that had gotten into his head and taken over his thoughts.

She wasn't the prettiest girl he'd ever seen. She obviously wasn't the most outgoing. He'd peg her as a shy type of girl. One who took life seriously, who didn't have many friends, didn't date much. She probably wore her heart on her sleeve and spent a lot of time nursing hurt feelings.

Getting involved with her would be pure stupidity on his part. He liked girls who knew he was looking for a good time. Girls who didn't care about things like commitment or romance. That type of girl piqued his interest. Not some sweet, sappy-eyed, fresh-faced doll who would bring his emotions out of hiding and quite possibly make him feel something.

Nope.

Girls like that were dangerous and that was why Brody was determined to forget all about Haven Haggarty. Starting now.

Just because he'd driven past her office twice in the past week, hoping to catch a glimpse of her, and spent an hour perusing her company's website looking at photos of her along with her work bio, it didn't mean a thing.

Neither did the photo he'd downloaded from the website or the way he stared at it before he went to bed, remembering how smooth and soft her skin looked, how much he wanted to touch her silky hair, how good she smelled.

Brody was through obsessing about the girl, though. He had better things to do with his time.

"You know who I'm talking about, man. Don't play dumb with me," Marcus said, raising an eyebrow at his friend. "I saw you give her that ball last week. I thought I might have to bring a towel up there and wipe your chin before you drooled all over her."

"Shut up," Brody said, glaring at Marcus. He hadn't been that obvious. "She works for one of the sponsors. I was just being nice."

"Sure you were. Correct me if I'm wrong, but you don't offer such personal service to any of the other sponsors, do you?"

Marcus had him there.

Brody generally didn't go out of his way to do anything for the sponsors. If a request arrived for the team to make an appearance at a sponsor's event, he went with a smile. He recommended sponsor businesses and shopped in their stores, but at a game, he didn't pay much attention to who was sitting in the sponsor seats and he never gave them personal attention.

He certainly never signed a ball and hand-delivered it to any of them.

Ignoring Marcus' comments, Brody tossed him the ball, but his friend wasn't ready to let the matter drop.

"Wasn't she the girl you decided was a high-maintenance trophy wife? Wasn't she with two big guys who looked like twins, or something?"

"Yeah, but one of the guys had a date and I'm not so sure she liked the guy she was with. He was obnoxious. And she didn't have fake nails or a gaudy ring," Brody added, wondering why he said anything at all. It only served to make Marcus grin with satisfaction.

"Yep. I can tell that you're not interested in her at all." Marcus tossed him the ball again. "So, do you think she'll be here tonight?"

"How would I know, dude? I barely know her name." Brody realized the error in admitting even that much to Marcus. Now he'd be like a dog with a bone, gnawing away until he got what he wanted.

"Ha! And her name is…"

"Haven," Brody said on a sigh. "Haven Haggarty."

"Well, la-di-da. That name sounds like one you'd find on the strip in Vegas. What did you say she does for a living?"

Brody glared at Marcus. "I didn't. Now why don't you quit flapping your jaws so we can finish warming up before the game starts?"

Marcus grinned and saluted his friend. "Yes, sir." He'd never seen Brody so worked up about a girl. He hoped the cute blonde could capture his buddy's interest. It was about time for the mighty Brody Jackson to take a fall.

They were a few minutes into the game when Brody saw Haven come in with two different men and a girl that looked like a supermodel. She was tall with flowing black hair, a great body, and a huge smile. He noticed the girl said something to make Haven laugh as they sat side by side. One of the guys sat next to Haven and the other sat by the black-haired girl.

Marcus elbowed him in passing, causing Brody to shake his head and return his attention to the game.

Working hard for the lead they earned by halftime, Brody was so busy playing he hadn't been able to observe Haven and her friends.

The last to head back to the locker room, he took a moment to watch Haven laugh at something the girl beside her said. Her face lit with joy and he thought she looked beautiful. Stealing one last look at her, he followed the team out of the arena.

"She's here," Marcus said in a singsong voice that grated on Brody's nerves.

"What's wrong with you?" Brody asked, giving Marcus a shove.

"Man, you've got it bad." Marcus glanced around to see with whom he could share this newsworthy tidbit of information. He felt Brody's hand grip the back of his neck and turned to see a look of unmistakable warning on his face.

"Do not say a word. You hear me, Marc? Not a word," Brody growled, dropping his hand and taking a seat on a bench while the coach talked.

"What's going on?" Marcus whispered.

"Nothing, dude. Just keep it to yourself," Brody said quietly. He couldn't explain to himself why he was so interested in Haven. He sure didn't want to try to enlighten anyone else.

Finally, halftime ended and they returned to the field. Brody made it a point to keep from looking in the direction of Haven's seat. Marcus studied him and tipped his head her direction, trying not to grin.

"Leave it alone, Marcus," Brody said, slapping him on the shoulder as he ran out on the field.

Brody played with incredible intensity as he channeled his frustrations and energy into the game. After one amazing catch, he could hear a group of particularly rowdy fans start to chant, "Jump it up, Jackson! Jump it up!" Soon the entire crowd seemed to be yelling it.

Catching a pass and running for all he was worth, Brody almost made it to the end zone when he felt a weight hit his back and knock him down. Keeping the ball gripped tightly in his hand, he heard the distinctive smack of bodies plowing into each other and helmets cracking as players piled around and over him. Trying to take a breath, he thought for moment he might smother before the guys got off him. Freed from the pile, he pushed himself to his feet and grinned.

He loved football.

Glancing into the stands, his gaze collided with Haven's. She stared at him wide-eyed from her seat, tightly clutching the hand of her friend. She looked relieved when he took a step back, bumping into someone.

Marcus walked by and tapped his helmet twice. "Focus, man. Game's almost over."

"I'm on it," Brody said, forcing his attention back to the last few minutes of the game.

Winning by one touchdown, the team was ready to celebrate. Brody knew he couldn't run up into the stands to see Haven again without causing a bunch of tongues to wag, but he couldn't let her leave without speaking to her.

Grabbing Marcus by the arm, he tugged him into the foyer where people were flooding out the doors into the parking lot. Shaking hands and accepting congratulations as they made their way over to the doorway of the section where Haven sat. Marcus didn't say anything, although he seemed to know what Brody was planning.

They didn't have long to wait as Haven appeared with her friends.

"Hey, good to see you again," Brody said, smiling at the group, although his gaze lingered on Haven. She wore jeans, a flowery blouse, and a navy blue coat that hid most of her figure from his view. Instead of the bun she wore the previous week, her hair was pulled back in a long ponytail.

He gave her an interested look, although he had to swallow twice to regain his ability to speak as her soft fragrance, redolent of spring flowers, drifted over him. "Haven, isn't it?"

"Yes, it is, Mr. Jackson. I'm surprised you remembered." Haven looked at him with big blue eyes and a questioning glance.

"I couldn't forget a name like that. And I thought you agreed to call me Brody," he said, watching her cheeks turn pink.

The girl next to Haven gave her a noticeable nudge. He thought he could detect a hint of irritation mixed with longsuffering in her voice when she spoke.

"Brody. This is my cousin, Allison," Haven said, making introductions. The tall dark-haired girl held out her hand.

"Everyone calls me Allie. You guys played a great game," Allie said, grinning as she shook Brody's hand.

"Thanks." Marcus said, introducing himself to the group.

"Oh, this is my boyfriend, Rick, and Haven's friend Seth," Allie said, pushing Haven so she had to take a step closer to Brody.

Glaring over her shoulder at her cousin, Haven wanted to smack her. If she wasn't her best friend, she just might have done it, too.

"So, Haven, my invitation from last week still stands if you'd like to come to the party later," Brody said, wanting desperately to reach out and rub his fingers along her pale cheek to see if her skin felt as soft as it looked.

Although she wasn't tall and willowy like her cousin, Haven was cute with an amazing smile. He watched as dimples popped into her cheeks and felt a growing need to kiss each one.

If she'd just agree to come to the party, he was sure he could manage to get some time alone with her, get her out of his system, so he could move on and return his focus to making it a winning season.

"Thank you, Brody, but we really do need to get going," Haven said, pushing Allie toward the door, leaving a bewildered Rick and Seth trailing along behind. "We appreciate the offer, but we just can't. Great game! Bye!"

Before Brody could offer any protest, Haven hurried outside, briskly marching across the parking lot. Allie was obviously stating her opinion about the matter while Rick and Seth followed the girls, shaking their heads.

"What just happened here?" Marcus asked as they walked toward the locker room to shower and change. "I could be wrong, but for the first time in history, the great and mighty Brody Jackson was just turned down. Hang onto something, I think the world just might be about to end."

"Just shut it!" Brody said, stomping into the locker room and yanking off his shirt followed by the rest of his uniform. He knew he was good-looking, he knew he could be charming, and he knew girls bought into that whole going-out-with-the-football-player thing.

What was wrong with Haven? She was the first girl in his twenty-seven years of living to turn him down, not once but twice.

He was sure the guy with her tonight wasn't her boyfriend because they acted more like coworkers. Besides, the dude was shorter than she was and that was just wrong in Brody's book of how things worked.

That book also did not include a page on being turned down by the only girl who had managed to hold his interest for more than a day or two since his first crush in high school.

Still ramped up on adrenaline from the game, Brody wanted to kick something or pound someone into the ground. He hadn't felt this tied up in angry knots since the practice squad dropped him three years ago.

Playing arena football and trying to work his way into an NFL training camp, he didn't have the time or energy to invest in a girl who obviously had no interest in him.

Yanking on a pair of shorts, Brody decided to go to the weight room and blow off some steam.

"Bro, what're you doing?" Marcus asked, putting a restraining hand on his arm. "You look like you're about to explode."

"I'm fine, man. I just need to work off a little energy," Brody said, attempting to give Marcus an encouraging smile.

It looked more like a grimace and Marcus shook his head. "Want me to hang with you?"

"No, go on to the party. I'm cool."

"You sure?" Marcus gave him a doubtful look.

"I'm fine, man. Go on, have some fun," Brody said over his shoulder, walking in the direction of the weight room.

Pulling on gloves, he beat the punching bag until his arms began to ache and he could feel a little of the tension slide off his shoulders.

Sitting on a bench, he used a towel to wipe the sweat from his face and felt the presence of someone near. Lifting his gaze, the coach stared down at him.

"You need to run a few laps, too?" the coach asked with a smile.

"No, sir. I don't believe I do," Brody said, realizing he was tired and much calmer than he'd been an hour ago.

"Good. Get out of here. Go home. Get some sleep." The coach walked off, knowing Brody would turn off the lights and shut the door behind him.

Returning to the locker room, Brody took a shower and dressed in jeans and the shirt he'd worn earlier before he changed into his uniform.

Finger-combing his hair, he realized he was starving and decided to skip the party and instead go get something to eat.

Driving toward his apartment, he stopped at a diner that looked quiet. The last thing he needed right now was to be swarmed by a bunch of people wanting to discuss the game or asking for his autograph.

Going in, he sat down at an empty booth and picked up the laminated menu on the table, waiting for the waitress to come over.

"Oh. My. Gosh," Allie said, squeezing Haven's arm in a death grip.

"Ow! What are you doing?" Haven asked, jerking away from her cousin and rubbing her forearm. She was certain it would sport bruises tomorrow.

"You won't believe who just walked in." Allie's gaze locked on someone behind Haven. After the game, the two girls, along with Rick and Seth, went to a diner near Haven's apartment to enjoy dessert.

With her back to the door, Haven had no idea who could have possibly inspired such a reaction in Allie.

"I'm sure I won't, so just tell me," Haven said, taking a sip of water as Seth and Rick both glanced up to see who captured Allie's attention.

"Oh, this is too good," Rick said, grinning at Allie. "You couldn't have planned this better yourself, Al."

"I know, it's like totally perfect," Allie agreed, beaming with pleasure.

"I'm going to kick you, hard, under the table if you don't tell me who came in," Haven demanded, wondering what had gotten into Allie.

Seth rolled his eyes and took another bite of his pie.

"It's the naughty hottie from the football game," Allie said, staring over Haven's left shoulder toward a booth. "He's even cuter dressed in normal clothes. I would pay money to see him without his shirt on."

"Hey, do you not see me sitting right here?" Rick asked, clearly offended as he frowned at Allie.

"Sorry, babe. Just trying to help out Haven."

"Sure you were," Rick said, glancing behind Haven. "I don't see what the fuss is all about. I could totally arm wrestle the dude."

Rick flexed his biceps and Allie squeezed them then kissed him soundly on the lips. Disgusted by the public display of affection, Haven wondered how she could possibly be related to her cousin. They were nothing alike. At all.

"Could you please stop that before I lose my dinner?" Haven asked, shoving her half-eaten piece of chocolate cake away from her. "And before you embark on more theatrical demonstrations, Allie, just tell me who came in."

"Brody Jackson. He's sitting three booths behind you, looking mighty fine and terribly lonely."

"How stupid do you think I am? Like he'd show up in a place like this when he has a party with adoring fans to attend. I don't think so, Al, but nice try," Haven said, sipping her hot tea and shaking her head.

Seth caught her eye and tipped his head, letting her know that she should turn around and look for herself.

Pretending to drop her napkin, Haven bent down to pick it up and looked behind her, sucking in a gulp of air as she discovered Allie was telling her the truth.

"What do we do now?" Haven asked, sitting up so straight in her seat, it looked like someone shoved a board up the back of her shirt. "How can we leave with him sitting there? Does this place have a back entrance?"

"Are you insane?" Allie asked, grabbing the bill the waitress brought to the table and motioning Rick to finish eating his pie. "It's obvious he's interested in you and you practically ran out the door when he invited you to that party. I still don't know why you wouldn't just say yes. I know you hate that type of thing, but the rest of us wanted to go."

"Fine. Next time, go without me. I suppose we'll have to stop and say something to him on our way out. It's the polite thing to do," Haven said, stabbing her fork into her cake and taking another bite.

"That's right. You wouldn't want to be impolite, would you, dear cousin?" Allie said, subtly motioning for Seth to put on his coat.

"Of course not. I just don't want to encourage him, is all," Haven said, lost in her thoughts of how gorgeous Brody Jackson looked up close. She couldn't believe he remembered her name and spoke to her after the game. She didn't think he'd noticed she was even there.

Caught up in Allie's antics and silliness, she missed the many glances he shot her direction while he was on the field, assuming he'd forgotten all about her.

Part of her hoped he would call about the modeling offer. She wouldn't have minded seeing him somewhere other than the football game. She didn't know why Brody had taken an interest in her, but guys like him just didn't ask girls like her on dates.

She might be inexperienced where men were concerned, but she wasn't stupid. With his good looks and the way his voice made delicious shivers run up and down her spine, she knew staying away from him was the intelligent choice.

Renewing her resolve to give him a wide berth, she'd smile on her way out the door and hopefully avoid running into him again.

Excusing herself to the restroom, she returned to find an empty table. Glancing outside, she watched as Allie and Rick pulled into traffic, and Seth followed right behind them.

Shocked the three of them would sneak out and leave her at the diner, Haven knew it was Allie's idea. Her cousin was in such deep trouble, she might never work her way back out of it.

Sighing, she turned around to find Brody standing next to his booth watching her.

"Haven?" he asked, stepping toward her. "Is everything okay?"

"Yes. No. I'm not sure," Haven said, letting him take her arm and lead her back to his booth with her coat and purse in his hand.

He motioned for the waitress to come over and she brought Haven another cup of tea as she settled onto the plastic-covered bench and looked across the worn table at Brody.

"What was that all about?" Brody asked, scooting his plate toward her so she could take a fry if she wanted. She shook her head and he slid his plate back.

"My cousin Allie thinks she is much more clever and amusing than she really is," Haven said, wondering what sort of retribution Tom would demand if she called and asked for a ride home. She'd call Hale, but knew he had a big date with Abby and didn't want to be bothered. Maybe she'd just call a cab.

Pulling out her phone, she started searching for a cab company.

Brody leaned over and glanced at the screen.

"Left you high and dry, did she?" he asked, thinking Allie was now among his favorite people. He'd have to remember to thank her the next time he saw her. He hadn't even noticed the group in the diner until Allie and the two guys ran by, smiling and waving on their way out the door.

Watching them sprint across the parking lot and speed off into the night, he wondered what they were doing then he noticed Haven. She'd obviously not expected to be left behind.

"Something like that. My brother would make my life pure misery if I call him to come get me, so I'll just call a cab," Haven said, wondering which cab company was more reputable. Deciding she was too tired to care, she would randomly choose one.

"Put down your phone. I'll take you home," Brody said, finishing his burger and smothering a fry in a puddle of ketchup before eating it.

"No. That's completely unnecessary. I wouldn't want to put you out," Haven said, looking at him with wide, frightened eyes.

He wondered what exactly about him scared her. He supposed it could be his height or his career. Maybe she'd gotten wind of his supposed reputation with women. Whatever it was, he could see the fear on her face and wished he wasn't the one who put it there.

"I insist," Brody said, glancing across the table and finding himself drawn, again, to Haven's pink mouth and soft skin. She looked so utterly feminine. If someone needed a visual of the words sophisticated or lady, he thought she'd be the perfect picture. "Really, it's no trouble."

"Well, I…"

"Come on. I have to be better than some random cab driver. I promise to get you home safely or you can have your brother beat me up."

Haven laughed and the dimples bloomed in her cheeks. Brody held his hands beneath the table to keep from reaching out and touching each indentation.

"I don't think you have to worry about that. He was very impressed with you after the game last week," Haven said, relaxing a little and taking a sip of her tea.

"Last week? How many brothers do you have?" Brody asked, wondering if the men with her were her brothers. If one was, they both had to be because they looked so much alike.

"Three, but Hale and Tom went with me to the game last week. I guess we didn't get around to discussing that during introductions."

"No, we didn't," Brody said, relieved that the two men who seemed quite familiar with Haven were her brothers. That knowledge improved his mood significantly. "What about the guy with you tonight? Seth? He your boyfriend?"

Haven laughed again and shook her head. "No. Seth and I are the lead consultants at the firm where we work. He's engaged. His fiancée hates sports of any kind, but he is a huge football fan."

"I see," Brody tried not to grin too broadly. So far, three of the men he thought were direct competition for Haven had been quickly eliminated.

"So does your boyfriend not like football?" he asked, fishing to find out if there was a boyfriend.

"I don't know if he does or not," Haven said, gifting Brody with a teasing smile.

"How can you not know? Didn't you invite him to the game?"

"No. It would be hard to do that when I've yet to meet him."

"You have a boyfriend you've never met? Wait. That's just weird," Brody said, puzzled by her words. "He's not one of those online stalker dudes, is he?"

Haven gave him a pointed look. "No, of course not, but I had you going, though."

Brody chuckled and finished his glass of soda. "So you don't have a boyfriend? Or a fiancé? Or a husband and three kids waiting at home for you?"

"Sadly, none of the above. It's just me and Mad Dog," Haven said, taking another sip of tea, glancing at Brody over the rim of her cup. The look on his face was priceless. His handsome brow wrinkled in confusion and he looked completely bewildered.

"Mad Dog?"

"I'm reading a book about a cop named Mad Dog and the bad guy she's trying to catch. It has gruesome murders and a crazed killer. Oh, there's some romance in there, too."

"Sounds great, at least up to the romance part."

"Don't tell me you're one of those guys who think romance is stupid."

"Guilty as charged," Brody said, taking the bill from the waitress and thanking her. Pulling money out of his wallet, he left a hefty tip on the table along with cash to cover the bill.

Haven slipped on her coat and looked at him, seeming hesitant to leave with a man she barely knew.

"If it will make you feel any better, you can call Allie and talk to her the whole time I'm driving you home. That way, you know I can't abscond with you," Brody said, offering Haven one of the sincere smiles he rarely shared. His mother and Marcus were among the privileged few who'd seen it.

"That won't be necessary, I'm sure," Haven said, surprised when Brody held the door for her as they walked outside.

"Where's your coat?" she asked, glad to be wearing her warm wool coat in the frigid air. The night was cold but clear as he took her arm and guided her toward a shiny pickup.

"I left it at home this afternoon. It was warm then, you know, and I didn't think about needing it later," Brody said, holding the pickup door while Haven slid inside. She was just tall enough she didn't require his assistance getting into the pickup. Disappointment trickled over him as he shut the door and walked around to the driver's side.

Getting in and starting his truck, he glanced over at Haven. Sitting primly against the door with her hands folded on her lap, she seemed ready to bolt.

"Seriously?" he asked, giving her a once over when she looked at him. "I promise I won't turn into a vampire, a serial killer, or whatever else is running through your head, between now and the time I drop you off. But you are going to have to tell me where you live."

Haven let out her breath and worked up a smile. For some reason Brody made her extremely nervous. She seemed to have that problem around really cute guys, particularly ones that actually spoke to her.

"Okay. But if I turn up with fang marks on my neck or my head missing tomorrow, you're gonna be in really big trouble," she said, making him laugh as he pulled out onto the nearly deserted street and followed her directions. She didn't live all that far from the diner. In fact, her apartment was only five blocks from his place.

"Got it. No biting or decapitating," he said, sitting at a red light. "At least tonight. I'm on my best behavior. See, I'm trying to impress this girl, but I get the idea she really isn't all that into me."

"Really?" Haven wondered what was wrong with a girl who wouldn't be flattered by attention from Brody. "Where did you meet her?"

"At a football game. I looked up into the stands and there she was."

"What does she look like?" Haven asked, curious as to the type of girl that caught Brody's eye. She pictured someone like Allie.

"She's got curly blonde hair, beautiful blue eyes, dimples in her cheeks, and the pinkest lips that just beg for a kiss," Brody said, trying to keep a straight face, realizing Haven didn't know he was talking about her.

He watched her processing his response then her gaze narrowed as she looked at him and shook her head.

"You ought to know I'm well-versed in being teased. I do have three older brothers, remember?"

"I know, but you're so gullible," Brody said, liking that fact. She was so innocent it was almost comical.

"I'm not either," she said hotly, turning her head and staring out the window. After a moment, she sighed and glanced back at him. He could see the hint of her dimples as she smiled. "Maybe a little."

"Maybe more than a little, Miss Haven Haggarty," Brody said, turning into her apartment complex and parking in an empty space close to her door.

Unfastening his seat belt, he jumped out and ran around the cab of the truck, determined to walk her to the door, wishing she'd invite him in. He'd enjoyed talking with her and hoped she'd be open to continuing the conversation for a while.

"You don't need to be out in this cold, Brody. I can get myself to the door," Haven said, taking his hand as he helped her out of his truck.

"I know, but I'll walk you to the door just the same. You never know when a vampire or crazed killer might jump out of nowhere," Brody said, walking down the sidewalk with her hand still held in his. He liked the soft, delicate feel of her fingers against his palm. That mere connection of her skin touching his sent a flurry of sensation zipping up his arm, right into his chest.

"How about that? Here we are at the door and we're both still alive with no madmen in sight," Haven said, pulling her fingers from his grasp so she could dig in her purse for her key and unlock the door.

Opening it a crack, she turned back to Brody and stuck out her hand. When he enclosed it in his big warm one again, she felt a tremor work its way up from her toes. She breathed in a whiff of his scent and was certain she'd never smelled anything so utterly masculine and divine.

"Thank you for driving me home. I apologize for the behavior of my supposed friends," Haven said, looking up at Brody's face in the dim porch light. She was beginning to think he might just be the most handsome man she'd ever seen in person. Certainly the most handsome one she'd ever seen this close.

An overpowering yearning to run her fingers along that chiseled jaw and chin made her take a step back, bumping into the door, sending it banging against the inside wall.

"No problem. I'm just glad I was there to drive you home," Brody said, realizing an invitation to go inside with her wasn't going to materialize. He should have known he was wishing for something that wouldn't happen.

"Thanks again. Have a good rest of the weekend," she said, tugging her hand from his as she backed farther into her apartment and flicked on a light. He could see a nice living room behind her and thought about walking inside, but knew instinctively that would frighten her.

"I will. You, too. Thanks for coming to the game tonight."

Brody took a step in the direction of his truck. The last thing he wanted to do was leave, but he knew he couldn't stay.

"I enjoyed watching you play, Jump It Up Jackson," Haven said with a teasing smile that brought out her dimples once more. She waggled her fingers at Brody, then shut the door.

Shoving his hands in his pockets, he hurried back to his truck and drove home, caught in a state between bliss and undeniable longing.

# *Chapter Five*

Hoping to catch Haven at home Sunday afternoon, Brody drove to her apartment and knocked on the door only to stand on her step and decide she wasn't there. Or, if she was, she wasn't going to let him in.

By Wednesday morning, every nerve in his body felt tightly strung and about to snap, so he pulled her business card out of his wallet and called her at ten minutes past eight. He assumed she'd be in the office by then. He'd bet she even showed up early, to get a jumpstart on her day.

Anxiously waiting for her to answer, he let out the breath he'd been holding when her soft voice came on the line.

"Good morning, Haven. This is Brody Jackson. I've given some consideration to your proposal about modeling. I was wondering if we could discuss it over lunch?" he asked, knowing he had no intention of doing any modeling, but grasped at any excuse to see her.

"Good morning, Brody. It's nice to hear from you." Haven said calmly, although her feet tapped out a happy dance beneath her desk. While her head kept telling her to stay away from Brody Jackson, her heart and the rest of her cheered at the opportunity to see him again. "Let me check my schedule and see what I've got open today."

Haven didn't care if she had to cancel every appointment on her calendar, she was having lunch with Brody. Fortunately, she had an opening between eleven and one.

"Sorry for the short notice. I just thought I'd take a chance and see if you could squeeze me in." Brody knew he sounded like an overanxious moron. Always in control, always smooth, Haven left him feeling like he'd just gotten off a rollercoaster. The constant state of highs and lows was entirely out of character for him.

Since the team had a rare day off from practice, he hoped to use the time to further his cause with the cute girl.

"I've got an opening if you'd like to meet at eleven. Would that work for you?" Haven asked, hoping like everything he'd say yes. That way, if they wanted to visit more than an hour, she would have time before her next appointment at half past one that afternoon.

"That works great. I'll come pick you up. See you then." Brody disconnected the call before Haven could disagree.

Shooting both arms up in the air, he pumped his fists in victory.

There wasn't a girl alive he couldn't win over and he sure wasn't going to let Haven be the first. He'd never had to work this hard to get a date, pretending to be interested in something he wasn't, or had a girl infiltrate his thoughts for more than a day or two like she did.

His unreasonable obsession with the fair-haired girl had lasted for almost two weeks. He figured once he kissed her he'd realize there was no spark and his life could return to normal. Her face would stop floating through his dreams, he'd stop imagining the feel of her soft sweaters or smooth skin beneath his fingers, and her tantalizing fragrance would cease to invade his senses.

His morning passed quickly and he was soon on his way to Haven's office to pick her up. Giving himself plenty of time, he sat down the street for ten minutes because he didn't want to seem too eager. At five minutes before eleven, he parked his truck in a space close to the door and walked inside.

A young woman glanced his way then looked again, staring openly at him as he stood by her desk.

"I'm here to see Miss Haggarty," he said, smiling at the girl as she sat unmoving, blinking her eyes at him like she was trying to decide if he was real. When she continued to stare, he repeated his statement. "I'm here to see Miss Haggarty. Could you please let her know Mr. Jackson is here?"

"Certainly, Mr. Jackson," the girl finally said, pushing a button on her phone then quietly stating Haven had a visitor.

"She'll be right out, sir. You may have a seat if you like," the girl said, pointing to a set of chairs and a sofa across from her desk.

"I'll stand, thanks," he said, stepping over near the door to look out the window. They were in a newer commercial area surrounded by well-maintained businesses. From all the brown grass and empty planter boxes, he assumed it was probably quite pretty in the spring when flowers bloomed and everything was green.

"Brody, you didn't need to come pick me up. I could have met you," Haven said, walking toward him with a smile that brought out her dimples. She already had on her coat and carried a large bag instead of a purse. "Shall we go?"

"You bet, doll," Brody said, grinning broadly as he held the door for her. Nodding to the receptionist, he caught her watching them open-mouthed as they walked outside.

"Is your receptionist always so helpful?" Holding the pickup door open, he gave Haven a hand as she climbed up in her skirt and heels. It was a lot easier in her jeans the other night.

Haven laughed and Brody stood gazing at her dimples, loving the way her smile lit up her face. "Usually she's very good, but alarmingly handsome men tend to distract her. We've had that problem a few times before."

"So next time, I'll just honk and not bother to come in," Brody teased as he pulled out on the street and headed to a restaurant not far from Haven's office. He wanted to have as much time with her as possible and the restaurant nearby seemed like a good choice.

"My boss would love that. Besides, who says there'll be a next time?" Haven asked, the teasing light in her eyes giving away the fact she was kidding. Seeing Brody in broad daylight did funny things to her ability to think, especially with a swarm of butterflies erupting into a frenzied flight in her stomach. With the way she felt, she wasn't sure she'd be able to eat any lunch.

Brody was good-looking in his football uniform. In his casual shirt and jeans the other night he'd been quite handsome. Today, in a nice button down shirt with a sports jacket, jeans, and cowboy boots, he looked gorgeous and rugged.

Haven had to remind herself this was a business lunch, not a date, even though she wished he was interested in her personally. Convinced he was going to kiss her Saturday night, she'd experienced acute disappointment when all he'd done was squeeze her hand and leave her at the door.

She knew she was naïve, but she was sure there was some little spark of interest between the two of them. When their hands touched, she could tell he felt something too. Apparently, it had been her own wishes making her fanciful.

Brody parked in front of a restaurant and she smiled at his choice. It was one of her preferred places to meet clients and the food was always good.

Rushing around the pickup, he politely held her hand as she got out of his truck and the sizzle from Saturday night returned, sending currents dancing up her arm.

Walking inside, the staff greeted Haven by name, a fact that appeared to surprise Brody.

"Do you have a reservation, Miss Haggarty?"

"No, Danielle. I don't today," Haven said, looking at Brody with a questioning glance.

"But I do. Brody Jackson," he said, taking a step closer to the host station.

"We've got you right here, Mr. Jackson. Right this way, please."

Seated at one of Haven's favorite tables overlooking the river, Brody sat smiling at her in a way that made her feel fidgety and uneasy.

Grateful to be pulled out of his entrancing gaze when the waitress appeared, Haven spent the next several minutes pretending to study the menu. When the waitress reappeared with their drinks, she took their orders and Haven was left with nothing to distract her from the extremely appealing Brody Jackson, local football star.

She wasn't one who cared to watch sports on the news, but she sat glued to the television when the sportscaster showed a clip of Brody catching a pass at Saturday's game. Seeing him on TV confirmed she hadn't imagined how good he looked in his uniform.

Needing something to draw her attention away from his perfect face, she took a notebook and pen out of her bag and placed them in front of her.

"You mentioned an interest in modeling. Is that correct?" Haven asked, prepared to take notes about the types of projects that attracted Brody.

"I did mention I wanted to discuss it," Brody admitted sheepishly. When Haven stared at him, puzzled, he reached across the table and took her hand in his. Although it made his thoughts jumble, he entirely liked the feel of her hand in his. Far more than he should. "What I wanted to discuss is that I won't be able to model for you."

"You won't?" Haven asked, confused. She was certain when Brody called to invite her to lunch, he indicated an interest in modeling. Playing back the conversation in her mind, he said he wanted to discuss it, which is what they were doing.

"No. Not with my football contract," Brody said, feeling pricks of guilt at the look on Haven's face. She attempted to tug her hand away from his, but he held on, rubbing his thumb across her palm soothingly. The movement must have worked because she didn't try to yank it away from him again.

"Then why did you lead me to believe otherwise and why did you bring me here?" Haven asked, eyeing him speculatively. "I'm beginning to think you coerced me into meeting you under false pretenses."

Brody knew it was time for a confession. "I'm sorry for misleading you, but I figured if I called and asked you on a date you'd tell me no. I was pretty sure if I called and you thought it was business, you'd agree to meet."

"Trickery, subterfuge, and manipulating the truth. My, my, Mr. Jackson, this doesn't bode well for you," Haven said, removing her hand from Brody's as the waitress approached with their orders. When the girl left them alone again, Haven looked from her salad to Brody, shaking her head.

She should be angry with him. She should tell him what she thought of his behavior. She should order him to stay far away from her and never call her again. But she couldn't.

Flattered by the amount of effort he went to just to have lunch with her, a little voice in her head whispered that maybe Brody Jackson was as interested in her as she was in him.

"I'm sorry, Haven. I promise I won't do that again, but I just wanted to see you," Brody admitted, despite the embarrassment it caused him. If she didn't smile soon or let him know she wasn't mad at him, he might end up on his knees, groveling. "I enjoyed talking with you the other night and just wanted to get to know you better."

"I see," she said, and turned her attention to her salad. Although she wasn't upset with him, he didn't necessarily need to know that, yet.

Eating their meal in silence, Brody felt like squirming in his chair when Haven finally leveled her gaze at him. She looked like a disapproving teacher and he was beginning to feel like a misbehaving schoolboy, about to receive a tongue-lashing.

"Well?" she finally asked, sitting back and crossing her arms in front of her. He didn't know how she did it, but he swore she used those glasses to look intimidating and formidable.

He was a grown man who let other grown men tackle him for a living, yet this sweet girl was about to make him break out in a cold sweat.

"Well, what?" he asked, using a napkin to dab at his suddenly perspiring forehead.

"You said you wanted to talk, so what was so important that you had to trick me into meeting you here?" Haven asked, staring into his face. She had to fight to keep a smile from breaking out of hiding, so she practiced the stern glare she used at work when the staff told her something couldn't be done. Amazingly, the glare enabled all sorts of impossible things to become possible.

With her delicate fragrance surrounding him, Brody could barely remember his name, let alone anything remotely close to witty conversation. Frantically searching for any topic to discuss, he remembered she had brothers. Trying not to cringe beneath the glare she sent his direction, he cleared his throat.

"Tell me about your brothers. You said you had three, but you only mentioned two. What about the third brother?"

Haven leaned back in her chair and took a sip of her water before deciding to answer Brody's question.

"My brothers are all older than me. Wes is the oldest and married to Tammy. They have two little boys who are holy terrors. I'm pretty sure they take after their father. I feel sorry for my sister-in-law being the only female in that house, but she doesn't let them get to her, at least too often."

Brody chuckled and she continued.

"You met Tom the other night. He's only a year older than I am, and the most obnoxious of the three. Actually, he and Wes are a lot alike. Wes works with Dad on the family farm. Tom is a licensed realtor. He's a good salesman, even if he is a pest of a brother. Hale was the mad chemist of the family and he's now a pharmacist." Haven leaned across the table and dropped her voice to a whisper. "And if you can keep a secret, I'll even admit he's my favorite brother. He and I always got along really well."

Grinning, Brody leaned forward, bringing his face so close to hers, he could see flecks of light and dark blue dancing in those luminous eyes behind her glasses. "Your secret is safe with me."

"Good," Haven said, sitting back in her chair. She felt the need to keep a little distance from Brody because the desire to kiss him nearly got the best of her when he leaned across the table. His eyes were dark and rich, and he smelled so good, it made her feel lightheaded.

"You know, the other night I thought your brothers were twins until I was standing next to you and could see there was some age difference there," Brody admitted. He refrained from telling her he thought she was dating one of them.

"People often mistake the three of them for triplets from a distance. They all look so much alike. They get their coloring from my mom."

"So, do you take after your dad?"

Haven smiled. "Only my eye color. No one seems to know where this mop of hair came from."

Unable to stop himself, Brody reached out and captured one of the curls that escaped the bun at the back of her head and rubbed it between his fingers. The silky strands were even softer than he imagined.

Seeing her shift uncomfortably in her chair, he released the springy coil and dropped his hand to his lap.

"What about you?" she asked, wanting to know more about the man who'd tricked her into having lunch with him. "Do you have any siblings?"

"Nope," Brody said, taking a long drink from his glass.

"Where do your parents live? Where are you from?" Haven asked, knowing many of the football players just lived in town for the season, returning to their homes for the remainder of the year.

"My mom raised me in a little town back in Kansas. She still lives there," Brody said.

"What about your dad?" Haven asked, noticing the angry sparks in his eyes at the mention of his father.

"He took off before I was born. He married my mom, Angelina, when they were both young and stupid. She got pregnant with me right away and that's when he left. She never saw or heard from him again and doesn't even know if he's alive or dead."

That was more information about himself than he'd shared with anyone other than Marcus. No matter what he did right or wrong in his lifetime, he'd never abandon a wife or child the way his father had.

Remembering how his mother worked so hard and struggled to take care of him, he wouldn't ever put someone through that.

"I'm so sorry, Brody," Haven said, placing her hand over his and giving it a gentle squeeze. He lifted his gaze and took in the moisture gathering in her eyes. The last thing he wanted was her pity, so he changed the subject.

"Tell me again what you do for a living. I get the idea you're pretty hoity-toity for someone barely out of school," Brody said, knowing that would distract her.

"I'll have you know I'm almost twenty-six and I graduated from college when I was twenty," Haven said, feeling a little defensive at Brody's comments. "I've been working for Mr. Young since then and you'll find, since his company is fairly new compared to some, that he has a relatively young staff."

"I see," Brody said, hiding his smile behind his glass. "What do you do?"

"I'm an image consultant and brand analyst."

Brody tried to figure out what that meant, exactly, and gave her a questioning look.

"We work with companies who want to rebrand themselves, need a new corporate image, or want to tweak certain areas of their marketing and publicity strategy. We do everything from creating logos and designing websites to brand positioning and ad campaigns."

"I don't even know what half that means, but it sounds impressive," Brody said, resting his arms on the table, studying Haven's animated face. He suddenly wondered what she'd look like without glasses. They complemented her serious, professional demeanor, but without them on he'd bet her eyes would look even bigger and more alluring.

Haven reached down and pulled an iPad out of her bag. Tapping it a few times, she scooted Brody's empty plate out of the way and placed the tablet in front of him.

"This is a project we just finished for one of our clients," she said, showing him what the client's logo, website, and advertisements looked like before and what they looked like now. The difference was remarkable and he could see she excelled at her job.

"So what do you do specifically with something like this?" he asked, still not sure what her job entailed.

"For this project, I met with the company president, discussed what they wanted to accomplish, reviewed what they were doing, and made suggestions on what could work better. I took my ideas and the company objectives to our design teams and we met, brainstormed what we wanted to do then got to work. I oversee the development of the specific components, although I don't do the creative work myself."

"So basically, you schmooze clients, come up with the ideas, and crack the whip to make them happen," Brody said, boiling Haven's job down to one straightforward statement.

"That's an accurate assessment," Haven said with a smile. "Now tell me about your job."

"You know what I do. I catch the ball and run. Sometimes I tackle or block. That's about it," Brody said, simplifying his career.

"I know a little about football from having three brothers. You're a wide receiver. Correct?"

"Correct."

"And from what I've seen and heard, you're a really good one. How in the world do you jump so high?"

"It's just something I was always good at. Jumping and catching things thrown at me," Brody said. Those two talents had been useful when he was a scrawny kid trying to get away from the bullies who hounded him after school.

"What's the highest you've ever jumped?"

"On the field, during a game, right at forty inches. But I've jumped a lot higher than that before. Once I even jumped over a backyard fence, but I had a good running start."

"Oh, my gosh! That is amazing," Haven said, trying to imagine jumping that high. "The highest I ever jumped was the time Tommy dumped a mouse down the back of my shirt."

Brody laughed and Haven smiled.

"No wonder Hale's your favorite." Brody winked and gave her a teasing grin.

"Shh. I told you that's a secret," she said, putting a finger on his lips to silence him. The impact of that innocent touch left them both reeling as Haven snatched her hand back and placed it on her lap.

"Don't worry. I won't tell." Glancing at his watch, Brody realized they'd been at the restaurant for more than an hour. He assumed he'd probably kept Haven away from work longer than he should have.

Placing his napkin on the table, he looked around for the waitress so he could pay the bill. While he waited to catch her eye, he apologized to Haven. "I'm sorry, I didn't realize the time. I hope I'm not making you late for your next appointment."

Looking at her watch, Haven smiled. "I've got plenty of time. No apology necessary, except maybe for leading me here under false pretenses. Care to explain what that's all about?"

"Let's just say I was convinced you wouldn't meet me here any other way and leave it at that. I'm sorry, Haven, really I am. But I'm not sorry you came or that we had the chance to visit for a while. I like talking to you."

"I like talking to you, too," she said, deciding to be bold and brave. "Next time, just ask if I want to have lunch with you instead of inventing some pathetic story."

"It wasn't pathetic," Brody said, pretending to be offended. "It got you to come and it wasn't a story. We did discuss modeling. We discussed how I won't be doing it."

"Technically, but still…"

Haven quieted as the waitress approached with the bill and Brody took it before Haven could protest.

"I can pay for my half," Haven said, fishing in her bag for her wallet.

"No. I invited you and I'm buying," Brody said, wishing he could spend the afternoon with Haven, but he needed to get going and she had to return to work.

Getting to his feet, he held Haven's coat for her and inhaled her perfume as she slid her arms in the sleeves.

Her scent made him think of sunny skies, warm breezes, and spring flowers. Resting his hands on her shoulders, he wanted to pull her back against his chest and rain kisses along the exposed skin of her neck.

Instead, he took out his wallet and left cash for the bill as well as a generous tip on their table.

Haven noticed the other night Brody seemed to leave hefty tips and wondered about the reason. She assumed it was because both times the waitress was young and pretty and he was the big jock looking to impress a girl. Somewhat miffed by his actions, she glared down at the money he casually dropped next to the bill.

Noticing Haven staring at the cash on the table, Brody shrugged his shoulders and looked down at his feet. "Mom worked two jobs as a waitress all the years I was growing up and to help put me through school. I… um…"

"I see," Haven said, reaching out and squeezing his hand, aware that Brody had cracked open the door to his heart and let her peek inside for a brief moment. She felt remorseful for thinking his generous gesture was about stroking his ego. Maybe there was more to the man than she originally thought. "I think that's nice, Brody."

He nodded and kept her hand in his as they exited the restaurant and returned to his truck. Driving back to her office, they chatted about the weather and spring arriving soon. He started to get out to walk her to the door, but she asked him not to.

"It will just distract the staff with unnecessary gossip and speculation if you do," Haven said, placing her hand on his arm before he could get out of the truck.

"Why? Surely this isn't the first time you've left with a man for lunch," Brody said, thinking someone like Haven should have men asking her out on a daily basis.

"Well, it's um…"

"Come on, Haven. You go to lunch with clients all the time, don't you?"

"Yes, but you aren't a client."

"And I'm really glad about that because I'm pretty sure you can't do this with your clients." Brody leaned across the cab and placed a soft, gentle kiss on her surprised lips.

Although the contact was brief, Haven felt like her lips were about to burst into flame, along with the rest of her body from the brush of his mouth against hers.

"Thanks for lunch today, doll. I'm going to be playing out of town this week and next, but maybe we can see each other for lunch again, or something," Brody said in a husky voice with his face just inches from Haven's. His gaze rested on those pink lips he'd just kissed. He wanted to take her in his arms and drink from them until his thirst for the lovely woman was finally quenched.

Aware of the longing reflected in her eyes, along with a hint of uncertainty, Brody sat back and looked around his pickup for a piece of paper. Cleaning it out before he took her to lunch, he didn't even have a stray gum wrapper anywhere in the cab.

Grabbing a pen, he took Haven's hand in his, turning it over so it rested open and flat on his thigh. He shot her a cocky grin after scribbling something across her palm.

"That's my cell number if you want to call or text me," Brody said, kissing her cheek as she opened her door and started to slide out. "I hope I don't have to wait until our next home game to see you."

"Thanks, Brody," she said, unable to say anything as she held her hand open, away from her body, hoping her nervous, damp palm wouldn't annihilate the ink before she could get to her desk and write down his number. "Bye."

Walking quickly inside the building, she forced herself not to look back at Brody's truck. Instead, she tipped her head politely to the receptionist and hurried to her office.

Plopping down at her desk, she grabbed a pen and wrote the number on a piece of paper.

Removing her coat, she hung it up then took her phone out of her purse and added the number to her list of contacts. Staring at it, she contemplated the significance of Brody giving her his personal number.

Knowing he wouldn't be in the area in a few months when the season ended, she needed to decide if she'd allow herself to enjoy his company while she could or keep guarding her heart.

## *Chapter Six*

"You're not still mad about us ditching you at the diner after the last game, are you?" Allie asked Haven as they walked across the parking lot to the arena.

"What do you mean left you at the diner?" Hale asked as he walked beside his cousin and sister. He'd picked up Haven at her apartment and they met Allie and Rick in the parking lot at the football game.

For some reason, Haven refused to ride with Allie and he wondered if this had anything to do with it.

"Allie thought it would be hilarious to leave me at the diner after the last football game because Brody Jackson happened to be there. She was under the assumption he'd give me a ride home if I was abandoned by my so-called friends."

Hale glared at Allie. "You didn't really leave her there, did you?"

"Well, yeah, we did. Rick and I parked across the street and then followed behind his truck to make sure she got home safely. He didn't even try to kiss her goodnight. I was, like, totally in shock," Allie said, speaking to Hale while ignoring the look of irritation on Haven's face.

"So not only did you dump me, you stalked me?" Haven said, looking from Allie to Rick. He at least had the grace to look embarrassed.

"It wasn't stalking. I wanted to make sure he wasn't like a crazed killer or something," Allie said, looping her arm around Haven's as they neared the door.

"Wouldn't that have been good to discover before you left me at the diner?"

"Maybe, but it was a spur of the moment thing," Allie said, grinning as they walked inside. "Besides, it worked out fine, didn't it?"

"I don't know what your definition of fine is, but it's not like we've gone out on a date or anything. I haven't even seen him for a couple weeks," Haven said. Although Brody gave her his number and said he wanted to see her again soon, between him traveling out of town for games and her work schedule, all they'd managed to do was speak on the phone a few times.

Brody called her last night to make sure she'd be at the game, and she assured him she'd be there. She'd hoped he'd want to talk a while, but he cut the call short and left her wondering what was going on with him. She still couldn't decide if he was interested in her or not.

Deciding now was not the time or place to worry about it, she focused her attention on their options for food.

Although Haven was still annoyed with Allie and her crazy ideas, she wasn't mad enough to keep from inviting her to attend the game that night. She knew both Allie and Rick enjoyed the last one. Hale hinted, when they had dinner together Tuesday night, he'd like to go since Abby was out of town for the weekend.

The four of them bought drinks and snacks then went to their seats. Eating doughy pretzels, they watched the players warm up out on the field, tossing balls and stretching.

"Look, Haven! There he is!" Allie grabbed Haven's hand as she was taking a sip from her water bottle, making liquid splash down the front of her shirt.

"Thanks, Al. Thanks a lot," she said, mopping water from her chin with a napkin and following Allie's pointing finger to the field where Brody tossed a ball with his friend Marcus.

From their conversations, Haven learned that Marcus was Brody's best friend. She'd even talked to him for a few minutes last week when Brody had to answer a question the coach asked in the middle of one of their calls. He was friendly and amusing, and seemed like a good balance to Brody's more dynamic personality.

Brody happened to look into the stands and catch her watching him. He lifted his hand just enough she knew he acknowledged her presence, although he didn't smile. His attention quickly returned to the ball in his hands and in another minute the field cleared and the drum line entered the arena.

Listening to the thump of the bass drum and the chiming clang of the cymbals energized the crowd then the players raced out on the field one at a time as the announcer called their names.

Surprised when Brody came out holding the hand of a little boy, she noticed a few of the players had kids with them. The announcer said something about the children representing those who had undergone treatment at the hospital's new cancer center.

Watching Brody squat down and put his arm around the little boy, talking to him while cameras flashed and music blared, she could see the child finally smile and nod his head at something Brody said.

Deeply touched by the interaction, Haven didn't know what to think about Brody Jackson.

He was intense, exciting, confusing, kind, and exasperating. Beyond that, she decided she'd hold off forming any other opinions until she actually went on a real date with him, if that ever happened.

Watching the beautiful cheerleaders strut their stuff, Haven swallowed hard, realizing she was so far out of Brody's league she had no business entertaining any thoughts about him. She also knew she was setting herself up for a fall when Brody would most likely be gone in a few months and she'd never see him again.

Closing the door on her worries and self-induced anxiety for one night, she thought she should follow Allie's example and live in the moment. At least until the end of the game.

Cheering as the game began, Haven was soon caught up in watching the players on the field.

She joined in the chanting as the rowdy fans started yelling, "Jump it up, Jackson! Jump it up!"

When the quarterback threw the ball to him, Brody jumped so high, Haven didn't know how he could do it. Catching the ball perfectly, he took off running. He gained several yards before a tackle felled him, but the crowd had already gone wild, stomping their feet and clapping noisily.

"Did you see him, Hale?" Haven turned to her brother, wearing a happy smile.

"I sure did, baby girl. Maybe you can ask him how he jumps like that. Does he put springs in his shoes?" Hale asked, giving Haven a one-armed hug, knowing she had more than a passing interest in the football player. Hale was all for her having fun, he just worried that Brody would break her heart before the season ended.

"He told me he once jumped over a backyard fence. Can you imagine?"

"Not really. Maybe we can take him out to the farm sometime and see if he could hurdle one of dad's big hay bales."

"That would be entertaining," Haven agreed, returning her attention to the game.

Allie nudged Haven and pointed to where Brody joined his teammates as they walked out of the arena and back to the locker room at halftime.

"You sure he doesn't play tight end, because, sweetie, that is definitely what he's got going on. Don't you just want to reach out and grab his bum?" Allie giggled as a blush colored Haven's cheeks.

"Hey, boyfriend sitting right here," Rick said, insulted and somewhat peeved as he glared at Allie.

She kissed him on the mouth and rubbed her hand across his shoulder. "And I've only got eyes for you, lover boy. I'm just pointing out the obvious to Haven. We all know she needs a little nudge now and then."

"Well, keep your nudging to yourself." Haven fanned her face with the program, trying to act indignant while secretly agreeing with Allie's assessment. She couldn't decide if she preferred Brody in his uniform or dressed up like he'd been when they went to lunch. She needed to see him in jeans and a T-shirt in the light of day before she made any lasting decisions, though.

Reining in her inappropriate thoughts where one handsome football player and his extremely attractive backside was concerned, she turned to Hale and talked to him about work and how things were progressing with Abby.

The teams returned to the field before Haven even had a chance to run to the restroom, so she stayed in her seat, waiting to see Brody again.

He made another amazing jump, catching the ball and gaining a few yards before a tackle ended the play. Getting to his feet, she saw his head turn her direction, so she smiled and nodded her head in approval, hoping he knew she thought he did well.

While the team was playing defense she excused herself to the restroom and returned with some of the mini doughnuts Hale loved so much. She purchased two orders of them, knowing she and Allie wouldn't get any if they had to fight both Rick and Hale for a bite.

Licking sweet chocolate frosting from her fingers, she cheered when the team made another touchdown, moving the score ahead in their favor. The final quarter of the game was brutal and she watched as the rival team slammed Brody to the turf and into the dasher boards repeatedly.

With just a few seconds left on the clock, his team took possession of the ball and made it to the end zone, winning the game. The crowd erupted in cheers and Haven clapped loudly as they stood on their feet, watching the players high-five each other then shake hands with the opposing team.

"That was wicked," Hale said, knuckle bumping Rick as they gathered up their things to leave.

"What a game! It was brutal," Rick said, kissing Allie's cheek as they waited for the aisle leading out of the arena to clear so they could leave.

"I'm too wound up to go home this early. You guys want to go out?" Allie asked as Haven slipped on her jacket and dug around in her purse for a piece of gum. Finding a half-empty pack, she passed it around before dropping it back in her bag.

"I'll pass, but Hale, you can go if you want to," Haven said, knowing Allie was a night owl while she preferred mornings.

"Nah. I'll take you home and then I think I'll turn in. I had to fill in at the pharmacy this morning and I'm kind of tired," Hale said, grinning as he watched Brody jump over the dasher board and run up the steps toward them. "Don't look now, but your hero has arrived."

"What?" Haven asked, turning to Hale then noticing Brody charging up the steps toward them.

"Haven!" Brody said, all smiles now that the game was over. "Did you like the game?"

"You played very well," she said, feeling unnerved under his penetrating gaze. He looked like he wanted something and she wasn't exactly sure what it was or if she would be willing to grant his wish if she did know.

"Man, that was amazing," Hale said, shaking Brody's hand. "Great game."

"Thanks," Brody said, returning his handshake. "Haven talks a lot about you."

"Then I'm surprised you'll even shake my hand," Hale said with a teasing smile directed at his sister. "You aren't telling tales are you, baby girl?"

"No, I'm not. But I might if you don't behave yourself," Haven said, glaring at Hale, embarrassed he called her baby girl in front of Brody. He'd always called her by that name and the family was used to it. However, she didn't think it sounded like a very dignified moniker for a business professional.

Brody laughed and shook Rick's hand then smiled at Allie, giving her a wink and leaning over to whisper his thanks for dropping Haven in his lap after the last game.

"If I beg and plead, will you guys come to the party? I'd really like to have you join me," he invited, seeing the hopeful look on Allie's face.

Haven started to say no but an elbow in her ribs from Allie and a shove at her back from Hale forced her to agree.

"Sure, why not," she said, turning a cold stare on her cousin.

"You mean it? You'll go?" Brody wasn't convinced he'd heard her correctly.

"We'll be there," Haven said, thinking it was a bad idea, but not knowing what else to do.

Brody told them where to go and said he'd meet them there as soon as he could. After pecking Haven's cheek, he hurried away, glancing over his shoulder once and giving her a pleased smile.

Allie was bouncing on the balls of her feet in excitement. "We get to party with the team. This is going to be so cool."

"Right. Cool," Haven said, feeling the beginning of a headache start at her temple. She hated big crowds and loud parties. All the drinking, and who knew what else, that went on was definitely not her thing.

Allie, however, fed off the energy and Rick didn't seem to mind either.

Turning to leave the stands, she looked at Hale. "If you want to go home, I can leave myself at the mercy of these two."

"I'll tag along," he said, throwing an arm around Haven's shoulders as they walked to the exit and went outside. "At least for a little while. That way if you want to leave early, I can take you home."

"Thanks, Hale. I appreciate it," Haven said as she climbed in his pickup.

They followed Allie and Rick to the sports bar just a few miles from the arena. They walked inside together and the jubilant atmosphere nearly sent Haven rushing back outside.

It was noisy and rowdy with many of the fans already enjoying the after game party. Finding a table in a back corner, Haven and Hale sat down while Allie decided to mingle and Rick went along to make sure she didn't get into any trouble.

Hale ordered them both sodas and a burger for himself. Haven didn't want anything, other than to go home. She couldn't fathom why Brody wanted her to come or how he thought they could talk here. The noise level made it impossible to think let alone converse.

Sitting next to Hale, she could see his lips moving as he said something to her, but she couldn't hear a word he was saying.

Releasing a sigh, she held a hand to her ear, indicating she couldn't hear him. He gave her an odd look and turned his attention to the burger the waitress sat in front of him.

Rifling through her purse, she pulled out a notepad and pen, scribbling a note to Hale, asking if they could leave as soon as he finished his burger.

Shoving it his direction, he read it and shook his head.

"Why not?" she yelled, annoyed by the noise and atmosphere. He was getting to be as bad as Allie at making her do things she didn't want to do.

Rather than answer, he pretended not to hear her and continued eating his burger. He motioned for her to take some fries and she shook her head. Picking up her purse again, she found a bottle of pain reliever and took two, hoping it would stop the throbbing in her head.

Growing more agitated by the minute, she was contemplating calling a cab when she felt a warm hand on her shoulder and looked up into Brody's handsome face.

He bent down until his lips nearly touched her ear, his breath warm on her neck, making a wild shiver work its way through her body.

"Hey, doll. Thanks for coming tonight. I know it's loud and not your scene, but if you can sit tight for just a little while we can escape," Brody said, hoping like everything she'd say yes.

Haven didn't know when her brain and mouth disconnected because she meant to tell Brody he was insane if he thought she'd spend even five more minutes sitting there, but she heard herself say, "Sure, that sounds great."

He patted her on the back then wandered off in the direction of the bar where several of his teammates were talking to fans. She saw him sign an autograph then signal to the bartender for a drink. Trying to ignore the women sidling up to him, she turned away and looked at Hale who focused his attention on his hamburger.

Allie and Rick returned to the table and Allie gulped down Haven's soda before she could utter a protest.

"It's warm in here. Made me thirsty," Allie said, waving her hand in front of her face, trying to stir the air. "Rick, would you get us something to drink, and maybe a snack?"

"Sure, babe. Be right back," Rick said, heading off in the direction of the bar.

Hale finished his burger and soda, wiped his mouth and hands on his napkin, and got to his feet, following Rick toward the bar. He stopped next to Brody and said something then they both looked her direction.

Brody appeared to be agreeing to something. Haven was sure her jaw dropped open when Hale waved at her and walked out the door.

"Guess you're either going home with me or maybe some tight end football player will take you," Allie teased, scooting her chair close enough the two of them could talk without yelling to be heard.

"Allie," Haven warned, but her cousin sat back in her chair and crossed one long leg over the other. "Lighten up, cuz. You need to let your hair down and have fun once in a while."

Allie tugged on Haven's ponytail and grinned.

"I do have fun, but you know I hate this sort of thing. I'd much rather go to a concert or a gallery opening or something remotely civilized," Haven said, looking over a few tables at a group of men who appeared to be having a belching contest. Tipping her head their direction, she gave Allie a pointed look.

"You of all people should know boys will be boys," Allie said, wondering how Haven could be such a prude when she grew up with the three rough and tumble brothers. "Could you try, just for one night, to have some fun?"

"I could try, but it's going to be impossible here," Haven said, about to lose her patience with Allie. She didn't force Allie to go with her to book club or any of the places she would have been bored to tears to attend with Haven. It seemed only fair Allie not try to include her in things that held no interest for her.

"Seriously? You've got that handsome hottie over there making goo-goo eyes your direction every few minutes and all you want to do is leave?" Allie asked, smiling as Rick returned to their table with a basket of chips and two drinks. "What's with that outfit, anyway? You look like a librarian with your little sweater thing and those glasses. Why don't you show a little skin?"

Allie reached over to undo one of Haven's shirt buttons and received a firm slap to her hand.

"Don't even think about," Haven warned, starting to get up from the table. Allie grabbed her wrist and pulled her back down. "Chill, cuz. I'm just giving you a hard time."

"I think maybe you better dial it down, babe," Rick said, noticing the angry flames shooting from Haven's eyes. He knew Allie pushed Haven out of her comfort zone sometimes because she wanted her to have more fun. What he didn't think Allie realized was the way she pushed Haven often had the opposite effect, like now.

Looking at Haven, Allie realized Rick was right and took Haven's hand in her own, patting it softly. "Oh, I'm sorry, honey. I did it again, didn't I?"

So angry, Haven couldn't even speak, she fought back the tears that were about to spill down her cheeks. Why couldn't Allie leave well enough alone? If she didn't love her so much, she might never speak to her again.

"You okay?" a deep voice asked near her ear and Haven turned to find herself just inches away from

Brody's concerned face. She felt his hand on her shoulder and he gave it a gentle squeeze, bending down beside her.

She nodded her head, but didn't trust herself to speak.

"Here, take a drink. It'll make you feel better," he said, handing her his glass.

Refusing it with a shake of her head, he pressed it into her hand, insisting.

Not knowing what else to do, she took a tiny sip, realizing she was drinking iced tea. Sweet iced tea. Looking at Brody over the glass, she took a long drink then handed it back to him. He finished the rest and set the glass on the table.

"You ready to get out of here?" he asked, pulling her to her feet.

She picked up her purse and gave Allie one last, disgusted look before taking Brody's hand and following him out the door.

The fresh air outside along with the quiet washed over her in a welcoming wave, helping release the tension from her neck.

"Sorry about that, but it's good for us to meet with the fans after the game," Brody said, helping her into his truck. He smelled fresh and clean, mixed with something warm and inviting that was uniquely him. Haven took a deep breath as he slid behind the wheel and started the engine.

Before he put the truck in first gear, he spent a moment studying her face. "You sure you're okay?"

"I'm fine," she said, realizing she was fine, now that she was away from the crowded party and Allie's unwelcome advice.

"Do you want to go anywhere or just home?" he asked, heading toward her apartment.

"Home, if you don't mind, please." Haven needed the comfort and rest of her home. She didn't even want to venture to the little diner where Allie had left her at Brody's mercy a few weeks ago.

Although she was great at her job and could socialize whenever necessary, large groups of rowdy people made her want to crawl in a hole and hide.

Small groups were fine, places like football games and concerts didn't bother her, but cram a bunch of bodies into a small, dark place, and Haven was ready to run screaming out the door.

Allie making fun of the way she looked hadn't helped her outlook or confidence. She knew her cousin meant well, but sometimes she went too far.

Quiet as they drove to her apartment, Brody parked in a designated guest parking space and ran around the truck to help her down. She took his hand as he walked her to her door then let it go to find her keys.

"Thank you for seeing me home, Brody. Hale could have dropped me off," she said, unlocking her door and pushing it open then flicking on the living room light.

"I know, but I wanted to bring you home. I… um… was really hoping to have a chance to talk to you," he said, looking everywhere except at her face, acting oddly nervous.

"Oh. Well, do you want to come in for a while, then?" Haven asked, stepping inside and motioning for him to join her.

Brody smiled as he walked into Haven's apartment and closed the door behind him.

## *Chapter Seven*

Haven set her purse on a small bench by the door and turned to look at Brody. Here in her apartment, he seemed larger than life as he stood next to the couch, filling up a large space of her living room.

Trying to gather her wits, she took a step toward the kitchen.

"Are you hungry? Can I get you anything?" she asked, wanting a cup of tea to calm her nerves. Something about Brody made her anxious and excited all at the same time.

"I don't want to put you to any trouble," he said following her into the kitchen and leaning against the doorframe to stay out of her way. She filled a cup with boiling water from an instant hot water dispenser on her sink and dropped a tea bag inside.

"How hungry are you? I can make a sandwich or fry a couple of eggs. I think I've got some leftover pasta and cake," Haven said, studying the contents of her fridge. She had no idea what big football players liked to eat, although it was probably similar to the things her three brothers enjoyed.

"A sandwich would be great. And maybe a piece of that cake," Brody said, giving in to the demands of his sweet tooth. "But I can make the sandwich. You don't have to wait on me."

"It's fine," Haven said, motioning for him to take a seat at her kitchen table. Folding himself into one of the chairs, he watched as she got out bread, meat, cheese, and condiments then set everything, along with a plate and knife in front of him. "What would you like to drink?"

"Got milk?" he asked, giving her a flirty grin.

He made a sandwich and waited while she poured his milk then got her cup of tea and sat across from him.

The first bite of his sandwich made him realize how hungry he'd been. Eating his simple dinner, he glanced over to see her staring at him.

She quickly looked down at her tea, appearing to study the contents of her cup before taking a sip.

Finishing his sandwich, he watched as she stood and cut a generous slice of cake, setting it on a plate in front of him then cutting a small piece for herself.

"Hope you like bananas," she said, forking a bite.

"I do, actually," he said, taking a bite of the deliciously moist cake. Unable to stop himself from wolfing it down, she grinned and cut him another piece. Eating it much slower than the first piece, he looked at her with a raised eyebrow. "Did you make this? I can tell it's homemade."

"I did. I'm going out to visit my folks tomorrow and my dad loves banana cake," Haven said, pleased that Brody enjoyed the treat.

"Do you bake like this all the time?" Brody asked, thinking Haven was one of the few women he'd met who could actually cook.

"No. I work so many hours, I rarely have time to cook. I tend to do more on the weekends, especially if I'm going to see my family."

"Did you say your parents have a farm? Is it nearby?"

"Yeah, it's about twenty minutes out of town. They raise potatoes mostly, but my dad also runs a few head of cattle and grows a little corn," Haven said, finishing her cake then setting their dirty dishes in the sink. She put away the sandwich ingredients and returned to her chair. "Do you need anything else?"

"No, I'm good. Thanks for that. The cake was one of the best things I've eaten in a really long time."

Blushing, she forced herself to look at him, seeing his praise appeared to be genuine.

She felt as if some force was drawing her closer to him as she gazed into his rich brown eyes. Sitting back in her chair, she tried to redirect her thoughts away from his sensual mouth and enticing smell.

"You said you wanted to talk. What about?" she asked.

"You. Us. This," Brody said, waving a hand around her kitchen before gently taking her hand in his. "I... um... well, you see..."

Brody let out a sigh and tipped his head back, staring at the ceiling.

In the last few weeks, he'd thought of little else besides Haven. It took every ounce of effort and concentration he possessed to focus on the games he played and block out the sight of her face, the smell of her fragrance, the silky feel of her hair in his fingers.

He hadn't even given her a real kiss, yet the woman had completely invaded his life.

Of course, she had no idea she had him so entangled he could barely think straight. That's why he'd cut short their last conversation and why he barely acknowledged her at the game. He had to block out thoughts of her or he might as well have not even played.

The idea of getting through the evening so he could see her and spend some time with her drove him to give his best to the game.

After winning tonight, he felt on top of the world, especially when Haven agreed to come to the party. Assuming she would hate it, he put in enough of an appearance to keep everyone appeased before slipping out with her. He was grateful Hale stopped to make sure he intended to spend some time with her, giving him permission to see her home.

Sitting across from her, staring into her beautiful blue eyes, he didn't know how to express his thoughts. He wasn't even sure what he wanted, other than to keep seeing her.

Thinking after one kiss she'd be out of his system, Brody had a strong hunch that one kiss would just lead to a desperate need for dozens more.

He was willing to take the chance, though. Especially as he watched the tip of her tongue moisten her lips.

"What is it, Brody? Just spit it out," Haven said, sensing his hesitancy to say what was on his mind. She had no idea what he was thinking or causing him to look so agitated.

"Look, Haven, I know you aren't the kind of girl who dates a bunch of guys. You're sweet and funny and a little naïve, so I want to be upfront about all this," Brody said, thinking he was doing a lousy job of expressing himself. "What I'm trying to say is that I'll be leaving when the season ends and don't even know if I'll be back next year. It all depends on if I get invited to an NFL training camp. There's also the chance I could end up with a different arena team."

"All right," Haven said, trying to make sense of what Brody was saying. So far, he'd pegged her and her dating habits accurately, but she didn't know why he was talking about leaving in a few months.

Brody got up and paced around her kitchen then leaned against the counter and ran his hand through his dark hair before staring at her for a long, intense moment. Returning to the table, he captured her hand in his again.

"What I'm trying to say, Haven, despite my obvious inability to get out the right words, is that I want to see you. I want to date you, but it would just be casual. For fun. No strings attached because we both know I won't be here by the time July rolls around," Brody said, rubbing his thumb across the inside of Haven's wrist and watching her face soften in response. "Unless I'm completely mistaken, I think you're attracted to me every bit as much as I am to you. But knowing you aren't one of those girls who take this kind of thing lightly, I wanted to be clear on what you can expect from me."

"I see," Haven said, trying to wrap her head around the notion that Brody Jackson just said he was attracted to her and wanted to date her. She knew from the first time he smiled at her he wasn't going to stick around which is why she fought to stay away from him.

Examining the two options before her, she could push him away and destroy a growing friendship, or she could enjoy what time she had with him before he left town.

Ignoring the whisper in her head telling her to shove him out the door and never see him again, for once in her life she chose not to play it safe.

"Okay."

"Okay, what?" Brody asked, confused by her response.

"Okay, I'd like to date you, too, with the understanding that it's just for fun and you'll be leaving. No strings attached." Haven said, smiling at him with such unguarded affection, Brody felt his temperature start to climb.

"That's good, doll," Brody said, running his hands up and down the arms of her soft sweater. "That's really good."

"Why do you call me doll?" Haven asked, anxious to distract herself from the look in Brody's eyes. It seemed dangerous and thrilling, and she had no idea how to handle it.

Laughing, Brody sat back in his chair and studied her from the blonde curls captured in a ponytail to her white and pink flowered blouse and light pink sweater. "Because you look like a beautiful doll with your curly hair, blue eyes, and perfect skin. You remind me of a doll my mom keeps in a box in her closet. I think it was something her grandmother gave her and told her to take care of, as a keepsake. It looks a lot like you."

"Oh," was all Haven could manage to say as Brody continued to stare at her in such a way it left her completely disconcerted. Before he could say anything further, she got to her feet and started walking to the living room. She could hear him scoot out his chair and his footsteps behind her. "Let's sit in the living room if you want to talk."

Her plan was to sit in the small chair by the couch and put some distance between her and Brody. Unfortunately, he had his own plans. Waiting for her to take a seat, he scooped her up effortlessly and plopped her across his lap on the couch.

"There, that's better," he said with a cocky smile.

"For whom?" she squeaked. Brody looked even better at this close proximity. She could see flecks of gold in his dark brown eyes and his scent flooded through her, obliterating her ability to think or move.

"Definitely me," Brody said, gently removing her glasses and setting them on the coffee table. Her eyes looked even bigger and bluer without her glasses on and Brody felt drawn to her in a way he'd never imagined feeling for any one. "Do you have to wear your glasses all the time?"

"Only if I want to see what I'm doing," she said with a nervous smile. Brody raised an eyebrow and she relaxed a little. "I have to wear them to see distances, driving, and to work on my computer, so yes, pretty much all the time."

"Can you see me okay with them off?"

"Yes," she said, thinking she could see him better than she probably should, but then again, her face was just inches away from his.

"Now, how about these sweaters you wear all the time? The only time I've seen you wear something else was the day we went to lunch. You had on a business suit that day."

"I like sweaters. They're soft and warm and pretty," Haven said, wondering why she was discussing her wardrobe selections with Brody. It certainly wasn't what she wanted to do.

Pressing her lips to his and seeing if they tingled like they did the first time he kissed her seemed like a much better idea.

"Pretty," Brody repeated, fascinated by the way her lips moved. Most of the girls he'd dated in the past wouldn't have been caught dead dressed in the modest attire Haven favored. On her, though, the soft, feminine clothes were definitely appealing.

Turning his gaze to her hair, his next objective was to lose the hair band binding that golden mane at the back of her head. He'd dreamed of what her hair would look like down, how it would feel with his hands buried in the curls, and he wasn't leaving until he found out.

"What about your hair? How come you've always got it pulled back?"

Reaching a hand up to her hair, Haven didn't even remember how she was wearing it. Feeling the hair band holding it in a ponytail, she tugged it out and stared at it lying on her palm.

"Old habit from growing up on a farm. Hair tends to get in the way when you're outside working. At work, I like to keep a professional image with it up, and I pull it into a ponytail at home most times without thinking."

"I see," Brody said, taking the band from her hand and dropping it on the table next to her glasses before slowly threading his fingers into her hair. It felt even better than he'd imagined and he drew closer, taking a deep breath, inhaling the sweet scent of it. He felt her lean into his hand and swallowed back a groan.

On the verge of devouring her with his growing longing, Brody gave himself a mental lecture to calm down and take things slow. He didn't want to scare Haven half to death the first time he really kissed her.

"Any more questions?" Haven smiled at Brody as he worked his hands through to the ends of her hair then wrapped a curl around one long finger.

The appearance of her dimples was his undoing. Grabbing her waist, he slid Haven closer then pressed his lips to each indentation in her cheeks before turning his passionate gaze to hers.

"No more questions. I think we should seal this deal with a kiss," Brody said, watching Haven's eyes drift shut.

Brody knew kissing her would be amazing. What he hadn't anticipated was the explosion of fiery heat in every nerve ending in his body. Her lips moving beneath his set him aflame with no hope of extinguishing the blaze.

In the next few seconds, Brody realized two important details. The first was that Haven touched places in his heart and soul he never even knew existed. The second was that he'd never, in his lifetime, get enough of her kisses.

"Haven," he whispered. His gravelly tone made a shiver rack through her with such force he could feel it. Folding her closer in his embrace, he deepened the kiss, thinking he'd finally found a perfect moment of pure happiness.

Out of breath and out of her mind, Haven knew she should jump off Brody's lap and show him to the door. She knew any more of his kisses would render her helpless and hopeless.

Despite what she knew, she couldn't force her languid limbs to move any more than she could force herself to focus on anything except how right it felt to be held in Brody's strong arms.

Finally, common sense took hold of her thoughts and dragged her back to reality. Lifting her head from Brody's she leaned away from him, trying to pull her unraveled composure together.

As long as he didn't say her name in that rough voice again, she might be able to let him leave with her heart and dignity still in one piece.

Her plans to get to her feet and move to the side chair were thwarted when Brody wrapped his hands around her waist again, keeping her on his lap.

"Don't get up yet. Please?" he asked quietly, moving until her head rested against his chest and his chin nestled against the top of her head. She could hear his heart pounding fiercely and knew it was keeping time to her own racing pulse.

She'd never felt so secure and cherished as she did at that very moment. No matter what happened with Brody, he'd given her a beautiful kiss to remember always.

Sitting quietly together until Haven's clock chimed twice, letting them know it was very late, Brody kissed the top of her head and gently pushed her back until she sat up.

"You have no idea how much I enjoyed the past few hours with you," Brody said, kissing Haven's forehead and her dimples one last time before setting her on her feet and getting to his own.

"I enjoyed being with you," Haven said, knowing Brody needed to leave but wishing he could stay.

"Can I see you tomorrow?" he asked, taking his keys out of his jeans pocket and standing at the door.

"I have church in the morning and then I'm going to see Mom and Dad in the afternoon. You're welcome to come along if you'd like."

"To which?" Brody asked, trying to remember the last time he sat in a church service, or met a girl's parents. It had been a long, long time for either one.

"Your choice," Haven answered with a saucy grin.

"Maybe I'll choose both," he said with a smirk. "Why don't you call me in the morning when you get up? I'll let you know if I'm awake enough to function, or if I'll catch up with you later."

"Deal," Haven said, holding out her hand to him. Instead of shaking it, Brody pulled her against his solid chest and breathed in her heady fragrance one more time.

"Have a good night, doll, and sweet dreams."

"Thanks, Brody. You, too."

He opened the door and ran across the parking lot to his truck, wondering what he was going to do about his growing infatuation with sweet Haven.

## *Chapter Eight*

Haven maintained a demure posture at church during the service but couldn't keep the smile off her face. Brody sat next to her with his arm draped along the back of the pew behind her, wrapping her in the warmth of his presence although he didn't actually touch her.

She knew he was uncomfortable, out of his element, but those glancing his way wouldn't notice. All they saw was a tall, incredibly good-looking man listening to the pastor's sermon.

Stifling a yawn, Haven felt weary from a lack of sleep. She went to bed soon after Brody left, but she kept replaying everything that happened from the moment he said he wanted to date her to the hug he gave her before walking out the door.

Reminding herself over and over that he just wanted to hang out and have fun, she couldn't stop her thoughts from lingering on how much she enjoyed his kisses, how right it felt to be in his arms, how the sound of his deep voice saying her name made her feel boneless and witless.

Casual. He wanted to be casual friends who dated. She could handle that. At least she tried to convince herself of it.

Brody was the most handsome man with whom she'd ever been on a first name basis. He was exciting and a little wild, although she knew him to be kind and gentle, too. She sensed a mixture of anger, longing, and regret fueling his drive to move on to bigger and better things.

Although he acted open and friendly, she knew he kept the real Brody Jackson removed and protected from most people. He'd started to let her have glimpses into who that person was and the more that was exposed, the more she liked what she saw.

She'd never have guessed she'd be sitting in church, struggling to pay attention to the sermon, with him at her side.

Calling him just half an hour before church started, she didn't want to wake him up too early, considering how late it was when he left her apartment. He answered on the second ring and told her he'd be ready when she got there, giving her directions to his place.

True to his word, she didn't even have to get out of her car. She'd barely pulled into a parking space when she saw him hurrying down the steps toward her. He wore the same sports coat he'd had on the day they ate lunch together, along with dress pants and shoes, and a button down shirt. She could see, from the glint of the sun, his hair was still wet and knew he'd probably raced to get a shower before she arrived.

"Hey, doll. Nice wheels," he said, dropping a duffle bag behind the passenger seat as he climbed in. "I didn't picture you as a crossover kind of girl."

Haven loved her vehicle that was a cross between a car and an SUV. It was perfect for hauling around her stuff, both personal and work-related, and it had four-wheel drive for when the roads were bad. The deep burgundy color made her smile every time she looked at it.

"What kind of girl did you picture me as?" she asked, backing out of the parking space and pulling into Sunday morning traffic.

"I don't know. Some kind of sensible sedan in a conservative color," Brody said, looking around the interior and appreciating that there was both ample leg and headroom for him.

"I'm thoroughly insulted. You thought I had a granny car? Like what? A big ol' boat in a blah shade of tan?" Haven asked, sounding offended, although she was amused.

Brody chuckled and squeezed her hand where it sat on the armrest between them. "My apologies. I should have known to expect the unexpected with you."

"What's that supposed to mean?" Haven asked, turning into the church parking lot and finding a space.

"It means, there is much more to you than meets the eye," Brody said, smirking at her as he got out of the car and followed her inside.

As they sat listening to the end of the pastor's sermon, Haven had to stifle a laugh when Brody's stomach grumbled in hunger. He shot her a sheepish look then turned his attention back to the pastor.

After singing the closing hymn, Brody stayed close to Haven as they worked their way to the back of the church where she introduced him to the pastor then walked outside into the bright spring sunshine.

"Would you like to have some lunch before we go out to the farm?" Haven asked, grinning at Brody as he held her door then ran around to the passenger side.

"If you don't feed me, there's no telling what might happen," Brody said, reaching over and trying to tickle her.

Haven jerked and smacked at his hand, trying to steer the car while grabbing his hands in her much smaller one.

"You behave, mister, or no lunch for you," she said, wondering if he'd rather go out to eat or get something to take back to her place.

"I might turn into a crazy vampire or some head-lobbing madman if you don't," he said, pretending to try to work his hands free from where she held them captive. Amused she thought her little hand could stop his if he really wanted to move, he stared at her delicate fingers. He liked the feel of them wrapped around his and left things just the way they were.

"Well, we can't have a blood sucker on the loose, so where would you like to eat?"

He suggested a restaurant she liked that was generally fast, affordable, and filling. They arrived a few minutes later and hurried inside, hoping to beat the after-church rush.

Seated at a booth, they enjoyed the meal then returned to Haven's apartment. Brody carried in his bag and Haven looked at it then back at him. "What's that?"

"You said we were going out to your family's farm so I figured I'd need to change before we go," Brody said, removing his sports jacket and untucking his shirt.

"I'll just go… um… change," Haven said, trying not to stare as Brody began unbuttoning his shirt.

"You look really pretty today, Haven." Brody reached out and ran his hand down the sleeve of the soft black sweater she wore over a black dress with bright pink trim. She looked so girly and cute, Brody almost had to sit on his hands at church to keep from reaching out and touching her during the pastor's sermon.

"Thank you, Mr. Jackson. You look quite handsome yourself," Haven said, stepping away from him and backing toward her bedroom door. "You're welcome to change in the bathroom if you want. I'll just be a minute."

He watched her close the door then carried his bag into the bathroom to change. He didn't mind changing in the middle of her living room, but for propriety's sake, he went in the bathroom and traded his dress clothes for a worn pair of jeans and T-shirt.

Folding his jacket and shirt, he stuffed them in the bag with his pants and shoes then tied on a pair of sneakers.

Opening the bathroom door and returning to the living room, he could hear Haven in the kitchen. Quietly stepping into the room, he stood admiring the view provided as she bent over a drawer, taking out a roll of plastic wrap.

She wore faded jeans, a pair of scuffed boots, and a T-shirt that clung to every womanly curve.

Swallowing hard, he shoved his hands in his pockets and cleared his throat. "Need any help?"

"No, I've got it," Haven said, smiling at him over her shoulder. She'd taken her hair down from the bun she'd worn to church and pulled it back in a long braid. Curls already attempted to escape the confines, bouncing around her ears and along her neck.

She quickly placed a piece of the wrap over a bowl then set it in a box followed by a cake pan.

"Can I carry something?" Brody asked, stepping closer to her, inhaling her luscious scent.

"Sure," she said, handing him the box then dropping the plastic wrap back in the drawer and closing it. "Ready to go?"

"I am if you are."

"Let's get to it, then," she said, picking up her purse and a denim jacket before opening the door and holding it for Brody to walk through. Locking it behind her, she opened the door to the backseat of her car and Brody set the box down before holding Haven's door for her.

He may have grown up lacking many things, but the one thing his mother made sure he possessed was good manners.

Right now, Brody was glad she'd drilled the lessons into his head, because Haven was a lady who deserved to be treated like one.

"Who'll be at the farm today? Just your folks?" he asked as they merged onto the freeway and headed out of town.

"No. Hale and Tom might be there. Wes and his family could be. It just depends on what they've got going on. Usually they all show up in time for dinner, though." Haven hoped meeting her parents wouldn't make Brody nervous. She'd never taken a boy out to the farm for them to meet before and she hoped they didn't read anything into the fact she had a man in tow today.

She'd have to find time to take her mother aside and tell her they were just friends. That Brody would be leaving in a few months and she'd likely never see him again.

Although he hadn't said anything, Haven sensed his need for friendship. To find something, or someone, that chased away his loneliness. She recognized it in him because that need was so strong in her own life. Even with her loving family and crazy friends like Allie and Rick, an emptiness lingered in her that Haven realized only someone special could fill.

Knowing that Brody had no plans to stay in the area, she had to remind herself he couldn't be that person. For the time being, she decided it wouldn't hurt to pretend he might be.

"Tell me about your brother's kids. You said they were a handful," Brody said, wondering how much trouble two little boys could make.

"They are more than a handful. Be forewarned, they can plow a wide path of destruction before you even realize they've moved," Haven said, making Brody chuckle.

"They sound like my kind of kids. How old are they?"

"Mason is six and Jed is almost five," Haven said, taking an exit and following a road out toward what appeared to be nowhere. "Don't let their sweet smiles and freckles fool you, though. They should be approached like you would a pack of bloodthirsty hyenas."

Brody laughed and shook his head. "You're hilarious, you know that?"

"No, I don't. I'm just telling you how things are," Haven said, slowing down as they turned onto a gravel road. She cast a glance at Brody and he caught her eye. "I want you to have fun today, so please don't take anything anyone says to heart and please, please don't believe the stories my brothers may tell about me. None of them are true and I'm not Dad's favorite."

Brody was still laughing when she pulled up in front of a large farmhouse with a landscaped yard and two big dogs lounging on the front porch.

"Wow! You grew up here?" Brody asked, looking around as he got out. Opening the door to the backseat, he picked up Haven's box of food.

"Yeah. Mom and Dad built the house when I was about seven. Our old house is where Wes and Tammy live. It's down the road that way," she said, pointing toward a spot in the distance Brody could barely see.

"You sure they won't mind me intruding on your family time?"

"Not at all, especially if you talk football with my dad. It's his favorite sport and he spends as much time during football season as possible watching games."

"Sounds like a man after my own heart," Brody said, realizing the gaping chasm of difference between the scroungy little house where he grew up and Haven's upbringing.

Sensing his hesitation, Haven looped her arm around his and tugged him down the front walk. The dogs raised their heads to see who approached, bounding off the steps and barking out a friendly greeting.

"Down boys. Down!" Haven commanded, as two chocolate labs approached and bumped into her, wanting attention.

"Who have we got here?" Brody asked, shifting the box so he had a free hand. Holding his fingers down for one of the dogs to sniff, he rubbed its head and scratched behind its ears.

"Don't laugh, but you're making friends with Minion and the one over here is Gru. You know, from the movie *Despicable Me*?" Haven smiled while Brody reached over to pet the other dog.

"Let me guess, your nephews helped pick the names," Brody said, giving each dog another pat on the head.

"Is it that obvious?" She offered him a cheeky grin. "Let's go in before they slobber us to death."

Haven led the way up the steps and was just about to open the door when it swung inward and a woman who looked a lot like Allie pulled her into a hug.

"Sweetie, we were hoping you'd get here soon. Tom and Hale both came for lunch and Wes and Tammy will be here for dinner," Rachel Haggarty said as she pulled Haven inside then stood with round eyes staring at the gorgeous man on her front step. "Please, come in. I'm Rachel, Haven's mother."

"It's very nice to meet you, Mrs. Haggarty," Brody said, trying to remember every lesson in manners his mother ever taught him.

"Please, Mrs. Haggarty is John's mother. Just Rachel is fine," she said, looking at Haven expectantly.

Haven finally noticed her glare and remembered her mother didn't know anything about Brody.

"Mom, this is Brody Jackson. We… um… well, he's a friend I met through work," Haven managed to say, taking the box from Brody so he could shake her mother's hand.

"Brody. That's a good, strong name. Now where did you grow up, dear?" Rachel motioned Brody toward the kitchen as they followed behind Haven.

"Kansas, ma'am," Brody said, taking in the big house with wood floors and sparkling windows that looked out on a huge backyard.

"Have you lived here long?"

"No, ma'am. Just a few months."

"And what is it you do?" Rachel asked, taking a bowl of salad from Haven and putting it in the fridge then smiling approvingly at the banana cake her husband loved so much.

"I play football. Arena football. Our season started a few weeks ago and wraps up around the end of June if we make the playoffs."

"Football, huh? Well, I'm sure you'll find plenty to talk about with my husband. He lives for football season," Rachel said, asking Brody if he wanted a glass of iced tea. He shook his head but offered his thanks.

"Why doesn't Dad go to the arena football games, then, Mom? I've got tickets if he ever wants to go."

"You know how busy he is this time of year getting ready for spring planting, honey. He just doesn't have time," Rachel said, giving Haven a look that said she'd be cornering her for a long discussion later.

"Where are the guys?" Haven asked, hoping to postpone explaining to her mother why she showed up on her doorstep with a man who could be a professional model if he ever gave up the desire to play football.

"In the man cave. Your brothers want to go shooting. If you hurry, you can catch them and go along," Rachel said, pointed at the back door.

"Come on, Brody," Haven said, grabbing his hand and hurrying out the door. He found himself standing in a large three-car garage and noticed a shiny new pickup parked alongside a newer SUV.

"It's down here," Haven said holding open a door. He followed her down a set of steps into a basement. Mounted deer and elk heads lined one wall. Another held a big screen TV and four big recliners sat in a semi-circle in front of it. Three men stood in front of the biggest gun safe Brody had ever seen.

"Hey, there. Mom said you're going shooting. Can we go along?" Haven asked, walking up behind her dad and brothers.

"Hi, sweetheart. How are you?" John Haggarty asked, engulfing his daughter in a warm hug. "You get prettier every time I see you."

"Daddy," Haven said, embarrassed. Before she could introduce him, Hale and Tom spied Brody standing by the steps.

"Brody, man! What are you doing here?" Tom asked, hurrying over to shake his hand before Hale could tell him to be quiet.

"Haven invited me to come along with her today," Brody said, returning Tom's handshake then walking over to shake Hale's hand.

"You're kidding, right?" Tom asked, looking from Haven to Brody. Hale gave him a not so subtle elbow to the ribs when he started to say something else, causing him to clamp his mouth shut.

"Daddy, this is my friend, Brody Jackson. He's a wide receiver on the arena football team," Haven said, smiling at Brody. "This is my dad, John."

"It's nice to meet you, sir," Brody said, noticing that Haven did indeed have her father's blue eyes although his tall, brawny frame closely resembled those of his sons.

"Pleasure's all mine, son. So you play football," John said, excited at the prospect of discussing the game with Brody. He tried to hide the shock of seeing his little girl with a big, strapping man who looked like he belonged in one of the advertisements she masterminded. It was about time some boy turned her head, though.

"You two want to go shooting?" John asked, taking out a pistol and handing it to Haven. She weighed it in her hand and returned it to the gun safe, selecting one that was smaller and lighter.

"You bet we do," Haven said, looking to Brody for agreement. He shrugged and smiled. He'd never gone shooting before and decided it might be fun.

"You'll need these then," John said as he dug around in a box and found a pair of safety glasses along with something that looked like headphones from the 1980s, handing them to Brody.

"What's this stuff?" Brody whispered to Haven while John, Hale, and Tom were discussing which guns they should take.

"The funky shades are eye protection and those big clunky things will keep your ears from ringing. You can turn these knobs on the sides to hear voices, but it filters out the shots," Haven said, showing Brody how to adjust the volume.

"Okay," he said, impressed Haven seemed to know what she was doing.

Seeing her dressed so casually, and so at home in this rural setting, made him rethink his opinion that she was one hundred percent girly. As she smacked Tom on the back of his head at something he said, Brody decided there might be a little tomboy in her as well.

"Ready to go?" she asked, taking the ear and eye protectors from him and stuffing them in a bag along with a couple of handguns, water bottles, and some ammunition.

"Are you going to join us, Dad?" Haven asked as they walked back up the steps to the garage.

"No, sweetie. I think I'll stick around the house with your mom this afternoon. You kids go have fun. Tom, be nice to your sister," John cautioned, grinning as they went out a side door of the garage to a carport where three four-wheelers were parked.

"Geez, Dad. I'm always nice to the kiddo," Tom said, jumping on a four-wheeler, starting it up and roaring off down the road.

"Have a good time," John called before going in the house.

"Looks like Brody will have to ride with you, baby girl," Hale said, securing the bag he carried to the back of the machine with a bungee cord before starting it and going at a much slower pace down the road in the direction Tom headed.

"I guess you're stuck with me," Haven said, running a bungee cord through the handle of the bag she carried and fastening it to a carrier on the front of the four-wheeler. She climbed on then slid up, making room for Brody to sit behind her. "Just hang on and you'll be fine."

"I trust you," he said, lightly placing his hands at her waist. He wondered if he could talk her into letting him drive the four-wheeler on the way back. He'd driven one during a job he had in high school for a few months, helping a man who had a sod farm. He learned more than he ever wanted to know about grass that summer.

"That's good to know," Haven said, starting the machine and speeding down the road after her brothers. Brody wrapped his arms around her and grinned, leaning closer.

"I think there's a wild woman hiding beneath those suits and sweaters you wear," he said in her ear as they sped down the road and turned into a stackyard.

Hale and Tom were setting up targets in front of a one-ton bale of hay.

"We shoot out here because there's no one around and the bale absorbs the shots," Haven explained as she handed Brody the earmuffs then pulled out a bright pink pair for herself. Giving him the safety glasses, she took out two handguns and set the boxes of ammo on the four-wheeler seat.

"Are we shooting for fun or money today?" Tom asked, loading a magazine and slipping it into his gun.

"Fun," Hale and Haven replied at the same time.

"Have you ever shot a gun before?" Hale asked as he stepped beside Haven and Brody.

Shaking his head, Brody listened intently as Hale gave him the basics of gun safety. It seemed every sentence ended with "never point it at someone and always make sure the safety is on."

Half-afraid to take the gun and half-excited to try, Brody watched Tom and Hale both shoot before Haven took a turn.

He knew she was right-handed but she seemed to be sighting with her left eye and shooting left-handed.

"I thought she was right-handed," Brody commented to Hale.

Hale nodded. "Haven's at a little disadvantage in that her dominant eye and her dominant hand aren't on the same side. She had to learn to shoot with her left hand because her right eye isn't strong enough for her to sight with."

They watched as Haven hit the center of the target several times in a row.

"Doesn't look like she's suffering too greatly from it," Brody observed, making Hale grin.

"Nope. If she wanted, I think she could outshoot all of us, but don't tell Tom or Wes. They like to think they're the best."

"Got it." Brody high-fived Haven when she came back, all smiles. He almost bent down to kiss her then decided she might not appreciate it with her brothers watching.

"Your turn, football man," Haven said, letting Hale take Brody out to shoot. He showed him how to hold his arm, site the gun, take off the safety, and smoothly pull the trigger until Brody felt comfortable with the gun.

His first few shots hit the dirt around the bale but the more he shot, the closer he came to the target. His last one hit one of the outer rings.

"Not bad for a first-timer," Haven said, taking a drink from her water bottle then holding it out to Brody.

Hale gave Tom a look that had them both watching Haven with interest, but they wisely refrained from saying anything.

Shooting several more rounds, Tom decided to go back to the house, leaving Hale, Haven, and Brody to practice.

"Try my gun. Let's see how you do with it," Hale said, handing Haven his gun.

"Oh, fancy. A new Ruger 9mm," Haven said, examining the gun while Hale filled the magazine with cartridges. "When did you get it?"

"A few weeks ago," Hale said, handing Haven the magazine and watching as she slid it in the gun.

The three of them walked out to where the target leaned against the hay bale. Hale and Brody took a few steps back, waiting for her to shoot.

She took aim and fired a few rounds, hitting the center of the target. Unexpectedly, her next shot missed the target as her arm jerked up. She dropped the arm holding the gun to her side, then bent over and madly clawed at her T-shirt.

"What's wrong?" Hale asked, as he and Brody rushed toward her.

"Stay away!" she yelled, turning her back to the two men while trying to fish a hand down the front of her shirt without them seeing. She finally tossed a shell casing to the ground and turned to face them.

Making sure the gun had its safety on, she handed it back to Hale. "I don't believe I like your gun. I'm done shooting for the day."

"What happened, baby girl? Are you okay?" Hale asked as he took the gun from her. He and Brody walked with her back to the four-wheelers. She grabbed a water bottle and held it against her chest.

"I'm fine. Just fine. Go shoot some more or something," she said, waving her hand in the direction of the target.

Understanding dawned and Brody barely contained his laughter while Hale didn't even try to hold his back. He laughed so hard tears streamed down his face and Brody couldn't keep a few chuckles from escaping.

Hale finally turned back to the target to finish shooting the rounds already in his gun while Brody stepped behind Haven and put his hands on her shoulders.

"You should have said something. I'd have been more than happy to help dig that casing out for you," Brody said in a low voice, peering down at the neck of her T-shirt.

"I don't think so," Haven said in a clipped tone, frowning at Brody although his words, delivered in that husky voice laced with gravel, made her feel weak yet oddly energized despite her current predicament.

Hale's gun ejected the shells to the right as she shot at the target. One of them just happened to go down the front of her shirt in the perfect funnel created by having her bosom compressed between her upraised arms.

The wicked piece of hot metal singed her tender skin multiple times before she managed to dig it out. Momentarily alarmed she might have to rip off her shirt to get to it, she would have died of embarrassment if Brody or Hale had actually seen anything.

Even though the cool water bottle helped ease the pain a little, she wanted to go back to the house and see if her mom had something she could put on the burns.

"You sure you're okay? Maybe I better take a look," Brody suggested, turning her around and slipping a finger under the neckline of her shirt.

She gave him a shove and stepped back, bumping into the four-wheeler. Trying to decide if she wanted to laugh or cry, she began loading the gear back in the bag then fastened it down in the carrier.

"I'm going back to the house. You can ride with Hale if you like," she said, standing next to the four-wheeler.

"I'm sorry, doll. Does something hurt?" he asked, giving her a hug. At her barely perceptible nod, he kissed the top of her head. "Did you get burned? Is that the problem?"

Another nod.

"Are you sure I can't take a look? I'm pretty good at doctoring due to my many injuries over the years," he said, not surprised when she raised a hand and smacked playfully at his chest.

"Hale's about done shooting. Go over there when he finishes the last round and pick up the shell casing," Haven said, motioning toward her brother.

Brody did as she asked and watched where the last one fell to the ground. He grabbed it in his hand and had to drop it because the metal was too hot to hold in his fingers.

"Hot little buggers, aren't they?" Hale said, removing his ear and eye protection. "Did she say what happened?"

"No, but she told me to come grab one and see how it felt. Man, that's got to be brutal on a woman's…"

"Don't say it! That's my sister, you know," Hale said, slapping Brody on the shoulder as they walked back to Haven.

"Why didn't you throw down the gun and yank off your shirt, baby girl?" Hale teased, knowing his sister would rather die than do either thing.

"Just be quiet. I'm heading in. You boys staying or going?" Haven asked.

"Going," Hale said, putting away his stuff. He started the four-wheeler and drove off, leaving Brody looking at Haven with a questioning glance.

"Are you…"

Haven cut him off before he could finish his question. "Let's just not talk about it. Ever. Again."

Brody nodded his head and looked around. With the warm spring day and sunshine overhead, he could get used to being out in the country. Breathing deeply, the air smelled earthy and new, with a hint of Haven's perfume mingling in.

"You waiting for something?" Haven asked, noticing him glancing around, taking in the scenery. She'd have to bring him out once the potatoes and corn started to grow. Before they went home after dinner, she should take him out to see the baby calves. They were cute and she thought Brody would enjoy seeing them.

"No. Just wondering if you'd mind if I drove back to the house?" he asked, giving her a charming smile.

"I don't mind and you don't have to waste one of those smiles on me. I prefer the real ones," Haven said, waiting for Brody to climb on before sitting down behind him.

"What do you mean real ones?" Brody asked, wondering if other people knew most of his smiles were fake or just Haven.

"You have a lot of different smiles, but the one you usually give me is a real one. That one was all fake and you know it."

"Guilty as charged and sorry," Brody said, grinning over his shoulder at her as he started the four-wheeler. "This one's real, though."

"I see that," she smiled in return. "Now how about you take me home?"

"Yes, ma'am," Brody said and turned back the way they came, enjoying the feel of the wind in his face and Haven's arms wrapped around his chest.

## *Chapter Nine*

Returning to the house, Haven's brother Wes and his family waited to greet them. Two little boys stood gaping at Brody for several minutes until Hale suggested everyone go out back and play football.

Brody grinned and squatted down so he was closer to eye level with the two youngsters.

"Will you two toss the ball to me? I'm much better at catching than throwing."

Mason and Jed enthusiastically nodded their heads, each grabbing one of Brody's hands and tugging him outside.

He grinned at Haven on his way out the door and she stared at him, amazed at how good he was with kids.

"Go on and join them," Tammy said, pushing Haven toward the door. "I'll help your mom get dinner ready."

Haven found herself caught up in the fun as they played a rowdy game of backyard football. Brody and the two boys, along with Hale, took on the rest of them.

So far, the little boys and their helpers were winning, hands down.

Watching their antics, Haven looked up to see the ball flying her direction.

"Catch it, sweetie," her dad yelled as he moved to block Hale. Wes tickled his two boys while Tom tried to take on Brody, but was quickly outmaneuvered. Brody chased after Haven, making her squeal.

She ran toward the makeshift end zone but found herself swept into Brody's arms before she could score.

"Isn't that cheating?" she asked, her eyes filled with laughter while dimples danced in her cheeks.

Brody wanted to kiss her so badly, he could feel his head dipping toward hers. Haven's eyes started to close, anticipating his kiss, then they both felt the impact of two little bodies latching onto Brody's legs.

"You're s'posed to tackle her," Jed said, looking up at Brody, shaking his head.

"Like this, Brody." Mason grabbed onto Jed's shirt and pushed him on the ground then flounced on top of him. The boys started throwing punches and shouting before Wes got them separated.

Still holding Haven in his arms, Brody felt her chest heaving against his and the sensation was about to push him beyond the edge of reason.

"I don't think your Aunt Haven would appreciate being pummeled, boys. How about if I just set her down?" Brody asked, reluctantly placing Haven on her feet. He wouldn't mind rolling around in the grass with her, but he'd prefer her entire family not be watching. She must have sensed a little of what he was feeling because she squeezed his hand and whispered, "thanks," in his ear.

"I think that's about enough football for one day. You boys run in and wash up for dinner," John said to his grandsons.

"Do we have to, Gramps?" Mason asked, dragging his toes as he walked through the grass.

"Only if you want to eat dinner instead of sitting out here by yourself."

"Well, that stinks," Jed said, earning a disapproving glare from his father.

"If I show you a trick, will you two wash up without any more complaints?" Brody asked, once again hunkering down on their level.

The boys looked at each other then back at Brody, nodding their heads.

"What kind of trick, Brody?" Mason asked, watching as Brody pointed to a section of fence on the side of the yard.

"A jumping trick. If I can jump over that fence, will you two wash your hands and faces, eat your dinner, and behave the rest of the evening?" Brody asked, giving the boys a serious look.

"You can't jump that high," Mason said doubtfully, crossing his arms over his little chest. "Nobody can."

"Yeah, nobody," Jed repeated, mimicking his brother.

"Do we have a deal, though?" Brody asked, holding out his hand to Mason.

The little boy nodded and shook Brody's hand then Jed took a turn.

Haven glanced at Brody. "Are you sure you want to do this? That fence is four feet high."

"I know. I've got this," Brody said, walking across the yard and eyeing both sides of the fence.

With a series of running steps, he launched himself over the fence and landed with a bounce on the other side. Repeating the action, he jumped back in the yard where the two little boys ran up to him, both talking excitedly and begging him to do it again.

"You two made a deal, now get to it," Wes said, propelling the boys toward the door. When they went inside, he turned to Brody with a broad grin. "Man, that was awesome."

"Just takes a little practice," Brody said, catching Haven's eye and recognizing her indulgent smile.

Sitting around the dinner table a short while later, the conversation ranged from the types of potatoes Wes and John were planting that year to how many home football games were left in the season.

"Can we go, Dad? Please?" Mason and Jed both begged their father.

If Brody hadn't met Wes and his family that afternoon and happened to run into them somewhere, he would have immediately known he was Haven's brother because he looked like a slightly older version of Hale and Tom. Mason and Jed looked just like him, too.

"We'll see. A lot will depend on how well you boys can behave for the next week or two," Wes said, winking at his wife. Since the two boys were so ornery and rambunctious, they used any advantage they could to keep them in line.

Eating Haven's banana cake for dessert with caramel-laced ice cream, Brody couldn't remember when he'd spent such a fun, relaxing day.

Once everyone was sufficiently full and couldn't eat another bite, Wes and Tammy took the boys home and Tom left to complete some paperwork he needed to have ready early the next morning.

Hale and Brody joined John in clearing the table while Haven and Rachel put food away and started doing the dishes.

Brody was walking out of the kitchen when Rachel began peppering Haven with questions. He grinned when he heard her say they met at a football game and yes, she was aware that he was extremely handsome and sweet.

Laughing to himself, he'd never considered himself sweet. He could be selfish and arrogant when the mood struck him, as well as callous, thickheaded, and stubborn. Fortunately, the mood didn't strike often.

Mostly, he felt a deep sense of gratitude for the way his mother raised him. Watching her sacrifice everything for him taught Brody a healthy respect for women, despite his bad boy reputation. A lot of that was just locker room talk and the wishful thinking of girls who liked to hang out with players.

Returning with the last of the dirty dishes, he heard Haven ask her mother why she gave her such an awful name. Brody stopped just outside the door and listened.

"You know I hate my name, Mom. What were you thinking? How many drugs did they give you during labor? It sounds like I should work in some tawdry club or escort service," Haven said, rinsing off a bowl and drying it.

"I happen to think your name is beautiful. There isn't a thing wrong with Haven Clarice Haggarty. I named you that because after three boys, I was grateful for the haven you would provide in my all-male world. You were so delicate and perfect," Rachel said, scrubbing a pot and rinsing it before handing it to Haven.

"Well, when you say it like that, it makes it sound better," Haven admitted, with a smile.

"Does Brody make fun of your name?" Rachel asked, giving Haven a concerned look. "He doesn't seem like the type to do that."

"No, he's never said anything about it," Haven said, sounding wistful.

"I bet when he says your name, your knees get all wobbly and butterflies swarm your tummy," Rachel teased.

Brody didn't wait to hear the response, feeling only marginally guilty for eavesdropping. Recalling what Marcus said about Haven's name, he'd have to remember to tell her how much he liked it. Just not now. Otherwise, she might catch on that he overheard the conversation she had with her mother.

Returning to the living room after leaving the dishes in the kitchen, Brody talked with Hale and John until Haven and Rachel joined the men when they finished the dishes. Discussing farming and football over cups of coffee, Haven finally glanced at the clock on the fireplace mantle and got to her feet.

"We better head back to town. I don't want to keep this guy out past his bedtime," Haven said, grinning at Brody.

Standing, he shook both Hale and John's hands then gave Rachel a warm hug, thanking the family for their hospitality.

"You're welcome to come anytime, Brody. The next time you're here, Haven will have to take you out to see the cattle or go for a horseback ride," John said, winking at his daughter.

"That sounds great. I didn't know you had horses, too," Brody said. Riding horses with Haven would no doubt be a great experience.

"Just a few," John said, looking at his wife. "Rachel rides them more than anyone. I guess they're kind of her pets."

"That they are, but I share," Rachel said, walking with Haven and Brody toward the door.

"Oh, I almost forgot my dishes," Haven said, running to the kitchen and returning with a clean bowl and an empty cake pan.

"You can fill that pan back up with cake, sweetie, and bring it next time you come," John said. He was partial to Haven's baked treats. Rachel didn't like to bake much and when Haven moved out, he rarely got homemade pie or cake, unless she brought something when she came to visit.

"I'll see what I can do, Dad. Thanks for everything," she said, hugging first her mom then her dad and finally Hale. Before he let her go, she whispered in his ear. "I hate your new gun. Don't ever ask me to shoot that thing again."

Chuckling, Hale shook his head and waved as she and Brody walked out the door.

On the way back to town, Brody asked her questions about her family.

"I know they can be a little much," Haven said as they arrived at her apartment.

Brody remembered he left his bag of clothes on her couch, grateful for an excuse to follow Haven inside. He wasn't ready for the evening to end.

Getting out of the car, he realized his phone had been quiet all day then he remembered he turned it off before they went in to church and never turned it back on. Going the whole day without calls or texts was nice. He might have to try it more often.

Being with Haven and her family had given him a sense of something he'd spent his life waiting to find. He felt at home with the friendly group of people and hoped that Haven would take him back to the farm again.

"Honestly, doll, it's been one of the best days I've had in a long, long time. Thank you for inviting me to tag along," Brody said, opening the back seat door on his side of her car. Picking up her bowl and cake pan, he carried them inside, going straight to the kitchen with them. Setting them down on the table, he turned to look at her.

"I'm glad you had a good day, Brody. I enjoyed spending my Sunday with you," she said, smiling at him, standing with her hands stuffed in the back pockets of her jeans.

He opened his arms and she stepped into the warmth and comfort of his embrace.

"You mean my family didn't scare you so badly you'll walk out that door and never call me again?"

"Not even close," Brody said, inhaling the smell of sunshine and something flowery in her hair. "Your nephews are awesome."

"They're a handful is what they are," Haven said, leaning back so she could look in Brody's face. "You are so good with kids. Where does that come from?"

"I suppose part of it was growing up alone. I always wanted to be around other kids. Part of it is from my degree," Brody said. He didn't often talk about his career options, beyond football.

"Degree? What do you have a degree in?" Haven asked, knowing Brody hadn't mentioned it before. She just assumed he'd left school to play football, like so many other players did.

"Education. I try to keep up my certification. When I'm done being a football player, I plan to teach and coach," Brody said, looking down at Haven and seeing surprise and approval on her face.

"That's fantastic. I had no idea," she said, giving him a warm hug. "What else are you keeping a secret?"

"Let's see," he said, taking off her glasses and setting them on the counter. He kissed one eyelid followed by the other. "I'm pretty sure it's not a secret now, but there's this girl named Haven who caught my eye and I spent the entire day wanting to do this."

Brody pressed his mouth to hers, teasing and tasting. He felt Haven's arms wrap around his neck and he held her closer, deepening the kiss. A moan of pleasure escaped from her and Brody thought he might lose all control right then.

Pulling back, he gave her a devilish smile, trying to lighten the moment. "I'm not the only one with secrets, Miss Haggarty."

"What am I hiding?" she asked, still languid from his kiss.

"The evidence of what happens when a hot shell casing goes down your shirt," Brody said, making her grin.

Taking a step away from him, she ducked her chin to the neck of her T-shirt and began backing toward the living room.

"And that evidence will remain hidden. No one, and I mean no one, is going to see it," she said.

"Is that right?" Brody asked, lunging toward her, making her giggle as he chased her around the coffee table and caught her waist between his big hands.

Gently tossing her down on the couch, he held her hands in his as he pressed his body next to hers, pushing the throw pillows out of his way.

"I might take a peek for myself. It is evidence, after all," Brody said, holding both her hands in one of his above her head while he used the forefinger of the other one to trace a line across her smooth jaw and trail slowly down her neck to the edge of her T-shirt.

"Brody," she said breathlessly, looking alarmed and uneasy although she held perfectly still beneath him.

"Relax, Haven. I won't do anything. At least not much," Brody said, coaxing her lips into a heated response with his.

Dropping his hold on her hands, he wrapped his arms around her, kissing her with more passion and yearning than he'd ever felt for anyone.

"Brody," she whispered again, causing him to raise his head and look into her soulful eyes. What he saw reflected there both frightened and encouraged him. He'd never seen such a beguiling mixture of love, longing, and acceptance before.

Picking her up, he switched places so she was lying on top of him, staring down into his face. He touched his finger to her dimples then kissed her again, thinking he'd never get the taste of her sweetness out of his mind if he lived to be a hundred.

She lifted her head and gazed at him again, then smiled. "For evidence," she said, pulling down the neck of her shirt just enough that Brody could see a bright red spot that closely resembled the round end of a shell casing. It looked tender and sore. Then he noticed two similar spots marring her creamy skin.

Before he could think about what he was doing, he pressed a kiss to each spot. Haven sucked in a gulp of air while his hands rubbed soothingly along her back.

Continuing to press kisses against her soft skin, he stopped before he took things too far and held her close.

Since Haven dressed so conservatively, he'd had to use his imagination to fill in a lot of the detail. Today, seeing her in a T-shirt and jeans helped define what he suspected all along. Beneath her business suits and sweater sets lurked a temptingly curved body.

That tiny little peek at the ivory skin on her chest left him feeling like he might die from wanting.

"I'm sorry, doll. Does it hurt?" he asked, trying to focus on the fact she'd been burned instead of the ache she created inside him.

"A little. Not like it did when it happened." She spoke quietly with her head resting on his chest.

His heart pounded out such a loud, rapid beat, she wondered that it didn't explode. While she felt limp and languid against him, his muscles tensed and tightened beneath her. Wanting him to relax, she scooted off him and the couch.

"Roll over," she said, pushing at his shoulder.

He stared at her, trying to figure out what she was doing. When he didn't move, she pushed at him again.

"Roll over, Brody. Please?"

"Why?" he asked, wanting to be sure what she had planned before he agreed.

"Just do it. What do you think I'm going to do? Clonk you over the head and paint your nails bright pink?"

"No," he said, chuckling as he rolled onto his stomach. Turning his head, trying to see her, she slid a pillow beneath his cheek.

Her breath was warm on his neck when she whispered close to his ear. "Just relax, football man."

If she thought brushing against him with her sweet breath blowing on his neck and her alluring scent teasing his senses would help him relax, he'd have to explain in detail how that wasn't going to work.

"Look, Haven, I…" Brody couldn't say another word as her hands began massaging the muscles of his back. She put strength behind her movements and he could feel her loosen a knot beneath his shoulder.

"That feels good," he groaned, thinking this had to be some form of exquisite torture.

Only then, it got worse.

She pushed his shirt up until his back was mostly exposed. Reaching back, he yanked the T-shirt over his head and worked to hold on to his self-control with a tenuous grasp as her hands caressed his bare skin.

Letting his body and mind unwind, he tried to calm down. Haven didn't say anything as she worked, kneading his muscles until they became pliant and lax.

Brody couldn't remember the last time he felt so completely relaxed and calm. When she finished and sat back, he tried to lift his head to look at her and couldn't. His arms didn't want to function either.

"Where'd you learn to do that?" he mumbled, feeling drugged. He absently wondered if her hands cast some sort of spell over him.

"I've got a hard-working dad and three brothers, remember?" Haven said, pleased to see Brody look entirely peaceful for the first time since she met him.

"That's right," he whispered, losing the battle to stay awake.

Haven could tell by Brody's breathing he'd gone to sleep. Smiling, she decided to let him rest for a while. It was barely eight and she didn't typically go to bed until after ten.

Picking up the book she'd started reading the previous afternoon, she curled up in the chair by the couch, trying to be quiet. Instead of getting lost in the story, her thoughts and gaze kept wandering to Brody.

Making herself a cup of tea, she finally abandoned efforts at reading and sat watching him. Fighting the urge to reach out and run her hand through his hair and along his face, she grinned when a corner of his mouth tipped up in a smirk she well recognized.

It was just wrong for one man to be so perfectly handsome. Admiring the muscles exposed on his back and arms, she looked forward to seeing those on his chest when he rolled over. Even though she'd seen her brothers without their shirts, it was far, far different to see Brody shirtless.

She recalled Allie's words about paying money to see him without his shirt on and stifled a giggle. She wondered if Allie would hand her a twenty-dollar bill to come over right now.

When it was almost ten, she decided she better wake Brody and take him home. He certainly couldn't stay at her apartment all night. The neighbors would have a heyday if he walked out with her in the morning.

Kneeling next to him, she brushed her fingers along his forehead then finger-combed his hair away from his temple.

"Brody," she whispered, hoping he'd stir. "Brody, time to go. I need to take you home now."

He didn't so much as flicker an eyelash at her. Leaning closer, she kissed his cheek and gently shook his arm.

"Please, Brody. I can't let you stay here all night. You have to wake up, now."

Still nothing.

Wondering if he was ticklish, she lightly grazed her fingers down his side and prepared to find out when he suddenly rolled over and grabbed her in his arms, blowing a wet, sloppy kiss on her neck.

"I wouldn't do that if I were you, doll," he said in a gravelly voice, sounding half-awake, as he pulled her down beside him and tickled her sides.

"Not fair using brute force," Haven said, squirming to escape and trying to contain her giggles. "That's definitely cheating."

"Who says?" Brody asked, nuzzling her neck then kissing her cheek.

"Me," Haven wrapped her arms around his neck and pressed against his chest. Warm and solid, he smelled so good, she struggled to keep her resolve to take him home immediately from rapidly unraveling.

"Is that right? Even so, I think I've overstayed my welcome today. I didn't mean to fall asleep," Brody said, setting Haven on her feet and getting to his, realizing he didn't have on his shirt. He vaguely remembered tossing it aside when magical fingers began massaging his back.

Haven grabbed something from the floor and hurried to the other side of the room. "Looking for this?" she asked, dangling his T-shirt from her finger.

"As a matter of fact, I am," he said, holding out his hand to her. "May I have that, please?"

"Mmm. No. I don't think so," Haven said, cocking her head and giving him a saucy smile. "I think I like you this way much better."

"Haven," he growled, taking two quick steps and grabbing both her and his shirt. Wrapping his arms around her from behind, he held her against his chest, his lips pressed close to her ear. "If you don't stop this nonsense, I won't be the only one without their shirt on."

He felt her stiffen as she grew still in his arms. Pushing against him, she took a step away and kept her back turned while he put on his shirt.

"I'll take you home," she said quietly, picking up her purse and fumbling with her keys. When she dropped them on the floor, Brody bent down to pick them up at the same time she did and their eyes locked. She looked confused and a little offended.

"Haven, I'm sorry. I was just teasing," he said, pulling her upright and folding her into a hug. He felt her arms wrap tightly around him and she breathed against his chest, making his temperature begin to climb again.

"I was teasing, too. I just didn't… I didn't think… I'm sorry, Brody," Haven finally said, realizing as much as she enjoyed looking at him, she didn't want to give him the wrong idea.

"No worries. I just don't want you to be upset. It's all in good fun, right?" he asked, helping her slip on a jacket since the night air was cool.

"Right," she said, stepping away from him and opening the door.

Brody grabbed the duffle bag he'd left earlier and followed her outside.

If he had a brain in his head, he'd avoid being alone with Haven. She provided a temptation he found extremely hard to resist. Then again, Brody hadn't always been known to avoid trouble.

## *Chapter Ten*

Haven looked up from her desk to see her assistant, Jordan, walk in carrying a vase of gorgeous pink and white tulips.

"It's starting to look like a florist shop in here," Jordan said, searching for a place to set the flowers.

Haven jumped up and cleared a spot on the corner of her desk for the vase. It was the third bouquet she'd received that week.

Monday, Allie sent her a bouquet in a smiley-face mug along with a note apologizing for acting like an idiot after the game.

A gift basket from a pleased client arrived Tuesday afternoon. After picking out the chocolates she liked, she put the rest in the break room for the staff to share.

Another client sent her a bouquet of daisies and carnations Thursday in thanks for a successful launch of an online campaign Haven developed for them.

The huge bouquet of tulips Jordan set on her desk was one of the loveliest she'd ever seen. Searching for a card, Haven had no idea who would have sent the flowers.

Finding the florist envelope, she read the short note then sank into her chair and stared at the bouquet.

"Everything okay, Haven?" Jordan asked, noticing her boss looked a little pale.

"Yes, fine. Thank you, Jordan. If you wouldn't mind taking that vase with the daisies to the reception area, they might look nice on the side table by the couch.

"Sure," Jordan said, taking the flowers from the top of Haven's filing cabinet and leaving even though she wasn't convinced the woman was fine.

Haven read the card again and smiled.

*To the sweetest girl I know.*
*Happy Birthday, doll.*
*Have a great day.*
*Love,*
*Brody*

She'd been disappointed to realize Brody would be out of town at a game this weekend. It was her birthday and she'd hoped to be able to see him. Instead, he'd left yesterday to go to a game across the country.

Not wanting him to think it would bother her if he missed her special day, she didn't mention her birthday was fast approaching.

Someone must have told him, though, because he'd just sent her the loveliest tulips she'd ever seen.

"Aren't you the popular one this week?" Mr. Young observed, walking in carrying a tastefully wrapped gift box in his hand.

"So it would seem," Haven said, smiling at her boss.

"These tulips are magnificent," he said, studying them critically. "Can we take some photos of them while they're fresh?"

"I guess so," Haven said, realizing they really were exceptionally lovely. No wonder Mr. Young wanted to take photos of them. She had no doubt they'd be used in some promotional piece or ad campaign.

"Great. Just take them to Adam and tell him I said to be careful with them," Mr. Young said, setting the box on her desk. "Happy birthday, Haven. You should leave early tonight. Celebrate! You're only young once, you know."

"Thank you, sir," Haven said, not certain if she should open his gift while he waited or save it for later. He made the decision for her when he smiled and left her office.

Taking the lid off the box, she was surprised to see a bowl she'd admired at an art show one of their clients hosted. Taking it out, she held it up and marveled at the way the light reflected through the glass.

Setting it back in the box, a slip of paper caught her attention and she pulled it out. Laughing when she read, "Go home early! Or else!" she vowed she would be out of the office before four.

Picking up the tulips, she carried them back to their small studio and found Adam trying to take photos of a client's cleaning products.

"Ah, sweet relief," Adam said, taking the tulips from her and setting them on a pedestal in front of a light gray backdrop. "These are far and above much more photogenic than that mess."

Haven smiled and looked at the array of cleaning products, agreeing with Adam. There was nothing appealing about any of them.

"What account are these for?" Adam asked, setting up his camera and lights.

"None at the moment," Haven said, watching Adam adjust a light. "I received them and Mr. Young suggested we take some stock photos, since they are so perfect."

"Good idea," Adam said, snapping a test photo and making a few adjustments. "I needed a break anyway."

Haven stood quietly while Adam worked and in a few minutes time, he handed the flowers back to her.

"Whoever sent those has excellent taste. Much better than someone who thinks I can make mops and bottles of cleaner look exciting."

"Lots of luck, Adam. Thanks," Haven said, feeling sorry for her coworker. Sometimes Adam got to shoot fun, cool stuff. Other times, he had to deal with a lot of boring photos.

Returning to her office, she sent a text message to Brody before anyone else could interrupt her, thanking him for the flowers.

Slipping her phone in the pocket of her skirt, she returned her attention to some online research she was doing for a client. She'd barely touched the mouse of her computer when her phone rang.

"Haven Haggarty," she said, politely, not bothering to look at the caller ID.

"Hi, doll. Happy birthday!" Brody said, sounding a million miles away, although the two thousand miles between them might as well have been that many. "Hope you're having a great day so far."

"Brody!" Haven said, surprised to hear his voice. "The tulips are gorgeous. Thank you so, so much."

"You're welcome. I didn't want you to think I forgot about you," Brody said, glad Hale mentioned something about Haven's birthday when they were at the farm Sunday. "Any other birthday surprises?"

"Mr. Young bought me a bowl I liked from an art show we attended. Other than that, the day is still young." Haven was thrilled Brody called but hoped she wasn't keeping him from something he needed to do. "I thought you'd be tied up all day."

"They gave us a few moments of peace for good behavior. I have to go in a sec, but I wanted to wish you a happy birthday. Have a really good one, Haven."

She could hear voices in the background and Brody mumble something about being off the phone in a minute.

"It sounds like you need to go now, Brody, but thank you again for the flowers and the call. I really appreciate both," she said. For a guy who made it clear he was keeping things casual with no strings attached, he seemed to be just as tied to her as she was to him.

"You're welcome. Maybe I can take you out for dinner or something when I get back."

"That sounds great," Haven said, wanting to thank Brody in person. If he were in town, she'd have no problem leaving the office early. "Have a great game. I hope you win. Jump high and catch everything that comes at you."

"I'll do my best," Brody said, yelling at someone in the background to leave him alone. "Bye, Haven. Miss you."

"I miss you, too. Bye, Brody." Haven stared at the phone in her hand for a while before stuffing it back in her pocket.

Feeling things she'd never before experienced, just thinking about Brody made her elated and keyed up. Although he tried to make people think he was tough and carefree, he had a tender heart.

Unable to concentrate on doing detailed research or any work involving her full attention, she decided to clean out some files while her thoughts lingered on Brody.

Allie showed up to take her to lunch and apologized again for being difficult after the game Saturday.

With a promise to go shopping the next afternoon, Allie gave her a hug and slipped a card in her hand as they parted ways in the parking lot. Returning to her office, Haven opened the card and laughed at the silly greeting, then smiled to see a gift card to her favorite store.

Working on some creative design ideas in the early afternoon, she lost her focus every time one of her coworkers stopped by to wish her a happy birthday. Finally giving up on getting any work done, she gathered her things, picked up the vase of tulips and locked her office at a little past three.

"Have a great weekend, Haven," Mr. Young said as he saw her leaving.

"I will, thanks!" she called as she hurried out the door.

Treating herself to a pedicure on the way home, she carried the tulips inside and set them on her coffee table, admiring how they brightened the whole room.

Staring at them a while, she finally got up and changed into jeans and a soft blouse, then drove out to the farm where her family would gather for dinner to celebrate her special day.

Walking in the door, Mason and Jed slammed into her legs, almost knocking her over backward.

"Aunt Haven! Happy birthday!" they said in unison, dragging her toward the family room where cheerfully wrapped packages sat on a side table, waiting to be opened.

"You've got tons of presents," Mason said, pointing to the festive-looking gifts.

"And Mom said we can't open them. They're all for you," Jed said, nodding his head for emphasis.

"Is that right? Well, that's pretty cool, isn't it?" Haven asked, ruffling the hair on one dark head and then the other.

"Where's Brody? We brought our football so he can throw it to us. Will he jump over the fence again?" Mason asked, dancing around her and tugging on her hand.

"Brody's gone to a game far away right now. Maybe you guys can come see him when his team plays at home in a few weeks," Haven said, walking with the little boys to the kitchen where her mom and Tammy finished dinner preparations.

"Happy birthday, sweetie!" Rachel said, hugging her daughter. "Did you have a good day?"

"I did, Mom. It's been really nice so far," Haven said, snitching a strawberry from a bowl of fruit salad.

"I heard you tell the boys Brody's out of town. Did he remember your birthday?" Rachel asked.

"Actually, he sent me the most gorgeous tulips," Haven said, taking her phone out of her pocket and showing her a photo. Adam sent her one of the shots he took and it made the flowers look even more beautiful.

"Oh, my gosh," Tammy said, grabbing the phone and looking at the flowers. "Those aren't just 'hey, I'm dating you' flowers, those are 'I'm in love with you, baby' flowers."

"You're insane," Haven said, laughing as she stuffed the phone back in her pocket. "Brody and I both know he'll be gone at the end of the season. It's not like either one of us expects this to be a long-term relationship. Allie informed me I need to get out and have more fun, and she's right. Brody wanted to be friends who date, so there it is."

Tammy gave Rachel a look that said neither of them were buying Haven's story, but they didn't say anything.

After dinner with her family, including Allie, Rick, a few other cousins, aunts and uncles, they all convened to the large family room where Haven opened her gifts.

The boys helped remove the paper and ribbons, leaving a path of shredded destruction in their wake while Haven opened the gifts and offered words of thanks.

"You've got one more gift," Hale said, handing her his laptop computer. Footage from a football game played and Haven suddenly realized it was Brody's game from that evening. With the time difference, he should have finished playing an hour or so earlier.

"Look, there's Brody!" Haven said, holding the computer so Mason and Jed could watch over her shoulder. He leaped high in the air and made a perfect catch before turning to run with the ball. Tossing the ball to a ref after the whistle blew, Brody looked into a nearby camera and held up his hand. The words, "Hi, Doll!" marched across his wide palm, for the entire world to see.

"He didn't!" Haven shook her head in disbelief then looked at Hale for confirmation. He nodded his head and grinned.

Everyone wanted to see, so Haven passed around the laptop and they watched the video over and over.

"Yep, he's just a dating kind of friend," Tammy said to Rachel while both of them gave Haven a knowing glance.

Unsure how Hale knew to show her the clip, he explained that Brody had a friend make sure the clip was posted on YouTube and then sent Hale the link.

"Thank you for your sneaky involvement in making today extra special," she said, giving Hale a hug as he walked her to her car.

"I'm glad you had a great day, Haven," Hale said, holding her car door while she slid inside. "For the record, I like him."

"Me, too." Haven drove back to town floating on cloud nine.

Sitting down at her computer, too wired to sleep, Haven watched the video clip again and saw a string of comments had been added, the most common wanting to know whom Brody was calling a doll.

The secret knowledge that it was her warmed Haven from her toes all the way down deep into her heart.

Sending Brody a text message telling him he made her day amazing, she'd barely set down her phone when he called.

"Hey, Haven!"

"Brody, I can't believe you did that," Haven said, thrilled to hear his voice for the second time that day. An abundance of noise in the background, like he was somewhere with a lot of people, made it hard to hear. "You're awesome and I loved it."

"You're welcome," Brody said, flying high both from victory at the game and being able to surprise Haven. "Did you get a lot of good junk at the party?"

"Absolutely. Although I'm not entirely certain I'll remember who gave me what when it comes time to write thank you notes because Mason and Jed helped me unwrap my gifts."

Laughing, Brody could picture the two little boys ripping into the packages before Haven could read the card to find out the name of the giver. "I'm glad you enjoyed your day. Did you eat a piece of cake for me?"

"No, but I brought home a piece for you and stuck it in the freezer. You can eat it yourself when you get back," Haven said, uncertain as to when that would be. She knew Brody had another away game the next weekend.

"I'll look forward to it," Brody said, dropping his voice so quiet, she had to strain to hear him. "And I'm looking forward to seeing you, too. I'll call you tomorrow, Haven. Miss you."

"I miss you, too, Brody. Travel safe and know I'll be waiting to see you."

Disconnecting the call, Haven smiled dreamily and reached out to place a finger on her computer screen, touching Brody's face, thinking how much he'd enriched her life in such a short amount of time.

Refusing to think about the end of June when he'd leave, she went to bed dreaming of his gravelly voice, strong arms, and tender smile.

## *Chapter Eleven*

Flying home on a red-eye flight after the game Friday night, Brody crashed from exhaustion within minutes of walking in his apartment door. Afternoon rolled around on Saturday before he opened his eyes and stretched in bed.

The guys razzed him all the way home about his "doll" and kept asking who she was. Marcus was the only one who knew and refused to say anything, aware of the fact that Brody would do serious damage to him if he did.

Arriving home in the wee hours of the morning, he hoped after getting some sleep to surprise Haven and see if she wanted to go out on a real date, with dinner and a movie.

Wondering if she'd be home or at the farm or at some event put on by one of her clients, he reached for his phone and sent a text to Hale. Her brother had proven to be an especially helpful ally, and one he genuinely liked.

He could see why Hale was her favorite of the three brothers. Wes was all wrapped up in his little family, and rightfully so, while Tom spent most of his time focused on himself.

Getting up and going to the kitchen, he drank orange juice straight from the carton then made an omelet. After eating it, he checked his phone and saw a message from Hale saying he thought Haven was shopping with Allie at the mall.

Sending Hale a brief message of thanks, he hurried to take a shower, dressed, and then drove to the mall.

One of the last places he thought he'd be on a sunny Saturday afternoon was in the midst of busy stores packed with people, but he really wanted to see Haven.

He wondered if she liked seeing the message on his hand as much as she said. Then again, she wasn't the type of girl to be coy or play games with him, which was one of the many reasons he found himself so attracted to her.

Going inside, the noise level was somewhere between a football game and a rock concert. He watched a handful of kids screaming as their mothers tried to drag them from the play area.

Walking toward one of the big department stores, he took out his phone and sent Haven a text message, asking what she was doing.

She quickly sent a text back that she was shopping with Allie.

He asked her where. When she named one of the boutique stores located outside the mall, he stopped and bought three Italian sodas. Strolling to the front of the store, he waited for her to come outside.

When she and Allie walked into the sunshine a few minutes later, they both stood staring at him, open-mouthed.

"Oh, my gosh, Brody! What are you doing here?" she asked, wanting to give him a hug, but his hands were full of drinks. She settled for kissing his cheek.

"We took a red-eye flight home and now that I'm awake, I wanted to see you," he said, holding out the drinks. The girls each took one.

"Nice to see you, Brody." Allie gave him a flirty smile before taking a sip of her drink.

Haven rolled her eyes as they strolled toward the next store. Standing outside, she looked from Allie to Brody, uncertain what to do.

"Hey, don't let me interrupt your shopping adventure. I just wanted to surprise you," Brody said to Haven, taking her hand in his and giving it a squeeze. "If you don't have plans later, I thought maybe we could have dinner and catch a movie."

"Oh, please," Allie said, plopping down on a bench and motioning for the other two to join her. "Cool your heels for a minute there, handsome. We'll finish these drinks and you can just shop with us then I'll let you kidnap Haven and do what you will with her."

"Excuse me?" Haven looked at her cousin, flabbergasted.

"I'm not so sure shopping with you girls is a good plan. I'll just... um... give you a call later, doll, and we'll decide...

"Scared of a little retail therapy, Mr. Jackson?" Allie asked in a tone that dripped with challenge.

"No. I just don't want to horn in on your girl time." Brody said, thinking that sounded convincing. He'd never had a steady girlfriend to force him to accompany her on trips to the mall and his mother never had the money to waste on anything that wasn't absolutely necessary. Brody didn't think this particular afternoon seemed like the right time for an initiation into the rituals of tagging along with women intent on shopping.

"Watch this, Haven. He's about to tuck his tail between those long legs of his and run," Allie said, bumping Haven's arm with her elbow.

Glaring at the girl who was too pretty for her own good and far too opinionated for his, he finished his soda and dropped the cup in a nearby garbage can. He'd never run from a challenge and today would not be the exception.

If any of the guys saw what he was about to do, they'd probably roll on the ground laughing, but odds were high he wouldn't run into any of his teammates in the girly stores he'd no doubt be dragged to before the afternoon was over.

Walking back to the bench, he gave Haven a hand and helped her to her feet, then kissed her cheek. "Lead on, fair lady. I'm here to serve this afternoon."

Haven looped her arm around Brody's then shot her cousin a smug smile. "Told you he wouldn't run off."

"Let's just see how long he lasts. Rick can't even make it through Macy's shoe department," Allie said, going to Brody's other side and looping her arm through his. "I bet I can break you before the afternoon is over."

"Give it a try, Allie. Bring it on," Brody said, holding open the door to a shoe store as the girls preceded him inside.

An hour and a half later, as he sat in a chair by the dressing rooms waiting for the girls to finish trying on outfits, he realized he wasn't having a terrible time. In fact, he'd learned a lot about Haven by listening to her and Allie talk, and by observing the types of things that grabbed her interest.

While Allie went for the flashy, super trendy pieces, Haven gravitated to either career clothes or outfits that were much more conservative.

This store was a mix of both and Allie was like a whirlwind, grabbing a handful of hangers and insisting Haven go back to the dressing rooms with her.

Spying a few other men sitting around waiting, Brody joined them. So far, no one recognized him. If a video of him packing shopping bags around ended up online, his carefully cultivated reputation as a partying bad boy was as good as dead.

After a few more minutes of waiting, Allie appeared and motioned Brody to come closer to the dressing rooms.

"I've been trying to talk Haven into modeling an outfit to see what you think. I'm pretty sure I've finally got her convinced to stick her nose out the dressing room door, but she refuses to walk all the way out to the sitting area," Allie said, speaking quietly with a hint of conspiracy. "If you don't mind waiting right here. I'll shove her out the door and you can share your thoughts on how it looks."

"What's she trying on that's such a big deal?" Brody asked, unfamiliar with the trauma women endured in front of dressing room mirrors.

"I told her this dress would make your eyes pop out of your head and she's convinced it's a little too... me!" Allie said, hurrying back to a dressing room halfway down the hall.

Brody received a glare from an older woman who came out of a dressing room to look in the big mirror at the end of the hall. When she saw him in the reflection, she quickly returned to her dressing room and slammed the door.

Allie poked her head out and nodded at him before shoving Haven into the hall.

Staring at the girl in the mile-high heels wearing a dress that accented every generous curve in her figure, Allie was almost right.

His eyes didn't pop out of his head, but it felt like they might. Brody's jaw dropped as he ogled Haven from the top of her golden head to the tips of the "notice me" shoes.

"Haven," he said, his voice unusually husky and rough as he reached out a hand to her. She walked his direction, looking a little uncertain and a lot self-conscious. The dress was cut lower than anything he'd seen her wear, but it still provided more coverage than the clothes many women wore.

He knew nothing about women's fashion, except that the cut of this particular dress was made for Haven, not to mention the rich blue color that perfectly matched her eyes.

"Whatever it costs, you've got to have it," he said, knowing Haven needed this dress. Not only because she looked so hot in it he was afraid he might singe his fingers if he touched her, but also because he knew, intuitively, it would boost her confidence whenever she wore it.

"Do you really like it?" she asked, delighted at the look on his face when she stepped out of the dressing room. Starting to feel a heady sensation from the way he couldn't take his eyes off her, she wondered if that was how Allie felt all the time.

"No, I don't like it. I love it. I don't care what else you planned to buy today, you've got to have that dress, doll." He bent down so he could whisper in her ear. "And you have to promise you'll wear it on a date with me."

Haven nodded her head and turned to go back in the dressing room, noticing her reflection with Brody in the big hall mirror. He placed a hand on her waist and smiled as she looked at their images.

"We look good together, don't we?" he said, admiring the view of her in the mirror as well as the feel of her waist beneath his hand.

"Yes," she whispered, then hustled back in the dressing room.

Allie winked at him. "You can thank me later," she said before following Haven back in the room.

Returning to where the other men waited, Brody felt the need for some fresh air and a cold shower.

Stepping outside, he took several deep breaths then returned inside to see Haven at the cash register with the dress. Walking up beside her, he noticed she was buying a few other things as well.

"Don't you want the shoes, too?" he asked, hopeful she'd get the entire outfit.

Haven shook her head. "No. I've got some at home that will work."

"Okay," Brody said, feeling a little disappointed. The shoes that made her legs look a mile long wouldn't be on her feet in the near future. He somehow doubted she had anything similar in her closet. From what he'd seen, she had tasteful heels she wore for work, flats for casual events, and boots she wore out to the farm.

"You want me to buy your dress?"

Haven and Allie both looked at him in surprise.

"Thank you, but I've got it," Haven said, shocked by Brody's offer. She knew playing arena football didn't make him a fortune and he didn't have unlimited funds. That he'd even offer melted another piece of her heart.

At this rate, he'd have it entirely dissolved before he left in June.

Brody was impressed when he discovered the dress was on sale and Haven had a gift card from Allie she was using to purchase it.

"I think we should quit while we're ahead," Allie said, taking pity on Brody. He'd not complained once, carried their bags without comment, and the way he reacted to Haven in the dress was more than she'd hoped for.

"Want to make it dinner for four and go to the movies?" Brody asked as he walked Allie and Haven to where Allie parked her car.

"I'd love that. Rick and I were planning something similar anyway. Why don't we get a little fancy so Haven can wear her new dress?" Allie suggested.

"Sounds good to me," Brody said. The three of them decided on a restaurant and agreed to meet there in two hours. Allie planned to help Haven get ready before running home to change.

Brody really wanted to take Haven home himself, but knew he needed to go back to his apartment and change.

Giving her a kiss on her cheek, he walked around the side of the mall to where he parked his truck. Remembering something he thought might make Haven smile, he ran back inside and found what he was looking for in one of the stores he'd browsed through with the girls.

Driving home, he dug his sports jacket from the back of his closet, changed from his T-shirt into a button down shirt, swapped his faded jeans for a new pair, and spent a few minutes polishing his boots before pulling them on.

Glancing at his watch, he still had time to kill so he turned on the television, but couldn't get interested in anything. He absently thumbed through a magazine, paid a few bills, and paced the floor.

Unable to wait any longer, he tried to walk slowly down the steps to his truck, but he was anxious to see Haven in that dress again and couldn't keep himself to a sedate pace.

Arriving fifteen minutes early, he forced himself to sit in his truck for a few minutes before knocking on her door.

At first, he wasn't convinced he had the right apartment when the door opened.

Expecting to see his curly-haired sweetheart, a blonde bombshell offered him a warm greeting. Haven's shiny hair hung sleek and straight down her back. She wore more makeup than usual and he could see Allie's hand in it, from the dark eyeliner to the smoky eyes that didn't look like Haven's usual innocent, fresh face. Her lips weren't the soft pink he was accustomed to, but instead a deep red.

She wore the figure enhancing blue dress with a pair of heels even sexier than the shoes she had on at the store.

"I'm sorry. I think I got the wrong place. I was looking for my girlfriend." He made the tone of his voice teasing, although intense desire crashed over him as he stood staring at her.

"Well, that's too bad. I thought maybe I'd opened the door and my dreams were finally coming true," Haven said, deciding Brody got more handsome every time she saw him, but she didn't know how it was possible. She stepped back so he could enter her apartment and closed the door.

Taking her arms in his hands, he gave her a slow, thorough once-over that made her feel exposed and wanted all at the same time.

"Haven, you take my breath away," he said, kissing her lightly on the cheek, not wanting to smudge her makeup. He'd gone out with enough high maintenance girls to know messing up their lipstick on the way out the door was something they considered a cardinal sin.

"You look very nice, too," she said, wondering why he didn't pull her close and kiss her like he usually did.

"I've got a little something to go with your new dress," Brody said, removing a small box from his jacket pocket and holding it out to her.

"Another present? Really, Brody, you've done more than enough already," she said, accepting the box and opening the lid. Inside was a necklace she'd admired earlier that afternoon when she and Allie were shopping with Brody. "I can't believe you bought this for me. Thank you."

"You're very welcome," he said, picking up the necklace and moving so he could drape it around her neck.

Haven lifted her hair so he could fasten the necklace and he planted a warm kiss to the back of her neck before she dropped her thick, golden mane back in place.

"I've never seen your hair straight before," he said, running a hand over the back of her head. Although it looked very nice, he thought he liked her untamed curls better. They looked more natural and like Haven.

"Once in a great while Allie talks me into straightening it," she said, brushing a strand of hair out of her face. "Shall we get going?"

Putting on her glasses, Haven picked up an evening bag, grabbed her keys, and walked out the door Brody held open for her.

"Do you need a jacket?" Brody asked as he shut her door behind him. "It still gets cool in the evenings."

"We're not going to be sitting outside anywhere, are we?" She took Brody's hand as they walked over to his pickup.

"Not that I know of, but with your cousin involved, anything could happen."

Haven laughed and smiled at him. "I'll throw a fit if she tries anything."

"Right. Because you're given to bouts of hysteria, especially in public," Brody said, opening his truck door. He smiled at Haven before picking her up and setting her on the seat. There was no way with her tight skirt and those heels she could possibly get in the truck without his help, which was exactly why he didn't suggest taking her car.

"You never know. There's a first time for everything." Haven gave him a flirty smile as he shut the door and hurried around the truck.

A few minutes later, they pulled up at a popular Italian restaurant where Allie and Rick stood waiting outside the door. As usual, Allie looked like she belonged on a magazine cover with her short skirt, spiked heels, perfect makeup, and flowing hair.

For once, though, Haven didn't feel like the ugly stepsister standing beside her. With Brody's hand warm against her back, she felt almost giddy.

Dinner was delicious with the four of them enjoying pleasant conversation. They were just leaving the restaurant when Brody ran into a couple of his teammates with their dates.

"Dude!" one of them said, giving him a knuckle bump as they all stood outside the door. Noticing Brody's arm around Haven, he smiled broadly. "So, is this *the* doll? You didn't mention she was super-sexy Barbie."

Brody never considered himself a barbaric, jealous type of guy, but having his friends check out Haven like they'd all looked at any number of girls made him want to beat them into the ground.

Stepping protectively in front of her, he gave the men a long, dark glare, before telling them to enjoy their evening and escorting Haven down the walk.

"Told you you'd rock that outfit, cuz," Allie said, as she and Rick walked behind Brody and Haven.

Brody sent her a warning glance over his shoulder. It was one thing for him to think Haven looked like a mouth-watering confection he was dying to taste. He didn't want anyone else ogling her that way. No one.

"Don't you think she looks amazing, Brody?" Allie prodded.

Before Brody could answer, Rick asked what movie everyone wanted to go see and steered the conversation to a much safer topic.

"We'll meet you at the theater," Rick said, smiling at Haven while hurrying Allie toward his car before she could say anything further to upset Brody.

Watching Brody slide behind the wheel, Haven tilted her head with an impish grin as she fastened her seatbelt. "You didn't answer Allie's question."

"I didn't think I needed to," Brody said, starting the truck and driving in the direction of the movie theater. "If you can't tell by the way I keep touching you or the fact that I can't keep my eyes off you, you don't deserve an answer."

"Oh," Haven said, surprised by Brody's honesty. "I just… I wasn't…"

"I know, doll," Brody said, picking up her hand then bringing it to his lips, kissing her fingers. "For the record, you do look amazing. And hot. And exactly like the Barbie my buddy described."

"Brody," Haven said, her cheeks heating with embarrassment.

"It's true, Haven. Every word of it."

Arriving at the movie theater, Haven didn't have a chance to say anything else as Brody helped her out of the truck and they walked toward the door. Rick and Allie were right behind them.

Paying their admission, they ordered sodas and water before going in to watch an action movie. It wasn't what the girls would have chosen to see, but the guys wanted to and it started in a few minutes, rather than waiting almost half an hour for another movie to begin.

Throughout the movie, Brody either held Haven's hand or managed to touch her in some way like putting his arm around her shoulder or resting his hand on her leg. Pleased by his apparent need to be close, she breathed deeply of his scent and absorbed his warmth at her side.

Brody also managed to sneak in a few kisses, although they landed on her neck and cheek. She wondered that he didn't try a little harder to press one to her lips. He seemed like the kind of guy who wouldn't mind kissing a girl in a dark theater.

Deciding not to dwell on it, Haven turned her attention back to the movie.

When it ended, the four of them were discussing where else they could go when Haven excused herself to the restroom. On her way back to rejoin the group, two men walking behind her whistled loudly and one of them reached out like he was about to grab her rear.

Before Haven could say or do anything, Brody was there with a look on his face that frightened her. He gently pushed her behind him before stepping forward with a clenched fist.

"Don't even think about it," Brody threatened, looking at the men.

Deciding they didn't want to take on someone who was clearly angry, looked like he could flatten them both with one hand, and towered over them, the two men turned around and went back the way they came, mumbling an apology.

Brody considered going after them and knocking their heads together, but the coach frowned on that kind of publicity, so he instead took a deep breath, trying to calm down.

"Brody?" Haven asked, placing a hand on his arm. "Are you okay?"

"Yeah. I'm good." He inhaled deeply before turning around and taking her hand in his. "Are you okay?"

"I'm fine. They didn't actually do anything," Haven said, aware that at least one of the men would have grabbed her if Brody hadn't suddenly appeared. While most of her was disgusted and annoyed by their lack of manners, some little part of her was thrilled the two men found her attractive.

"They almost did. Have you ever taken a self-defense class? Do you know how to take care of yourself?" If Haven was going to go out in public looking like she did at that particular moment, she might need to know how to defend herself. He wouldn't always be there to take care of her.

Ignoring the pang of regret shooting through him at the thought of not being around for more than a few months, they rejoined Rick and Allie.

"My red-eye flight is catching up with me. If you all don't mind, I think I'll take Haven home and get to bed at a decent hour tonight," Brody said. He was tired, but it wasn't fatigue that had him taking Haven home. It was the thought of other men staring her direction. He didn't know if he could control his anger or jealousy much longer without somebody getting punched in the face.

"I'm sorry, Brody," Haven said, looking up at him apologetically. "I should have realized you'd be exhausted. I can catch a ride home with Allie if you want to go now."

"No, I'll take you home first," Brody said, smiling at Rick and Allie, even if it was a little forced. This whole fiasco was Allie's fault.

If she hadn't been trying to turn Haven into a shorter, light-haired version of herself, none of this would have happened. Haven would be dressed in one of her soft sweater things with her curls pulled back and her lips all sweet and pink, looking like the innocent girl she was instead of some temptress.

Waving to the other couple as he helped Haven in his truck, they both were quiet on the drive to her apartment. When he pulled into a parking space, Haven opened the door and started to get out.

"Wait, Haven, I'll help you. You might break a leg getting out in those shoes," Brody said, grinning at the thought of her trying to slide off the seat with the tight skirt of her dress hampering her efforts. Hurrying around the truck, he lifted her down then walked her to the door.

"Thank you for a lovely evening, Brody, and the necklace. I love it," Haven said, resting her hand against Brody's chest. Other than a few kisses to her neck and cheek at the movie theater, Brody hadn't tried to kiss her all evening and she'd been thinking about his kisses since he spent the day with her last Sunday.

Knowing she'd never get any rest unless she had at least one, she started to pull his head down to hers, but a throat clearing nearby made her raise her head and smile half-heartedly at one of her elderly neighbors. The woman stood in her bathrobe, glaring disapprovingly from her open door.

"Good evening, Mrs. Humphrey."

"Don't do anything I'd have to tell your mother about," the woman said, shutting her door.

"Friend of yours?" Brody asked, as Haven opened her door and pulled him inside. She tossed her keys and evening bag on a side table then turned to look at Brody.

"Not exactly. My mom is friends with her daughter so if I do anything Mrs. Humphrey deems unacceptable or inappropriate, Mom gets to hear about it."

"Does she ever tattle on Allie?" Brody asked, thinking if the woman needed someone to snitch on, Allie was the girl to watch.

"Well, most of the stuff she complains to her daughter about me doing is because Allie is involved," Haven admitted.

"Just think how boring your life would be without your cousin around to liven things up," Brody said, removing Haven's glasses before wrapping his arms around her. He didn't care if her carefully applied lipstick ended up smeared from ear to ear, he was done waiting to kiss her.

From the way her hands slid up his arms and looped around his neck, he thought maybe she was tired of waiting too. Her eager lips were as giving and demanding as his when they met with an electric jolt.

"Why'd you wait so long to kiss me?" she asked in a breathy whisper.

"I didn't want to mess up your makeup." Brody nuzzled her neck, making her sigh with pleasure.

"I'll never let Allie do my makeup again," she said, pressing her mouth to his.

Brody blindly maneuvered her toward the couch where he sank down, pulling her on top of him without breaking the seal of their lips. He ran his hands across her shoulders, down her back, and along one leg, dragging the hem of her dress up with his hand.

Suddenly stopping, he placed his forehead to hers and drew in a deep breath.

"Haven, I… um… need to go home now," he said, unable to move, barely forcing words out of his lips, wanting more than anything to hold Haven all night long.

"Okay," she said, moving until she was sitting on the couch instead of sprawled across his body.

Brody raised himself into a sitting position and almost lost the feeble grasp he had on his self-control. Clenching his hands together seemed to be the only way to keep from putting them all over her.

"Is something wrong?"

"Yes. something is wrong and before it goes from a little wrong to completely wrong, I'm going to leave." Brody got to his feet and held his hand out to her.

She took it with a look of trepidation on her face and walked him to the door.

"Look, doll, the problem is that between you looking so flamin' hot and way too many other guys noticing, I can't promise I won't do something in the next few minutes I'd pound one of them for even thinking about," Brody admitted, staring at the floor instead of Haven's face.

Placing her hands on either side of his face, she forced him to look into her eyes and see her smile.

"Thank you, Brody, for making me feel beautiful and wanted," Haven whispered, kissing his cheek.

"You've got no idea, none at all, how much I want you right now and that's why I've got to go." Brody drew her into his embrace again then kissed each dimple in her cheeks before opening the door. "The next time you wear that dress, I think we better just plan dinner at your place or mine. It's too potent to be seen in public. On second thought, maybe you'd better not wear it when I'm around. That's probably a much better idea."

Giving her one more appreciative look, he hurried out to his truck and was soon gone.

Haven watched his taillights disappear down the street before closing the door and sighing. Wielding the power of her feminine charms had left her exhilarated, particularly when Brody said he thought she was beautiful.

She couldn't remember ever hearing any words that had pleased her more.

Although she'd promised herself not to let her heart get involved, she was head over heels in love with Brody. From that gravelly voice that made her tingle all over to his tender heart and quick wit, she loved everything about him.

She wondered if he didn't feel something for her, too, with the possessive way he behaved all evening.

Wrapping her arms around herself, she hummed as she went to make a cup of tea. Maybe Allie wasn't as crazy as Haven thought.

## *Chapter Twelve*

Forcing himself to stay away from Haven all day Sunday and then again on Monday, Brody couldn't stand the thought of not seeing her again before they flew out of town for another game.

He'd sent her a text message Sunday morning telling her he was tied up all day, although he spent part of it doing laundry and hanging out with Marcus. The other part was spent lost in his daydreams of Haven.

He had no idea how one incredibly sweet, entirely desirable woman worked her way so completely into his head that he could think of nothing else but the taste of her lips and the feel of her soft skin beneath his hands.

Monday he sent a text telling her to have a great day, then somehow managed to make it through the day without calling her, sending her another message, driving past her office, or camping out on her doorstep, waiting for her to get home.

Sitting up in bed, knowing he couldn't go another day without seeing her, he tried to decide what to do. So far, he'd been honest with Haven, being more open with her than he had anyone.

If he applied that same level of honesty with himself, he'd have to admit that when it came time for them to part ways at the end of June, they were both going to have broken hearts.

She wore her feelings for him on her sleeve and as hard as he worked to keep the feelings she evoked in him buried, they refused.

Trying to decide if he should break up with Haven now or just let things go until they had to say goodbye, he wished he could step outside himself and see the best plan of action.

He knew he should never have said hello to her, never looked into those deep blue eyes, never fallen in love.

Concluding that his current misery was a by-product of being in love for the first time in his life, he didn't have a clue what to do about it.

Every time he closed his eyes, he saw Haven with her hair down in that blue dress, smelled her perfume, felt the intense impact of her lips against his.

Grabbing his head, wanting to shake thoughts of her loose, he picked up his phone and called the one person he knew would listen to him and offer good advice.

"Hello?" a woman answered the phone.

"Hey, Mom," Brody said, grateful to hear his mother's voice. He knew if he never had another living soul to turn to, his mom was always there for him.

"Baby, what's wrong?" Angelina Jackson asked, knowing by the tone of his voice something was off in her son's world.

"What makes you think something's wrong?" he asked, getting out of bed and walking to the kitchen where he filled a glass with water and sat down at the table.

"A mother knows things, Brody. Now tell me what has you upset. Did something happen with your team or at a game?"

"No, Mom. Everything with football is great. It's um… I kind of…"

"Do you need money? Did you get hurt? What's going on? Spit it out, baby."

Brody sighed and jammed a hand through his hair. "I met this girl and she's, I don't know, just awesome. I told her I wanted to date but made sure she knew I'd be leaving as soon as the season is over and she seems okay with that."

"Okay," Angelina said, trying to decipher the problem from what her son shared. "And you like this girl?"

"Yeah, Mom. A lot. Too much." Brody released a sigh. "She's smart and funny, innocent and nice. You'd definitely approve of her."

Angelina laughed. "Go on, son."

"I've met her family, played with her nephews, even gone to church with her," Brody said, still hesitant to tell his mother everything.

"She sounds wonderful. So what's the problem?"

"I think I'm in love with her," Brody said, waiting for his mom to comment on that statement.

"Why do you think you're in love with her?" Angelina finally asked after a moment's pause, knowing Brody hadn't ever said that before.

"I can't stop thinking about her. When I close my eyes, she's all I see, her perfume is stuck in my nose, and the sound of her voice keeps playing in my head. I look in the mirror and see me with this stupid grin on my face that just doesn't go away. I want to be with her, make her smile, see her laugh, just get to know her more," Brody said, sure he'd just bared his soul.

"I see. And how does she feel about you?"

"I'm pretty sure she feels the same way, although she hasn't said anything. She's one of those girls with a completely readable face. Everything she feels is right there for all the world to see," Brody said, realizing it was true. He could tell just by looking at Haven what kind of day she'd had, what sort of mood she was in, and that she was thrilled to see him.

"Well, then, what's the problem?"

"The problem is that at the end of June, I'm out of here. Even if I end up playing with this team next year, I'll still be gone for months. What if things work out like I'm hoping and I get signed for a training camp? I may never come back here again. How can I just walk away from her like that?"

"I don't know, baby. How can you? If you love her as much as you say you do, don't you think you both deserve the opportunity to see where your relationship will go? One thing I know is that love will find a way even when our heads tell us something is impossible. If you truly love her and she loves you, what happens at the end of June won't matter," Angelina said.

"Do you really think so, Mom? I know I have no right to ask anything of her, but I've never felt this way before and don't know if I want to again."

"Have you told her that?"

"Of course not," Brody said, feeling defensive. "We agreed this was just casual dating for fun until I leave. No strings attached."

"Sounds to me like there are plenty of strings. All wrapped around your heart." Angelina tried to keep the smile out of her voice. Although she'd fallen in love with the wrong man, it didn't mean she wouldn't be overjoyed for Brody when he found love with the right girl. She'd raised him to know the difference between the two.

"What should I do, Mom? I can't even go three days without seeing her. I've turned into a pathetic wimp. I'm trying to decide if I should just break up with her now or wait until I leave."

Brody grimaced when his mother's laughter echoed through his phone.

"Baby, you're not a wimp. You're one of the finest men I've ever met, and I'm not biased in the least. However, I do think you should continue seeing this girl, but tell her how you feel. Be open and honest with her. You can't ever go wrong doing that."

"Thanks," Brody said, then talked to his mother about a few other things before thanking her again for her advice.

"Just remember I want to see a picture of this girl. I expect you to send me one the next time you see her," Angelina said, anxious to see the girl who finally turned her son's head.

"Okay. Love you, Mom."

"Love you too, baby."

Brody disconnected the call and sent Haven a text message, asking if she wanted to have dinner with him.

She quickly texted him back, telling him she'd cook if he wanted to come to her place.

Wanting to do a victory dance, he instead sent her back a message letting her know he'd be there.

Hurrying out the door to practice, he decided to take part of his mom's advice and just let nature run its course. Maybe by the time June arrived, he'd have Haven worked out of his system, or maybe she'd be tired of him.

The thought of her not wanting to see him made his gut clench, so he focused his attention on getting through the next several hours of spending time with his teammates.

Surprised to receive the text from Brody asking if she wanted to have dinner that night, Haven wasn't sure what to think where he was concerned.

After leaving her apartment so abruptly Saturday night, she'd hoped to spend time with him Sunday, but the message he sent let her know he was busy all day. She'd even anticipated him stopping by her office or home unannounced Monday, but his simple text that morning made it clear she wouldn't be seeing him.

Wondering if she'd done something to drive him away, relief poured through her when she received his text wanting to get together.

As she sat completing a client profile report, her thoughts wandered to what she could make for dinner. She wanted it to be something special, yet it would also have to be fast and easy to prepare because she wouldn't have much time once she got off work.

Knowing how much he liked sweets, she also wanted to make dessert.

On her lunch break, she searched online for any recipes that might work and realized trying out a new recipe on Brody wasn't the best plan.

Finally deciding to keep things simple, she made a shopping list, satisfied with her menu.

Rushing to the grocery store after work, she hustled back to her apartment, hurried to change her clothes then whipped up dessert.

She was setting the table when she heard a knock on the door. Pushing the curls away from her face, she rushed to open it, expecting Brody. Her smile quickly turned into a frown when she saw Hale standing there, holding a carton of her favorite ice cream.

"Want to pool our efforts for dinner?" Hale asked, stepping inside and closing the door behind him.

"No, I don't. And you bringing ice cream isn't exactly pooling efforts. You can't always bribe me with caramel-laced confections, you know," Haven said, glaring at Hale. She needed him to leave, now. She'd been looking forward to spending the evening with Brody and her plans didn't include one of her brothers, even if it was Hale.

"Did the grumpy bug bite you today, baby girl?" Hale asked, strolling in her kitchen and putting the ice cream in the freezer, noticing she already had the table set for two and dinner started.

"Am I interrupting something or did you expect me to come?" Hale asked, turning around to look at Haven.

"Brody's coming for dinner, if you must know." Haven stirred a pan of ground beef on the stovetop, adding taco seasoning as it cooked.

"Sorry, kiddo. I'll just leave and maybe we can have dinner another night," Hale said, walking toward the front door.

"Thanks, Hale. Brody's out of town this weekend, so maybe we could do something whatever night you aren't spending with Abby," Haven said, giving her brother a hug. "You want to take the ice cream with you?"

"No," Hale said, shaking his head as he reached for the door. "I buy that just for you."

"I know, that's why you're my favorite," Haven said with a laugh. Hale opened the door and almost walked into Brody who was raising his hand to knock.

"Hey, man. Nice to see you," Brody said, shaking Hale's hand. "You're not leaving, are you?"

"Haven told me she's cooking for you and kicked me out," Hale said with a grin, stepping aside so Brody could enter.

"Don't leave on my account," Brody said, avoiding direct eye contact with Haven. "You don't mind if Hale stays, do you?"

"I don't suppose," Haven said, minding more than either of the men could possibly know. Irritated that Brody didn't want to be alone with her, she left the two men talking in the living room while she finished cooking dinner.

Setting another plate on the table, she filled glasses with water then walked out to the living room, letting the guys know dinner was ready.

Hale and Brody dominated the conversation and neither seemed to notice she was quiet through the meal.

After eating the lemon bars she made for dessert with scoops of the ice cream Hale brought. Hale put the leftovers away while Brody helped Haven with the dishes.

Returning to the living room, Hale bid his goodbyes and hurried out the door, knowing he was in trouble with his sister.

Watching her brother leave, Haven sank down on the couch and tried to keep an expressionless face as she stared at Brody.

Although Haven thought she was hiding her emotions. Brody could tell she was miffed and had been since he asked if Hale was staying for dinner. Knowing the volatile state of his emotions where Haven was concerned, he didn't think it was an entirely bad idea for them to be chaperoned through dinner.

Now that he was alone with her, all he wanted to do was take her in his arms and lose himself in a fragrant, loving embrace.

The way she sat glaring at him, though, indicated that wasn't going to happen anytime soon. Sitting down on the opposite end of the couch, he leaned back and looked at her.

"Wanna watch TV?"

"Not particularly," Haven said in a clipped tone. She had no idea what was wrong with Brody, but he definitely wasn't acting like himself. She wished she'd never let Allie talk her into buying that stupid dress let alone wearing it out to dinner. Things with Brody hadn't been the same since the moment he saw her try it on.

"Have any projects for work you brought home with you?" he asked, knowing she often brought the remnants of her workday home to finish.

"Nope," she said, wishing Brody would move a little closer, at least put his arm around her. He hadn't given her as much as a hug since he arrived.

"Want to go for a walk?"

"Not really," she said, chewing on her bottom lip. Finally, she blurted out what she was thinking. "If I in some way offended you Saturday, I'm sorry. I don't know what I did, but whatever it was, I didn't mean to, and I'll never wear that awful dress again."

Stunned by her outburst, Brody gave her a shocked look. Once he processed what she said, he scooted across the couch, pressing against her side.

"Don't make any hasty decisions. You looked amazing in that dress. I'm sorry I went all cavedweller on you while you were wearing it." Brody buried his face in her hair and inhaled the scent that was so ingrained in his senses he could smell it when he was alone in his apartment in the middle of the night.

Haven turned tear-filled eyes his direction, making his heart ache. He couldn't do tears. Not big, roll-down-her-cheeks tears.

"I'm sorry, Haven, for acting distant the last few days. You didn't do anything wrong. I just had some stuff I needed to work out in my head." His thumbs brushed away the tears from her cheeks.

Sniffling, trying to keep from crying more, Haven nodded her head, slipping her arms around Brody and giving him a warm hug. He gladly wrapped his arms around her and held her close, resting his cheek on the top of her head.

Relaxing with her in his arms, nothing had felt this right since the last time he'd held her.

"Forgiven?" he asked and felt her nod against his chest.

Tipping back her head, Haven smiled at him with a watery gaze and pressed a soft kiss to his chin. He took that as all the encouragement he needed to kiss her the way he'd imagined doing since he walked out her door Saturday night.

All thoughts of anything beyond kissing Haven flew out of his head and his lips met hers in a fervent blending that eventually left them both breathless.

Haven opened her eyes and looked at Brody, every nerve in her body tingling and alive as he gazed back at her with those rich, dark eyes. She'd watched him around others enough to know he generally kept shutters over them, blocking the world from seeing into his heart. With her, though, he opened up and let her glimpse his soul.

"Maybe we should go for that walk," Haven said, knowing if they stayed on the couch she could be in big trouble where Brody was concerned.

"Good idea," he said, getting up and giving her a hand, then waiting as she grabbed a sweater in case it cooled down outside before they got back. Stuffing her keys and phone in her pockets, they strolled down the street in the direction of Brody's apartment. He didn't think hanging out there was any smarter than staying at hers, but there was a park close by and determined that might be a good place for them to talk for a while.

"How are things going with the team? It seems like you're having a great season," Haven said, seeking a safe topic of conversation.

"We are having a great season. Usually it takes a while for new members to mesh, but we all fit together and play together really well. It's a good group of guys," Brody said, then talked about his upcoming schedule with Haven. After the away game that weekend, the team had a bye week where they wouldn't play any games. Haven invited him to go out to the farm with her, if he wanted. He quickly agreed then asked her about some of her client projects.

"I was just thinking, Brody, if you want to generate some good publicity for the team, and the guys were up for it, you could do a football camp for the local high school kids. Don't you have another bye week later in the season?" Haven asked as they reached the park and headed toward a set of empty swings. "I'm sure the local news outlets would be all over it and you'd be helping the kids at the same time."

"That's a great idea. I'll mention it to the coach," Brody said, thinking again how smart and successful Haven was in her line of work. "Any other ideas for the team?"

"Not at the moment, but if I think of any, I'll let you know." She was quiet for a moment then asked, "Do you have a list of your corporate sponsors?"

"There's a page on the website that lists them all. Why?"

"Just thinking," Haven said, looking distracted as she took out her phone and typed in a message.

"What are you doing?" Brody asked, trying to see what she was writing, but unable to make it out when she kept turning away from him.

"Sending myself some notes so I won't forget."

"Forget what?" Brody asked, waiting until Haven sat on a swing before taking a seat on the swing next to her.

"I'll tell you later," she said, sliding the phone back in her pocket.

"How about now?"

"So, what else is new with you?" she asked, changing the subject and still trying to distract her thoughts from Brody's tempting lips and strong arms. His scent drifted around her and she breathed it in, savoring every whiff.

"I talked to my mom this morning. She insisted I send her a photo of you," Brody said, pulling out his phone and taking a photo of Haven before she could refuse.

"Good grief, Brody. At least let me comb my hair before you do that. I've probably got stubble burn on my chin from our kissing session at the apartment. What will your mother think?" Haven asked, exasperated.

"That you're sweet and pretty and wonderful," Brody said quietly, reaching out a hand to stroke over Haven's head.

"You have a habit of saying the nicest things," she said, glancing at him with a soft smile that turned his heart into a mushy mass in his chest.

"Only because they're true. You can ask Marcus. I don't tell him he's pretty or sweet."

Haven laughed and pushed back in the swing, making it soar forward when she lifted her feet.

"What else did your mom have to say?"

"Not much. She… um… gave me some advice about a problem I've recently encountered."

"Oh? What kind of problem? Is there anything I can do?" Haven asked, continuing to swing back and forth while Brody watched her.

Although Brody knew his mom was right and he needed to tell Haven how he felt, this wasn't the right time. He didn't want her to think he was expressing his feelings because of how she looked Saturday night. He wanted to be clear she understood what he felt for her had very little to do with how she looked and everything to do with how she made him feel.

If he told her he loved her now, she'd think it was because of the way Allie dressed her up for their date. Although how she looked that night nearly drove him mad with longing, it wasn't why he wanted to be with her.

Spending time with her and getting to know her better was the best way to show her how he felt. Then, when the time came to tell her, she'd know he was sincere.

For now, though, he needed to quit acting like a weirdo or she'd know something was up.

Getting off his swing, he stepped behind Haven and gave her a big push, making her laugh as she soared upward.

"Do it again, please," she called over her shoulder before she came back toward him.

He grinned and pushed her for several minutes before she challenged him to an obstacle course of sorts.

Since no one else was in the park, Haven tried to utilize as many pieces of the playground equipment as possible as she made the rules. They had to cross the monkey bars, race across a balance beam, work their way over a chain climbing wall, jump over the teeter-totter then whoosh down the slide. The first one at the bottom of the slide would receive the title of winner.

"So, what's my prize when I win?" Brody asked, stretching then shaking his arms to loosen up his muscles.

"Who said you're gonna win, football man?" Haven took off her sweater, and set it with her keys and phone near the bottom of the slide. "You're going down, big guy."

"Is that right? You and whose army is taking me down?" Brody asked, giving Haven a look meant to be threatening that only made her laugh.

"Me, so you better stop talking and start running," she said, racing toward the monkey bars. She was halfway across when Brody caught her, his long arms able to cross much faster than her shorter ones. She jabbed him in the ribs with her elbow as he tried to pass her. The surprise of the action made him lose his grip and fall.

"You have to get across without touching the ground or it doesn't count," she said, swinging across the far end, then running for the balance beam.

She'd barely taken two steps when Brody grabbed her around the waist and slung her over his shoulder, carrying her across. He set her down then leaped toward the climbing wall, his long arms and legs giving him a definite advantage as he scurried upward. Near the top, he almost fell off when his feet didn't want to work.

Looking down, he saw she'd somehow managed to tie his shoelaces together.

"You're such a cheater," he said, unable to move forward with his shoes laces in a knot. Hanging by one hand, he reached down and worked until his laces were free then hurried to finish his climb and drop down the other side. By then, Haven was running toward the teeter-totter. He would have passed her, but she stuck a foot out and tripped him.

He rolled in the grass before coming to his feet with a growl.

"You are in such trouble, doll," he said, running at top speed toward the slide. He tried to grab her foot as she climbed in front of him, but she kicked at him while pulling herself upward and swooshed down the slide.

He watched her raise her arms in the air and do a little dance as he slid down and sat at the bottom of the slide.

"Remind me not to race against you again. You cheat and you're mean. You do know I need this body in working order to be able to play football," Brody said, holding his hand against his chest and doing his best to look wounded.

"Did I really hurt you?" Haven asked, stopping her dance and kneeling in front of him, looking at him with concerned eyes. "I'm sorry, Brody. I'm used to playing with my brothers and I didn't mean to…"

Leaning down, Brody silenced her with a kiss. When he pulled back, they were both smiling.

"I think you need to kiss all the wounds you inflicted and make them better," he said, holding out a scraped elbow.

She placed a soft kiss there and looked at him with a flirty grin. "Any other boo-boos?"

"Right here," Brody said, pointing to the back of his hand. She kissed the spot. "And here," he indicated a place on his forehead.

"Anywhere else?" she asked, her heat-filled gaze making his internal thermometer spike.

"Yep. You missed this spot," he said pointing to his lips.

She gave him a skeptical look, but pressed her lips to his. When she did, Brody picked her up in his arms and settled her across his lap. Lost in each other, they stayed on the bottom of the slide, kissing, until dark settled in and Brody acknowledged he needed to walk Haven home.

"Come on, cheater-girl, let's get you home," he said, setting her on her feet and picking up her sweater. Holding it for her, she slid her arms in the sleeves then grabbed her keys and phone. Taking his hand, they walked back toward her apartment.

When she unlocked the door, he knew if he stepped inside to kiss her, he wouldn't want to leave, so he kissed her fingers and gave her a look he hoped conveyed what he felt for her in his heart.

"Good night, Brody," she whispered, closing the door behind her.

"I seriously doubt it," Brody muttered to himself, walking back to his apartment, thinking sleep wouldn't come easy.

## *Chapter Thirteen*

Bright sunlight peeking around the edges of his blinds flickered in Brody's face, drawing him from his dreams.

Not quite ready to leave behind his visions of Haven, he stretched then rolled over. Her scent lingered in his nose, her voice echoed in his ears, and he could feel her soft skin beneath his fingers.

Wide-awake, he finally opened his eyes and got out of bed. Going to his kitchen, he dug through the fridge for something to eat and ended up pouring a bowl of cereal. Eating soggy corn flakes, he looked around, and decided to spend some time cleaning. He tried to keep things somewhat orderly, but the furniture needed dusted, the floor hadn't seen a vacuum for weeks, and he couldn't remember the last time he'd cleaned the bathroom.

Starting a load of laundry, he picked up anything that could be considered garbage and filled a large bag. Setting it by the door, he went to work on the bathroom, did a second load of laundry, and vacuumed every surface of the floor that was visible. Using one of his dirty T-shirts, he wiped the dust off the furniture. After scrubbing the kitchen sink and wiping down the counters, he decided that was the extent of his cleaning abilities.

Taking a shower, he made sure to shave then slapped on some aftershave, and tousled his hair. Pulling on a pair of basketball shorts and a T-shirt, he folded his clean laundry and put it away then gave his apartment a critical appraisal. It didn't look too bad for a single guy who didn't really care if it was clean most of the time.

He picked up his keys and phone, shoving them in his pocket, and grabbed the garbage bag on his way out the door.

Leaving it in the dumpster at the apartment complex, he walked toward Haven's, thinking about how much he'd enjoyed seeing her the previous evening. Since it was the week they didn't have any football games, they hung out with Marcus and his date.

The four of them went out to eat at a popular Mexican restaurant, then went back to Haven's apartment after dinner and played Pictionary. Haven and Brody trounced the other couple so thoroughly, Marcus said he wouldn't play with them ever again, so Haven put on a movie and they watched it before everyone called it a night.

Marcus sent him a text after he got home saying his little "doll" was sure sweet. Knowing his best friend liked his best girl made him smile as he crossed Haven's parking lot and tapped on her door. She wasn't expecting him until late afternoon, but he had something he wanted to do with her before they met Hale and Abby for dinner and a concert.

It didn't take long after meeting Haven for him to realize she loved to read. She had a bookcase against one wall by the kitchen filled with books and he'd seen her using an electronic reader on more than one occasion.

He shouldn't have been surprised when she opened the door with a paperback in her hand, unaware of who was standing in front of her until Brody reached out and grabbed the book away.

"Oh, hi," she said, smiling as she noticed who now held her book.

"What are you doing answering the door like that?" he asked, stepping inside and closing it behind him. He set her book on an end table and stared at her. "What if I'd been a vampire or a serial killer or who knows what? You need to pay attention."

"I was. I just… it was…" Haven realized Brody was right and let out a sigh. "What am I supposed to do, beat somebody over the head with my umbrella?"

"No. You can't just open the door like that. If it were someone intent on doing you harm, you'd have already let him into your home. You can't go around oblivious to what's going on. You're going to learn to defend yourself. Go change into some workout clothes," he ordered, not leaving any room for argument, although it didn't stop her from trying.

"Maybe I don't want to," she said, crossing her arms over her chest.

"Maybe I'll throw you over my shoulder and take you wearing those jeans and that blouse. I guarantee you'd much rather be wearing comfortable clothes."

Haven stood her ground, giving him the glare that made her coworkers jump into action without question. On Brody, however, it didn't seem to faze him at all.

"Go change," he said again, taking a step toward her.

Turning, she ran into her bedroom and slammed the door but soon emerged wearing a T-shirt, yoga pants, and running shoes.

"You know you're a bully, don't you?"

"Fully aware of the fact, now move it," he said, opening her door. Taking her hand, he made sure she had her phone and keys, then shut the door behind them.

"Where are we going?" she asked as he led her out to the street and started walking in the direction of his apartment.

"My place," he said, tugging her along behind him.

"Why?" she asked, wondering what Brody had planned. A thundercloud had settled on his face and he hadn't even tried to kiss her since she opened her door.

Looking forward to spending the evening with him, she wasn't sure she was in the mood to put up with his surly looks and bossy attitude for the remainder of the day.

Curious to see what his apartment looked like, though, she followed along not saying anything. Hale's apartment was generally clean but sometimes messy while Tom's was always a smelly disaster. She wondered if Brody's would be a mixture of the two.

Going up the steps to his apartment, he unlocked the door and motioned for her to precede him inside.

Glancing around, she was impressed that his apartment was not only clean and orderly, but it smelled like him.

Breathing deeply, she turned and offered him a smile. "Very nice. I'm impressed."

"Thanks," he said, shoving his living room furniture around until he had a large open space on the floor.

"Take off your glasses and set them with your phone and keys over there," he said, motioning to the coffee table he'd just pushed up against the counter dividing the kitchen from the living room.

"Fine, but I still think I deserve to know why you made me change and marched me over here like some drill sergeant."

Although she couldn't see distances or do computer work without her glasses, standing just a few feet away from Brody, she could see him just fine. Studying him from his tousled hair and square jaw to his long legs and the muscles that bulged beneath his shirt, she felt her cheeks warm and looked away.

"The night we were at the movies and those two guys were heckling you, what would you have done if they followed you outside? How would you have handled it if they grabbed you?" Brody asked, feeling his anger rise just thinking about anyone touching Haven.

"I'd have screamed," she said, thinking that was a good answer.

Before she knew what was happening, Brody stepped behind her and wrapped one strong arm around her waist and clamped his hand over her mouth, holding her tightly against him.

"What would you do if they grabbed you like this?"

Haven yanked at the hand across her mouth, but Brody didn't budge. She tried kicking at him but he somehow locked her legs between his. To prove his point, he tightened his hold around her waist.

She clawed at his hand over her mouth until he grabbed both her hands with his other hand and pinned her arms down, while still holding her tight against him. Unable to move, she started to cry in frustration.

Brody let go, turning her around and giving her a gentle hug. Rubbing his hands across her back, he kissed her forehead and whispered to her soothingly.

When she calmed down, he stepped back and used his finger to tilt up her chin. He retrieved a paper towel from the kitchen and handed it to her to dry her tears.

"Haven, I didn't mean to scare you and I wouldn't hurt you, but I want you to be aware of how fast someone could take advantage of you. You can't just open your door like that and you can't go around not knowing some way to defend yourself. Didn't your brothers ever teach you?" Brody asked, surprised Hale hadn't at least given Haven some basics.

"Kind of, a little, I guess. Hale always said to kick a guy where it would really hurt, but Mom told me not to practice on the boys because she wanted grandkids someday," Haven said, mopping at her tear-stained cheeks and blowing her nose. She went to the kitchen and threw away the paper towel then rinsed her hands before going back to face Brody. "I'm good with a gun. I could always get a concealed weapon permit."

"No, you can't," Brody said, wondering what she was thinking. "Could you really pull out your gun and shoot someone? Really, Haven?"

"No. I couldn't do that."

"All right, then. Show me what you think you know," he said. Standing with his hands relaxed at his sides, waiting to see what Haven could do to defend herself.

"I don't want to hurt you," Haven said, studying Brody.

"Bring it on, doll. Let's see what kind of damage you can do," Brody said with a cocky grin, thinking Haven couldn't hurt a flea if she tried. She was too sweet.

Coming at him, she used the flat of her hand to push his chin up then jammed her thumbs into his eyes, just not with enough force to hurt him.

"Okay, that's a good start. I assume if you were really being attacked you'd put a little muscle into it," Brody said, smiling at her.

"You'd have two exploded eyeballs if you were a bad guy," she said, feeling smug.

"Do you have any other moves, besides kicking me where it will definitely hurt?"

"Not really. My go-to move is pretty much screaming and running."

"Those are both good things if you think you can outrun your attacker or at least run far enough away to get help," Brody said, stepping in front of her and holding out his hand so it looked like the letter "L."

"Hold your hand like this," he instructed, moving her fingers so they were close together, with her thumb extended at a ninety-degree angle. He moved her hand down so it was level with her arm. "Now make your hand stiff, and tense up your muscles. Then you take that hand and you ram it at my throat. You want to hit me right in the ol' Adam's apple. If you can land it, your assailant will probably drop to his knees, unable to breathe."

Haven tensed her hand and shoved it at Brody, again without the force to inflict any harm.

He made her practice the move a few times then picked up his cell phone and searched on it for a minute before handing it to Haven.

"You ever watch the movie *Miss Congeniality*?"

"Sure, hasn't everybody?" she asked, watching a clip from the movie on YouTube.

"You watch that and tell me what you learn from it," Brody said, smiling as Haven's eyes widened. She replayed the clip a few times then handed the phone back to Brody.

"Want to give it a try?" Brody asked, moving so he was standing behind Haven.

"Okay, but I'm still not going to hurt you."

"Fine. Just remember the acronym. Let's hear you say it while you do it," he said, stepping close behind her and wrapping an arm across her throat and placing the other around her waist.

Before he could pin her arm down, she jabbed him in the stomach and said, "Solar plexus."

Stepping on his foot, she said, "Instep," then turned with a fist and brushed it against his face, "Nose."

Blushing she said, "Groin," and lifted her knee, but didn't make a connection.

"Good," Brody said, kissing her cheek. "Try it again. And you can put some muscle in it. You aren't gonna hurt me."

They went through the routine again with Haven doing it just like she had the first time.

"Again," Brody said, grabbing her from behind.

He made her practice several more times until he could tell she was getting tired and irritated.

"Haven, if you don't put some oomph in it, all you're gonna do is make someone really angry with you."

"I know that, but I already told you, I'm not going to hurt you," she said, glaring at him with her hands on her hips.

"Fine, let's practice something else," Brody said, showing her a few more tricks.

"I won't remember half this and if I ever am in trouble, I'll probably be scared spitless and forget all of it," Haven said, panting from the exertion of the practice.

"Just remember to SING and you'll be fine," Brody said, watching the way her chest heaved up and down and her curls hung in wild disarray around her face. The hair band fell out a few moves back and her long blonde hair called out to him to bury his fingers in it.

"I think I better show you one more move," Brody said, instructing Haven to stand behind him. When she was in position, he reached back, flipped her over his shoulder and gently tossed her to the floor. Coming down on top of her, he held her hands in one of his above her head and grinned into her smiling eyes.

"I think I might like this one," she said, giving him a look that made his blood zing through his veins. "What happens next?"

"Something like this," Brody said. He lowered his lips to hers, rolled over until she rested on top of him, then sank his hands into her hair and growled. "I wanted to do that for the last hour."

"I've been wanting you to since I opened my door."

"Haven," he said in the gravel-laced voice she loved.

"Hmm?" she asked, kissing her way along his jaw.

"You're just about to push me beyond the ability to think straight," he said, closing his eyes as her teeth nipped playfully at his ear. "Baby, you're killing me."

Before she could do anything else to seduce him, he sat up and started tickling her to ease the tension.

When she begged for mercy, he stopped and helped her to her feet.

"Let's get you home. I'm guessing you'll want to clean up before we meet Hale and Abby for dinner," Brody said, watching as she put on her glasses and picked up her phone and keys.

"You guessed right. I can walk myself home. You don't need to," Haven said, opening Brody's door then turning back to kiss his cheek.

"Right. After all that, you think I'm letting you walk home alone?" He grabbed his keys and shut the door behind him. "March it out, doll."

Instead, Haven jogged down the steps and took off running in the direction of her apartment. Brody chuckled and followed, pacing himself to run just behind her, thinking she'd stop before she made it two blocks. He was surprised when she ran all the way back to her apartment without slowing down.

"Hey, speedy, that was pretty good," he said, grinning as she unlocked her door.

"You never asked me what I do to keep in shape," Haven said, going inside and taking a water bottle out of her fridge. She took a long drink then handed it to Brody. He finished it and handed the bottle back to her.

"You mean to tell me that knockout figure isn't a natural phenomenon?"

"Hardly," Haven said. Guys were so clueless about the amount of work women went to just to look like they put no effort into their appearance. "I get up before five every morning and run."

"Wait, wait, wait," Brody said, staring at her in disbelief. "You mean to tell me you go running alone, most of the year in the dark, without the ability to defend yourself?"

"Allie usually goes with me and I run at the gym most of the time."

"That makes me feel marginally better," Brody said, kissing her cheek on his way out the door. "I'll see you in an hour."

Haven was trying to decide what shoes to wear when she heard a knock at her door. Wielding one of the heels like a weapon, she opened the door, catching Brody off guard. He reflexively raised his arm to defend himself and she dropped the shoe, laughing.

"How's that for defending myself, big, bossy football man?" she asked as he stepped inside, glaring at her.

"If you scare the perpetrator to death, you'll be just fine," he said, thinking she might just be able to handle herself without his help.

Stuffing her feet into two different styles of shoes, she turned to Brody and held out one foot, then the other. "Which should I wear?"

"That one," Brody said, pointing to a pair of ballet flats she kept by the door to slip on if she needed to run outside.

"No. Come on, pick one," she said, thinking he was teasing.

"I'm serious. Both of those make your legs look long and way too… anyway, I don't want to spend half the night fighting off other guys," Brody said, ogling her legs. She had on a black knee-length skirt with a silky looking blouse in a soft shade of blue that just made him want to rub his hands up and down the length of it. She had two black high heels on and either one of them might push him beyond distraction before the evening was through.

"Fine," she said, shaking her head. Wobbling back to her bedroom, she reappeared in a pair of heels that weren't quite as high as the others. Although stylish, they looked a little more sensible.

Gathering up her keys and phone, she shoved them in a little evening bag and opened the door.

"Ready to go?" she asked, looking back at Brody who stood staring at her from his spot near the couch.

"Not quite," he said, moving close enough to gently brush his knuckles down the smooth line of her jaw. Bending down, he kissed the dimples in her cheeks then pressed a soft, tender kiss to her mouth.

"What was that for?" she asked in a breathy voice as he walked her outside and shut the door behind him.

Keeping a hand at her back as they took the few steps to his waiting pickup, he grinned down at her. "Because I like you," Brody said, opening his truck door then picking her up and setting her inside.

"I like you, too," she said, wanting to tell him she loved him, but afraid if she said the words he wouldn't want to see her again. She knew her time with him was limited and that loving him was going to end in heartbreak, but she couldn't stop herself anymore than she could keep from breathing.

"So, where are we meeting Hale and Abby?" Brody asked, pulling out of the parking lot.

"At that new place not far from the mall," Haven said, looking forward to an evening with two of her favorite guys. "Isn't it a steakhouse?"

"Yep. We had a team lunch there before the last home game and it was really good," Brody said, switching lanes as he neared an intersection.

"Team lunch?"

"On game days, we pick one of our sponsor restaurants, if possible, and go out to lunch together. It's nice," Brody said, pulling into the restaurant parking lot and finding a space on the end of a row. Hale and Abby stood by the door, waiting for them.

Haven waved after Brody helped her out of his truck and they hurried across the parking lot.

"Hey, it's great to see you guys," Abby said, giving Haven a warm hug. "Are you excited about the concert tonight?"

"Totally," Haven said, walking inside as Hale held the door for them.

They didn't have to wait long for a table and soon were enjoying their dinner. Their waitress recognized Brody and continued to cast flirty glances his direction. When she came to refill their water glasses, she placed a hand on his shoulder and leaned across him provocatively to fill Haven's glass.

Abby raised an eyebrow Haven's direction, but no one said anything. When the waitress brought their bill, she slid a piece of paper to Brody and winked at him.

Haven took a sip of water and pretended not to notice. She wished she could practice some of her newly learned defense moves on the brazen female. Disgusted with the way the waitress practically threw herself at Brody while she was sitting beside him, Haven thought the woman had no class at all.

Trying not to let her irritation show, she felt the building anger melt away when Brody reached beneath the table and took her hand in his, rubbing her palm with his thumb. His leg bumped against hers and when she turned to look at him, he gave her the smirk that let her know everything was right in the world.

Brody crumpled the paper with the waitress's phone number into a tiny wad then worked it into the leftover ketchup on his plate. Abby smiled approvingly.

Splitting the bill, Hale and Brody somehow silently agreed the waitress didn't deserve a tip, but each plunked down a dollar. Maybe she'd learn not to come on to her customers, especially when they weren't interested and already had a date.

The four of them left the restaurant and drove to the concert venue. The group performing was one they all liked.

Hale mentioned something about Tom being there with a group of his friends, but Haven didn't see him.

Excited after the concert ended, they decided to go out for dessert at the diner not far from Haven's place.

"Why don't you girls wait here and we'll get the trucks," Hale offered. The only parking spaces they could find were a long way from the door and it seemed like a nice thing to do since the girls were both dressed up, wearing heels.

While they were walking toward their pickups, Brody told Hale about teaching Haven some self-defense moves that afternoon.

"What?" Hale asked, stopping on the sidewalk and staring at Brody.

"She said you guys didn't really teach her anything, so I showed her a few basic moves," Brody said.

Hale started to laugh, looked at Brody, and laughed even harder. When he could finally talk again, he wiped his watering eyes and took a deep breath.

"She got you good, then," Hale said, slapping Brody on the back. "She used to wrestle with us all the time. Once she pinned Tom and wouldn't let him up. He finally started to cry and Mom told her not to hurt us anymore. We did, of course, discourage her from kicking vital body parts in defense, but she knows how to take care of herself."

"Really?" Brody asked, wondering if what Hale said was true. "She acted like she had no clue and refused to do anything that might hurt me. Seriously, though, I worry about her taking care of herself. That girl couldn't hurt someone even if she tried."

"Let's put your theory to the test," Hale said, pulling out his phone and placing a call to his younger brother.

who hadn't yet left the concert. He suggested it would be funny for Tom to sneak up on Haven while she waited for Brody. Giving his brother detailed directions on where to find the girls, he motioned for Brody to follow him back in the direction they came.

Hiding around the corner, they had a great view of Haven and Abby as they stood talking. They were standing side by side looking out at the parking lot when Tom and a group of his friends snuck up behind them.

Tom put his arms around Haven, as if he was going to attack her, and the next thing anyone knew, he was on his knees on the pavement, looking like he might cry or be ill. Haven had elbowed him in the stomach, stomped his foot, punched his nose and delivered a vicious blow to his groin before she realized it was her brother.

Not only did Haven remember the four steps of self-defense Brody taught her, she executed them flawlessly.

Brody slapped Hale on the back, grinning broadly. "That's my girl. Did you see that?"

"That was wicked. Did you teach her those moves?" Hale asked. "She's got some good ones, but I haven't seen that particular sequence before."

"Yeah, we worked on that this afternoon, but I couldn't get her to actually put some muscle in it. I think maybe she learned more than I thought, or knew more than she indicated," Brody said, watching Haven as she patted Tom on the back and gave his friends a lecture about sneaking up on people.

"I think we should go get the vehicles," Hale suggested, backing around the corner before anyone saw them.

"Good idea," Brody agreed, still grinning. "You might have to tell your mom the likelihood of Tom producing grandkids just decreased dramatically."

Hale laughed again. "I think we'll keep that quiet. Tom will be too embarrassed to admit Haven got the best of him, especially when it happened in front of his friends. I'm not admitting to any knowledge of her newfound skills, but I told you she can take care of herself."

"You were definitely right," Brody said, unlocking his truck and sliding behind the wheel.

Picking up the girls, they drove to the diner where they enjoyed dessert. Haven and Abby replayed what happened with Tom as they walked out the door to leave. The two men feigned surprise as the girls related the story then Brody drove Haven home.

"Will Tom hold a grudge?" Brody asked as he parked his truck.

"Probably. I feel kind of bad about hurting him," Haven said as Brody helped her out of his truck and walked with her to her apartment door. Mrs. Humphrey watched them, so Haven tugged Brody inside and closed the door behind her. "But at least he won't sneak up behind me again. Or any of his idiot friends, either."

"No. I don't see him trying that again," Brody said, encouraging her.

Haven kicked off her shoes, removed her glasses and sat down on the couch. The look she sent Brody's direction had him sitting down beside her and wrapping his arms around her before he even realized what he was doing. She snuggled against him, with her back against his chest.

"Tom mumbled something about Hale and his bright ideas. You wouldn't happen to know anything about that, would you?" Haven asked, keeping her tone light. She felt Brody's arms tense as he held her and knew Hale talked Tom into trying to scare her. Hale was fully aware she could take care of herself.

"Guilty," Brody said, pulling her closer against him. "I was telling Hale about your little lesson today and he informed me that you are already well-versed in defending yourself. He thought Tom would make a good guinea pig for a demonstration. We stood around the corner and watched."

"You did not!" She turned to glare at him with a shocked expression on her face.

He nodded his head and gave her a cocky grin. "Did you really wrestle with your brothers and make Tom cry?"

"Yes. The last time was when Tom was a senior. Mom said it was too emasculating to whip him so badly at a sport he lettered in, so I stopped," Haven said, enjoying the feel of Brody's strong chest against her back and his arms wrapped securely around her. "I didn't fib to you today. My two main forms of defense were poking them in the eyes or kicking them. I think I could still manage a few of the wrestling moves Hale taught me."

"Maybe we can practice those another day," Brody said, thinking if they did, he'd have an extremely hard time maintaining his self-control. The thought of being pinned by Haven made him feel like he was about to burn up with a fever. "Obviously, you can take care of yourself. Why did you let me make you practice all afternoon?"

"First of all, you taught me some things I didn't know. Although, I didn't appreciate your high-handed manner of showing me I had some things to learn. That was just mean," she said, lightly smacking his leg.

"Agreed, and I'm sorry," he said, kissing her neck. "Go on. What was your other reason?"

"I spent a couple of hours this close to you with your arms around me. Why would I not want to do that?" She glanced over her shoulder so he could see the impish grin on her face. "My mama didn't raise a stupid girl."

"No, she didn't," Brody said, turning her in his arms so he could give her a kiss. "Not at all. Just remind me not to sneak attack you or get on your bad side."

"If you do, I'll leave you crying on the sidewalk next to my wimpy brother," Haven said, smiling as Brody's mouth captured hers and all other thoughts flew right out of her head. All she wanted was for Brody to hold her tight, kiss her deeply, and never let her go.

## *Chapter Fourteen*

"He won't bite, you know," Haven said, trying to hide her smile as Brody let a calf suck on his fingers and stared at it with a mixture of revulsion and apprehension.

"Is it supposed to feel like wet, gritty sandpaper?" he asked, pulling his hand away. The calf immediately latched onto the leg of his jeans and started sucking the denim. Brody looked helplessly at Haven, unsure what to do.

"Let's go back to the house. I think you've had enough barnyard fun for one day," Haven said, grinning as Brody pushed the calf away then wiped his fingers on his jeans.

As they left the pen where her dad kept the bottle-fed calves, Haven climbed over the fence and laughed to see Brody glancing over his shoulder, expecting the calf to come after him.

"Be glad you're not a cow," she said. At Brody's narrowed glare, she giggled and jumped off the fence, walking toward the house.

Strolling in the kitchen together, both wearing broad smiles, Rachel looked up from the potatoes she was mashing. "Have fun out there?"

"Yep. Brody did great riding, but I don't think he liked the calves very much," Haven said, washing her hands at the sink then flicking water at Brody as he soaped his hands.

If they hadn't been in her mother's kitchen with the woman watching their every move, Brody would have soaked Haven with the sink's spray nozzle. Thinking about what she'd look like in a wet T-shirt made him shake his head to clear his thoughts.

"That's okay, Brody. The bottle babies can be a little demanding and a lot slobbery," Rachel said, handing Haven the potato masher to finish the potatoes while she took a roast out of the oven.

"That smells great, Rachel. Thank you for inviting me for dinner," Brody said, looking around to see if he could do something to help. Noticing gravy bubbling on the stove, he walked over and gave it a stir. He wasn't a great cook, but he used to help his mom in the kitchen when she was home to make him a hot meal between her jobs.

"Thank you, Brody," Rachel said, watching him stir the gravy. "Would you mind lending me your muscle for a minute?"

"What can I do?" he asked, stepping over to the counter where Rachel handed him two large forks and pointed to a cutting board.

"Can you lift the meat out of the roaster and set it on the cutting board? We'll let it rest a few minutes before we slice it."

Brody wasn't sure what she meant by letting the meat rest, but managed to get the roast where she wanted without dropping it. He knew she or Haven could have lifted it, but appreciated her giving him something to do to feel useful.

Rachel made a tent out of foil and set it over the roast, then turned to take the gravy off the stove.

"If you wouldn't mind carrying the bowls to the table, it would be a big help," Rachel said, smiling at Brody as he picked up a bowl of green salad and one of green beans then went into the dining room. Lowering her voice,

Rachel smiled at Haven. "He's just a big sweetheart, Haven. And such a cutie patootie."

"Mom!" Haven whispered, glaring at her mother. "Hush! He'll hear you."

"Hear what?" John asked, walking into the kitchen with Brody.

"None of your business," Rachel told her husband with a smile. "Help this boy set the water glasses on the table while Haven and I finish up."

"Yes, ma'am," John said, winking at Brody and picking up glasses full of water, carrying them to the dining room.

It took just a few minutes for Rachel to have the meat carved and on a platter while Haven poured the gravy in a boat and spooned the potatoes into a bowl.

Hale and Tom came in the door as Haven took a seat at the table. "You two almost timed it too late. Losing your touch?"

Hale laughed as he and Tom took seats cross from Brody and Haven.

"Nope. Perfect timing, I'd say," Tom said, looking over the delicious smelling meal. "We didn't have to help do anything, yet we're just in time to sit down and eat while everything is still hot."

"They don't like to help in the kitchen. At all." Haven leaned toward Brody, explaining her brothers' last-minute arrival. "It's become an art form for them, trying to time it down to the last second to arrive at the precise moment all the food is on the table."

"Seems like they do a good job of it," Brody said, grinning at Hale.

After John asked a blessing on the meal, conversation around the table was lively. Talk eventually turned to football and why Brody didn't have a game that weekend.

"We get two bye weeks, when we don't play. I think I'd rather be tackled repeatedly the entire four quarters, though, than spend more time out in the calf pen," Brody said, making everyone laugh.

"It's an acquired thing, I think, getting used to the slobbers," Hale said, helping himself to more mashed potatoes and gravy. "Did you go riding?"

"Yeah, I put Brody on old Fred. If you can wake him up enough to move in a forward motion, he does fine," Haven said.

"Who? Fred or Brody?" Tom asked, earning a glare from his sister while the rest of them laughed.

"Did you enjoy your weekend off?" Rachel asked Brody, passing him a basket of rolls.

He took one and nodded his head. "I did. It was nice to have some free time."

"You two do anything fun?" Rachel asked, knowing Brody and Haven went to a concert with Hale and Abby.

"Just the concert, Mom," Haven said, smiling at Brody, then at Hale.

"Don't forget about beating up Tom in the parking lot," Hale said, grinning wickedly at his sister.

"What?" John asked, looking between his two youngest children. Their faces were both red - Haven's from embarrassment and Tom's from anger.

"Brody decided Haven needed to learn some self-defense moves and she didn't tell him about all the times she wrestled with us. To prove that she could take care of herself, I sort of suggested that Tom sneak up behind her and pretend he was an attacker," Hale said, leaning back in his chair and smiling as he recalled the look on his brother's face when Haven took him down. "Evidently, she's still a quick learner."

"What did you do?" Rachel asked, looking at Haven, trying to hide her amusement in her baby girl once again getting the best of her brother.

"I kind of... um... well, I sort of..." Haven stammered.

"She jabbed an elbow into his stomach and knocked the air out of him while stomping on his foot. When he bent over she popped his nose and then kicked him where it counts," Hale said, gleefully telling the story. "It was awesome."

"It wasn't awesome," Tom said, shoving his brother so hard, Hale had to grab the edge of the table to keep from ending up on the floor. Tom looked at his mother with a scowl. "Don't plan on me ever giving you grandkids."

John laughed so hard, he had to use his napkin to wipe his watering eyes. "I wish I'd seen it."

"If I'd been thinking, I would have recorded it on my phone," Hale said, ducking as Tom reached out and swung a fist his direction.

"You boys stop it," Rachel admonished, attempting to hide her grin. "I think we need to change the subject. You've picked on poor Tom long enough."

"Yes, ma'am," Hale said, winking at Haven.

She felt Brody's hand on her leg, giving her a gentle squeeze. Casting a sideways glance at him, she caught his smile and nodded her head.

The rest of the dinner conversation centered on Brody's upcoming game schedule, some of the interesting things Haven and Hale experienced through their work, and John talking about potatoes.

Preparing to leave later that evening, Brody shook John's hand and gave Rachel a warm hug as they stood at the door.

"I hope you'll come to a game with Haven soon. She really does have great seats," Brody said, knowing her dad would enjoy watching a game as much as he seemed to love football.

"We might just do that," John said, waving as Brody walked Haven to his truck and held the door as she jumped inside.

On the ride home, she leaned back against the seat and studied him.

"What?" he asked, running a hand over his head under her intense perusal. Wondering if he had food on his face or something equally embarrassing, he tried to catch a glimpse of himself in the rearview mirror but couldn't see anything amiss.

"Nothing." Haven continued staring at him and he decided she looked happy and content.

"You're looking at me for some reason," he said, sliding his hand across the seat and trying to tickle her. She pulled away, just beyond his grasp then grabbed his fingers, holding them between her own. "Tell me what's going on in that pretty little head of yours."

"I just wondered if you had fun today." Haven hoped Brody honestly enjoyed being with her at the farm. She thought the time spent with him out in the fresh air and open spaces was almost magical, but then again, she found any time spent with him to be exceptionally special. "I monopolize your free time and don't want you to feel like it's wasted."

"I'd never think time spent with you was wasted. Not ever," Brody said, pulling her fingers to his lips and kissing the back of them before turning a heated gaze her direction. "And I did have a great time today. It's nice to get out of town and just hang without a bunch of people around. Horseback riding was a lot of fun, but the jury is still out on your slobbery calves."

Haven laughed and smiled again. "I'll make sure we skip bottle-feeding the babies next time. I could always sign you up to work in the potatoes with Dad and Wes."

"I think I'll pass, but thanks for the offer," Brody said, parking near Haven's apartment. Getting out of his truck, she jumped down before he could get around to her side and ran to her door.

Watching her, he appreciated how she seemed more playful and relaxed around him than she did with many people. While she liked the world to see her as a confident, serious, business professional, she'd slowly opened up to him, letting him see a fun and funny girl who loved to tease and laugh, was loyal to her family, and let animals suck on her jeans.

"You coming in?" she asked, standing in the open doorway, waiting for him to follow her.

"Just for a minute, doll," Brody said, jogging to her door and following her inside. Closing it behind him, he turned to see Haven walk into the kitchen. He heard her shut a cupboard then ice clanking as it filled a glass.

She returned carrying two glasses of iced tea and handed him one before sitting down on the couch.

"Thanks," he said, taking a seat, all the while thinking he should go home. Drinking a deep gulp of the tea, he set his half-empty glass on the coffee table and studied Haven for a few minutes.

As the desire to taste her lips created an urgent, unappeasable yearning in him, he reached out and took the glass from her hand, setting it next to his. Removing her glasses, they joined the tea on the coffee table, then he gave in to his need to hold her, to kiss her, to bask in the extraordinary excitement she stirred in him.

"Brody," she whispered, as he ravished her neck with moist, hot kisses. Grabbing his head with both hands, she lifted it until she could press her lips to his.

Surprised by her hungry, driven kiss, Brody wrapped her tightly in his arms and returned her fervor. As the passion between them escalated, Brody felt his self-control slipping. Perilously close to losing the last shred keeping him from carrying Haven into her bedroom and shutting out the world, he lifted his head, kissed her nose, and set her back from him.

"I need to go home," Brody said, getting to his feet before he could change his mind. He felt his resolve waver when Haven looked up at him with wide eyes still stormy with longing. Could she really be that innocent? Could she really not know what she did to him? How she tortured him with her looks, touches, and kisses?

Seeing the sweet gaze on her face, he knew the answer to his questions.

"I'll talk to you tomorrow. Thanks for a fun day at the farm," Brody said, opening the door as he bent down to kiss her cheek. "Sweet dreams, Haven."

"You, too, Brody. Good night," Haven said, watching him walk back to his truck.

Wondering what she'd done this time to chase Brody away, she was starting to think she must be a bad kisser. Every time they got involved kissing, he would pull away, make some excuse, then leave.

If she could work up the courage, she'd ask Allie what she thought it meant. Her cousin had plenty of experience while Haven felt woefully inadequate in the art of understanding men.

## *Chapter Fifteen*

"Looks like you met the parents," Marcus observed as Brody waved to Haven, Hale, and their parents where they sat in Haven's sponsor seats at the game.

"Yeah. No big deal," Brody said, stretching before the game began. Marcus stopped mid-stretch and stared at him.

"No big deal? Are you sure about that, bro?" Marcus asked with a mocking grin. "Seems to me meeting the parents and hanging out with the brother is a big deal. At least to her. What are you doing?"

"What do you mean?" Brody asked, standing straight and raising his arms over his head, in a nice long stretch. "I'm not doing anything except getting ready for this game."

"I mean with Haven," Marcus said, jerking his thumb in her direction. "She's a good kid, Brody. I like her and I don't want to see her hurt when we leave. You know how women get all attached and stuff. Don't you think hanging out with her family kind of hints that you plan on sticking around for her?"

"They all know I'm leaving at the end of the season. I haven't made any secret of that fact." Brody felt irritation with Marcus begin to flood through him. He knew his friend was trying to help, but right now his words only put him on the defensive. "If I want to spend time with a pretty girl who seems to enjoy my company until then, why shouldn't I?"

"Why indeed." Marcus clamped his mouth shut, knowing when Brody got the look on his face he was currently sporting, there wasn't a thing he could say or do to change his mind. Giving up, he broached a new subject, slapping Brody's shoulder. "Did she really take out her brother at the concert?"

"You should have seen her, man. Bam! Before anyone knew what happened, ol' Tommy boy was on his knees looking like he might cry."

"I'll be sure to stay in front of her at all times, then," Marcus said with a laugh, glad to see Brody smile and nod his head in agreement.

Called off the field, the game soon began. Brody forced his thoughts away from Haven and what Marcus said about hurting her. He'd worry about that later.

Right now, they had a hard-playing team to beat and an arena full of cheering fans.

Keeping an eye on the quarterback, Brody was ready when the ball sailed his direction. Leaping up, he easily caught it, hit the ground, and turned to run. He'd taken just a few steps when he felt the air rush out of him as a tackle took him down.

Waiting for the player from the other team to get off him, Brody was glad when welcome air filled his lungs again. Marcus walked over and offered a hand, helping him to his feet.

"You okay?"

"Yep. Let's rock it!" Brody playfully thumped Marcus's helmet twice and ran off.

"My goodness, Haven, this is such fun," Rachel said, patting her daughter's leg as they watched the players leave the field for the halftime entertainment to begin.

"Why's that boy playing arena football?" John asked, leaning around Rachel. "He's good enough to play on some NFL team. How did he end up here?"

"He said something about being cut from a practice squad and trying to work his way back," Haven said, not sure what a practice squad was, why he'd been cut, or how he planned to work his way back. Brody hadn't been inclined to elaborate on the details, even though she didn't understand what they meant.

"Practice squad, huh? Well, I guess that makes a little sense. Who'd he play for?" John asked.

"I don't know. He didn't say. A practice squad is for a specific team?" Haven asked, realizing she really knew very little about professional football.

"Yes," Hale said, entering the conversation. "And I don't know why he was on a practice squad instead of playing. He's really got the talent."

"That's what I'm saying," John said, leaning around his wife and daughter so he could see Hale. The two of them talked football stats for a moment, leaving Rachel and Haven to stare helplessly at each other before a group of dancing girls entered the arena.

Dressed in jean shorts and boots, the girls began a routine to a lively country tune. Haven had seen them do the dance before, but her parents' eyes widened in shock when several of the die-hard male fans whipped off their shirts and swung them over their heads, whooping and cheering as the girls danced.

Haven laughed and pointed to two little boys who stood on their seats, waving their T-shirts over their heads, dancing along to the tune.

"That's quite something," Rachel said, trying not to look at a portly man nearby swinging his shirt and hips to the music.

"Quite," Haven agreed, turning her head away. She much preferred to watch the drum line to this over-enthusiastic display.

The teams returned to the field and the third quarter began with Brody's team making a fast touchdown.

By the middle of the fourth quarter, they were far ahead of their opponents. Haven watched as Brody jumped high in the air and caught a ball tossed his direction with such ease and grace, it made her hold her breath.

He came down and she saw his knee buckle beneath him as some huge oaf from the other team sailed into him, knocking him on his back.

"Something's wrong with Brody," Haven said, getting to her feet. Hale pulled her back down.

"He's fine. You know he gets tackled all the time."

"I know, but I'm telling you something is wrong," Haven said, near hysteria as she watched Brody lie motionless on the arena floor.

Finally, he got to his feet and left the field, leaning on the shoulder of a medic as he limped along.

"Let's hear it for Brody Jump It Up Jackson. His old knee injury looks like it just may have made an unwelcome reappearance," the announcer boomed over the crowd.

"Knee injury? What knee injury?" Haven asked, to no one in particular.

"He didn't mention that before?" Hale asked, looking with concern at his sister. He knew she was in love with Brody and he was sure the football player felt the same about her. What the two of them were going to do when Brody left at the end of the season was anyone's guess, but even he could tell there were some deep feelings between the two.

Talking about football with Brody on any number of occasions, he realized the man generally avoided discussing what happened between playing college ball and ending up in an arena league. Obviously, there was an injury he didn't like to discuss.

"I'm sure he'll be fine," Rachel said, squeezing Haven's hand as the game continued.

"I hope so." Haven wanted to run down to the locker room and see for herself if Brody was okay. Knowing he'd hate the intrusion, even if it were an option, she stayed in her seat.

Haven couldn't have been more correct about Brody not wanting her to see him hurting.

As he sat with ice on his knee, Brody wished Haven and her family hadn't even been at the game, watching him limp off like some decrepit old man.

"You should be fine with a day or two of rest," the doctor said, probing Brody's knee again. "Has it been bothering you?"

"No more than usual," Brody said, frustrated that he had the old injury and angry that it had held him back from his dreams. There was no way he would let it get in the way now. Not when he was so close to getting back into the NFL.

"Just take it easy, keep it elevated and iced tomorrow. You'll be ready for next week's game."

"Thanks, sir," Brody said, hearing the cheers of the crowd. Glancing at the clock on the wall, he knew the game had to be close to over. He wondered if Haven and her family would leave immediately or if she'd hang around, wanting to see him.

In no mood to be friendly or keep his longings for Haven in check, he knew the best thing he could do was beg off seeing her for a few days.

The sounds of hurried footsteps along with the loud rumble of excited voices drew nearer and the team arrived in the locker room, pumped up from winning another game.

"Man, you missed out on a great final play," one of his teammates said, thumping him on the back.

"Yeah, we were awesome, even without Jump It Up Jackson,'" Marcus teased, knowing Brody was mad and in pain. The combination of the two would make him short-tempered and anxious to be away from everyone. "Hang on a minute and I'll help you get out of here."

"Thanks, man, but I can take care of myself," Brody said, getting up and removing his uniform. Not bothering to shower, he dressed and limped out to his pickup before anyone could say anything else to infuriate him. Driving home, he dragged himself up to his apartment and collapsed on the couch.

Taking out his cell phone, he sent Haven a brief text, telling her he went home and he'd talk to her in a day or two.

He took a shower then dressed in a pair of shorts and shuffled to his kitchen, digging around in the freezer for an ice pack. Finding one, he limped to the couch and attempted to prop up his knee before placing the ice pack on it. It slid off and Brody muttered darkly.

Reaching down to grab it off the floor, a knock at the door made his frown turn into a growl. Ignoring whoever was at the door, he put the ice back on his knee and bit back a string of words his mother would slap him silly for saying when it again slid off to the floor. The knocking resumed.

"I'm not home. Go away," he yelled, flopping back against the cushions with the ice pack still in his hand. If someone pounded on his door again, he might just throw it at him.

"If you're not home, then maybe you should lock your door," Haven said, sticking her head around the edge of the door. Seeing him on the couch with the ice pack and his knee propped up, she stepped inside and shut the door behind her.

Setting a bag on the kitchen counter, she rearranged the pillows beneath Brody's leg then retrieved a dishtowel from the kitchen and wrapped the ice pack in it before placing it on his knee.

"Better?" she asked, sinking down on the floor beside him.

Brody answered with a grunt, not quite ready to be civil, even to Haven. As much as it galled him to admit, his knee was more comfortable.

"So you're going to do the whole mad and pouting thing, is that it?" she asked, getting up and going to the kitchen. He heard her opening cupboards and the sound of water running then she returned with two glasses of water, setting them down on the side table by his head.

Returning to the kitchen, she opened the bag she'd set on the counter and divided the contents onto two plates and came back, sitting down in front of the couch and handing Brody one of the plates.

He stared down at the sandwich, made just the way he liked from one of his favorite restaurants, and realized he was hungry.

Haven watched him struggle to sit up. She went into what she assumed was his bedroom and returned with her arms full of pillows. Propping them behind Brody, it allowed him to sit up while keeping his knee elevated.

"Thanks," he said, picking up his sandwich and taking a bite.

"You're welcome," Haven said, glad she'd braved the lion's den.

Marcus caught her after the game while she waited for Brody to appear, letting her know he went home in a foul mood. When she asked Marcus what happened, he told her she needed to get the story from Brody, then wished her luck if she planned to go see him anytime soon.

She told Hale and her parents to have a good night, then drove to Brody's favorite restaurant and ordered two sandwiches to go, making sure his was just the way he liked.

Taking a deep breath, she'd climbed the stairs to his apartment, hoping she was doing the right thing. When she heard him yell to go away, she almost turned around and left, but something in his voice, something that sounded pleading to her, made her stay.

Surprised his door wasn't locked, she knew he needed help when she saw him on the couch, attempting to ice his knee with it bent in an awkward position.

Making him more comfortable was simple enough. She just hoped he wasn't in too much pain. Quietly eating her sandwich, she wondered what else she could do to help Brody.

"Are you going to be okay?" she finally asked as she took his empty plate and hers to the kitchen. He was drinking from the glass of water she'd set by him earlier when she stepped back beside him. Bending down, she took the empty glass from him then ran her hand across his forehead, brushing back his hair. He grabbed her wrist in a firm yet gentle grip and stopped her.

"I'm fine," he growled, letting her wrist go, settling into the pillows behind him.

"I'm pretty sure you aren't fine. Even if your knee was fine, which it obviously isn't, your attitude is definitely not fine. Or nice. Or even okay." Haven placed her hands on her hips and gave him a long glare. "What's wrong?"

"Nothing you need to be concerned about," Brody said, glaring right back at her. "I appreciate you coming over, but I can take care of myself. Why don't you go home?"

"Is that what you really want? For me to go home?" Haven asked, fighting to keep her own temper in check.

"Yes," Brody lied. What he wanted was for her to run her cool hands over his warm forehead again. He wanted to rest in the comfort of her tender embrace. He wanted to know that anytime he had a problem she would be there to help him through it. What he wanted and what he could have were two completely different things, as far as he was concerned. "I know you're trying to help, but I don't need it and I don't need you. Go home."

Shock and anger blended with raw pain at his words. Haven hoped he would say he needed her, wanted her to stay, and appreciated her concern. Instead, he'd made it clear he didn't want her there. Didn't want her at all.

As his eyes took on a cold gleam, she knew it was past time to go. Losing her bravado and unable to conceal her dejected feelings, she picked up her car keys and purse, taking a step toward the door.

"Sorry I bothered you," she said, opening the door and closing it quietly behind her.

Brody felt like the world's biggest jerk, but he knew he needed to let her go. He wasn't fit company for her at that moment and having her there with him just felt too comfortable, too good, and way too right.

## *Chapter Sixteen*

Wednesday morning found Haven still brooding over Brody's behavior Saturday night.

He'd hurt her feelings and made her question how much he truly cared for her.

If she was smart, she'd use this little upset as an excuse to break things off with him before her heart became any more entwined with his.

For once in her life, though, Haven didn't want to be smart. Or safe. Or cautious.

She wanted to love Brody with all the passion he aroused in her and not worry about what the consequences might bring.

Instead, she sat at her desk, trying to figure out if she'd misinterpreted his interest in her or if he truly just needed some space after being injured at the game.

Reading the same report for the third time, hoping to pay enough attention to retain some of the information, she looked up at a knock on her door.

Forcing a smile, she waved a welcoming hand at her assistant. "Come in, Jordan. What have you got there?"

"Some files Mr. Young wanted you to review. It's a new account and he wanted you to share your thoughts on the notes he placed on the top page," Jordan said, handing Haven a stack of folders.

"Great. I'll get on these before lunch," Haven said, lacking her usual enthusiasm.

"I'll let Mr. Young know," Jordan said, backing out the door, thinking Haven seemed awfully quiet and subdued, but kept her thoughts to herself.

Haven was finishing the last of her notes to send to Mr. Young when the man himself stopped by her office.

"Jordan said she gave you the files on the McClaskey account. Did you have a chance to review them?"

"I did, sir. I was just finishing up a report for you," Haven said, printing her notes and handing the page to her boss, along with the stack of files.

"You okay, Haven? You've seemed kind of down in the dumps this week," Mr. Young observed, standing in the doorway.

"I'm fine, but thank you for asking." Haven made a mental note to do a better job of concealing her feelings.

"Anytime. If there is anything I can do to help, just let me know," Mr. Young said then disappeared down the hall.

Releasing another sigh, Haven sat for a moment with her forehead resting against her palms when she heard a throat clear. She looked up to see the receptionist standing in the doorway.

"You've got a call on line two. He's been on hold a while."

"Did he give you a name?"

"I believe he said Brad Jackson?" The receptionist often failed to get the right name and her habit drove Haven crazy.

"Brody Jackson, perhaps?" Haven suggested with a note of annoyance in her voice. "Please tell him I'm unavailable."

"But you..."

"I'm unavailable. I'm leaving for an appointment," Haven said, jumping up and grabbing her purse. She shut the office door behind her and walked outside so fast, it left both the receptionist and Jordan gaping after her.

Driving home, she didn't bother to change before throwing herself down on her bed and allowing herself to have a good cry. She hadn't done that in ages and once the tears subsided, she got up and washed her face with cool water. Changing into a pair of shorts and a T-shirt, she called Allie and asked her to stop by after work, throwing in the added bribe of making her dinner.

Fixing her cousin's favorite noodle and chicken casserole, she sat and waited for Allie to arrive, staring out the front window but not seeing anything, lost as she was in her thoughts.

A part of her wasn't surprised Brody resorted to calling her at the office.

He hadn't bothered to call or text her all day Sunday or Monday. By Tuesday morning, Haven wasn't sure if she should be devastated or angry.

Tuesday afternoon, he sent her a text with a brief apology for his curt behavior. When she ignored it, he called her cell and left two messages that she also ignored. She'd barely arrived home from work that evening when she heard a knock on her door.

Looking out the peephole, he stood on her doorstep, looking contrite, but she still wasn't ready to talk to him. Not after he ignored her for two and a half days, kicking her out of his apartment, when all she was trying to do was be a good friend.

Pretending she wasn't home, she tiptoed to her bedroom and shut the door, waiting for him to leave. She was glad she always locked the door behind her or he'd have no doubt come inside.

Her cell rang while he was knocking, so she turned it off. He finally gave up and left, but not before she heard her nosy neighbor yelling at him to stop all the knocking when Haven clearly wasn't answering.

She woke up that morning to find two text messages and another voice message from Brody. Ignoring them, as well as the three messages he left on her office phone throughout the day, she thought maybe he'd finally get it through his head she didn't want to talk.

Her traitorous heart, though, longed to see him. To breathe in his enticing masculine scent. To feel his arms around her, and his lips teasing hers.

Shutting down those thoughts, she smiled as she watched Allie hurry across the parking lot to her door through the filmy curtains covering her front window.

Opening the door to her cousin and friend, she gave her a big hug and invited her in.

"What's up? You hardly ever invite me over for dinner unless you've got something you want to talk about," Allie said, in her normal blunt fashion.

"Let's eat first and then you can give me some advice," Haven said, closing her front drapes then escorting Allie into the kitchen.

They talked about family and upcoming activities while they ate. As they did the dishes, Allie shared something funny Rick had done that made them both laugh. Taking glasses of lemonade to the front room, they sat on the couch and Haven released a sigh.

"I know you've said it before, but I'll admit I'm completely hopeless and clueless when it comes to men," Haven said, trying to keep her tone light although tears stung her eyes.

"It's beyond my ability to comprehend how a girl with three older brothers and many obnoxious male cousins has no idea how men think, act, or operate, girl. It's just not right," Allie teased. The look on Haven's face made her reach out and grasp her cousin's cool hand in hers. "What did Brody do?"

"What makes you think Brody did anything?" Haven said, pulling her hand out of Allie's grasp and cuddling a pillow to her chest, leaning back into the couch cushions.

"For starters, Aunt Rachel told Mom that you didn't want to go out to the farm Sunday afternoon because you had some flimsy excuse about having stuff to catch up on for work. You haven't called me since Saturday afternoon and we usually talk at least once a day or text. Hale said you nearly took his head off when he stopped by Monday and I know for a fact you've been crying because your eyes were still all red when you answered the door," Allie said, listing off the reasons for her accurate assumption. "The only person I can think of who could upset you that much is Brody. I say that only because any moron can see you're totally gone for the hunky football hottie."

"Oh," Haven said. She was reminded, once again, she had no talent for hiding her feelings. None whatsoever.

"Spill. What did he do that's got you so worked up?" Allie asked, sitting up with a concerned look on her face. "You didn't catch him with one of his fan club who hang around after the game, did you?"

"No! It's nothing like that. It's just…" Haven tried to find the words to express her feelings.

"Just what? Come on, you know you can tell me anything," Allie said, patting Haven's knee. "What's the matter?"

Haven sighed again before the words burst out of her mouth. "I think I'm a terrible kisser. Every time we get… involved, Brody pulls back then goes home. Every time. One minute I'm convinced he really does like me, and then the next, he acts like he wants to be anywhere except with me. The other night he got hurt at the game and I went to his apartment afterward to make sure he was okay. He wasn't, but he kicked me out. Told me he didn't need or want me. What am I supposed to think?"

Haven sniffed, trying to curtail her tears before they morphed into full-fledged sobs.

"Oh, honey," Allie said, scooting over and giving Haven a hug. When she patted her on the back, Haven couldn't keep her tears contained any longer and reached for a box of tissues she kept on a side table.

"I'm so confused and hurt and don't know what to do. Am I really that awful at kissing?"

Much to Haven's dismay, Allie laughed. "I don't think that's your problem. Not at all."

Haven looked at her, irritated, and shook her head. "I didn't ask you to come over so you could laugh at me. I need your help!"

"I know. Just calm down," Allie said, confirming her suspicions that Haven was completely over the moon for Brody. "When you and Brody are kissing, who usually initiates it?"

"He does, most of the time. Why?"

"Just answer my questions," Allie said, looking thoughtful. "Does he hold you close, act like he's enjoying it?"

"Yes, at first. Then the more… fervent the kisses become, the more he tenses up and then he pulls away," Haven said, thinking about how Brody seemed to enjoy their encounters, to a point. "A lot of times he looks frustrated or upset, then he'll kiss me on the cheek or nose or forehead and tell me he has to go home."

"I see," Allie said, pleased at the information Haven was sharing. "Now about the other night, when you said he kicked you out… did he seem to be in pain?"

"Well, yeah. When I got there, he was trying to get an ice pack to stay on his knee on this lump of pillows. I fixed it so he could rest more comfortably, wrapped the ice in a towel so it would stay on his knee, and got him a sandwich to eat, because he's always starving after the game."

"Okay, then what happened?"

"We ate. He was grumpy the whole time. When I asked him if he'd be okay, he said he was fine. I may have commented on him not being fine and his bad attitude and that's when he said he didn't need or want me there and ordered me to go home."

"And you did?"

"Of course. I'm not going to stay where I'm not welcome or wanted," Haven said, indignantly.

"Have you talked to him since Saturday?" Allie knew Haven and Brody often talked or texted several times a day.

"No. He made no effort to contact me until yesterday afternoon and then he got quite persistent about it. He sent me texts, voice messages, came over, and even called the office and left messages."

"So why don't you talk to him?" Allie asked, listening to the mixture of anger, hurt, and fear in Haven's voice.

"Because he needs to know he can't treat me like I don't matter and then expect me to fall all over myself when he decides he wants to talk. That's not how things work," Haven said, slapping her hand down on the pillow she still held. Taking a calming breath, she looked at Allie. "Is it?"

"No, it isn't how it works," Allie said, fighting the grin trying to fill her face. "So let's go over that list of concerns. First, I'd say you are probably a good kisser. From what I've seen of Brody, you'd have to be excellent to keep him coming back for more. Second, you are correct that you are totally clueless when it comes to men. I'd have to guess that Brody enjoys your affectionate attentions so much, he's probably struggling to keep from dragging you into the bedroom like some chest-banging caveman and ravishing you."

Haven's mouth dropped open and her eyes looked like saucers at Allie's statement. "You're kidding, aren't you?"

"No. Not so much. He must be an honorable kind of guy to leave when he does. It's not a bad thing, Haven.

Brody cutting things off and going home is a good thing. Especially with you being so naïve. Seriously, though. How do you not have a clue?"

"You know I was much more interested in studying than boys in high school, then it was finishing my degree early and starting my job," Haven said, recalling the many times over the years she chose advancing her education or career over her personal life. "I just never had time for dating or learning all the rituals."

"It's about time you figured it out, then." Allie said, grinning at Haven then taking a sip of her lemonade. "You really shouldn't hold what he said the other night against him. Some men are complete babies when they get hurt and Brody might just be one of them. He's not used to being on the receiving end of help. You know he likes to be large and in charge. You probably put a huge dent in his ego when you went over there and played nursemaid to him."

"Right," Haven said, realizing there was some truth to what Allie was saying. "So what do you think I should do?"

"You could go on ignoring Brody, but then you're really just depriving yourself of his attention. Is that what you really want? Besides, isn't their game away this week?"

"Shoot. I forgot about that. He's leaving tomorrow," Haven said, remembering Brody's game schedule. "But what about the kissing thing?"

"Why not just ask him?" Allie shrugged her shoulders, as if it was no big deal to ask a man if he liked the way you kissed him.

"Are you insane? You can't just ask someone a question like that!"

"Sure you can, if you want to know the answer." Allie pulled her cell phone from her pocket and placed a call.

Haven could tell from the way she was talking the person on the other end of the line was Rick.

"Hey, babe, I've got a question for you," Allie said, turning on the speaker so Haven could hear his response.

"What do you need to know?" Haven heard Rick ask.

"Do you like the way I kiss you?"

"Honestly, Al? We've been together for two years and you just now are asking that question? Don't you already know the answer?" Rick's voice sounded disappointed.

"Please, can you just give me your response?" Allie asked amiably.

"You know I love the way you kiss me. It makes me..." Allie switched the phone off speaker and held it up to her ear but gave Haven a thumbs-up sign as she told Rick to hold that thought and she'd be at his place soon.

"See, that wasn't hard, was it?" Allie asked as she got to her feet and picked up her purse. "If you want answers to your questions, you need to ask Brody. He's the only one who can tell you what you want to know."

"Whatever," Haven said, giving Allie a hug before her cousin hurried out the door.

Returning to the couch, she picked up a magazine and thumbed through it with her thoughts wandering aimlessly. Mostly, they kept circling back around to Brody.

A knock on her door made anxiety flood through her. Part of her hoped it was Brody and the other part was afraid it would be.

Fluffing her hair, she brushed at her cheeks to make sure all traces of her earlier tears were gone then she opened the door.

A bouquet of fragrant lilacs greeted her and she inhaled their wonderful scent. Brody stuck his face around the large arrangement, looking at her with an awkward grin.

"Please don't slam the door in my face or make me leave, Haven. I can't take another lecture from your neighbor," Brody said quietly, inclining his head toward Mrs. Humphrey where she stood glaring at him from her doorway.

"I can at least spare you that," Haven said stoically, motioning for Brody to step inside the living room.

He set the vase of flowers on her coffee table and shoved his hands in his pockets to keep from reaching out and touching her.

It seemed like it had been weeks since he'd seen her instead of a few days. He knew he'd hurt her feelings Saturday, knew he'd said things that weren't true, but he was too wrapped up in obsessing over his knee to do what was right by her. He babied his knee all day Sunday then spent Monday moping around, realizing he handled the whole situation with Haven badly.

Tuesday morning, he was still out of sorts and lost his temper at Marcus before practice. His friend proceeded to tell him he needed to snap out of it and apologize to Haven.

Mulling over Marcus' comments, he decided to follow his advice and let Haven know he hadn't meant what he said. Only she wouldn't talk to him.

She ignored his messages, and even went so far as to pretend to not be home when he dropped by the previous evening. He knew she was home, even without Mrs. Humphrey nodding at him when he quietly asked her if Haven was in her apartment.

If Haven wanted to get his attention, she certainly had it now. He'd spent the entire day tied up in knots, wondering if she'd give him the opportunity to apologize.

He had so much riding on this season being successful, on his success with the team, sometimes it was hard for him to think beyond it. Somehow, though, Haven had infiltrated his defenses and wound her way into his heart. Brody didn't want to think about what would happen at the end of June. He couldn't.

The pain it created in his chest was too much to bear, so he pushed the thought away and focused on the moment.

This particular moment was begging for him to pull Haven into his arms and kiss her until they both forgot there was anything else going on in the world except what the two of them shared.

"Thank you for the flowers. They're lovely," she said, bending over to inhale their fragrant scent. "Where did you find them? It's still pretty early in the season for them to be bloomed out like this."

"Let's just say some people will sell anything," Brody said, recalling the house he drove past that had a huge lilac bush in full bloom in a sunny spot that appeared to be blocked by much of the weather. He assumed that was why the plant was already full of blossoms when most of the other lilacs around were just starting to bud.

In a move not like him at all, he boldly went to the front door and begged the little old woman to sell him a few flowers. She was so taken with him, she told him to cut as many as he liked and even gave him a vase for the twenty-dollar bill he handed her.

Seeing the look of pleasure on Haven's face as she enjoyed the flowers, he was glad he went to the effort of bringing them to her. He wasn't sure she'd let him in her apartment, or even answer the door, but he thought flowers couldn't hurt his cause any.

"Would you like anything to drink? Have you had dinner?" Haven asked, taking a step toward the kitchen.

"I'm fine, Haven. Would you mind sitting down so we can talk?" Brody asked, pointing toward the couch.

Haven took a seat in a side chair and looked at him expectantly. Forcing down a sigh, he sat on the couch and ran a hand over his head. She wasn't going to make this easy.

"I'm really sorry about Saturday night. I've had... let's just say it wasn't my first knee injury and I was worried about the extent of it. Turns out a day of rest was all I needed, but I acted like a jerk and I apologize. I didn't mean what I said to you then."

"Which particular thing?" Haven asked, wanting to be clear on the extent of Brody's apology.

"About not needing your help or you." Brody held her gaze, although with her sharp glare, he really wanted to drop his to the floor. "You were a huge help to me then and a good friend, not to mention brave. Marcus wouldn't even come see me until Sunday night."

The barest hint of a smile lifted the corners of Haven's mouth.

"I do need you, Haven, in whatever capacity you'll have me. At the very least, I still want to be your friend." Brody knew that wasn't exactly true. He wanted to be her friend, a good friend. He also wanted to be the man she kissed, held, and loved.

"I see," she said, picking up a half-empty glass of lemonade and taking a drink. He watched her run her tongue out and lick her pink lips, fighting down the urge to do the same.

"So, can we still be friends?"

"I suppose so," she said, brushing at some imaginary spot on her shirt.

"And you forgive me?"

"I suppose so."

Brody let out the breath he was holding and conjured up a smile. It quickly faded when Haven pinned him with another glare.

"Why don't you like kissing me? Allie said I needed to ask you directly, so here goes. Am I really that bad that you always have to leave?" Haven asked, feeling her cheeks heat with embarrassment, but unable to go another minute without knowing the truth.

Haven let out a small squeak when Brody abruptly picked her up and sat back down on the couch with her across his lap, his hands buried in her hair and a groan that bordered on misery escaping his mouth.

"Haven, how could you… why would you ever think that?" he asked, knowing no woman's kiss would ever affect him the way Haven's did. She tipped his world off kilter and sent him into a tailspin every time their lips connected.

"Because anytime we kiss for very long you get all tense, pull back, and leave. What am I supposed to think?" Haven asked quietly, her forehead resting against Brody's chin.

He gently pushed her back until she looked him in the eye. The smile on his lips reached his eyes and she felt some of her embarrassment melt away.

"Baby, you do things to me that no one else is even capable of," Brody said, shocking Haven with his words. "I know you're a good girl and I intend for you to stay that way. That's why I go home. You push my ability to think rationally right up to the very edge. When I'm about to fall over, I have to leave."

"I… um… Oh…" Haven said, unnerved by Brody's statement. Allie was right. She was completely clueless. "I'm… I'm sorry, Brody. I didn't mean…"

His finger on her mouth cut off her words.

"I know, doll. I know. I'm sorry if you felt like it was something you were doing wrong," Brody said, kissing her cheek. "It's just the opposite. You do everything all too right."

Haven didn't know what to say to that and sat looking up at Brody with a probing gaze.

"Like right now, when you look at me with those beautiful blue eyes all liquid and hot," Brody said, tracing his thumb along the column of her throat before nibbling her lips.

Haven wrapped her arms around his neck and pulled him closer, not ever wanting to let him go.

"This is exactly what I mean," Brody mumbled against her mouth before kissing her with a fierce eagerness that stole the air from her lungs and ended with her panting for breath.

Resting her forehead against his chin again, she sighed. "I suppose now is when you're going to give me that spiel about needing to go home. Could you throw in a fake yawn or two to make it more believable?"

Chuckling, Brody set Haven down on the couch beside him and gave her a wet, sloppy kiss on her neck.

"Maybe later. How about we watch some television or go for a walk or you can even tell me all about the latest book you're reading?" Brody suggested, not wanting to end the evening too soon. It would be almost a week before he could see her again.

"How about we watch a movie," Haven suggested and let Brody pick one while she went to the kitchen to get him a glass of lemonade and refill her own.

A few hours later, with the evening long gone and a darkened sky outside, Brody stood at the door and held Haven close to his heart, wishing he didn't have to leave but knowing he had to.

He was grateful they were back on even footing because he wasn't sure he could have focused on the game if he thought she was still upset with him.

"I'll call you when I get back. Maybe we can have dinner before I have to leave next week," Brody said, wishing they didn't have two back-to-back away games. It meant he hardly had any time to spend with Haven and he wanted to make the most of every day he had left with her. In two months, he'd be packing his bags and leaving.

"Be safe and have fun," Haven said, kissing Brody one last time before he walked out the door.

Waving as he strolled out of the parking lot and down the street toward his apartment, she felt relief wash over her.

At least now she could stop worrying that he didn't like the way she kissed. Her new worry was on maintaining control of her emotions and not pushing him too close to the edge of his.

## *Chapter Seventeen*

Haven tossed a green salad and set it on the table before taking pork chops out of the oven and covering them with foil to stay hot. Glancing at the clock on the kitchen wall, she hurried to her bedroom and changed, then spent a few minutes primping in front of the mirror.

Brody was back from his away games and this would be the first time they'd spent any time together since he brought her lilacs two weeks ago.

Taking one last look in the mirror, she pinched her cheeks then gave herself a goofy grin before hurrying back to the kitchen.

"Hey, doll? Anyone home?" Brody asked as he knocked on the door and let himself inside. Haven gave him a key the last time he was there, letting him know she trusted him not to abuse the privilege.

"In the kitchen," she called, pouring iced tea into glasses then placing hot rolls in a basket. She covered it with a napkin to keep the bread warm.

"Something smells good," Brody said, wrapping his arms around her and kissing her neck. "And dinner smells pretty good, too."

"You're a tease," Haven said, eating up every word he said. Turning around, she smiled at him, placing her hands on his cheeks and gazing into his face. "I missed you. It seems like you've been gone for months."

"Tell me about it," Brody said, hugging her and resting his chin on top of her head. "But we're home for the next two weeks before we have another away game."

"I know, and I'm really glad. Wes and Tammy are bringing the boys to your game this weekend and I think Mom and Dad are coming again, too."

"Really? That's awesome. I'll try to do something to make the game special for the boys," Brody said, thinking he could give the kids an autographed ball.

"Just getting to watch you play will be excitement enough for them. They don't know they're going because they'd drive Wes and Tammy crazy with questions between now and the game."

Brody chuckled, releasing Haven so he could wash his hands at the sink then waited for her to sit at the table before taking a seat.

"You didn't have to go to all this trouble for me, Haven. I'd eat anything," Brody said, looking forward to a home-cooked meal. He knew Haven, like her mother, was a good cook and couldn't wait to cut into what appeared to be a juicy pork chop.

"I wanted to," she said, smiling at him as he took a bite and closed his eyes, savoring the tender bite of meat.

"That is so good," Brody said, quickly cutting another bite. "I shouldn't be so glad you're domesticated, but I am. This might be the best pork chop I've ever had."

"You are so full of it," Haven said, grinning at Brody as he winked at her, helping himself to more salad and another hot roll.

"Did you make the bread?" Brody asked, slathering it with butter.

"No, the bakery did," Haven said, glad Brody enjoyed her culinary efforts, as basic as they were. "Just don't get any ideas that I cook like this all the time. I just happened to finish with a client earlier than planned and had time to actually prepare something for dinner rather than give you a cold sandwich or tacos again."

"I don't mind those either," Brody said, enjoying every bite he was eating, as well as seeing Haven's lovable face across from him at the kitchen table. He could get used to having dinner with her every night, knowing she was waiting for him at home.

Squelching those thoughts, Brody instead asked her about her job, her family, and if Allie had done anything crazy since he'd been gone.

As they did the dishes, Haven asked Brody about his mom, Marcus, and if he had plans for Easter, inviting him to spend it with her family.

Walking into the living room, Haven noticed one of Brody's football jerseys tossed on the couch.

"What's up with your shirt?" she asked, pointing to the jersey.

"The game this weekend is 'Go Pink Night' and all the players are supposed to add some pink to our jerseys," Brody said, picking up his shirt and holding it to his chest. Lifting his gaze from it to Haven, he grinned. "I was hoping you could help me out. Adding pink to my wardrobe isn't among my particular skill set."

Laughing, Haven took the jersey from him and returned to the kitchen, spreading the shirt on the kitchen table and eyeing it critically.

"I don't have stuff here to do anything. Want to go with me to the craft store?" Haven asked, looking at Brody.

"Sure, let's go," he said, motioning for Haven to go out the door. Since he walked to her apartment from his, they took her car to a store Brody had driven past many times but never entered.

It was a mega-store out of every man's nightmares. He entered the warehouse-type space filled with row after row of sparkly doo-dads, fabric and yarn, wall décor, fake flowers, and more girly stuff than he wanted to see in a lifetime.

Haven grabbed Brody's hand before he became rooted to his spot next to the exit door, and tugged him down an aisle. What seemed like hours later but was less than thirty minutes they were on their way back to Haven's apartment with a bag full of supplies.

"You look a little traumatized," Haven teased as she pulled into her parking space and opened her apartment door.

"I am. Please don't ever take me there again," Brody begged in a pleading tone. "No man should have to suffer like that."

Smacking playfully at his arm, Haven giggled and went to the kitchen where she dumped the supplies out on the table. Using pink glitter paint, she highlighted both his name and number on the jersey. She added pink stripes down the sides of the shirt and along the collar as well as some pink embellishments on the sleeves.

Brody watched her efforts and shook his head when she finished. "I'm going to look like Tinkerbell's long lost cousin. The guys are definitely going to make fun of me."

"No, they won't," Haven said, grinning at Brody, enjoying the time she spent with him as well as the opportunity to do something crafty. "You said they all have to add pink to their shirts, so you won't be the only one."

"True, but only a few of the guys are married or have girlfriends to help them."

"See, then you won't be the only one there with pink on your shirt. I promise," Haven said, washing her hands at the sink to remove paint residue then filling two glasses with iced tea. "Now did I hear that the shirts will be up for bid after the game?"

"Yep. We have to surrender them at the end of the game, sweat and all," Brody said, taking the glass Haven handed him and going to sit on the couch.

She sat beside him and curled her legs to the side. "And the money raised goes to the local cancer center for women?"

"That's right," Brody said, looking at Haven and smiling at her pink lips and rosy cheeks, thinking she looked prettier every time he saw her. "Tell everyone to wear pink Saturday when they come to the game."

"I will, but you should know my dad and brothers don't own anything pink. I might talk them into wearing a pink ribbon pin, but that will be the extent of it."

Brody took a drink of his tea and nodded his head. "I'd be right there with them, except for me, it's mandatory. The footballs will be pink and we even have pink laces for our shoes."

"No way." Haven giggled, picturing all the rough and tough players running around with pink shoelaces. "I can't wait to see it."

"I'm sure you can't." Brody poked Haven in the side, making her giggle even more.

They visited for a while then Brody said he needed to leave. Haven let him get all the way to the door before she pulled down his head and gave him a long, lingering kiss.

"What was that for?" he asked, his voice gravelly and deep.

"I really, really missed you, Brody. I'm so glad you're home for a few weeks," she said, leaning into his strength and the place she was coming to realize felt like home - wrapped in his arms.

"Me too, Haven. Me too."

## *Chapter Eighteen*

"Did you see that? Did you see it?" Hale asked, excitedly grabbing Haven's arm as they jumped to their feet and watched Brody run the ball to the end zone.

Leaping high in the air and catching the ball, he somehow managed to evade a tackle and score a touchdown. The pink glitter paint on his shirt sparkled in the arena lights and made Haven grin.

The crowd went wild, yelling. "Jump it up, Jackson! Jump it up!"

Brody's teammates knuckle-bumped and backslapped him before turning their attention to the next play. She watched as Marcus tapped Brody's helmet twice, they're way of saying "great job!"

Haven smiled Brody's direction and felt her heart go soft when he looked her way and held up his hands for a brief moment, just long enough for her to see he'd written her a message that said, "Hi, doll!" across the palms of his gloves.

She waved at him and he lifted his hand in acknowledgement.

At halftime, Hale and Haven went to get a refill on their sodas and some sweet mini doughnuts to share. Starting back toward their seats, her nephews grabbed her around the waist, both talking a mile a minute. Wes managed to get seats just a section over from where Haven sat with Hale and her parents.

"Did you see Brody make a touchdown?" Mason asked, dancing off one foot to the other in his enthusiasm.

"I did. It was pretty cool, wasn't it?"

"Yep. And I saw him wave at you, Aunt Haven." Jed said, eyeing the treats in her hand.

"You did? How'd you know he was waving at me?" Haven asked, smiling at Tammy and Wes as they walked up behind her.

"Because he calls you doll and Mommy said he wrote 'doll' on his hand. I wanna write stuff on my hand," Jed said, turning to look at his parents. "Can I write on my hand when we get home?"

"Not tonight." Tammy said, rolling her eyes at Haven and tugging her boys back toward their seats.

"He's an amazing player, Haven. Tell him we're having a great time watching him," Wes said, patting her back then following his wife and sons back to their seats.

"Looks like Brody's fan club just got four new members," Hale said as he and Haven returned to their seats next to Rachel and John. Haven handed them a soda and one of the containers of doughnuts.

"So it seems," Haven agreed, using her fork to stab a chocolate-covered orb. She felt her mother's elbow bump her side and looked at her.

"These little doughnuts are really tasty. You think they'd give me their recipe?" Rachel asked, forking another bite.

"Mom, seriously?" Haven said, laughing at her mother.

"Here they come," John said, pointing as the players entered the field. The third quarter flew by with the teams tied going into the fourth quarter.

The last few plays were brutal, with Brody tackled twice. Haven watched as he caught the ball and took a few steps. An opponent flew at him, forcefully shoving him into the dasher boards surrounding the field.

"Looks like tempers are flaring as the game nears the last vital moments of the fourth quarter. It's going to come down to the wire to determine a winner unless someone scores soon," the announcer said.

The other team almost made a touchdown before the home team took possession of the ball. From there, they became an unstoppable force, working their way down the field and scoring the final touchdown mere seconds before the buzzer signaled the end of the game.

Stomping their feet and yelling loudly, the fans had no problem proclaiming their excitement.

"That's what I'm talking about," John said, high-fiving Hale as he stretched across Rachel and Haven.

"Can we stay a few more minutes?" Haven asked, looking at Hale and then her dad. "The players are auctioning off their shirts for the cancer center and I want to see how much they earn."

"Did you bid on Brody's?" Rachel asked, smiling at her daughter. Haven already told her she helped Brody decorate his shirt. She'd made ribbon pins and forced Hale and John to each put one on before coming to the game. Rachel and Haven both wore pink blouses and Haven had a pink ribbon tied around her ponytail.

"No. It's too rich for my blood, but I thought it would be fun to see who gets their sweaty, smelly ol' shirts."

"When you say it like that, they don't sound particularly appealing," Rachel said, wrinkling her nose.

The announcer talked about the silent auction and asked the players to return to the arena with their shirts so they could present them to the winners.

As his teammates returned to the arena, wearing regular jerseys while carrying their pink adorned shirts, she didn't see Brody among them.

Glancing around, she happened to see him run into the stands with two autographed footballs and hand them to Mason and Jed. He'd made sure they weren't pink, since that was the color of ball used for the game that night. The players passed out as many of those as they could during the game. Rachel sat holding one Brody delivered into her hands during the first quarter.

When he leaped over the dasher board and ran up the steps to hand it to Rachel, he winked at Haven and squeezed her hand before returning to the game.

Now, he was receiving hugs from both boys as their dad held the footballs and Tammy tried to get them to let Brody go. He ruffled their hair, ran down the steps to the field and jumped over the dasher board into the arena.

Still wearing his shirt, it was obvious Brody spent the time he should have been changing in getting his teammates to autograph the balls for Mason and Jed.

The announcer proclaimed the winners starting with the lowest jersey number and working his way up. Since Brody's jersey was number 15, it didn't take long before the winner ran out to claim the shirt he wore. Taking it off, he handed it to a young woman dressed in a tight, short skirt and an even tighter knit top. She brushed against him and kissed his cheek before sashaying away, giving him a long look over her shoulder.

Haven sat watching the whole thing, clenching her fingers into a fist.

"You gonna take her out, baby girl?" Hale teased, observing the tense set of Haven's shoulders and the annoyed look on her face.

Turning to look at Hale, Haven released the breath she didn't even realize she'd been holding and relaxed. "No, of course not."

"Good. I wouldn't want everyone to see my sister in action. It would be a shame for you to mop the floor with her before she even realized what hit her," Hale said, making his mom and dad both laugh.

"Shall we go?" Rachel asked, getting to her feet and nudging Haven's leg.

Haven nodded her head and followed Hale out of the stands and to the parking lot. She knew Brody would make an appearance at the after-game gathering. He told her he'd give her a call, if it wasn't too late, when he left the party.

An hour later, Haven sat on her couch reading when she got a text from Brody asking if she'd come pick him up. She sent a message saying she'd be right there, then hurried out to her car. Ten minutes later she pulled up outside the sports bar, hoping Brody would be waiting outside, but he wasn't.

Resolving herself to going inside and finding him, she got out of her car and walked in the dimly lit interior. Several of the players hung out talking to fans.

She finally spied Brody standing at the end of the bar with the woman who'd entered the winning bid for his shirt. She wore it and had her hands looped around Brody's neck, pressing close against him. When she grabbed his head and pulled it down for a kiss, red rage along with a potent dose of jealousy rushed through Haven.

Wanting to run over and pull the woman's brassy hair out by the roots, Haven instead spun on her heel and hurried toward the door, running into Marcus.

"Hey, Haven. I thought Brody would be gone by now. He said he was going to have you pick him up," Marcus said, giving her a friendly smile.

"I see he's got his hands full right now, so I'll be leaving," Haven said, pulling her arm away from Marcus. "I'm sure he can find a ride."

"Oh, man," Marcus said, watching as Brody tried to disentangle himself from his zealous fan while Haven rushed out the door. Hurrying over to Brody, he pushed between the woman and his friend, telling him Haven was leaving.

Running out to the parking lot, Brody caught Haven as she tried to push the right button on her key to unlock the car. Between her trembling hands and tear-filled eyes, she wasn't having much luck.

"Haven!" Brody said, putting his arms around her. She stiffened and pushed against him, but he held on. "This isn't what you think and definitely not what it looks like."

"What do you think it looks like?" she asked, angrier than she'd ever been in her entire life.

"It probably looks like I was kissing that woman, but I wasn't. Honest. You can ask the guys, she's been on me all evening. Marcus borrowed my truck to take someone home who didn't feel well and I told him just to drop my keys off in the morning because I was tired of dodging her. That's why I asked you to come. I couldn't take anymore," Brody said, hoping Haven understood.

"Is that why you smell like cheap perfume and have lipstick smudges on your neck?" Haven asked, clenching her hands to keep from slapping Brody's handsome face.

"I already told you, it's not my fault. She honestly wouldn't leave me alone. I tried foisting her off on Baker or Johnson and they didn't want anything to do with her either." Brody raised his hands in an innocent gesture, wishing Haven would stop glaring at him and calm down. He'd never seen her angry before. Her eyes were narrowed, her lips parted as she took short, sharp breaths, and tense hostility radiated from her stance.

"And I'm supposed to believe you didn't welcome her attentions, not even a little bit?"

"Yes, because it's the truth," Brody said, starting to lose his patience. He hadn't done anything wrong and he wasn't going to stand out in the parking lot defending himself if Haven didn't want to believe him. "Have I ever lied to you?"

"Not that I know of," Haven said, not ready to let go of her anger or be reasonable.

"What's that supposed to mean?" Brody asked, stepping back and crossing his arms over his chest. "Care to explain that?"

"No, I don't care to. And I don't care to spend more time with you this evening, especially when you smell like that… that… woman," Haven said, poking a finger into Brody's bicep. If his arms hadn't been covering his chest, he wondered if she would have punctured a lung with the force of that one dainty little finger now turned into a weapon. "I'm going home."

"Fine. You just do that," Brody said, grabbing Haven's keys from her hand and pushing the button to unlock her door then handing them back to her. "Have a great night."

"You, too!" she yelled before getting in her car and peeling out of the parking lot.

"Stubborn, frustrating woman," he muttered, deciding he better follow her home to make sure she made it in one piece, since she was driving like a crazy person.

Remembering Marcus still had his keys, he ran back inside and found his friend then turned to leave, only to have the drunk, persistent woman try to kiss him again. Brody set her aside, none too gently, and gave her a cool glare. "For the last time, I'm not interested!"

With that, he ran outside and got in his truck, hurrying to catch up to Haven and hoping he didn't get a speeding ticket. He watched her blow through a stop sign and prayed she would make it back to her apartment without causing a wreck or killing herself.

Pulling onto the main street running toward her place, he saw her car zipping through traffic then watched as she took a corner a little fast and wide, almost smacking into another car. Brody arrived at her apartment complex in time to see her slam her front door.

Deciding there was no reason to talk to her when she wouldn't listen to what he was trying to say, he went home and took a shower. He agreed with Haven - the woman's perfume did smell cheap and tacky.

## *Chapter Nineteen*

Haven rubbed her gritty eyes, sat up in bed, and looked at her clock with a sigh. If she didn't hurry, she was going to be late for church and she felt an overwhelming need to be there this morning.

Reviewing the previous night's events, she decided she'd been unfair to Brody, refusing to believe him when she knew he was telling the truth. She realized her jealousy fueled her anger and from there, she quickly lost the ability to think rationally. Tossing and turning most of the night, she kept seeing that woman kissing Brody.

Sending him a text message apologizing, she took a shower, dressed for church, and ate a quick breakfast. Rushing out the door, she stopped short as Brody walked toward her dressed in nice slacks and a polo shirt.

"Good morning," she said, subdued.

"Morning, doll," he said, kissing her cheek. "Can I go with you to church?"

"Absolutely," she said, her face brightening at his words.

Neither one of them mentioned the previous evening on their way to church, nor after when they returned to Haven's to eat lunch.

Instead of sitting around trying to avoid the topic, Brody asked Haven if she'd like to go for a walk. It was a beautiful, sunny spring afternoon and he thought the fresh air would do them both good.

They strolled along at a leisurely pace toward the park near his apartment complex. Stepping off the sidewalk onto the green grass, he noticed a few families enjoyed picnic lunches.

Brody took Haven's elbow and guided her away from three rambunctious youngsters playing on the slide. Taking seats side by side on a set of swings, neither of them spoke until Brody finally broke the silence.

"I think we should talk about last night," Brody said, looking at his feet as he let the swing move slowly back and forth.

Haven smoothed down the skirt of her blue and white dress, nodding her head. "I suppose we should and since I was the one who acted unreasonable, I guess I'll go first. I'm sorry, Brody. I shouldn't have gone off mad and I shouldn't have judged you."

"Thank you, Haven. In retrospect, I should have called you sooner or taken our friend home myself instead of letting Marcus borrow my truck," Brody said, thinking back over everything that happened from the point he arrived at the bar to the moment he saw Haven.

Some little part of his ego, the part that occasionally needed stroking, liked having a woman so enthralled with him she couldn't leave him alone. He was disgusted with himself for letting the woman get close enough to kiss him, especially when Haven was watching. He knew she would be there any minute. He should have gone outside to wait for her instead of making her come inside, aware of how much she hated to be there.

"It seems we both could have made some better choices last night," Haven said, twirling a stray curl around her finger.

Brody watched her work the strand around her finger and let it go, repeating the process. She wore her hair down, and with the sun throwing golden highlights through it, she had an almost angelic appearance. It was a far cry from the infuriated woman who faced him head-on last night.

"I agree."

"Brody, I really am sorry. Seeing that woman throw herself at you made me so angry and… jealous. I couldn't even think straight," Haven admitted, as much to herself as Brody. "Is there anything I can do to make it up to you?"

"Actually, there is something you can do, sort of."

"Well, that was terribly informative, Mr. Jackson. Would you care to elaborate?"

Brody sighed and ran a hand through his hair before returning his gaze to Haven. His mom said to be open and honest the last time he'd talked to her about Haven, so he'd give it a shot and hope it didn't backfire.

"Haven, I'm in love with you. I considered walking away to save us both some heartbreak later on, but Mom suggested I discuss it with you," Brody said, watching as Haven got to her feet, standing in front of him.

"You… you're in love with me? Brody, you hardly know me. We've only… you…"

Brody stood and took her hands in his, looking intently in her eyes. "It doesn't matter if I've known you a day, a week, or a year. What matters is how I feel about you right now. Today. At this very moment."

"But… are you sure?" Haven asked, wishing more than anything for him to be certain.

Instead of responding to her question, he began asking his own.

"Does your heart pound when you see me? Have you found it increasingly difficult to think of anything besides me? Does just the thought of seeing me make you smile? Have you lost your ability to concentrate? Do I invade your dreams? Do you feel like you could reach out and touch me at night even though you're home alone?"

Haven blinked at him, wondering how he could have read her mind so thoroughly.

"Do you, Haven? Do you? Do you feel like you've finally found the place where you belong? The one person who makes you feel different? Special? Better?"

When Haven didn't answer, he took her arms in his hands and pulled her closer. "Because that is what you do to me, Haven. I can't get you out of my head or heart, and to be honest, I don't want to."

"Brody," she said on a sigh, pressing her head against his chest as her arms went around his waist, holding him tightly. "I didn't know… I had no idea you felt that way, too."

"You mean you really do have… feelings for me?" Brody asked, desperately wanting the answer to be yes.

"It's no secret that I wear my feelings on my sleeve. How do you not know I care for you, you crazy man?" Haven asked, smiling at him. "If I didn't, do you think I would have been so upset last night? I've loved you from the moment you handed me that autographed football."

"Really? Seriously?" Brody asked, picking her up and swinging her around as the tension that had settled into his shoulders suddenly melted away.

Coming back to reality, he set her down and took her hands in his again. "But what about when the end of June comes? I don't want to break your heart, Haven. We both know I can't stay."

"I know. Let's worry about June when it gets here. Until then, we've still got a couple months to enjoy each other, to really get to know one another."

"Okay," Brody said, kissing her cheek. "We'll just take it a day at a time and not worry about then."

"It's a deal," Haven said, thinking if Brody let go of her hand she might float away. A glorious happiness filled her, knowing he cared for her, knowing he needed her as much as she needed him. "Maybe we should seal it with a kiss."

"Are you sure? Out here in front of the whole wide world?" Brody teased, knowing how Allie's public displays of affection for Rick annoyed Haven.

"I'll risk it," Haven said, grabbing a handful of Brody's shirt collar and pulling his lips to hers. Something new mingled in with the familiar passion and longing. Something that felt like acceptance and love.

Brody was the first to pull back and swung Haven around in his arms one more time before setting her down and lacing her fingers with his.

"Before you risk more than you meant to, let's get you home. There's too big of an audience here today for my liking," Brody said, leading the way back to Haven's apartment.

Walking her to the door, he stepped inside to kiss her again, not wanting to give her nosy neighbor anything scandalous to report to Rachel. The kiss he gave Haven definitely would have been gossip worthy had anyone witnessed it.

Haven had to grasp the back of the chair next to her to keep herself upright when Brody stepped away.

Smiling at her with a new light in his eyes, he brushed his thumb across her well-kissed lips then grasped her chin in his hand.

"I love you, Haven Clarice Haggarty, and I never once thought your name sounded like you should be a stripper," Brody said, with a devilish smile.

"How did you know I hate my name?" Haven asked, realizing Hale must have said something to Brody.

"A little bird told me," Brody said, hugging her again. "I think it's a beautiful name for a beautiful girl, but if you ever want to try out that stripper theory, you can practice on me."

"You're awful!" Haven grabbed a pillow from the couch and began hitting Brody as he laughed and tickled her sides. He wrapped his arms around her and pulled her against his chest, breathing in her soft fragrance, soaking her warmth into his soul.

"I know, but I make you laugh," he said, kissing her ear then her neck. He felt her melting against him and reveled in the knowledge he could make her knees weak with his kisses.

"Yes, you do, and I love you, too."

"I can't believe he wrote that on his hand for the entire world to see," Allie said, looking at Haven's flushed cheeks.

Brody had flashed his hands after he made a touchdown and this time his palms read, "Luv U, Doll!" The camera crew caught it and played it on the big screen for every person in the arena to see.

Haven's cheeks immediately turned red, but she was thrilled Brody no longer tried to hide his affection for her.

After declaring their love for one another Sunday, he'd sent her flowers at work on Tuesday and a box of decadent truffles Thursday.

Although he'd been busy getting ready for the game, she knew she'd see him after and he planned to spend the following afternoon with her.

She had no idea he'd make their recently revealed feelings such public knowledge. She could hear two girls a few rows behind them loudly speculating on who could possibly be the love of Brody's life. When they pointed at Allie and suggested someone like her might capture his attention, Haven didn't know whether to laugh or be insulted.

Allie's nudge to her ribs and eye rolling made her smile and they both laughed.

"I still don't know why he likes me," Haven said to Allie, whispering quietly in her cousin's ear.

Allie turned and stared at her. "You're kidding, right? This is like the idiotic kissing question."

"No, I'm not," Haven said, suddenly embarrassed she'd voiced her thoughts.

"Let's hear the reasons why he wouldn't like you," Allie said, nudging Rick and waiting for Haven to speak.

"I'm not gorgeous like you, or tall, or thin, or even remotely trendy. I'm not outgoing or super friendly. I'm not the life of the party and truthfully prefer to stay home with a good book than be forced to attend one. I'm not the smartest, funniest, or wittiest girl on the planet. I'm just me - plain ol' Haven, with a ridiculous name."

Even Rick looked at her with a raised eyebrow before glancing at Allie and shaking his head.

"I could be completely off base, but I think what Brody sees in you, why he likes you, are all of those reasons," Allie said, grabbing Haven's hand in hers. "You're sweet and innocent, hard-working and loyal. You aren't vain or pretentious, and everything isn't all about you. You're funny and super smart not to mention all those domestic skills you have my mother wishes I possessed. As for your name, I'll bet you ten bucks that Brody likes it and doesn't think it's ridiculous."

"I second all that," Rick said, smiling at Haven. "I can tell you there is a certain appeal in a girl who lets us do the chasing, who isn't all wrapped up in herself, and is a good person."

"Did I hear you say appealing girls?" Tom asked as he returned with a box loaded down with snacks.

"We're talking about your sister," Allie said, giving Tom a look that said now was not a good time for his usual sarcastic remarks.

"I'm definitely not interested then," Tom said, grinning at Haven as he handed her a bottle of water. "What brought all that up?"

"Haven doesn't know why Brody likes her," Rick said before Allie could tell him to be quiet.

"Me neither," Tom said, picking up a slice of gooey pizza. "I mean he's got women falling at his feet and can choose from any he likes and he decides on this kiddo. She's a total goofball nut-job who's also miss snooty business professional. What fun is that?"

Allie glared at Tom, shaking her head slightly.

He glanced down at Haven to see if she knew he was teasing and saw, for the first time in his life, that his words did wound his sister. Although she smiled, he knew it wasn't genuine.

"I'm kidding, Haven. You have a lot to offer a guy, especially one who isn't interested in the one-night stand types. There's a lot to be said for the wholesome, sweet whatever thing you've got going on."

"Thanks, I think," Haven said, patting Tom on the arm before they returned their attention to the halftime show.

They watched as a group of the die-hard fans started a balloon around the arena. It made it through three sections before one of the security guards appropriated it. They found another one and started it around. The guard also captured it. Out of balloons, Haven and Allie laughed as one of the guys paid a child five dollars for his balloon and started it around. It made it around four sections before the guard appeared.

The crowd started chanting, "Pass it around, pass it around," before the guard could catch up to it. Clapping loudly as he tried to chase it across sections of seats, the balloon quickly made it all the way around the arena back to the group of guys. After cheering in victory, they willingly surrendered it to the guard, who gave them a contemptuous glare then stalked off.

"That was great," Tom said, high-fiving Rick.

The team appeared back in the arena and Brody looked Haven's direction as he entered the field. It made a smile bloom in her face to know he was thinking about her.

Only a few minutes into the fourth quarter, Brody stood waiting for a pass. The rowdy fans split the arena into two sides. The first side chanted," Jump it up!" then the second side yelled, "Jackson!"

This went on until Brody leapt high in the air, catching the ball with one long arm extended and brought it back to his chest. He hit the ground running and made almost ten yards before a tackle drove him down right on the twenty-yard line, directly below Haven.

When he got to his feet, he looked up at her and lifted his hand slightly. She discreetly waved back at him, but smiled broadly when he nodded his head and returned his attention to the game.

"So what's going on with you two?" Tom asked Haven as her eyes followed Brody's every move.

"Going on?" Haven asked, distractedly.

"Yeah. I mean it's obvious you're a goner for Brody and for reasons I'll never understand, he seems to like you, too. What's gonna happen when he leaves at the end of the season?" Tom asked, sounding concerned.

Haven pivoted her head to the side and studied her brother. Although Tom could be a jerk and a dork, she knew he cared about her even if he'd never come right out and say it.

"I try not to think about what will happen when he leaves, but we both know it's going to happen. I suppose I'll go back to being lonely and a workaholic, except then I can add broken-hearted to the description."

"So why keep seeing him, knowing you'll wind up hurting?" Tom asked, thinking his sister was truly crazy.

"I'd rather spend a few months loving someone like Brody, and being loved by him, than never know what it would be like to experience true love," Haven said. Tom didn't miss the wistful look on her face or the soft light in her eyes.

"Still seems like you're just setting yourself up for a mental breakdown," Tom said, keeping his tone light and teasing.

"And I'm sure you'll be the one to suggest a straightjacket when the time comes," Haven said, playfully slugging his arm.

"You know it, kiddo."

Watching as Marcus scored a touchdown, they got to their feet and cheered along with the rest of the fans.

The game ended soon after that with Brody's team winning. They were on fire for the season and had a chance at making the playoffs. If they did, it meant Brody would be around for a few extra weeks.

Haven hoped they did make it not only for the team, but because it would keep Brody near for just a little while longer.

He looked her direction as he left the field and she nodded her head at him, indicating she'd wait while he changed. Deciding to skip out on the after-game celebration, they instead went to a late movie then to the diner near their apartments where Brody ate a full meal and Haven indulged in a piece of cake.

"So you're gone next week, is that right?" Haven asked, already knowing the answer. She had the team's schedule memorized and could rattle off their travel dates, when they'd be home, and approximately how many hours between times she could see Brody.

"Yep, but we've got a home game Easter weekend, so I plan on chasing the Easter Bunny to your place that Sunday morning," Brody said, giving her a teasing smile.

"Maybe he'll skip by me. I'm getting a little old for the Easter Bunny business, don't you think?"

Brody put a hand over her mouth, dropped his shoulders down, and looked cautiously around the restaurant. "Shh. He's got spies everywhere checking up on who's good and who's not. You better be careful or no goodies for you."

Haven laughed as Brody sat back up and took another bite of his burger.

"I guess I better be careful about who I'm seen with, too," she said, starting to get up from the table.

Brody shook his head and grabbed her wrist, tugging her back down across from him. "Too late. He already knows you associate with riffraff like me."

"Hey, don't go calling my boyfriend riffraff," Haven said, giving him a saucy smile. "He's a pretty great guy."

"You think so?" Brody was inordinately pleased she thought well of him. "I heard he was one of those jerk kind of jocks, full of himself, that sort of thing."

"Oh, he is, don't get me wrong," Haven said, gazing at Brody with an innocent look on her face. "He's completely conceited, thinks he's always right, is single-minded in his focus on football, and can be a little overbearing."

"Then why do you hang out with him?" Brody asked, trying to decide if she was teasing him or not. When she grinned, he knew she was.

"Because he's also funny and sweet, caring and gentle, and he's really, really cute."

"Don't forget a good kisser. You forgot that part," Brody said, finishing his fries.

"I didn't forget. I was just naming off the things he is good at, not thinks he's good at," Haven said, trying not to squeal when Brody grabbed her leg beneath the table and started pulling her down.

"I'm kidding, football man. Just kidding," she said, giggling as she scooted back up in the booth. Lowering her voice, she gave him a sideways glance that made him feel a little overheated. "He happens to be an amazing kisser. I actually never thought someone's kisses could be so... mesmerizing."

"So he puts you in a trance?" Brody asked as he paid the bill and left a generous tip for the waitress.

"Not exactly. More like enchants," Haven said, meshing her fingers with Brody's as he walked her across the parking lot to his truck. He opened the door and helped her in. She held onto his hand and looked at his palm in the glow from the streetlight above them. She traced the words he'd written there and smiled. "I love you, too, you know."

"I know, doll. And it makes me really happy that you do."

## *Chapter Twenty*

A thumping noise yanked Haven out of her dreams of Brody and brought her wide awake.

Carefully getting out of bed, she listened, but all seemed quiet. She quickly decided she'd imagined the sound.

Climbing back between the sheets, she closed her eyes and rolled onto her side when she heard another thump and what sounded like a muffled voice.

She grabbed a key and small flashlight out of her nightstand drawer and tiptoed across the room. Pulling a gun case from its hidden spot at the back of her closet, she quietly unlocked it. Taking out her handgun, she made sure it was loaded, and inhaled a deep breath.

Turning off the flashlight, she slowly opened the door, maneuvering around until she could see into the living room. She watched her front door swing shut as someone exited in the dim early morning light sneaking around the edges of her drapes.

Her foot connected with something that rolled away as she stepped into the room. Listening, she didn't hear anything, so she hurried to turn on a light.

She put the safety on her gun and set it on a side table by the door, looking around her living room with a big grin on her face.

Apparently, she'd been extra good as far as the Easter Bunny was concerned because she had a huge basket full of treats on her coffee table along with three vases filled with fresh flowers. The bright pink plastic egg near her foot must have fallen out of the basket.

Hoping when she kicked it that she hadn't broken anything, she opened the egg to find a piece of candy. Unwrapping the treat and popping it in her mouth, she searched the basket for a card. She finally found a note, scrawled on a sheet of plain white paper.

*Haven,*

*Despite your questionable choices in companions, you've been a very good girl. Enjoy your Easter treats and don't forget to share them with your good-looking, talented, super smart, completely awesome boyfriend.*

*The Easter Bunny*

She laughed aloud then dug through the basket, finding all of her favorite candy and treats. Had Brody paid that much attention to her likes and dislikes, or had he checked with Allie or her mom to discover her favorites? Whatever the reason, she knew he'd gone to a lot of work and effort to make her Easter morning special.

Sending Brody a text, she knew he was awake, even though it was much earlier than he was accustomed to rising.

He answered back that he'd be at her place in time to go to the sunrise service if she'd still let him go. She answered she would, then hurried to shower and dress before he arrived.

She heard him knock and come in while she slipped on her shoes. Grabbing her watch on the way past her dresser, she rushed into the front room to see him looking quite handsome in a suit and tie.

"Wow! You look great," Haven said, kissing his cheek, afraid to hug him and wrinkle his pressed shirt.

"You look amazing," Brody said, holding her hand and making her twirl around, showing off her new dress.

In a shade of blue that looked like a robin's egg with a style that accented her curves. Brody swallowed hard, thinking about how attracted he was to her. She'd left that mass of golden curls hanging loose and smelled so luscious, he had to force himself to be on his best behavior, instead of sweeping her into his arms like he wanted to do.

"Looks like the Easter Bunny thought you were really good this year," Brody said, pointing to the huge basket of treats.

"So it seems. He left a note about sharing this with some good-looking, talented, smart boyfriend. I guess I'll have to put it all in the freezer until I meet this guy." Haven grinned at Brody over her shoulder as she dug through the basket for a piece of candy.

He grabbed her around her waist and tickled her until they both were breathless.

Plopping down on the couch, Brody noticed the gun on the side table and stared at it wide-eyed.

"What are you doing with the gun?" Brody pointed at the gun, taken aback by the sight of it.

"Oh, I forgot to put it away earlier," she said, getting up and taking it to her bedroom. When she returned to the living room, Brody continued to stare at her. "What?"

"Why did you have the gun out?" Brody asked, glad he knew she had a firearm in her apartment. He definitely wouldn't ever sneak in again.

"I heard a noise out here and thought someone broke in."

"Seriously? You were going to kill the Easter Bunny?" Brody was shocked by the revelation that she could have shot him or Marcus when they were leaving her morning surprises.

"No," she said with a smile. "If I'd known it was you, I wouldn't have felt it necessary to protect myself."

"Did you see us?" Getting to his feet, he wondered when exactly she opened her bedroom door. Marcus had bumped into the coffee table in the dark and Brody wondered if that was what awakened Haven.

"Us? Who else was with you? And no, when I opened the bedroom door, the front door was just closing," she said, taking another piece of candy from the basket and holding it out to Brody. He shook his head, too focused on Haven's gun to think about candy.

"Marcus helped me. We left some stuff for his girlfriend, too."

"Oh, that's so sweet," Haven said, not realizing the turmoil she'd set off in Brody.

He started to say something about her being more careful, but realized she really could take care of herself. He'd just be more mindful about prowling around her apartment in the dark.

Giving in to his longing to kiss her, he gently took her lips with his, in no rush or hurry to do anything else. She tasted rich, dark, and sweet, like the chocolate candy she'd been eating, making a deep hunger gnaw at him.

Finally, Haven pulled back and tugged him toward the door. "We better hurry it up or we're going to be late."

"Yes, ma'am," Brody said, taking her hand and rushing across the parking lot.

Returning to Haven's place after church, she gave Brody a basket filled with things she thought he'd enjoy like jerky and a movie he mentioned he'd really liked when he was in high school. After eating a few more treats, they drove out to the farm for a big brunch.

While the women worked in the kitchen, Brody joined the men outside where they hid eggs for Mason and Jed then stood watching as the two boys raced around trying to find them all.

"Remember the year it was raining and you hid the eggs in the house for us, Dad?" Hale asked, grinning at his father.

"Yeah, I remember, all right. A month later, we kept smelling something odd in the living room and finally found a rotten egg that fell down beneath the couch. After that, your mother forbade any egg hiding activities in the house," John said, smiling at the memory.

"A month old hard-boiled egg?" Brody asked, thinking that had to smell awful.

"It was raunchy," Tom said, remembering he was the one his mom made carry it outside to dispose of it. "Even the dog wouldn't get close to it."

"Did we get them all, Dad?" Mason asked as he and Jed approached the group of men with baskets full of eggs.

Wes did a quick count and nodded his head. "Yep, you boys found them all. Good job."

"Will you hide them for us again?"

"Sure," Wes said, telling the boys to go in the house and not to peek.

The men waited until the boys went in the back door and then Wes checked to see if the boys were peeking. He could see their heads lurking around the edges of the curtain in the family room.

"The boys are watching our every move. No wonder they found all the eggs so fast the first time," Wes said, grinning at his dad.

"Just like you three always did. Poor Haven hardly ever found an egg because you boys would come tearing out here, already knowing where most of them were hid." John shook his head as he smiled at Wes.

"She made up for it when she'd sneak eggs out of our baskets," Tom said, recalling past Easter egg hunts.

"Haven always was a tough little thing," John said, thinking about his plucky daughter.

"She had to be around us," Hale said, taking one of the baskets Wes held in his hand. "I think we need a distraction while someone hides the eggs on the front lawn."

"Good idea," John said, slapping Hale on the back. While Tom and Wes pretended to have a fist fight, Brody and Hale snuck around the side of the house to the front yard and hid all the eggs.

Returning to the back yard, Mason and Jed were standing on the back step cheering for Wes while the women shook their heads and returned to the kitchen.

"Lick 'im good, Dad!" Mason yelled.

"They do know it's a pretend fight, don't they?" Brody asked.

"I don't think so," Hale said, watching as Jed threw out his arm, almost hitting Mason as he copied the movements of the adults roughhousing in the yard.

Hale handed the two boys the empty baskets and told them to go find some eggs.

Wes and Tom stopped their mock fight and watched the youngsters search high and low not finding a single egg.

"Why don't you two try the front yard?" Hale suggested. The men followed along as the boys raced around to the front of the house.

It took a little work and a lot of searching but they finally found all the eggs.

"Look, Brody, we got all of them." Jed held his basket out for Brody to admire the brightly colored eggs.

"You sure did. That was a great job of hunting."

Turning to their father, the boys began pleading for another round of searching for eggs. Tammy stepped out the door and announced the meal was ready, saving Wes from having to hide the eggs again.

Gathered around the big dining room table, the conversation was lively as they ate.

After the food was put away and the dishes done, Rachel announced it was time for the adults to hunt for eggs. She sent the boys out to hide them, telling the two little livewires they couldn't go beyond the edge of the lawn in any direction.

She divided the group into three teams.

"Why do I have to be Hale's partner," Tom whined, making them all laugh. Wes and Tammy partnered together while Brody and Haven made the third team.

"Would you rather be Haven's?" Rachel asked, arching an eyebrow at her youngest son.

"No, anything but that," Tom said, raising his hands in defeat. "What are we searching for and who wins?"

"You're searching for the same eggs the boys found earlier. Whoever finds the most eggs, wins a nice prize, if I do say so myself. Oh, and you have five minutes. The finish line is the back door."

Rachel handed each of the teams an empty basket. When the boys ran back in after hiding all the eggs, John yelled, "Go," and the adults hurried outside.

Tom gave Wes such a hard shove on his way out the door, he fell down the last two steps and rolled across the lawn.

Undaunted, Wes reached under a bush and came up with an egg, doing a victory dance. Tammy shook her head, but dropped the egg in their basket.

Brody grabbed Haven's hand and ran around to the backyard. Between the two of them, they found several eggs. Brody was good at running interference and blocking her brothers while she darted in and grabbed eggs. She also snitched a few out of Hale and Tom's basket when they weren't paying attention.

"You've got ten seconds to reach the finish line or you're disqualified," John yelled from the back door where he'd drawn a line across the cement in chalk.

On the far side of the lawn, Brody knew they wouldn't make it with Haven trying to run in the heels she still wore from church.

Swinging her up in his arms while she held their basket, she grinned and wrapped an arm around his neck while he sprinted across the grass and crossed the line in the nick of time.

A quick count of eggs revealed Brody and Haven had the most.

"She cheated!" Tom said, pointing a finger at Haven. "You know she did. She always does. And she's got her personal bodyguard on duty helping out."

"Oh, quit your bellyachin' and be a good sport," Wes said, giving Tom a shove.

"Yeah, be a good sport, Tommy," Haven said, sticking her tongue out at him. Brody worked to hide a smirk at the sibling rivalry.

"What's the prize, Mom?" Hale asked, anxious to see what the winner would get.

"Actually, there are three prizes and you all win. Your father and I just wanted to watch you fight over the eggs like old times," Rachel teased, giving each team a basket.

Hale and Tom's basket contained two of everything, including two tickets to a monster truck show and two big chocolate rabbits.

The baskets she gave the two couples had a few pieces of candy along with movie tickets and gift certificates for dinner at a nice restaurant.

"These are great, Mom. Thanks so much," Haven said, hugging Rachel.

"Thank you, Rachel. This is really nice," Brody said, hugging the woman who patted his back and made him miss his own mother. "And the egg hunt was fun, too."

"You kids are so predictable," John said. "Although Brody carrying Haven across the finish line was new.

Thanks for throwing in that unexpected touch to the finale."

"Anytime. Glad I could be of service," Brody said, grinning as John slapped him on the back.

They sat around visiting for a while then the women set out dessert. Brody zeroed in on what appeared to be a chocolate cream pie, one of his favorites.

Accepting a piece, he sat eating it, lost in sugar-induced bliss. Haven sat beside him and offered him an occasional look or grin as he quietly ate.

"Like your pie?" she finally asked as he forked the very last crumb to his mouth.

"I think it may be the best I've ever eaten," Brody said, looking with longing at the few pieces of pie left on the counter. Still full from brunch, he didn't think he could hold one more bite, but the pie was so good.

"You can have another piece if you'd like," Haven said, starting to get up to bring him one.

"I'd love another one, but I can't eat another bite right now. I'll probably kick myself later, but I'm going to pass."

"Suit yourself," Haven said, shrugging her shoulders and taking another bite of her cheesecake.

"Mom used to make pie when I was a kid. It was kind of a special celebration thing for us. I haven't had chocolate cream pie in years," Brody said, squeezing Haven's hand beneath the table.

A short while later, Brody and Haven were on the road back to town. Helping carry her things into her apartment, they sat and talked for a while about fun memories from their childhood.

Haven knew without asking, Brody had grown up poor without anyone except his mom. She wondered what it would have been like to grow up without her rowdy brothers or her dad. All of them could be ornery and teasing, but Haven couldn't picture life without them in it.

"Did you talk to your mom yet today?" Haven asked as Brody took a piece of candy from the basket still sitting on her coffee table.

"I called this morning, but she was working so I left her a message. I'll call her when I get home."

"I have something I thought you might like to send her." Haven said, picking up her cell phone and sending a text to Brody.

He opened it to find a photo of him carrying Haven with the basket of eggs. Both of them were laughing and the photo clearly showed the love they shared as they looked at one another.

"This is awesome. Mom will love it." Brody grinned at Haven.

"Mom said she couldn't resist taking it. I'm glad she did." Haven looked at the photo on Brody's phone as she sat next to him. He moved so he could wrap his arm around her and she cuddled against him. "I'm so glad you came with me today."

"Me, too. It was the nicest Easter I've ever had." Brody gave Haven a smile that made her limbs turn languid.

Her heart hurt to think Brody didn't have any great Easter memories as a child. She assumed his mom probably spent a lot of them working. She could picture him as a boy, sitting home alone with a tiny little basket of treats, maybe not even that, with no eggs to find or loved ones to keep him company.

Biting her cheek to keep the tears filling her eyes from spilling, she rested her head on Brody's chest and let out a sigh.

"What's wrong, doll?" Brody asked, easily reading her emotions. He knew she thought of something that made her sad.

"It's just… I was thinking that if today was the best Easter you ever had, how sad the ones you experienced as a boy must have been," Haven said quietly, wrapping her arms around Brody and holding him tight.

He rubbed her back and pressed a kiss to the top of her head. "Don't be sad. My Easter's weren't all bad. Mom most always worked, but she usually brought home a bunch of great leftovers and the Easter Bunny always brought me something, even if it was just a package of those marshmallow chicks. I don't think I'm scarred for life or anything. Today was special because I got to spend it with you."

"Brody," Haven whispered, looking up at him as a few tears rolled down her cheeks. He wiped them away with his thumb then kissed each cheek before he gave her such a soft, tender kiss, she was sure he could hear her heart sigh with contentment.

"I think I better go home, though." Brody kissed her forehead before getting to his feet. He pulled her upright and she handed him his Easter basket, walking him to the door.

"You'll have to let me know who you're going to take to dinner and the movies with the certificates you got from your mom," Brody said, pointing to the basket sitting on the floor by the couch.

"Maybe I'll take Mom or Allie," she said, pretending to study her fingernails.

"Sure, that sounds nice." Brody kissed her cheek as he opened the door. "You should have a girls' night out."

"Maybe I will," she said, knowing Brody would be the one to go with her. "Unless you happen to be available."

"I might be able to work it into my busy schedule. I'll have my people give your people a call," Brody teased, stepping outside and backing toward his truck.

"You just do that." Haven grinned at him as he almost tripped over a parking curb. "I'll be waiting for that call."

"Love you, doll," Brody called before climbing in his truck.

"Love you, more," Haven replied, then shut her door before Mrs. Humphrey could come outside and scold her for yelling across the parking lot.

"Are you sure I'm doing this right? Fred doesn't really seem to like it," Brody asked as he brushed the old horse.

"Oh, Fred's too old to care, but yeah, you've got the hang of it. Just give him a few more strokes on that side and you can be done," Haven said as she finished brushing her horse and patted the mare's neck. Leading the horse through the barn, she turned her out in the fenced pasture, watching the horse shake her mane and trot off in the direction of the other horses.

When Brody finished brushing Fred, she led the horse into a stall, making sure he had plenty of feed and water before closing the door.

"One of the other horses picks on Fred, so Dad decided to keep him in here for now. I don't think Fred minds at all. He gets extra feed and attention," Haven said, rinsing her hands at a sink in a far corner of the barn and wiping her hands on a paper towel. Brody washed his hands and turned to find Haven leaning against the wall, studying him.

"Where'd you get that hat, cowboy?" Haven asked, watching as Brody pushed a straw cowboy hat back on his head. She knew he had a pair of cowboy boots from seeing him wear them before, but the hat was a surprise.

"It's mine. I don't usually have anywhere to wear it."

"Are you more country than you led me to believe?" she asked, giving him a probing look.

"Maybe I am, maybe I'm not," he said, thinking Haven looked like a cute little country girl in her form-fitting jeans, scuffed boots, and soft, summery blouse. She wore her hair in a long braid down her back, but curls escaped and bounced around her face.

"I know one way to find out," she said, holding out her hand.

"What?" he asked, wondering what she wanted.

"Your phone, if you please." Haven wiggled her fingers his direction.

"My phone?" he asked, digging it out of his pocket and handing it to her.

She scrolled through the apps until she found his downloaded music then grinned.

"Ha! Just as I suspected. You've got more country tunes on here than anything else," she said, handing the phone back to him.

"So. Your point is…"

"That you're not this bad boy from the big city like you want everyone to think you are. You're a small town country boy. I've got you figured out." Haven shook a finger at him while giving him a flirty smile.

"If you've got me figured out, then you probably know I like to dance to a good country song once in a while." Brody picked a song and turned up the volume on his phone.

Holding out his hand to Haven, he swung her into his arms, dancing her around the aisle of the barn while Easton Corbin sang *Lovin' You is Fun* in the background.

"I love that song." Haven grinned at Brody as he twirled her around. "It makes me think of you."

"It does? Why?" He dropped her into a dip and pulled her back up with a kiss.

"Because loving you *is* so much fun. Allie thinks we're doing something wrong because we aren't fighting and making up all the time, but I like the even keel of our relationship. I know when I'm with you we'll laugh and have a great time. You're fun to be around and you make me happy."

"I'm glad you think so, Haven. I agree. Loving you *is* fun and one of the best things that's ever happened to me."

"Where'd you learn to dance?" Haven asked, impressed with Brody's moves, even if they were in the barn and the music was playing on his phone.

"Mom taught me. It was something we could do for entertainment that was free. We spent a lot of evenings dancing around our little living room," Brody said, grateful his mom made him learn how to dance.

"She did a great job teaching you." Haven twirled into Brody's chest and hugged him as the song ended. "Speaking of your mom, did she like the Easter picture?"

"No." Brody picked up his phone and shoved it in his pocket before taking Haven's hand in his as they walked out of the barn. The afternoon sunshine was bright and warm, and fields sprouting with green covered the gently rolling hills as far as Brody could see. It was a perfect Sunday afternoon, especially since he was spending it with Haven.

At her dejected look, he grinned. "She didn't like it, she loved it. She said you are a beautiful girl and she could tell from our faces that you care for me."

Haven smiled and let out a breath of relief. Although she'd likely never meet Brody's mother, she still wanted the woman to like her. "I'm glad she loved it. How's she doing?"

"Really well. She's working at a high-end restaurant these days with better hours and makes a lot more in tips. I'm glad she doesn't have to work so hard," Brody said, stopping to pet Minion and Gru, the two family dogs. "I try to help out, but she's refused to take any money for a while. When I go to visit her, I buy things she needs instead."

"Like what?" Haven asked, scratching Minion behind his ears. The dog wagged his tail so hard, Brody thought the animal might beat himself to death with it.

"You know, just stuff. Like when I was there for Christmas, her old fridge was about to die, so I bought her a new one. I also had a new front door installed." Brody hunkered down to give Gru a rub on his belly, missing the tender look Haven gave him.

Hearing him talk about his mom with such love and concern, learning that he did such caring, helpful things for the woman, made her heart puddle at her feet.

"You're a good guy, Brody Jackson. Don't ever let anyone tell you otherwise," Haven said, stepping behind him and hugging him around the neck while he pet the dog.

He stood up before she could move and gave her a piggyback ride to the house, making her laugh.

"And you're a sweet girl, Haven Haggarty. Don't you ever forget it."

## *Chapter Twenty-One*

"We've got a problem."

Haven looked up from the report she was typing as Mr. Young walked in her office. "A problem, sir?" she asked, standing behind her desk.

"A big problem," Mr. Young said, motioning for her to sit before taking a chair across from her. "We need to shoot the photos for the new campaign we're doing for the plumbing company. You remember sitting in with Seth on the brainstorming session, right?"

"Yes. Isn't this the campaign to give plumbers a new, younger image? The company wanted to use buff guys to get overweight, plumber's crack visions out of their customer's heads." Haven thought the creative ideas for the campaign were fresh and would probably be quite effective.

"That's correct. The problem is the model we had lined up for the photo shoot got food poisoning and can't come in today. We've got to get this rolling and I don't want to wait even one more day to make it happen. Do you have any contacts you could bring in on short notice?" Mr. Young asked, knowing Haven had a handful of models she frequently worked with.

"Let me see what I can do," Haven said, picking up her phone. "If I can get someone in here today, does it matter what time?"

"No. This project is top priority so if you can get someone in, we'll put everything else on hold while they're here. The photo shoot should only take thirty minutes or so." Mr. Young said, walking to the door. "Thanks, Haven. I know I can always count on you."

"I hope so," Haven muttered under her breath as she began calling models. Leaving messages with several, the few she actually spoke with said they'd do it if they weren't already busy.

In a moment of desperation, she called Brody. It was the team's second bye week and she knew he had a little more free time than usual.

"Hey, beautiful doll, what's up?" Brody asked when he answered her call.

"I need some help," she said, getting right to the point. "If I begged and pleaded and asked nicely, do you think the coach would let you pose as a model for an ad we need to shoot today?"

"What?" Brody asked, sure he'd heard Haven incorrectly. "Did you just ask me to model for you?"

"I did," Haven said, taking a breath then speaking so fast Brody had a hard time keeping up with her. "The model we hired got food poisoning and Mr. Young wants to finish the photos for the campaign today and the fourteen other models I called didn't answer or can't come in and I'm desperate because he's counting on me to find someone and I don't know who else to call."

Brody got the part about food poisoning and Haven being desperate. "I'd love to help, but you know there's a policy against us doing that kind of stuff."

"I know, but the company is one of your sponsors. Does that help my cause?" Haven asked, ready to cry.

She heard Brody sigh and knew he was running his hand over his head, thinking.

"I can't make any promises, but I'll ask the coach. Just don't get your hopes up." Brody held the phone away from his head when Haven squealed. "And you better tell me exactly how I'll be posing and what I'll be wearing."

Haven gave him the basic ideas for the photo shoot and what she knew about the planned attire.

"Sit tight. I'll call you back as soon as I get an answer from the coach," Brody said, disconnecting the call.

Haven tried to go back to working on her report, but couldn't concentrate. She tidied her already neat desk, filed a stack of papers she would normally have left for Jordan, and reviewed her appointments for the rest of the week.

Glancing at her watch, sure an hour or more had passed, she realized it had only been about ten minutes.

When the phone rang, she raced across her office and snatched it up so fast she almost dropped it.

"Haven Haggarty's office," she said in a voice left breathy from her rush to answer the phone.

"We'll don't you sound all sexy. You sure I didn't call the wrong number?" Brody teased. "What's going on over there I need to know about?"

"Brody! What did the coach say?" Haven asked, impatient to know the coach's response.

"Well, hello to you, too," Brody said, prolonging Haven's agony.

"Hello, Brody. I'm sorry." She took a calming breath. "Can you bail me out or not?"

"I can. But I won't be able to make it until this afternoon. I'm at practice now and we've got a lunch thing. I should be able to be there around three. Will that work?" Brody asked.

"That's perfect. You're my hero," Haven said, gratitude and relief evident in her voice.

"I thought I was already your hero." Brody tried to sound hurt although he was inordinately pleased she called him her hero. The relief in Haven's voice made him glad he'd talked the coach into letting him do the photo shoot, although he wasn't so sure he wanted to pretend to be a plumber.

"You are. Every single day, and I love you," Haven said. "I'll see you at three and make you dinner tonight."

"It's a date, doll. See you later," Brody said, disconnecting the call

Haven jumped to her feet as she hung up the phone and hurried to Mr. Young's office. He was on the phone but motioned for her to come in and take a seat. She did, trying not to listen to his one-sided conversation. It was easy to tell he was talking to his wife. When he rolled his eyes at something Mrs. Young said, Haven tried not to grin.

Wrapping up the call, he hung up and looked at Haven with a hopeful expression.

"I assume by the spark in your eye and spring in your step you found me a model," Mr. Young said, giving her a hopeful glance.

"I did, sir. But he can't be here until three."

"That's fine. I don't care when he gets here as long as it's before five today."

"Great. Do you want me to let Adam know?"

"If you don't mind, I'd appreciate it," Mr. Young said, picking up his phone to make a call as he smiled at Haven. "Great job, once again, Haven."

"Thanks, sir," Haven said, walking out of his office and down the hall to the photo studio. Absorbed in his work, taking photos of a plate of fries, Adam didn't notice Haven's approach until she stood beside him.

"You get all the fun projects," Haven said, pointing to the fries as Adam took a couple shots.

"Yeah, right," Adam said, grinning at Haven. "To what do I owe the pleasure of your visit today?"

"Mr. Young asked me to let you know a substitute model for the plumber campaign will be here at three," Haven said, staring at the fries. They looked gross with whatever substance Adam sprayed on them to make them look a steamy golden brown in the photo.

"Great. Is this model going to be hard to work with? I can't say I'm sorry the original model ended up sick. The last time that dude was here he was a nightmare," Adam said, taking a few more shots of the fries while Haven watched.

"He should be easy to handle. I'll personally make sure he behaves," Haven said, turning to leave.

"Is this model a friend of yours?" Adam asked, suddenly interested in who was coming.

"As a matter of fact, he is."

"He wouldn't, by chance, be the beefy boyfriend Jordan's been raving about?"

"Beefy? Nice. I'll have to tell him what the girls in the office are saying about him," Haven said with a grin as she left Adam and his fries.

Back in her office, Haven focused on her work and was surprised when she looked at the clock to see it was almost three.

Hurrying to the restroom, she touched up her makeup, fixed her hair, and brushed her teeth. Satisfied she looked refreshed, she returned to her office to find Brody sitting at a chair in front of her desk, waiting for her.

"Hi, Brody," she said, dropping her cosmetic bag in a desk drawer before kissing his cheek.

"Hey, doll," he said, wrapping his arm around her waist and pulling her down on his lap. He kissed her before she could tell him she shouldn't be sitting on his lap and definitely shouldn't be kissing him.

At a clearing throat, she looked up to see Mr. Young standing in her doorway, wearing a huge smile.

Heat flamed into her cheeks as she hastened to her feet, tugging on her suit jacket and skirt to straighten them. "Mr. Young, this is Brody Jackson. He's the one who'll be modeling for us today."

Brody stood and stepped across the room to take Mr. Young's outstretched hand.

"Nice to meet you, young man. I've heard a lot about you playing with the team this year. Sounds like you're destined for big things," Mr. Young said, pleased to meet the man who finally caught Haven's attention. He could see why the tall, athletic football player would turn her head.

Although he knew he shouldn't be, he was glad the original model was sick. Haven's young man would be the perfect model for his client's campaign. In addition to his fit physique, he had a face that was absolutely unforgettable.

"Shall we get started?" Mr. Young asked, motioning for Brody and Haven to step into the hall. "I'll take Brody to change if you want to let Adam know he's here."

"Yes, sir," Haven said, leaving Brody with Mr. Young as she walked to the photo studio.

"Adam, the model's here. Mr. Young took him to wardrobe, but they should be ready in a few minutes."

"Thanks, Haven. Can you help me set up the screen?" Adam asked, motioning across the studio.

"Sure," Haven said, helping Adam put up a big blank background with smooth fabric that extended across the floor. He would Photoshop in a kitchen or bathroom after taking the photos.

She was helping Adam stretch the fabric so there weren't any wrinkles when Mr. Young walked in with Brody. Haven's jaw dropped open and she quickly snapped it shut.

If the plumbing company's objective was to find a model who could sell their services, Brody was the man for the job.

Dressed in a pair of dark blue bib overalls with the company logo on the front pocket, Haven didn't think it mattered what he was selling, women would buy it.

Since he wasn't wearing a shirt under the overalls, the straps crossing his broad shoulders accented the muscles in his neck and arms as well as along his chest. A tool belt fastened low around his hips drew Haven's gaze down so she forced it back up again.

As tan, fit, and devastatingly handsome as Brody appeared, she had no doubt the client would be pleased with the photos Adam was about to take.

"You might want to stop gawking at him," Adam whispered as he walked by Haven to shake hands with Brody.

Exchanging introductions, Adam positioned Brody in front of the screen and had him stand in a variety of poses. Haven's favorite was of Brody appearing to lean back with one arm across his chest holding a pipe wrench, showcasing his biceps, while the other hand rested on the handle of a plunger in his tool belt.

Since women made up the majority of people who called the plumbing company, Haven knew this campaign would be successful. There was no way it could be anything else once advertisements started appearing with Brody as the model.

With the barest hint of a smile on his face, Brody stood wherever Adam asked without a word of complaint.

They were almost done when Haven took a step closer to Adam to see what Brody looked like in the camera. She lifted her gaze and caught his. The smile on his face then was genuine, along with the fire in his dark eyes.

Adam almost yelled in his excitement at capturing the raw emotion in a photo.

"That's it. We're done," Adam said, knowing nothing else would compare to that particular photo.

"That wasn't so bad, was it?" Mr. Young asked, shaking Brody's hand.

"No, sir," Brody said, feeling exposed and a little vulnerable. He hoped Haven never asked him to pose again. He didn't like the idea of thousands of people seeing him holding a pipe wrench or a plunger, of all things.

"If you stop by the receptionist desk on your way out, I'll have a check ready for you," Mr. Young said, starting toward the door.

"No, sir. The only way the coach agreed to this was if I did it without compensation. The plumbing company is one of our sponsors, so we're just saying it's a sponsorship bonus for them."

"I wouldn't feel right not paying you, Brody," Mr. Young said, shaking his head.

"Can you donate what you would have paid me to a charity? Something for kids?" Brody suggested.

"I can do that," Mr. Young said, liking Haven's young man. Smiling at her, he gave her a wink as he walked out the door.

"If you want to go change, I'll wait here for you," Haven said, knowing Adam would show her the photos he took.

"I'll be right back," Brody said, leaving the studio.

"Did you get anything good?" Haven asked, stepping beside Adam.

"You bet I did. He's a perfect model and the best part is he didn't bring a bucketload of attitude along for the ride."

"Yeah. He's pretty great," Haven said, looking at the photos as Adam scrolled through them. When he got to the last one, Haven grabbed his hand. "Stop!"

Adam knew she'd love the last photo. "You want me to get you a copy of that one?"

"How'd you know?"

"I just had an idea you'd like that one," Adam said, smugly. It was plain to see the football player was head over heels in love with Haven and that she felt the same. Wanting to do something nice for the two of them, he asked Haven if she'd like him to take a photo of her and Brody together.

"Are you sure you've got time?" she asked, knowing Adam was on a deadline to process Brody's photos for the plumbing campaign.

"It will only take a minute," Adam said, leaving the screen in place and adding a few more lights.

When Brody returned, he walked over to where Haven waited. Adam made her remove her suit jacket and pull a few curls out of her bun to give her a softer look.

"I'm gonna snap a few shots of you two together, just for fun," Adam said, positioning Brody so he stood just behind Haven and had him wrap his arms around her waist. "Perfect! Don't move."

He had them pose in several different ways then Brody tickled Haven and she started to laugh, which brought a big smile to his face. Adam took photo after photo, grinning as he watched them interact with each other.

"Okay. I've got something to work with," Adam said, shaking Brody's hand. "It was great to meet you. If you ever want a career modeling, I'm sure we can help you out."

"Thanks, but I'll pass," Brody said, smiling as he took Haven's hand and started toward the door. "It was nice to meet you, Adam."

Walking to Haven's office, she found a note on her desk from Mr. Young telling her to leave early and thanking her for coming to the rescue with such a great model.

"It appears I'm done working for the day. Do you have plans?" Haven asked, turning off her computer and picking up her purse. Brody stepped into the hall as she locked her office door then followed as she went to tell Jordan she was leaving.

"My only plan for the rest of the day is hanging out with you," he said, wrapping an arm around her shoulders as he walked her to her car.

"Why don't I see about making you that dinner I promised?" Haven said, kissing Brody's cheek before she slid behind the wheel of her car.

"I'm right behind you," Brody said, shutting her door and walking to his truck.

Two hours later, he sat on Haven's couch, rubbing his full stomach. Not only had she made him dinner, he was surprised to find she'd already made him a chocolate cream pie. Indulging in two slices, he knew he'd eaten more than he should.

"Want to walk off your meal?" she asked, smiling as she sat beside him.

"I'm too stuffed to move. If you try to force me, you might have to roll me down the sidewalk." Brody shifted so his head rested on Haven's lap while his feet hung over the end of the couch.

"Poor Brody. Gluttony has a price, doesn't it?" she teased, poking a finger into his tight stomach.

"Don't do that, doll," he said, taking her hand in his then kissing her fingers. "It could have disastrous results."

"I guess I'll just sit here and rub your head while you look pathetic," she said, brushing his thick, dark hair off his forehead. She worked both hands through the hair on the sides of his head then massaged his neck.

The feel of her cool, gentle fingers rubbing away his tension made Brody so relaxed and comfortable he drifted off to sleep.

When he opened his eyes, the room was dark. A nightlight plugged in near the bathroom provided the only illumination and silence filled the apartment.

Looking around, Haven was noticeably absent. He glanced in the kitchen and didn't see her. The bathroom door was open, so he stuck his head in her bedroom and found her asleep in bed. A glance at the clock on the nightstand showed it was after eleven.

Brody realized he'd been sleeping for more than four hours. He wondered why Haven didn't try to wake him. Then again, she probably had.

For whatever reason, being with her made him so content and at ease, he could fall into a deep sleep that eluded him the rest of the time. Since meeting Haven, he'd gone to sleep several times on her couch.

Studying her in the light filtering in from the nightlight in the hall, he took in the tumble of uncontrollable curls spread across her pillow beneath her. Her cheeks appeared so smooth, like porcelain, in the muted light. Her slightly parted lips looked so soft, Brody couldn't stop from bending over and kissing them lightly.

"Brody," she whispered, then reached up and put a hand to his cheek, touching it lovingly. "I'm so glad you're here."

He didn't say anything, not sure if she was asleep, awake, or somewhere in between.

She rolled onto her side, tugging on his hand. "You promised you'd hold me close, Brody. Won't you please hold me right now?"

Wondering if she was trying to kill him as he glanced down at her creamy shoulder and the thin strap of her silky gown running across it, he knew holding her at this particular moment was a very bad idea.

Her insistent tugging along with her pleas had him kicking off his shoes and sliding down beside her. He stayed outside the covers, but slid one arm beneath her shoulders and wrapped the other around her waist, pulling her against him.

Breathing in the soft fragrance of her hair, he kissed her shoulder. "I love you, Haven, for now and always," he whispered.

"I know. I love you, too." She snuggled closer against him.

He felt his eyes drift shut and before he could force himself to get up and leave, he joined her in slumber.

The sound of someone gasping and the feel of something jerking in his arms brought Brody wide awake.

"My gosh, Brody. What are you doing?" Haven asked, wide-eyed as she scooted across the bed, away from him, clutching the sheet beneath her chin.

"Sleeping," he mumbled, rubbing his eyes, trying to recall what happened the previous evening. He remembered falling asleep on Haven's couch and waking up to find her asleep. He realized he'd fallen asleep holding her when he only planned to stay for a few minutes, until he was sure she'd gone back to sleep.

"I meant in my bed," she said, absently brushing a hand over her hair.

"You asked me to hold you, so I did. I guess I fell asleep. That's all that happened. I didn't plan to stay all night."

"I should say not," Haven struggled to decide if the whole thing was funny or terrible. When the corners of her mouth lifted in a smile, she let out a giggle.

"Mrs. Humphrey will burn up the phone line calling to tell Mom about your truck still being here if she sees it."

"It's only five," Brody said, rolling onto his back and stretching.

Haven started to reach out to rub his shoulder, then decided better of it.

"I asked you to hold me?" She often talked to Brody in her dreams, asking him to hold her or kiss her, and in her dreams, he always complied. She must have thought the real Brody was just part of her dream when he came in her room to tell her good night.

"You did," he said, thinking he felt well rested even though he'd slept in his clothes, with Haven in his arms.

Or maybe he slept so well because he'd spent the night holding her close.

"I'm sorry. I didn't mean…"

"Don't say anything, Haven. It's fine. I didn't mind," he said, giving her a wicked grin as he got off the bed and stood looking down at her. "If I hurry, I might make it out of here without anyone seeing me leave. That way, you won't have to explain to your mom why I was here."

"Want to run with me this morning?" Haven asked, thinking since Brody was already awake, he might like to go with her.

"Why not? I'm not going to get any more sleep now." Brody bent to kiss Haven's cheek. She looked like a temptress with her hair mussed and the strap of her gown sliding off her shoulder. Before he did or said something he shouldn't, he backed toward the door. "I'll go home and change. Why don't you meet me at the park in twenty minutes?"

"I'll be there." Haven nodded her head while she pulled the sheet higher beneath her chin. "And thanks, Brody."

"For what?" he asked, turning to look at her as he stood in her bedroom doorway.

"For being you."

"Thanks for coming up with this idea, Miss Haggarty. I appreciate it," the coach said, shaking Haven's hand.

Brody took Haven's suggestion of the team providing a football camp for local high school kids to the coach. The team scheduled it for the last weekend in May. It was their second bye week, so they put their time not playing in a game to good use with a project that definitely generated community goodwill.

The coach contacted Haven to thank her and invited her to visit the all-day camp. She'd arrived an hour ago and sat watching Brody and his teammates work with several young men.

When Brody saw her sitting in the stands, he ran over and kissed her cheek then insisted on introducing her to the coach. He left her talking to him, returning to help the kids.

Brody was in his element with the teen boys. He seemed not only to relate to the kids, but also had them looking up to him as a leader and mentor.

It was easy for Haven to see why he chose to major in education. She was sure he would excel as a teacher and coach. If he ever left football, at least he had something to fall back on that would bring him joy.

"He's a natural with the kids," the coach said, pointing to Brody as he worked with two boys in particular. "Of all the players, he's the one that seems the most interested in events that help youth."

"I suppose that's why he has a teaching degree," Haven said, admiring the way Brody interacted with the kids. He had a group of them laughing while they followed his direction.

"Yeah, I guess so," the coach said, thanking Haven again then turning to speak with one of the sponsors attending the event.

Haven turned to go back to her seat but the team's sales director stopped her, giving her his card and asking her to call if she came up with any other ideas, since the football camp was such a success.

She assured him she would, then went back to watch the boys play for a while before leaving to meet Allie for lunch.

Arriving at the restaurant, she saw Allie wave at her from a booth and quickly joined her.

"So how is the kid camp going?" Allie asked, knowing Haven spent part of her morning watching Brody with the boys.

"It was awesome. You should see the players with the kids. Most of them looked like they were having a great time," Haven said, smiling as the waitress approached their table. Placing their orders, Haven smiled when Allie returned to the topic of the camp.

"So was Brody helping?" Allie asked.

"Of course. He loves kids and had them eating out of his hand."

Allie could hear the pride in Haven's voice as she spoke. Grinning, she nodded her head. "Isn't it hard to throw the ball if he's got a bunch of teenage boys slobbering on his hand?"

"You know what I mean, you dork," Haven said, tossing the paper from her straw at Allie.

They talked about family, plans for the coming week, and their jobs. Finishing their lunch, the two girls were trying to decide if they wanted to go shopping or to see a new art exhibit when Haven's cell phone rang.

"Hi, Brody," she said, wondering why he was calling. She knew he had a few more hours to go before the camp ended.

"Hey, Haven, it's Marcus. I'm on Brody's phone."

"Oh, hello, Marcus. What's up?" Haven asked, thinking it odd Marcus would call her, especially from Brody's phone.

"Brody had a little, um... mishap, this afternoon and several of us rode together today. I was wondering if you could come get Brody and take him home," Marcus said. Haven could hear a rumbling noise in the background that sounded like a disgruntled male voice speaking. Brody's deep, gravelly voice, if she wasn't mistaken.

"Sure. I'll be there as quick as I can," Haven said, ending the call.

"What's wrong?" Allie asked as Haven threw some money on the table to pay her part of the bill along with a tip and got to her feet. Allie tossed down some cash and followed Haven out the door.

"Marcus indicated Brody got hurt and needs a ride home. I'm going to get him. Maybe we can catch the art exhibit one day this coming week," Haven said, opening her car door and sliding behind the wheel.

"Sure, Haven. Whenever. I'm sorry about Brody. Hope it's nothing serious," Allie said, waving as Haven shut the car door and left the parking lot.

Arriving back at the football camp, Haven hurried her steps to where the boys and players practiced. Looking around, she spied the coach. He waved her over and told her where she could locate Brody and Marcus.

Following his direction, she found the two men sitting just outside the locker room. Brody held an ice pack on his knee, scowling, while Marcus wore a broad grin.

"Hi, Haven. Thanks for coming to his rescue," Marcus said, giving her a hug before helping Brody to his feet. "Where are you parked? I'll help get him to your car."

"I'll drive up to the door," she said and hustled outside to bring her car around to the side exit while Marcus and Brody slowly worked their way to the door. She got there as the two men stepped outside.

Opening the passenger door, Marcus steadied Brody until he could slide in, then handed Haven his ice pack.

"He just needs to stay off it and keep ice on it today," Marcus said, giving Haven a thumbs-up sign for luck before he rushed back inside.

"What happened?" Haven asked, driving toward his apartment.

"I was doing some drills with a group of kids and one of them hit my knee just right," Brody said, clenching his jaw from both pain and frustration. He was mad about his knee, mad that it hurt, and mad at Marcus for calling Haven. He didn't like her to see him in this kind of shape.

"I'm so sorry," Haven said, remembering the steps at Brody's apartment. There was no way he could navigate them in his current condition. Changing direction, she soon pulled into her own parking space and hurried to open her door. Coming back to the car, Brody limped toward her, holding the ice bag in one hand while the other formed a tight fist.

"What are we doing here? I thought you were taking me home." He worked his way inside, slumped onto the couch, and stretched his leg out in front of him.

"I was, but I remembered you live on the second floor and didn't want you to have to go up the steps." Haven cleared off her coffee table, pushed it closer to the couch, then disappeared into her bedroom. She returned with her arms full of pillows and placed them on the coffee table, gently lifting Brody's leg until it rested on the pile.

Taking the ice pack from him, she settled it on his knee then went to the kitchen and poured him a glass of sweetened tea, setting it on the side table at the end of the couch.

"What can I do for you, Brody?" she asked, feeling somewhat helpless as she stood looking at him.

"Nothing," he said, in the tight, closed tone she knew meant he was pushing her away and retreating into himself. "Unless you'll take me home."

"Why? So you can kick me out and wallow in your misery alone?"

Brody looked up at her and tried to fight back the smirk on his face. "Something like that."

"Sorry, no can do." Haven sat down beside him, taking his big hand between both of hers. "You're stuck with me for the rest of the day."

"Lucky me." Although his tone was derisive, the way he relaxed his head against the back of the couch and turned his dark gaze her direction let her know he wanted to be with her.

"I think now would be a great time for you to tell me about this knee injury that keeps bothering you," Haven said, pointing to his leg. She'd tried asking Brody several times about it but he either ignored her questions or said he didn't want to talk about it.

"I suppose you won't quit asking until I do." He lifted an eyebrow at her then took a drink of the tea before setting the glass back on the table beside him.

"Nope. I'll hound you relentlessly until you break beneath my iron will," Haven said, trying to sound menacing and making Brody chuckle.

"You win, you dastardly villain," Brody said, scooting down a little until he rested more comfortably against the couch cushions. He lifted his arm and Haven cuddled against his side with her head resting on his chest.

He'd never admit it if anyone asked him, but sitting with her like that, with her head pressed against his heart, was one of his favorite things in the world.

"I think you already know I went to college on a football scholarship," he said. When Haven looked up at him and nodded, he continued. "I was a good player. A really good player. My sophomore year, I already had recruiters talking to me about the NFL. My junior year, I was cocky and confident, knowing I'd be playing pro ball before long. We were in the second to the last game of the season when I tore my ACL."

"What's that?" Haven asked.

"ACL is the anterior cruciate ligament. When the ligament is torn, you can lose stability in your knee, and it really messes things up," Brody said, rubbing his hand up and down Haven's back as he talked. "It was a bad injury and cost me my guaranteed ticket to play football in the NFL. After months in therapy, I barely played my senior year, still trying to rehabilitate my knee. I finally worked my way into an NFL training camp and made the team's practice squad. Then I screwed up big time."

"What happened?" Haven asked, trying to imagine what Brody could have done.

"I went out partying with a few of the guys, stayed out too late, and had too much to drink. The next day at practice, I could barely function and it just happened to be the day the team was making cuts. Between my knee injury and my lack of ability that day, I was out."

"That's why you don't drink, isn't it?" Haven asked, knowing when Brody went to the after-game parties, he always had the bartender give him iced tea.

"Yeah. I learned my lesson the hard way," he said, shifting his leg. The ice fell off and Haven picked it up, taking it to the kitchen and putting it in the freezer since it needed to refreeze.

Returning to Brody's side, she once again curled up next to him. "Then what happened?"

"After going home and moping for a while, Mom told me to either keep chasing my dream or find a new one. She said the one thing I couldn't do was sit around pouting for the rest of my life, so I worked at it until I got on with an arena football team. This is my third year playing. I spent two years on a team in Nebraska until I was picked up by this team."

"Do you wish you were still there? Closer to your mom?"

"I wish I was closer to Mom, just because I worry about her, but I'm not sorry I ended up here, Haven. One of the best things that ever happened to me was meeting you," Brody said, tipping up her chin so he could look into her blue eyes. Filled with love and acceptance and longing, Brody knew he'd never get tired of staring into their vivid depths.

"I love you," she whispered, stretching up and giving him a kiss that made him temporarily forget about football, injuries, and everything else except how right it felt to hold her in his arms.

"I love you, too," he said, rubbing his thumb across her cheek.

"What happens next, Brody?"

"I keep playing to the best of my ability and keep praying I get chosen for a training camp. From there, I'm confident I'll make it to the playing field," Brody said, knowing it sounded simple, but the process was so uncertain and difficult.

"For your sake, for the sake of your dreams, I hope it happens."

"Me, too. I've wanted this for so long, I don't know what I'd do if it doesn't happen."

As they both sat thinking about Brody's career, and his impending departure from the area, neither voiced their thoughts.

Instead, they watched a movie and pretended they'd always be able to spend time together.

## *Chapter Twenty-Two*

"This is super exciting," Allie said, sitting next to Haven as they watched the beginning of the football conference semifinals.

Ranked as the number one seed, Brody's team hosted the semifinal game. Depending on if they won, the championship could play out the following week on their home turf.

Haven's entire family came to the game to cheer Brody on to victory.

Hale sat beside her and they both leaned forward and waved to their parents who sat in a section on the other side of the arena along with Wes, Tammy, their two boys, Tom, and some of his friends.

"I guess we should have let Uncle John and Aunt Rachel sit with you," Allie said, waving at Haven's parents.

"Mom wanted to sit with the boys," Haven said, bumping Allie with her elbow. "Besides, I like sitting with you when you behave yourself."

"I'm always a well-behaved lady," Allie said, pointing her nose in the air, affecting a haughty demeanor.

Rick choked on his soda and almost snorted it on the people sitting in the row in front of them. Allie whacked him on the back with more force than was necessary.

"Find something amusing, babe?" she asked, glaring at him.

"Not at all, miss prim and proper lady," Rick said, making Haven and Hale both laugh.

"Oh, just be quiet," Allie said, turning away from Rick and focusing on the game.

Haven jumped to her feet and cheered when Brody caught a pass and ran it to the end zone for a touchdown. The crowd chanted the now familiar "Jump it up, Jackson! Jump it up!"

The game was close, but the home team pulled ahead to win. Haven was thrilled for Brody and his teammates.

After the game, as they sat in her kitchen eating ice cream and cookies, the excitement rolling off Brody was a palpable force. They'd spent a few minutes celebrating at the after-game gathering with his friends then escaped to the quiet of Haven's apartment.

Wound up from both excitement and good news he'd received earlier that day, he was full of energy.

"Want to go for a walk?" he asked as they finished the ice cream and put their dirty dishes in the dishwasher.

"Now? It's almost midnight," Haven said, glancing at the clock.

"Why not? It's warm out and I'm too pumped to sit still," Brody said, grinning at Haven. "If you're tired, I'll leave so you can go to bed."

"No. I'll go with you," she said, stuffing her cell phone in her pocket and grabbing her keys as Brody opened the door.

Strolling toward the park, the moon was bright and the air warm, even for a June night. Instead of heading toward the swings when they reached the park, Brody walked toward a display of flowers. He'd noticed the roses were in full bloom when he ran past the park yesterday.

The heady scent of the blossoms floated in the night air and Haven breathed deeply.

"Mmm. There's nothing like the scent of roses on a summer breeze," she said, looking up at Brody.

He could see her perfectly in the light of the moon and thought of some old poem his mom used to recite about love and June nights. He suddenly understood what it meant. The author had to be outside near a fragrant flower garden with a beautiful girl in the moonlight when he composed it.

Haven squeezed his hand and smiled at him. "Congrats, again, about winning tonight. One more game and you guys could be the champions. It's so exciting!"

"Yeah, it is exciting," Brody said. Winning the game wasn't nearly as exciting as the thought of kissing Haven in the moonlight, though.

Recalling how she looked the night he'd accidently fallen asleep in her bed, he imagined seeing her with moon beams spilling across crisp sheets, highlighting her soft skin and tempting curves. Shaking his head to dislodge the tantalizing vision, he picked her up and swung her around.

Tipping back her head, she laughed and wrapped her hands around his neck.

"You're going to make me dizzy, football man," Haven finally said in a breathy voice, causing Brody to swallow hard. Desire for the sweet, lovely girl in his arms swept over him with a brutal force.

Setting her on a bench, he sat down beside her and took her hand in his, twining their fingers together.

"I have something I need to tell you," he said, looking at her with a serious expression on his face.

"Okay." Haven felt her smile slip away as she waited for Brody to say what was on his mind.

"I just found out I'll be going to an NFL training camp. I…um… I'll be leaving the first of July."

"Congratulations! I'm so happy for you. It's what you've been working toward, but Brody, that's just a few days after the championship game. I… I hoped…" Haven's voice caught and tears burned the back of her eyes.

"I know, baby. I know," Brody said, pulling Haven into the comfort of his arms. "I don't want to leave you. I can't ask you to go with me, and we both knew this is what would happen."

"Why can't you ask me to go with you?" Haven asked, pulling back and looking at Brody.

"Because I don't know where I'll be six months from now. They could cut me loose and I'd end up with nothing. I have no certainty or stability in my career at this moment in time," Brody said, shaking his head. "The last thing I would do is uproot you from your family, your friends, and a good, solid career to chase my dreams. I won't ask it of you, Haven. It's crazy to even think about it."

"Crazy or not, I'd go with you," Haven said, surprising them both.

Brody stared at her for a while before he kissed her temple and sighed. He rubbed his hands up and down the length of her back, trying to offer comfort. "It makes me happy to know you'd go wherever I go, Haven, but I can't do that to you. Maybe when I know for sure where I'll be, we could talk about something more permanent. For now, though, I won't ask and I can't stay."

"I'm going to miss you so much, Brody. I know we both said no strings attached, but I didn't plan on loving you so much," Haven said, burying her face against his neck.

Brody felt the moisture of her tears and it made his heart ache with acute pain.

"Come on, doll. No crying for me. Let's just be glad we have a little more time together," Brody said, brushing away her tears with his thumb. "I think we should pack as much fun as we can into the next ten days. What do you say?"

Haven couldn't speak around the lump in her throat, but nodded her head, realizing Brody was right. She'd have plenty of time for crying once he was gone. Now was the time to make as many memories with him as she could.

"Is that a yes?" he asked, tilting her chin up so he could look in her eyes. She gave him a lopsided smile that tugged at his heart. He kissed each damp cheek then traced her dimples with his finger.

"Yes," she whispered.

"Well, let's start right now," he said, standing up and bowing to her. "May I have this dance, Miss Haggarty?"

"What are you talking about?" she asked, brushing the last of her tears from her cheeks.

"Don't all girls want to dance in a rose garden in the moonlight? Did you lose your Romance 101 guidebook?" Brody teased, holding out his hand to Haven.

"I guess I did. Maybe you'll have to coach me." Gazing at him with her heart in her eyes, she tipped her head and smiled. "For a man who told me when we first met he thought romance was stupid, you're really quite talented at being romantic."

"So it seems," Brody said, finding the song on his phone that often made him think of Haven, a song about building dreams with a pretty girl. He set it to play then took her in his arms and danced among the roses with moonbeams swaying around them.

"What's on the agenda for tonight?" Allie asked as she sat on the corner of Haven's desk at her office.

"What agenda?" Haven asked, absently typing the last line of a report she needed to finish before she left for the afternoon.

After mentioning to Mr. Young about Brody only being in town for another week, he told her to take off all the time she needed. She'd left work early every afternoon. Brody was busy with practice and finalizing arrangements for when he left town during the day, but the evenings they spent together, making memories.

"Oh, give it up," Allie said, spinning Haven's chair around to face her. "I know you and Brody are trying to cram as much fun and excitement into the time you have left as humanly possible. Aunt Rachel told my mom that the two of you went on a picnic in the mountains, you took a boat ride on the river, and she mentioned something about paintball."

"Yeah, that was Brody's idea. Hale and Abby went, too. It was a lot of fun," Haven said, turning her chair back around and quickly finishing her report, then sending it to Mr. Young before she turned off her computer and cleared the top of her desk. Picking up her purse, she nudged Allie off her desk and the two of them walked outside. "Brody's never been fishing, so I'm taking him out to our fishing hole."

"Cool. Can Rick and I come?" Allie asked, standing next to Haven's car.

"Why do you want to come? You hate to fish."

"I know, but Rick likes it and I think it would be nice to hang out with you both. We haven't got to spend much time with Brody since you usually keep him all to yourself."

"Fine," Haven said, knowing Allie would show up whether she invited her or not. "But you two have to drive your own vehicle, leave when I tell you, and bring the bait for the fish."

"Yes, boss," Allie said, winking at Haven before she walked to her car and left.

Haven stopped at the grocery store on her way home. By the time Brody walked in her door, she had a cooler filled with sandwiches, chips, cookies, and fruit, along with bottles of soda pop and water.

Hefting the loaded cooler, Brody pretended it was too heavy to carry. "Are you feeding an army?"

"No, but Allie and Rick are joining us," Haven said, picking up the fishing poles and box of tackle Hale dropped off for her to use, along with a stack of towels and an old quilt she took on picnics.

"Will Allie scare the fish away?" Brody asked, setting the cooler in the back of his pickup and taking the fishing poles and tackle box from Haven, placing them in the back as well. He helped her in his truck and shut the door.

She set the towels and blanket on the seat between them as Brody backed out of the parking space and pulled out on the street.

"Just tell me where we're going," he said, following Haven's directions that took them out toward her parents' home, although they turned before they reached the house and went down a dirt road toward a creek.

Parking beneath an old cottonwood tree, Haven spread the blanket on a flat grassy spot while Brody got out the cooler and set it on one corner of the blanket. Opening the cooler, she removed a bottle of soda and handed it to Brody before closing the lid.

"Don't you want one? It's hot out here," he said. The air was sticky and humid as they sat close to the water. The area Haven chose was secluded from view by the trees, though. Despite the heat, green grass, blue sky, and an earthy smell provided the perfect summer backdrop.

Haven grabbed the bottle from his hand and took a drink. "I'll share yours for now."

Brody grinned at her as she handed the bottle back. He screwed on the cap then set the bottle on top of the cooler before stretching out on the blanket and tugging Haven down beside him.

"I bet I can find more shapes in the clouds than you," she said, pointing to the clear blue sky.

"If you can find any clouds, more power to you," he said, turning his head so his lips were almost brushing hers. "Personally, I can think of more entertaining things to do."

"Like what?" Haven asked, softly trailing her fingers along the inside of his arm, making a familiar tingle race all the way from his fingers to his toes.

"Like this," he said, rolling onto his side and pulling her against his chest, kissing her deeply.

"Don't let us interrupt," Allie said, looking down at them.

"Oh!" Haven said, disentangling herself from Brody as they both got to their feet. "Couldn't you honk or something?"

"I could, but where's the fun in that?" Allie grinned at Brody. He smiled and stepped forward to shake Rick's hand.

"We forgot the bait, so you're either going to have to dig for worms or forget about fishing for tonight."

"I don't need to fish," Brody said. His main interest in going fishing with Haven was to get her somewhere secluded and have her to himself for a few hours. Now he was going to have to share her with Allie and Rick. Not that he minded too much. Haven's cousin was always entertaining.

"How about we eat?" Haven suggested, pointing to the cooler. Getting out the food, the four of them talked and ate, laughing at funny stories Allie and Haven told on each other.

"Are you planning on swimming, Haven?" Allie asked, eyeing her cousin. They used to spend as much time swimming in the fishing hole as they ever did fishing.

Haven shrugged her shoulders. "Maybe," she said. Allie knew then that Haven wore a swimming suit beneath her T-shirt and shorts because she would have said no if she didn't want to get wet.

"You swim in that?" Brody asked, pointing his thumb over his shoulder at the water. "I figured it was only a foot or so deep."

"It is close to the bank but out in the middle there's a spot that's several feet deep," Haven said. "You wouldn't want to dive in it, but you can definitely get wet out there."

"I'm game if you guys are," Rick said, helping put away the remnants of their meal and looking around.

"You're always game, babe," Allie said, patting his arm. "Come on. I'll introduce you to the wonders of a redneck swimming pool."

"Is that what you call this?" Brody asked, grinning at Haven.

"Among other things," she said, brushing crumbs off her shirt as she stood.

Studying Brody, she thought he looked good in his T-shirt and cargo shorts. When he pulled the shirt over his head and stood like a bronzed statue with the sun backlighting him, Haven decided there were no words to describe how astoundingly handsome or virile he looked.

Allie's mouth dropped open. She dug in her pocket, pulling out a twenty-dollar bill and slipping it in Haven's hand.

Haven looked at it and turned a curious glance to her cousin. "What's this for?"

"I told you I'd pay money to see him without his shirt on and that really is worth twenty bucks," Allie whispered so only Haven could hear.

Grinning, Haven tucked the money in her pocket and watched as Rick and Brody kicked off their shoes and walked to the edge of the water. The two girls discarded their shirts, shorts, and shoes before going to join the guys. Allie wore a revealing bikini while Haven was in a much more modest tankini.

"Dare you to go first, Al," Haven said, giving her cousin a nudge toward the water.

"Dare accepted," Allie said, grabbing Rick's hand and tugging him in the creek. They took several steps then dropped into the water.

Rick came up still wearing a look of surprise, but Allie was laughing.

"That's priceless," Brody said, grinning as he and Haven walked into the water. Taking the last step into the hole, they both were prepared for the drop. The four of them splashed and played in the water for a while until they decided the air was starting to cool off. Allie said Rick needed to get home because he had to get up early for work, so they grabbed two of the towels Haven left on the truck seat and took off.

Brody and Haven stayed in the water a few minutes longer, splashing each other. Brody went beneath the surface and when he came back up, it was right in front of her. He pulled Haven against him and kissed her, holding her close.

His lips were cool against hers at first, warming with the intensity of their passion.

Haven wrapped her arms and legs around Brody, holding to him tightly as their kiss deepened. The next thing she knew, Brody was laying her down on the blanket, never breaking the contact of their lips.

Cool and hot all at the same time, Haven knew she'd never felt like this before in her life and fleetingly wondered if she ever would again.

Brody's lips worked their magic down her jaw, along her neck, trailing his searing touch across her shoulder and along the edge of her swimming suit.

Haven sighed and dug her fingers into his hair, pulling his head back up to her lips, kissing him with an urgency that couldn't be denied.

She felt Brody's long fingers tracing a tantalizing pattern across her side and shuddered when he lifted the hem of her top just enough to expose her stomach and press a kiss there.

"Brody," she moaned, grasping his head between her hands, forcing him to look at her.

"I'm sorry, Haven. I didn't mean to… I wasn't planning on…" he said, rolling onto his back and breathing hard, tightening his hold on his self-control.

"I think we better call this a night." Haven said, knowing she would never forgot the look of wanting in Brody's eyes, the feel of his skin against hers in the water, the untamed desire he stirred in her.

"I think you're right," he said, getting up and putting on his shoes. He walked to the truck and retrieved two towels, handing one to Haven then using the other to dry off his hair and chest. There wasn't much he could do about wet shorts and he didn't really care.

Haven dried and dressed, wrapping the towel around her head to squeeze some of the moisture from her hair before tossing it in the pickup.

Gathering up the blanket and cooler, Brody helped her in the truck, watching as her golden tresses curled in an uncontrollable mass around her head.

He'd seen Haven in many different ways, wearing a variety of outfits and hairstyles, but those wild, wet curls along with her damp T-shirt and cut-off shorts had to be at the top of his list of favorites.

Thinking about never seeing her again made a sharp, severe pain wrench his heart so hard, he had no idea how he was going to make himself leave without her.

## *Chapter Twenty-Three*

"You have the sweetest daughter in the world," Angelina Jackson said as she gave Rachel a hug and shook John's hand at the airport.

As a surprise for Brody, Haven contacted his mom to see if she'd like to watch him play in the championship game.

Angelina assured her she would, but still sounded hesitant about making the trip, explaining she held a strong fear of flying and didn't like to stay alone in a hotel. When Haven said Angelina could stay with her or her parents, the woman finally agreed.

Now, Haven and her parents stood in the airport, giving Brody's mom a warm welcome.

Observing the tall, slender woman, Haven could see where Brody got his dark hair and eyes. He also had his mother's lips and smile.

Thinking about how surprised Brody would be to see his mother, she clasped her hands beneath her chin to keep from rubbing them together in excitement.

"And you're sure he doesn't know I'm coming?"

"Absolutely and positively sure," Haven said, looping her arm around Angelina's.

Haven knew Brody was going to stay a few days with his mom on his way to the training camp, but this would be a special way to end his season with the local arena football team.

The four of them went out to dinner at a restaurant near the arena. Haven enjoyed the opportunity to visit with Brody's mother and get to know the woman who raised such a fine man all alone.

"So my boy tells me you raise potatoes?" Angelina said, talking to John and Rachel about farming. From what she shared with them, she apparently grew up on a farm where her family raised corn and soybeans. When her father died, her mother sold the farm to pay off outstanding loans, and moved into a small house in town.

After Angelina's husband left her, she moved in with her mother, who passed away when Brody was only three. Inheriting the little house, it was the home where Brody grew up. She still lived there, although it sounded like he had made many improvements in the last few years.

As John paid the bill for dinner, Haven walked with Angelina outside into the warm summer evening.

"I'm so glad you called me, Haven. Brody thinks the world of you and now I can see for myself why. You're just a sweetie and I know Brody's heart is safe in your hands," Angelina said, giving Haven a hug around her shoulders.

"Brody did tell you he's leaving here and I'm staying, didn't he?" Haven asked, wondering if he'd forgotten to tell his mom about his plans.

"Oh, I know what he said," Angelina said, then gave Haven a knowing smile. Abruptly, she changed the subject, inquiring about Haven's job. As they discussed what she did, Angelina asked if she could see the photos from Brody's modeling stint for the plumbing campaign.

Haven took out her phone and scrolled through the photos until she opened the file with the photos Adam sent to her.

"Oh, my goodness. I can't believe that is my boy," Angelina said. "He looks like he belongs on one of those show posters in Vegas."

Haven laughed, taking back her phone when Angelina held it out to her. "We make quite a pair then, because I always told Mom my name sounded like something a showgirl in Vegas would use."

"I think it's a lovely name," Angelina said, turning to Rachel with a warm smile.

"See, Haven, I'm not the only one who likes it," Rachel said, given her daughter a satisfied look.

Arriving at the arena, Haven asked Angelina if she wanted to see Brody before the game or wait until after.

"I don't want to disrupt his routine," Angelina said, walking beside her as they entered the arena. "Let's just wait."

"If you're sure," Haven said, leading the way to the seats. John and Rachel sat down and Angelina took the next seat while Haven hurried to the concession area to get everyone a drink.

When she returned, Hale was sitting in her seat, chatting with Brody's mother.

"This is really cool, baby girl," Hale said, patting her shoulder as he stood, stepping into the aisle so Haven could take her seat. "Nice to meet you, Mrs. Jackson."

"You, too, Hale," Angelina said, turning to Rachel. "What a nice family you have. No wonder Brody is so taken with you all."

"We're pretty fond of him ourselves," Rachel said, patting Angelina's hand.

The two mothers visited before the game started. Brody came out to warm up, but kept his back turned to their section of seats. Haven knew he often did that because he said looking at her scrambled his thoughts and messed with his focus.

The game soon started and Angelina clasped Haven's hand as Brody jumped up and caught a ball. He gained a few yards before he fell under a tackle.

Near the end of the second quarter, a tackle brought him down on the twenty-yard line where he'd first met Haven's gaze.

Haven couldn't keep from smiling as he looked her direction and waved a hand. When he realized who sat beside her, shock spread over his face.

Torn between playing and rushing into the stands to see his mom, Brody lifted a hand in greeting and played out the remaining seconds of the quarter. As soon as it ended, he jumped over the dasher boards and ran up the steps as he took off his helmet. Dropping it on Haven's lap, he crushed his mom in a big bear hug and kissed her cheeks.

"Mom! What are you doing here?" he asked, his joy at seeing her evident on his face.

"Haven thought I should see your last game this season, especially since you're playing for the championship," Angelina said, sitting back down, but holding on to Brody's hand.

He turned his gaze to Haven and lifted an eyebrow. "You did all this, doll? You got my mom to get on a plane and fly out here just to watch me play?"

"Well, it seemed like the right thing to do." Haven toyed with his helmet instead of making eye contact.

Brody kissed her on the mouth, not caring that their parents and a good portion of the crowd were watching. "You really are the best, Haven. Love you."

He grabbed his helmet and disappeared out of the stands, joining the rest of the team in the locker room.

Infused with excitement to have his mom and his girl sitting side by side in the stands cheering him on, Brody had an amazing second half in the game, catching numerous passes and making two touchdowns.

Their team won and the cheers that went up at the end of the game were deafening.

Brody waved to his mom and Haven before going to the locker room to shower and change.

"I can't believe your mom is here. How did Haven manage that?" Marcus asked as they dressed.

"I don't know, but it was awesome to look up and see her sitting in the stands. Haven is something else."

"How is it you think you can just get in your truck and leave her next week?" Marcus asked, knowing how closely tied Brody's heart was to Haven's. Much closer than his friend was willing to admit.

"Because I have to and we both knew all along that was the plan," Brody said, combing his hair.

"But that was before you two fell in love. Do you really think you're going to find what you've got with Haven again? It's not something that happens multiple times, man. It's a once-in-a-lifetime kind of thing."

"Like the opportunity to play for an NFL team?" Brody asked defensively. "I know what I have with Haven is special, but I can't ask her to go with me. I don't know if this is going to work out and if it doesn't she'd be stuck with an unemployed bum who can't make his dreams a reality. She needs her family and she has a great career here. Why would I ask her to leave all that?"

"You wouldn't. But any man with sense in his head and not rocks would," Marcus said with a teasing smile.

Brody grinned and gave him a playful punch to the arm on his way out the door. He found his mom and Haven waiting near the door with John and Rachel.

"Your mom is going to stay with us, Brody. You're welcome to come out tonight and stay, too, if you want," Rachel offered.

"I don't want to impose. Besides, if I know Mom, by the time you get her home, she'll be ready for bed."

"You know me well, son," Angelina said, patting his cheek.

"Do you all want to go out for some dessert before you go back to the farm?" Haven asked, looking around the group.

"I could go for a piece of pie," John said, looking at Rachel and then Angelina. At the nod of heads, they agreed to meet at a restaurant just down the street. Angelina went with Brody and Haven rode with her parents.

After visiting for an hour over coffee and pie, Angelina couldn't stifle her yawn and Rachel patted her back.

"You poor thing. You're probably exhausted after traveling all this way today. Let's get you home."

"That sounds great," Angelina said, following John and Rachel out the door. Brody paid the bill and took Haven's hand in his as they walked outside.

He hugged his mom again and kissed her cheek, telling her he'd see her in the morning, then he helped Haven in his pickup and took her home.

"I can't believe you brought my mom out here," Brody said as they stood in her living room. "It meant so much to have you both at this final game. Thank you, Haven. Thank you for making it happen."

"You're so welcome," Haven said, giving Brody a warm hug. "For the record, I love your mom. She's great."

"She is pretty awesome. Kind of like another strong, determined, wonderful woman I know."

"Really? Do I get to meet her, too?" Haven asked with mock seriousness.

"No, you nut." Brody tickled her sides until they collapsed on the couch together.

"I'm going to miss this, Brody, to miss you. I had no idea I could…"

Brody silenced Haven with a kiss.

"Don't tonight, Haven. Please. Let's just enjoy this moment and not think about later."

Haven nodded her head and pulled his lips back to hers.

An hour later, Brody stood at her door giving her one last, long kiss good night.

"See you in the morning?"

"You bet," Brody said, walking backward to his pickup. He'd done it so many times, he didn't even trip over the parking curb.

They spent the next day at John and Rachel's, hanging out with Angelina. She would leave the following morning to go home. Brody would see her again the next weekend when he drove through Kansas on his way to the training camp.

Sitting around a big bonfire away from the house with all of Haven's family surrounding them, Brody felt at home, at peace.

Angelina patted his hand and smiled at him, as if she could read his thoughts.

Later, she walked him out to his pickup while Haven gathered the dishes she'd contributed to lunch and dinner.

"Thanks for coming in the morning to take me to the airport, baby. Haven said I could stay with her, but it's nice to be out here in the country, you know?

"Yeah, Mom. I do know. I'll be here in plenty of time to get you to the airport. I'm so glad you came. It meant a lot to me," Brody said, giving his mom a hug.

"I'm glad Haven talked me into coming. She's one of a kind, son."

"I know, Mom, but don't give me a lecture about making choices and leaving her behind. Marcus has worn out my ears trying to tell me I'm about to mess up the best thing that's ever happened to me."

"Well, as long as you're aware of what you're doing," Angelina said, giving Brody a look that he'd hated as a boy and disliked even more now that he was a man.

"Mom, she and I both knew whatever was between us was for the football season. That's it."

"Right, baby. You just keep telling yourself that and I'm sure you'll both be fine," Angelina said, turning and giving Haven a hug before walking in the house.

"Ready to go?" Haven asked in an overly cheerful tone as Brody helped her into his truck.

"Yep," he said. Their drive back to town was quiet, both lost in their thoughts.

Brody carried Haven's things inside and hugged her so tightly, she felt like she couldn't breathe. Or maybe it was the thought of him walking out of her life for good that choked the air from her lungs.

"I love you, doll. Good night," he said, kissing her cheek and rushing out the door.

## *Chapter Twenty-Four*

"Are you sure you got everything?" Haven asked, looking at the suitcases and few boxes in Brody's pickup. The cooler she'd packed with his favorite treats sat on the front seat of his pickup, within easy reach if he needed something while he was driving.

"Yep. It's all loaded," he said, leaning against the door of his pickup. He told Haven he wanted to say goodbye at her apartment, so he'd driven over that morning before she had to go to work. He wanted to get an early start on the road.

She offered to fix him breakfast, but he wasn't hungry. She wasn't either.

They sat for hours the previous evening, holding each other until Brody couldn't take any more and told her he needed to go home. If he'd stayed any longer, he would have given up his dreams of football and made new ones with Haven.

Now, looking at the unshed tears in her bright eyes and the hair surrounding her head like a golden halo, he wished he'd held her all night long.

"Brody, I know you don't want me to talk about it, but I want you to know the past few months with you have been the best of my entire life. No matter what the future brings, I'll always, always be grateful to have had this time with you," Haven said, stepping into his arms and resting her head on his chest one last time.

Inhaling his scent, she knew it would be with her for the rest of her life. His scent, his laugh, the sound of his gravelly voice, the smirk he gave her when he thought no one else was looking. They were all etched deeply in her heart and in her memories.

"Haven, if things were different, if I was different, I would never say goodbye. I'd stay here forever with you. But I've got to do this. Fail or succeed, I have to try."

Brody was certain if he looked down, he'd see his heart lying in pieces at his feet. It hurt so badly, it was almost more than he could stand. If Haven's heart ached with even half the ferocity as his, he didn't know how she managed the pain.

"I know, Brody, and I won't be the thing that held you back. You're going to go and be great and become one of the best NFL wide receivers the world has ever seen," Haven said, working up a smile, even if it didn't reach all the way to her eyes. "Just remember me once in a while."

"I won't ever forget you, doll. Ever," Brody said, knowing what he said was true. Haven had somehow become a vital part of him in such a short time.

"I almost forgot," Haven said, hurrying back in her apartment and returning with a wrapped package.

"What's this? It isn't my birthday," Brody teased, trying to make her smile.

She shook her head and pressed the gift into his hands.

"I want you to open it when you get where you're going. The first time you feel lonely, you open it up and know that wherever you are, there's someone right here that loves you."

Brody set the gift on the seat and turned back to the girl who was going to be his undoing if he didn't leave soon.

"Haven," Brody said in a husky voice, raspy with emotion. "I love you so much. Please don't ever forget that."

"I won't," she said as the first tears trickled down her cheeks.

Not bothering to wipe them away, Brody kissed her with all the longing, all the love, all the passion he possessed for her. Holding her as close as he could, he memorized every detail about how she looked with morning sunlight dancing through her hair while her soft fragrance surrounded him.

"I love you, Haven Clarice Haggarty, and always will." Brody climbed in his truck and shut the door before he decided to throw away his career and his dreams for the girl who had so thoroughly captured his heart.

Haven couldn't stop crying.

She somehow managed to keep herself together the first few hours at the office but then she bumped into Adam in the hall. The folder he carried fell to the floor, scattering pages around them. She started to help him pick up the papers only to see Brody's photo in the plumber ads.

Mumbling an apology, she ran to her office and shut the door as tears streamed down her face.

Thinking she'd be fine in a few minutes, she couldn't get the tears to stop. Jordan tried to calm her down, making things worse. Finally, Mr. Young called Hale.

He took her home and walked her to the bedroom where she curled up around a pillow and continued sobbing until she fell asleep.

She awoke to find her mother sitting with her and started crying all over again.

For two days, she couldn't do anything but cry and miss Brody.

He hadn't called or texted and she knew he wouldn't. It was their agreement that it would be easier if they just cut things off and went their separate ways.

Only now, as she sat on her couch staring mindlessly out the window, she'd give anything to hear his gravelly voice on her phone.

A knock on her door forced her to get up and answer it. Her mom stood on the step with a bouquet of bright flowers and a pint of her favorite ice cream.

"Are you feeling better today, sweetie?" Rachel asked. The fact that Haven was up, showered, and dressed seemed like a marked improvement over the past few days.

"I guess, Mom," Haven said, setting the flowers on her coffee table and putting the ice cream in the freezer. "Thanks for the flowers and ice cream."

"You're welcome, sweetheart. Your dad and I are worried about you. Why don't you come out and stay at the farm through the weekend?"

"No, Mom. I just need some time alone to think." Haven said, not wanting to have to pretend she was anything but miserable. If she went to the farm, her family would hover around her even more than they were now, trying to cheer her up, and she'd be forced to act like they succeeded.

"You've had plenty of time to think," Rachel said, exasperated. "Honestly, Haven, what did you believe was going to happen? You and Brody both knew he'd be leaving and you both knew going into the relationship it was going to end sooner rather than later. Did you have some fantasy that he'd give up all his dreams, his career, to stay here with you?"

"No," Haven said, grabbing a tissue as she started to cry again. "I knew he'd leave. I just didn't realize he'd take my heart with him. And the only fantasy I had was that he'd let me go along."

"Oh, honey," Rachel said, folding Haven into a mother's tender embrace. "Give it some time and it will quit hurting so badly. I promise."

"How are you holding up, bro?" Marcus asked.

Brody had been in his new apartment for a week and couldn't find enough things to do to occupy his time or mind. He'd started to call Haven multiple times, but stopped himself before he did.

He missed her with every breath he took, and wondered, more than once, if a body could die from a broken heart. He was quite certain he didn't even have a heart anymore. Convinced Haven still held it in her hands, he realized he'd never, ever love anyone the way he loved her.

In a moment of desperation, he called Marcus, just to hear a friendly voice.

"I'm fine, man. How are you?" Brody asked, trying to keep the conversation light.

"I'm good. I start a new job tomorrow but it looks like I'll be back playing arena football for our team next season. I'm pretty excited about it."

"That's great, Marcus," Brody said, pleased for his friend. "How are your folks?"

"They're good. My baby sister just got engaged so she's planning to have her wedding before football season begins."

"Tell her congrats for me," Brody said. Thoughts of engagements and weddings brought visions of Haven to mind and made Brody's chest ache with renewed force.

"Are you sure you're doing okay? You don't sound like yourself," Marcus said, concerned. He could hear something in his friend's tone that gave him reason to worry.

"I'm fine, but thanks for caring," Brody said, not wanting to get into a discussion of how much he missed Haven and how he should have listened to Marcus and found a way to make things work with her.

"What did the doc say about your knee? Didn't you have an appointment yesterday to get it checked by the team physician?"

"Yeah. He basically told me what I already know. That my knee could hold up for ten more years of playing or ten minutes, but at some point it's going to give out and possibly leave me crippled."

"And why is it that you think doing this is a good idea?" Marcus asked, aware of the fact that football had been Brody's life for as long as he'd known him.

"I have to try, Marcus. You know I have to try."

"Yeah, man, I guess I do. You take care and be sure to keep in touch, though," Marcus said.

"I will." Brody searched for the right words to say what was on his mind. "Look, Marcus, I just want you to know how much I appreciate your friendship and support. You've always been there for me and it means a lot."

"You're welcome. Now hang up before you make us as mushy as a couple of schoolgirls."

"Bye, man."

Brody went for a long run, lifted weights, and tried to keep his mind occupied, but his thoughts circled back to Haven repeatedly.

Forcing himself to eat dinner and watch television, his gaze continued to go to the package Haven sent with him.

Unable to stand it any longer, he slowly removed the wrapping paper and sat looking at a plain white box for a while before lifting the lid and finding a digital photo frame inside.

A note from Haven, redolent of her soft fragrance, sat in the bottom of the box.

Lifting it out, Brody breathed deeply, closing his eyes to savor her scent.

Opening the plain card, it read:

*Always remember there's someone who loves you...*

Switching on the frame, Brody watched images of the two of them together scroll across the screen. There was the photo her mom took at Easter, the studio photos from Adam, pictures Allie and Hale had snapped with their phones. There was even a photo of them riding horses out at the farm.

The last photo, though, was one Brody hadn't seen before.

One that made every square inch of his body ache with longing for Haven.

It was obvious Allie had done her hair and makeup, because she looked like she was a model ready for the runway. She wore the dress that had almost driven him beyond the point of no return, along with a pair of sexy heels. Leaning against a marble counter she didn't look anything like his sweet, innocent Haven. This woman had a fiery look in her eye and a smile on her face that was pure invitation.

Brody wondered when or where she'd had the photo taken, then thought he recognized the backdrop from one of the plumber shots Adam took of him. It made sense that Adam would do the photo for her.

Although seeing her in that dress definitely made his temperature rise, Brody scrolled back to the photo of her in jeans and boots, laughing as he carried her piggyback across her parents' front yard. That was the one that made a lump he couldn't swallow form in his throat and filled him with regret so strong it made him want to get in his truck and drive straight back to the woman he loved.

## *Chapter Twenty-Five*

"How can autumn be here already?" Allie asked as she and Haven looked through a rack of sweaters at the mall. Although it was still warm, the October air carried a crisp tartness that signaled fall had arrived.

"I don't know, but here it is. Have you noticed how the trees are already turning color?"

"I did. We should totally plan a bonfire at the farm. It's so fun this time of year."

"Sure," Haven said, turning away, not wanting her cousin to see the look on her face at the mention of a bonfire. All she could think of was the bonfire at the farm when Angelina and Brody were there.

Haven hadn't heard a word from Brody since he left. She wondered if he liked the digital frame she'd sent with him or if he ever looked at the photos and missed her.

It took every ounce of courage she had to let Allie do her hair and makeup and ask Adam to take photos in the dress that Brody had liked so well. She did it because she hoped it would make him smile and remember her.

A month ago, a package arrived in the mail from Brody's mother. Inside, she found copies of photos of him as a little boy, wearing his first football uniform, and more photos and newspaper clippings from his teen and college years.

She sat on her living room floor and cried for three hours after seeing the photos.

Now that Brody played for an NFL team, she watched every televised game his team played, hoping to catch a glimpse of him. She kept track of his stats and combed through Hale's sports magazines searching for the mention of his name.

Her mother continued to assure her the pain in her heart would eventually lessen and then stop. So far, it hurt every bit as much as it did the day Brody left. She'd just learned to hide it better.

No longer the innocent girl with stars in her eyes, Haven was now a woman. One who experienced real heartbreak, true love, and devastating loss.

If someone were to offer her the option of taking away the pain by turning back time and erasing the months spent with Brody, Haven knew she'd go through it all again.

Some of the most wonderful moments she'd ever known were spent with him and she wouldn't trade those memories for anything.

What she needed to do, however, was get on with her life.

Taking a deep breath, she turned back to Allie and looped their arms together. "Hey, want to go see that new comedy movie that's out? I heard it's really funny."

Hours later, after she and Allie had dinner with Rick and they'd gone to a corn maze, Haven returned to her quiet apartment and got ready for bed. Sitting up, against her pillows, she couldn't stop herself from scrolling through photos of Brody on her phone. Kissing the tip of her finger, she touched the screen and wished him good night before turning out her light and sliding down in the covers. As she had every night since he left, she cried herself to sleep.

Dreaming Brody was with her again, holding her close, Haven breathed deeply, inhaling his masculine scent.

Rolling onto her side, she felt his arms around her and snuggled back against him.

The dream was as vivid as life when she felt his lips, warm and moist, press a kiss to her cheek then trail down her neck.

"Haven," his gravelly, deep voice whispered in her ear. "Haven, I love you, doll. Please wake up."

Opening her eyes, Haven prepared for the feel of Brody to linger for a moment before disappearing, as it always did.

Tonight, though, she still felt his warmth. His scent was strong and she could still hear him saying her name in the husky voice she loved.

Tears spilled down her cheeks and she started to roll over, bumping into something solid.

Blinking her eyes, she reached up and turned on the light beside her bed, holding back a scream at finding a pair of dark eyes staring back at her.

Realizing Brody was there beside her, not just in her dreams, she threw her arms around his neck and held him close.

"Brody! What are you doing here?" she asked, lavishing his face with kisses. "How long can you stay? How did you get in?"

"Slow down," Brody said, wrapping his arms around her, holding her close. She rested her head against his chest and listened to the steady beat of his heart. "I still have the key you gave me, so I hope you don't mind me using it."

"Not at all," she said, giving him a little squeeze. "Why are you here?"

"If you'll have me, Haven, I'm back to stay," Brody said, gazing into her sweet face. The face that haunted his every waking moment and invaded all his dreams.

He thought once he left town, cut off all ties to Haven, he'd be able to get her out of his system and focus on his football career.

Instead, with each passing day he missed her more and more. He missed her laughter and her smile, her innocent way of looking at life, her innate goodness, and sense of humor.

He sniffed the note she sent with the digital frame so many times, the paper was nearly worn out and he'd sat every night watching her face scroll across the screen of the frame, remembering every moment he enjoyed in her company.

The months spent with Haven were the happiest he'd ever known. She not only filled his heart with joy, she gave him a place to belong. In every sense of the word, she was his safe haven against the world.

A few weeks ago, he reached the point when he realized his love for her was greater than his love for football.

Finally accepting the fact that his knee could end his football career at any moment, he came to the conclusion there were other things he could do to make a living, but there was only one girl who could make his life complete.

Officially retiring from football, Brody packed his belongings and drove to his mom's place, telling her of his plans before driving straight through to see Haven.

Now he was here, where he belonged, right by her side.

"What are you saying, Brody? What do you mean you're back to stay?" Haven asked, trying to process Brody's words.

"I mean I'm done with football. I'm so sorry, Haven. I should never have left. It took me all this time to finally admit the only thing I can't live without is you," Brody said, framing her face with his hands and looking into her eyes. "My place is right here, beside you, holding you in my arms."

"But that's your dream, Brody. You can't just give it up. Not for me," Haven said, concerned that Brody would come to resent her if he quit football now.

"I didn't give it up for you. I gave it up for me. You see, I discovered there is something more important than football. Something I want far more than to play in the Super Bowl. Something that I love more than anything in this world, and that is you," Brody said, taking her lips with his in a possessive, passionate kiss that cleared Haven's mind of any thoughts except Brody.

"I can't let you do it," Haven whispered, clinging to him. "You have to go back. You have to try."

"I'm done trying, Haven. My knee isn't going to cooperate and I might as well face that fact now," Brody said, gently rubbing his hands up and down her back. "I've been in touch with a couple of the schools in the area. One of the coaches is retiring at the beginning of the year and they offered me a job. If you think you could spend your life with a high school football coach, I'm asking you to marry me. Will you?"

Haven sat up and stared at him, at the face of her beloved, and felt a smile tip the corners of her mouth. "Of course I'll marry you!"

Brody kissed her dimples then her mouth again as he held her close. "I love you so much, Haven. More than you could possibly know."

"I love you, too, Brody. Ever since that day you looked up at me from the twenty-yard line."

###

## *Banana Cake*

If you love bananas, this rich, flavorful cake is one you'll really enjoy. Captain Cavedweller likes it best when I add walnuts, but it's good without nuts, too!

**Banana Cake**

1 1/2 cups very ripe bananas, mashed
2 tsp. lemon juice
3 cups all-purpose flour
1 1/2 tsp. baking soda
1/4 tsp. salt
3/4 cup butter, softened
2 cups sugar
1 tsp. vanilla
3 eggs
1 tsp. banana flavoring
1 1/2 cups milk
1 cup walnuts, chopped (optional)

Preheat oven to 275 (yes, 275) degrees. Grease and flour a 9 x 13 baking pan.

Mash bananas with lemon juice and set aside. Mix flour, baking soda, and salt together and set aside. In an extra-large mixing bowl (really, you need a big one), cream butter and sugar until light and fluffy. Beat in eggs one at a time then blend in vanilla and banana flavoring.

Stir in flour mixture, a little at a time, alternating with the milk. Stir in bananas (and walnuts, if you are adding them) then pour into pan and bake for one hour or until a toothpick inserted in the center comes out clean.

Remove from oven and place directly into the freezer for about an hour (heightens the moisture of the cake). Remove from freezer and frost with cream cheese frosting.

Serve or refrigerate.

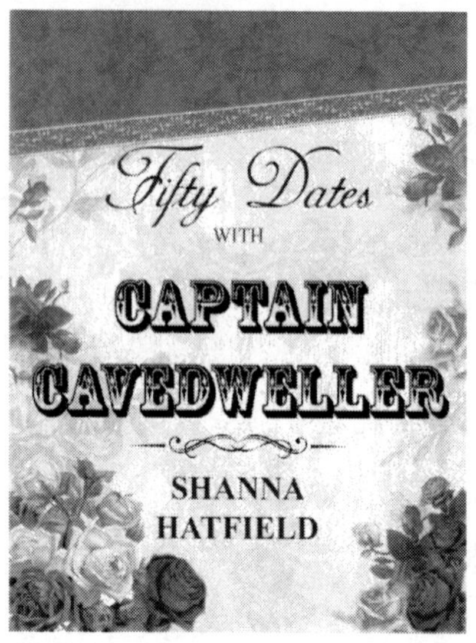


***Fifty Dates with Captain Cavedweller*** - Waking up one day to discover they'd gone from perpetual honeymooners to a boring, predictable couple, author Shanna Hatfield and her beloved husband, Captain Cavedweller, set out on a year-long adventure to add a little zing to their relationship.

This G-rated journey through fifty of their dates provides an insightful, humorous look at the effort they made to infuse their marriage with laughter, love, and gratitude while reconnecting on a new, heart-felt level.

*Enjoy an excerpt ...*

## *Date Eight*

For Captain Cavedweller's birthday, I purchased season tickets to the local arena football games.

Today's big date, hosted by CC, was to drive to the city to pick up the tickets, visit a couple of car dealerships since we are hunting for a new vehicle, and then take me out to dinner.

Picking up the tickets was fun. The team members were so gracious and friendly.

Car shopping also went pretty well considering we never saw a single car salesman. Generally, we can barely get out of the car before one swoops in, trying to talk us into vehicles you would never see me ride in dead or alive.

Apparently, the forty-mile-an-hour winds coupled with the frigid temperatures kept them inside the showroom where it was warm and toasty, and their hair wouldn't turn into a wild mess, resembling a "do" specially created by Medusa's own hairdresser.

Once I started crying and begging for mercy from the wind (okay, I wasn't crying, but the wind *did* make my eyes water. A lot.), CC offered to take me to the mall. I was not in a shopping mood at this point, much more interested in sitting down somewhere warm.

Since it was late afternoon and we still hadn't eaten lunch, we went to a barbecue restaurant. That would be my first pick once in a blue moon. However, the moon was not blue that day…

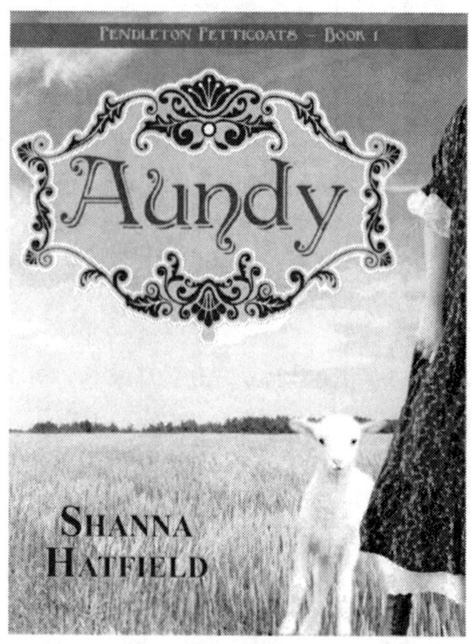


***Aundy (Pendleton Petticoats Book 1)*** - Desperate to better her situation, Aundy Thorsen agrees to leave behind her life in Chicago to fulfill a farmer's request for a mail-order bride in Pendleton, Oregon. A tragic accident leaves her a widow soon after becoming a wife. Aundy takes on the challenge of learning how to manage a farm, even if it means her stubborn determination to succeed upsets a few of the neighbors.

Born and raised on the family ranch, Garrett Nash loves life in the bustling community of Pendleton in 1899. When his neighbor passes away and leaves behind a plucky widow, Garrett takes on the role of her protector and guardian. His admiration for her tenacious spirit soon turns to something more. Can he convince the strong-willed Aundy to give love another try?

*Turn the page for an exciting excerpt…*

by

SHANNA HATFIELD

## *Chapter One*

*1899 - Eastern Oregon*

*Clickety-clak. Clickety-clak. Clickety-clak.*

The sound of the train kept perfect time with the runaway thumping of Aundy Thorsen's heart. Each beat took her closer to an uncertain future and she wondered what madness possessed her to make such a rash decision.

"Miss?" A gentle tap on her arm brought Aundy's head around to look into the friendly face of the porter. "We'll be in Pendleton soon. Just wanted to let you know."

"Thank you," Aundy said with a smile, nodding her head. The porter had been helpful and kind, answering her many questions and making two rowdy salesmen intent on bothering her relocate to a different car.

Aware that she was asking for trouble traveling alone, Aundy figured since she was taller than most men were and not considered beautiful, she wouldn't have any problems. The persistent salesmen had been the only nuisance in an otherwise uneventful, yet exciting, adventure.

Growing up in Chicago and never traveling any farther than her aunt's stuffy home across town, Aundy was trying to commit to memory each detail of her trip that would soon end in Pendleton, Oregon. Once there, she would marry Erik Erikson, a farmer who wanted a Norwegian bride.

Her betrothed, a man she had yet to meet, offered to travel to Chicago so they could wed there then make the trip to Pendleton as a married couple. Aundy assured him she would be safe traveling alone, although she was grateful for the train ticket and generous sum of money Erik provided to cover her expenses. So far, Aundy had saved most of it, used to living frugally and making each penny count.

Wishing she'd purchased something to eat at their last stop, Aundy willed the rumbling in her empty stomach to discontinue.

Suddenly overcome with the thought that she would soon meet Erik and become his bride, nerves replaced her hunger.

Although Erik wasn't the first man to whom Aundy found herself engaged, he would be the first she married. Not willing to think about the tender glances and gentle smile of the playful boy who had stolen her heart, she instead focused her thoughts on the man awaiting her.

Six months ago, desperate to make a change in her life, Aundy happened upon a discarded newspaper and her gaze fastened on an advertisement for a mail-order bride.

Normally one to ignore such nonsense, Aundy felt drawn to the words written by a farmer named Erik Erikson.

*Wanted: someone to build a future with and share in my dreams. Seeking loving wife with a tender heart and gentle spirit. Must be willing to move to Pendleton, Oregon. Hard worker, good cook, and Norwegian ancestry preferred. Farm experience helpful, but not essential. Outward beauty irrelevant. Please reply to...*

Ripping the advertisement out of the paper, Aundy carried it around in her pocket for two weeks, debating if she should send a reply. Finally, she sat down and composed a letter to Erik Erikson of Pendleton, Oregon, a place she'd never heard of and certainly never dreamed of seeing.

She wrote about her life, how she worked as a seamstress at a factory during the day and helped cook and clean mornings and evenings at a boardinghouse in exchange for her room and board. Explaining she was not beautiful by any sense of the word, Aundy assured him she had a strong constitution, a tender heart, and a willingness to work hard. She described how her parents, both from good Norwegian families, made certain their three children knew their heritage.

Not expecting to receive a reply, Aundy was surprised when a letter arrived from Erik. He invited her to correspond with him so they could get to know one another better before making any decisions or commitments.

Writing back and forth, sharing bits of information about themselves, their families, their hopes and dreams, Aundy came to like the man in the letters penned with a confident hand.

Erik wrote he wasn't much to look at, had never been married, and owned a farm that was on its way to being prosperous. He shared how lonely his life seemed and how much he wanted to have a family of his own.

When he wrote saying he was in love with her letters and asked if she'd agree to marry him, she quickly replied with her consent, changing the course of her future. Bespoken for the second time in her young life, Aundy had no delusions about being in love with Erik. Love died along with her beloved Gunther two years ago.

Admiration and respect, though, she had plenty to share with Erik along with her devotion and loyalty. She would be a caring, gentle wife even if she never brought herself to love the man.

Bringing her thoughts back to the present, Aundy took a shallow breath in the train car filled with the mingling odors of stale food, unwashed bodies, and smells from the washroom.

Longing to press her warm cheek against the cool glass of the window, she instead tipped her head so she could see over the sleeping woman who sat beside her to admire the brilliant blue sky, pine-dotted mountains, and snow-covered ground outside.

As the train chugged through the rugged Blue Mountains of Eastern Oregon, Aundy realized she was farther away from her familiar world than she ever thought she would be.

Tamping down her fears of what waited ahead, she pulled a handkerchief out of her reticule, carefully rubbing at her cheeks, hoping to remove the worst of the soot. Convinced grime covered every inch of her being from the long trip, she couldn`t wait to soak in a hot tub, wash her hair, and dress in clean clothes.

She sincerely hoped Erik wouldn't mind if she did that before she put on her wedding dress and exchanged nuptials with him. He didn't mention his plans for when they would wed, but Aundy assumed Erik would want to do so as soon as possible. If that was true, she supposed she would most likely be Mrs. Erik Erikson before the end of the day.

That thought made her grip the reticule so tightly in her hands, she felt her fingers cramp through her soft leather gloves.

Feeling a light touch on her arm, Aundy turned her gaze to the woman who sat beside her for much of the trip.

"You`ll be fine, dearie," Mrs. Jordan said, her kind brown eyes twinkling. "Nothing to worry about at all."

"Thank you, ma'am," Aundy said, patting the hand resting on her arm and offering the woman a small smile. With mile upon mile of nothing to do but stare out the window and watch the incredible changing scenery, Aundy and Mrs. Jordan discussed their individual reasons for being on the train. The elderly woman was going to Portland to live with her only daughter.

"You're a smart, brave girl," Mrs. Jordan said, sitting straighter in her seat. "I have no doubt that everything will work out for the best. If it doesn't, you know how to get in touch with me."

"I'm sure all will be well," Aundy said, grateful she did have a slip of paper in her possession with Mrs. Jordan's new address. If she ever needed somewhere to go, at least she had one friend on this side of the Rocky Mountains.

Shaking herself mentally, Aundy adjusted her hat, brushed at her skirt and the sleeves of her jacket then moistened her lips. Although Erik said looks didn't matter to him, she certainly hoped he wouldn't be terribly disappointed when he met her. Perhaps she shouldn't have refused when he asked for her photograph.

Afraid he would break off their commitment once he realized she was no beauty, she figured he would take her as she was or she'd be in an even bigger mess than the one she was leaving behind in Chicago.

If she looked anything like her younger sister, Ilsa, men would be falling all over themselves to do her bidding. Both blond with blue eyes, the similarities ended there.

Gathering her belongings along with her courage, Aundy glanced out the window to see the snow had disappeared leaving random patches covering the ground as the train made its way out of the mountains. The sky was so blue and wide open, she wondered, briefly, if she could see up to heaven. Would her father and mother be looking down and giving their approval to what she was about to do? She prayed if Gunther could see her, he wasn't disappointed with her for marrying someone she would never love.

Trapping a sigh behind her lips, she brushed at her skirt one last time and sat back to wait as the train rumbled to a stop, willing her pounding heart to slow as well.

The porter finally announced their arrival and stood outside the car, helping the women disembark.

Giving Mrs. Jordan a quick hug, Aundy slipped on her coat, grabbed the Gladstone bag that had been her mother's, and stepped off the train into the bright sunshine and brisk February air.

"Best wishes, Ms. Thorsen," the porter said as he helped her down the steps.

"Thank you, sir," Aundy said, tipping her head at him before turning her attention to the platform where a sea of people churned back and forth. How was she ever going to find Erik?

Cowboys and farmers, businessmen and miners, Indians covered with colorful blankets, Chinese men wearing long braids and strange hats, and women dressed in everything from plain calico to ornately stitched dresses milled together, all blending into a mass of varied colors.

Taking as deep a breath as her corset allowed, Aundy wished, again, she had exchanged photographs with Erik when he asked. His description said he was tall, blond and plain. She'd basically written him the same portrayal of her own appearance.

Looking around, she counted four men who were several inches taller than the majority of the crowd. One had dark hair that fell down to his shoulders, one was an extremely handsome cowboy, one wore a nice suit, and the last one appeared to be a farmer in mud-splattered overalls who was not only dirty, but had a mean look about him. She certainly hoped he wasn't her intended.

When the man in the suit removed his hat, clutching it tightly in his big hands, his white-blond hair glistened in the mid-day sun. Flecks of mud on his boots and the hem of his pants didn't detract from his crisp shirt, handsome vest or well-made tie.

Studying him a moment, Aundy hoped he was the man she was about to wed. Despite his obvious nerves, he had a kind face, even if it was older than she anticipated. Erik never stated his age, never asked hers.

Considered a spinster at twenty-one, she guessed Erik's age closer to forty from the lines time and life had etched on his face.

Although not handsome, he had a gentleness about him that held Aundy's interest. If this was, in fact, her betrothed maybe she hadn't lost her mind after all.

Squaring her shoulders and straightening her spine, she marched up to the man as he continued to search the sea of faces around him.

"Mr. Erikson?" Aundy asked, stepping beside him. The surprised look on the man's face when he turned his attention her direction made her smile. "Erik Erikson?"

"Yes, I'm Erik Erikson," he said, studying Aundy cautiously. "May I assist you?"

"I certainly hope so," Aundy said, with a teasing smile. "You did say you needed a bride and asked me to marry you."

"Oh! Ms. Thorsen? Is it really you?" Erik asked, sandwiching Aundy's gloved fingers between his two work-roughened hands.

"It is, indeed."

"I had no idea... I didn't think..." Erik stuttered, trying to chase his thoughts back together. "You said you weren't comely and when I saw you get off the train, I thought you were much too lovely to be my bride. It's a disservice, Ms. Thorsen, calling yourself plain. You look like one of the Viking queens in the stories my mother used to read me at bedtime - tall, strong, and beautiful."

Erik's comments made her blush. No one had ever called her lovely or compared her to a Viking queen, although her father used to tell her she had the tenacity of her ancestors running through her veins.

Looping her hand around his arm, Erik took her bag and escorted her off the platform over to a wagon hitched to a hulking team of horses.

"Meet Hans and Henry," Erik said, setting her bag in the wagon then giving her a hand as she climbed up to the seat. "I would have brought the buggy, but I assumed you'd have luggage. If you wait here a moment, I'll get your trunks."

"Thank you," Aundy said, warily eyeing the horses. Growing up in the city in an apartment, she had no experience with animals. She told Erik from the beginning of their correspondence he'd have to teach her about his farm and livestock. Writing about his day-to-day activities, she gleaned information about his horses and Shorthorn cattle, as well as the pigs and chickens he raised.

Wanting to crane her neck and stare at everything she could see, Aundy instead glanced around inconspicuously, taking in a variety of interesting faces and places. Erik wrote the town was growing and was one of the largest cities in Oregon. Hoping she'd have time to explore her new home another day, she smiled to see Erik walking head and shoulders above much of the crowd.

Erik soon returned, easily carrying one of her trunks while two younger men struggled to carry her other trunks. He set them in the back of the wagon, tossed each man a coin with a nod of his head, and climbed up beside Aundy.

"I let the pastor know to expect us as soon as the train arrived," Erik said, turning the horses so they began lumbering down the street.

"The pastor?" Aundy asked, trying to keep from swiveling her head back and forth as Erik drove past stores and business establishments. There were so many interesting buildings and fascinating people.

"Pastor Whitting," Erik said, trying not to stare at Aundy. She was young, tall, and much prettier than he'd anticipated. Not that her looks mattered, but her smooth skin, dusted by a few freckles across her nose, golden hair, and sky blue eyes made him glad he'd placed an advertisement for a bride.

Although most of his friends thought he had lost use of his mental faculties, Erik was tired of being alone and didn't have time to find a wife or court a woman properly. He vowed to make it up to Aundy by spending the rest of his life showing her she was special to him. Falling in love with the girl in the letters she wrote, it was easy for him to see he'd love the woman beside him even more. "I thought we could get married, have lunch, and then head out to the farm. I wanted to have time to show you around the place before it gets dark."

"Oh," Aundy said, absorbing the information. It looked like her mother's wedding dress would stay firmly packed in the trunk and a bath would have to wait. Resigning herself to exchanging vows with Erik in her current state of disrepair, she smiled at him and put a hand on his arm. "That sounds fine."

"Good." Erik said, grinning at her in such a way he took on a boyish look as he turned the horses down a side street. Aundy could see the church ahead and tried to calm her nerves. The warmth of the sun beating down, despite it being February, forced her to remove her coat. Erik tucked it behind the seat, placing it on top of one of her trunks.

Stopping the horses close to the church steps, Erik walked around the wagon and reached up to Aundy. When she started to put her hand in his, he gently placed his hands to her waist and swung her around, setting her down on the bottom step.

The breath she was holding whooshed out of her and she looked at Erik with wide eyes. She'd never been handled so by a man and wasn't sure if she liked it or not. Part of her thought a repeat of the experience might be in order for her to make up her mind.

"Shall we?" Erik asked, offering her his arm as they went up the church steps.

Before she could fully grasp what was happening, she and Erik exchanged vows, he slid a plain gold band on her finger, and the pastor and his wife offered congratulations on their marriage. Walking back out into the bright afternoon sunshine, Aundy had to blink back her disbelief that she was finally a married woman.

"We can eat just around the corner, if you don't mind the walk," Erik said, gesturing toward the boardwalk that would take them back toward the heart of town.

Aundy nodded her head and felt Erik place a hand to the small of her back, urging her forward.

Taking a seat in a well-lit restaurant, they were soon enjoying a filling, savory meal. Several people approached their table, offering words of congratulations. Aundy smiled when a few of the women invited her to stop by for a visit sometime soon. It appeared that Erik was a well-liked member of the community and for that, Aundy was grateful. She'd never lived in a rural town before, but assumed getting along with your neighbors spoke well of a man's character.

Watching Erik finish his piece of pie, Aundy hoped this marriage would be a blessing to them both. She didn't know what had prompted her to act so boldly, writing to a stranger, but right at this moment she was glad she sent Erik that first letter.

"Well, Mrs. Erickson, are you ready to go home?" Erik asked as she took a last bite of cherry pie and wiped her lips on a linen napkin.

"I suppose so," Aundy said, realizing she was no longer Aundy Thorsen, but Erik's wife.

Leaving money for their lunch along with a tip on the table, Erik stood and put on his hat, offered Aundy his arm, and escorted her back to the wagon.

Expecting him to help her into the wagon, Aundy was surprised when Erik pulled her into his arms, right there in front of the church for any and all to see as they passed by.

"Thank you for coming, Aundy. For marrying me," Erik said, kissing her quickly on the lips. He seemed unable to stop himself from giving her a warm hug. "I promise to be a good husband to you."

Looking into his eyes and seeing the questions there, Aundy tamped down her unease at having a man who was still a stranger kiss her. She placed a hand to his cheek and patted it with a growing fondness. "I know you will be. And I'll do my very best to be a good wife to you."

"You could start by giving me a kiss," Erik teased, waggling a blond eyebrow at her.

Aundy smiled and kissed his cheek, grateful that Erik seemed to have a fun, playful side. "You'll have the town gossiping about me and I haven't even been here two hours."

"Everyone knows I came into Pendleton to marry you today and I can't see a thing wrong with a husband kissing his lovely new bride."

Blushing, Aundy accepted Erik's help into the wagon and sat down, pleased at his words.

Heading out of town, Aundy relaxed as the noise and activity of Pendleton fell behind them, and the rolling fields opened before them. Releasing a sigh, she gazed up at the sky and breathed in the fresh air.

"Anything you want to know? Any questions?" Erik asked, watching Aundy as she settled against the wagon seat.

"I don't think you ever told me how old you are," Aundy said, studying Erik's profile.

"I'll be thirty-nine next month," he said, turning to look at Aundy.

"And you've never been married?"

"Never. I got so busy building the farm after my parents died, I kept putting off finding someone to court. I woke up one day and realized if I wanted to have a wife and a family, I had better do something about it. So I placed the ad and you know the rest of the story."

"I guess I do," Aundy said, looking with interest at the fluffy clouds drifting across the azure sky overhead and the fields that surrounded both sides of the road. If the land had been flat, she was sure she could have seen for miles. Instead, the gently rolling hills provided their own unique perspective to the landscape. Unfamiliar with wide-open spaces and such clean air, Aundy breathed as deeply as she dared and soaked up the sunshine.

"How old are you?" Erik asked, breaking into her thoughts.

"Twenty-one, although people often mistake me for someone older," Aundy said, then let out a soft laugh at a memory. "Someone once asked if Ilsa, my sister, was my daughter. I didn't know whether to be insulted or pleased."

Erik chuckled. "Pleased, I would think. People can't help but see the way you carry yourself with confidence and strength. That's a good thing."

"It is?" Aundy asked, thinking she liked the sound of Erik's laugh. Although she'd only just met the man, it wasn't hard for her to imagine spending her future with him. Since stepping off the train, what she'd seen and experienced led her to believe Erik was gentle and mannerly. He might not be handsome or young, he might not make her heart pound or butterflies take flight in her stomach, but she thought he would treat her with respect and care. If they were fortunate, they might even come to love one another someday.

"Certainly, it is. I wouldn't want some flighty young thing, so wrapped up in herself that she wouldn't take proper care of a home or her husband. It's easy to see that you'll be a good wife, Aundy. You're a sensible girl and I appreciate that," Erik said, turning to look at his new bride with a teasing smile. "I also appreciate your fine figure, beautiful eyes, and that sweet smile."

Feeling her cheeks turn pink and grow hot at Erik's words, Aundy lifted her gaze across the fields, dotted with a few skiffs of melting snow.

She heard Erik chuckle again before she felt his fingers on her chin. He gently, but firmly, turned her to face him.

"I didn't mean to embarrass you, but I want you to know I think this marriage is going to work out just fine," Erik said, leaning over and pressing another quick kiss to her lips.

Aundy closed her eyes and waited to feel something, anything. Instead, Erik pulled back and she opened her eyes to see him studying the road ahead.

"Do you think… if it isn't… what I…" Aundy stammered, trying to figure out a way to ask if she could take a bath when they reached his farm.

"What is it? Go ahead, Aundy. Don't be afraid to ask me anything."

"May I please have a bath? I feel like I'm wearing dust from way back in Wyoming and half a train car of soot."

"Yes, you may," Erik said, bringing his gaze back to Aundy with an indulgent smile. "You can do that while I take care of the evening chores after I show you around the farm. How does that sound?"

"Wonderful," Aundy said, excited at the prospect of being clean. "As soon as I'm finished, I can fix the evening meal."

"No need. One of the neighbors said she'd have a basket waiting on the table for a cold supper so you wouldn't have to cook on your wedding day."

"How thoughtful," Aundy said, thinking Erik must have some good neighbors. "I'll have to thank her later for her kindness."

"It's Mrs. Nash. She and her husband and son live on the farm to the south of us. They're good folks. Ol' Marvin Tooley lives on the farm to the west but he's cantankerous on a good day, so stay away from him if you can."

Aundy nodded her head, wondering what made Mr. Tooley crotchety.

Passing a lane that turned off the road, Erik inclined his head that direction as the horses continued onward. "That's the Nash place. Been here for many years. Raise mostly cattle and wheat. Good folks and good friends as well as our closest neighbors."

Aundy again nodded her head and gazed up the lane, catching a view of the top of the barn over a rise in the road. Pole fences ran along a pasture down to the road and she could see dozens of cattle grazing lazily in the sun.

"Are those..." Aundy's question was cut off when a sharp crack resonated around them and the horses spooked, lunging forward as they began flying down the muddy road.

"Whoa, boys! Whoa!" Erik called, pulling back on the reins, frantic to get the team under control.

Aundy clung to the side and back of the seat, praying for the runaway horses to stop.

"Get down, Aundy," Erik yelled, motioning for her to climb beneath the wagon's seat. She followed his orders, wedging herself into the space, as she listened to the thundering of the horse's hooves and Erik's shouts for them to stop.

The wagon veered sideways then slid back before hitting the side of the ditch bank and flipping over, sliding in the mud.

Aundy's screams mingled with Erik's shouts before everything went black…

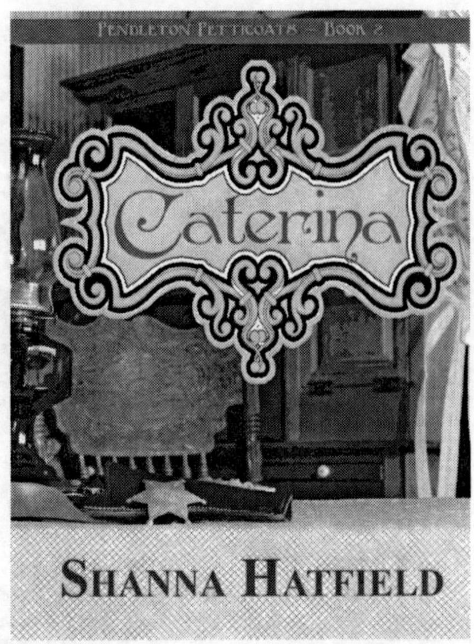


***Caterina (Pendleton Petticoats Book 2)*** - On the run from the Italian mafia in New York City, feisty Caterina Campanelli travels across the country to the small town of Pendleton, Oregon, trying to hide her past while she decides what to do about her uncertain future. Seeking comfort in her cooking, she battles her attraction to one of the town's most handsome men.

Kade Rawlings is dedicated to his work as a deputy in Pendleton. Determined to remain single and unfettered, he can't seem to stay away from the Italian spitfire who rolls into town keeping secrets and making the best food he's ever eaten. Using his charm, wit, and brawn to win her trust, he may just get more than he bargained for.

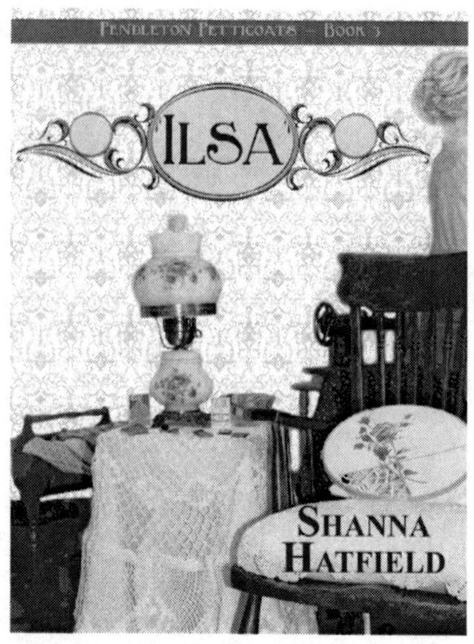


***Ilsa (Pendleton Petticoats Book 3)*** - One of the most talented seamstresses of her time, Ilsa Thorsen could sell her creations anywhere in the world, but she ends up on her sister's ranch in the western town of Pendleton, Oregon. Disgusted with the dust, smells, and nearly every aspect of rural life, Ilsa wonders how she'll survive, particularly with the arrogant Tony Campanelli constantly underfoot.

Enterprising and hardworking, Tony Campanelli embraces life in the small community of Pendleton with his sister and their friends, especially since Ilsa Thorsen moves to town. The uptight seamstress just needs to learn to have some fun and Tony's convinced he's the man for the job.

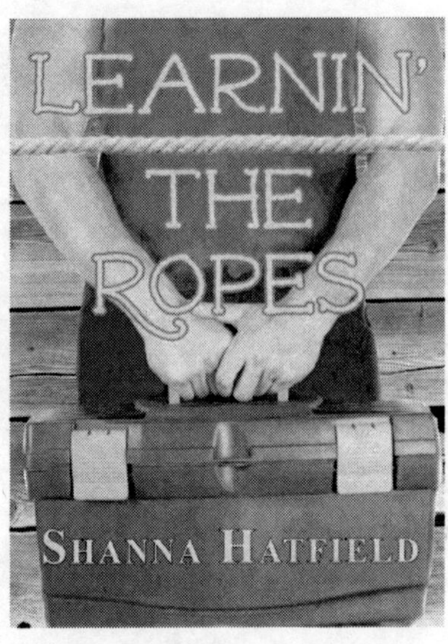


***Learnin' The Ropes*** - Out of work mechanic Ty Lewis is out of options. Homeless and desperate to find work he accepts a job in the tiny community of Riley, Oregon. Leaving everything he's ever known behind in Portland, he resolves himself to this new adventure with an elusive boss, Lex Ryan, someone he has yet to speak with or meet.

Lexi Ryan, known to her ranch hands and neighbors as Lex Jr., leaves a successful corporate career to keep the Rockin' R Ranch running smoothly after the untimely death of her father. It doesn't take long to discover her father did a lot of crazy things during the last few months before he died, like hiding half a million dollars that Lexi can't find.

Ty and Lexi are both in for a few surprises as he arrives at the ranch and begins learnin' the ropes.

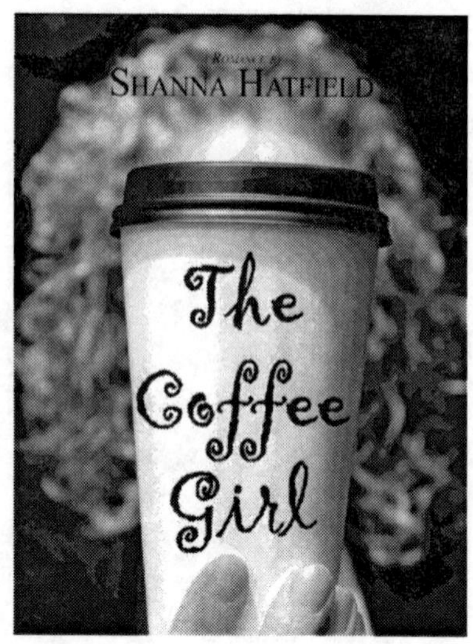


***The Coffee Girl*** - Former barista Brenna Smith dreams of opening a bistro where she can bake her specialty pastries and serve delicious coffee. Envisioning a rich, aromatic life full of savory moments, she instead lives at home with her parents, making a long commute each day to work for a boss who doesn't know beans about his job. If it wasn't for the hunky guy she sees each morning at the coffee shop, her bland existence would be unbearable.

Charming, smart, and good-looking, Brock McCrae is a man comfortable in his own skin. Owner of a successful construction company, he decides to move to the small town where his business is located and immerse himself in the community. Brock doesn't count on his new client being the cute and quirky woman he knows only as the Coffee Girl from his daily stop for coffee.

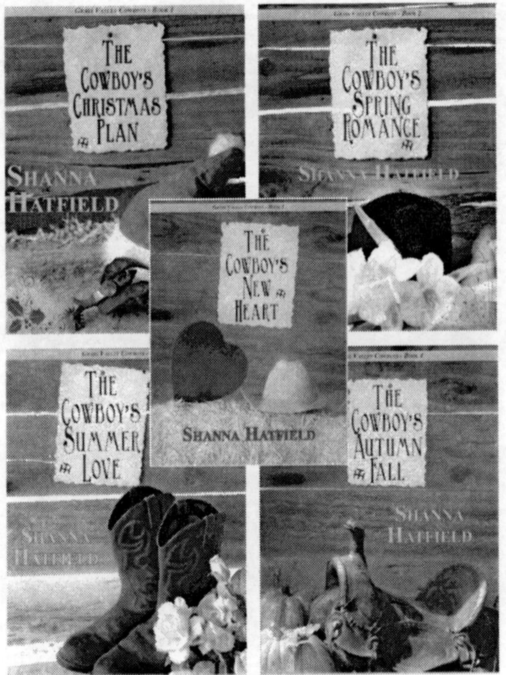


**Grass Valley Cowboys Series**

Meet the Thompson family of the Triple T Ranch in Grass Valley, Oregon.

Three handsome brothers. their rowdy friends, and the women who fall for them are at the heart of this contemporary western romance series.

Book 1 – ***The Cowboy's Christmas Plan***
Book 2 – ***The Cowboy's Spring Romance***
Book 3 – ***The Cowboy's Summer Love***
Book 4 – ***The Cowboy's Autumn Fall***
Book 5 – ***The Cowboy's New Heart***

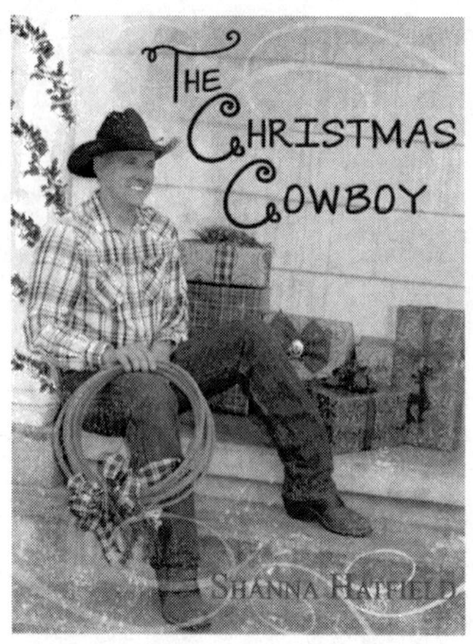


***The Christmas Cowboy*** - Flying from city to city in her job as a busy corporate trainer for a successful direct sales company, Kenzie Beckett doesn't have time for a man. And most certainly not for the handsome cowboy she keeps running into at the airport. Burned twice, she doesn't trust anyone wearing boots and Wranglers, especially someone as charming and handsome as Tate Morgan.

Among the top saddle bronc riders in the rodeo circuit, easy-going Tate Morgan can handle the toughest horse out there, but dealing with the beautiful Kenzie Beckett is a completely different story. As the holiday season approaches, this Christmas Cowboy is going to need to pull out all the stops to win her heart.

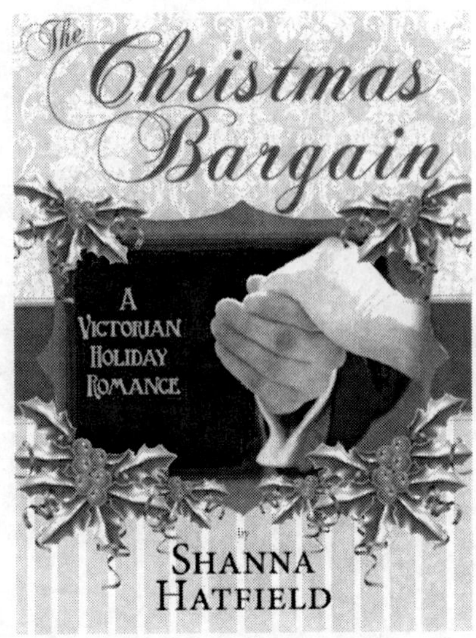


***The Christmas Bargain** (Hardman Holiday, Book 1)* - As owner and manager of the Hardman bank, Luke Granger is a man of responsibility and integrity in the small 1890s Eastern Oregon town. Calling in a long overdue loan, Luke finds himself reluctantly accepting a bargain in lieu of payment from the shiftless farmer who barters his daughter to settle his debt.

Philamena Booth is both mortified and relieved when her father sends her off with the banker as payment of his debt. Held captive on the farm by her father since the death of her mother more than a decade earlier, Philamena is grateful to leave. If only it had been someone other than the handsome and charismatic Luke Granger riding in to rescue her. Ready to hold up her end of the bargain as Luke's cook and housekeeper, Philamena is prepared for the hard work ahead.

What she isn't prepared for is being forced to marry Luke as part of this crazy Christmas bargain.

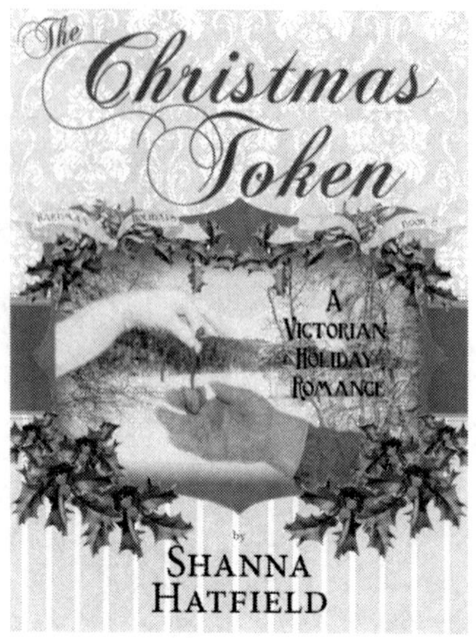


***The Christmas Token* (Hardman Holidays, Book 2)** - Determined to escape an unwelcome suitor, Ginny Granger flees to her brother's home in Eastern Oregon for the holiday season. Returning to the community where she spent her childhood years, she plans to relax and enjoy a peaceful visit. Not expecting to encounter the boy she once loved, her exile proves to be anything but restful.

A talented carpenter, Blake Stratton enjoys a simple existence in the small western town of Hardman. With honest work and good friends, his life is nearly perfect, at least until the day Ginny Granger arrives, setting him on his ear and turning his world upside down. Infuriated by her meddling presence, he's further exasperated to discover she kept a Christmas token he gave her along with his heart the day she left town many years ago.

***<u>The QR Code Killer</u>*** - Murder. Mayhem. Suspense. Romance.

Zeus is a crazed killer who uses QR Codes to taunt the cop hot on his trail.

Mad Dog Weber, a tough-as-nails member of the Seattle police force, is willing to do whatever it takes to bring Zeus down. Despite her best intentions, Maddie (Mad Dog) falls in love with her dad's hired hand, putting them both in danger.

Erik Moore is running from his past and trying to avoid the future when he finds himself falling in love with his boss' daughter. Unknowingly, he puts himself right in the path of the QR Code Killer as he struggles to keep Maddie safe.

From the waterfront of Seattle to the rolling hills of wheat and vineyards of the Walla Walla Valley, suspense and romance fly around every twist and turn.

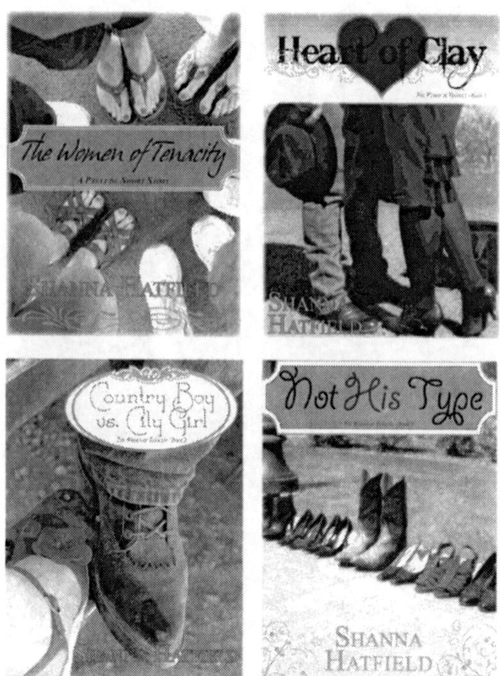


## The Women of Tenacity Series

Welcome to Tenacity!

Tenacious, sassy women tangle with the wild, rugged men who love them in this contemporary romance series.

The paperback version includes a short story introduction, *A Prelude*, followed by the three full-length novels set in the fictional town of Tenacity, Oregon.

Book 1 – ***Heart of Clay***
Book 2 – ***Country Boy vs. City Girl***
Book 3 – ***Not His Type***

**Savvy Entertaining Series**

Discover seasonal ideas for decorating, entertaining, party themes, home décor, recipes and more from Savvy Entertaining's blogger!

# ABOUT THE AUTHOR

SHANNA HATFIELD spent ten years as a newspaper journalist before moving into the field of marketing and public relations. Self-publishing the romantic stories she dreams up in her head is a perfect outlet for her lifelong love of writing, reading, and creativity. She and her husband, lovingly referred to as Captain Cavedweller, reside in the Pacific Northwest.

Shanna loves to hear from readers.
Connect with her online:

Blog: shannahatfield.com
Facebook: Shanna Hatfield
Pinterest: Shanna Hatfield
Email: shanna@shannahatfield.com

If you'd like to know more about the characters in any of her books, visit the Book Characters page on her website or check out her Book Boards on Pinterest.

CPSIA information can be obtained at www.ICGtesting.com
Printed in the USA
LVOW10s2222180115

423395LV00014B/102/P